ANGELA CARTER

The Infernal Desire Machines of Doctor Hoffman

PENGUIN BOOKS

PENGUIN BOOKS

Published by the Penguin Group
Penguin Books Ltd, 27 Wrights Lane, London W8 5TZ, England
Penguin Books USA Inc., 375 Hudson Street, New York, New York 10014, USA
Penguin Books Australia Ltd, Ringwood, Victoria, Australia
Penguin Books Canada Ltd, 10 Alcorn Avenue, Toronto, Ontario, Canada M4V 3B2
Penguin Books (NZ) Ltd, 182–190 Wairau Road, Auckland 10, New Zealand

Penguin Books Ltd, Registered Offices: Harmondsworth, Middlesex, England

First published in Great Britain by Rupert Hart-Davis 1972
First published in the United States of America under the title
The War of Dreams by Harcourt Brace Jovanovich, Inc., 1973
Published in Penguin Books 1982
10

Printed in England by Clays Ltd, St Ives plc
Set in Monotype Ehrhardt

For the family, wherever they are, reluctantly including Ivan who thought he was Alyosha.

Les lois de nos désirs sont les dés sans loisir.
                                    Robert Desnos

(Remember that we sometimes demand definitions for the sake not
of the content, but of their form. Our requirement is an architectural
one: the definition is a kind of ornamental coping that supports
nothing.)
                    Ludwig Wittgenstein, *Philosophical Investigations*

Imagine the perplexity of a man outside time and space, who has
lost his watch, his measuring rod and his tuning fork.
                              Alfred Jarry, *Exploits and Opinions of*
                                    Doctor Faustrall Pataphysician

Contents

Introduction

I remember everything.

Yes.

I remember everything perfectly.

During the war, the city was full of mirages and I was young. But, nowadays, everything is quite peaceful. Shadows fall only as and when they are expected. Because I am so old and famous, they have told me that I must write down all my memories of the Great War, since, after all, I remember everything. So I must gather together all that confusion of experience and arrange it in order, just as it happened, beginning at the beginning. I must unravel my life as if it were so much knitting and pick out from that tangle the single, original thread of my self, the self who was a young man who happened to become a hero and then grew old. First, let me introduce myself.

My name is Desiderio.

I lived in the city when our adversary, the diabolical Dr Hoffman, filled it with mirages in order to drive us all mad. Nothing in the city was what it seemed – nothing at all! Because Dr Hoffman, you see, was waging a massive campaign against human reason itself. Nothing less than that. Oh, the stakes of the war were very high – higher than ever I realized, for I was young and sardonic and did not much like the notion of humanity, anyway, though they told me later, when I became a hero, how I had saved mankind.

But, when I was a young man, I did not want to be a hero. And, when I lived in that bewildering city, in the early days of the war, life itself had become nothing but a complex labyrinth and everything that could possibly exist, did so. And so much complexity – a complexity so rich it can hardly be expressed in language – all that complexity . . . it bored me.

In those tumultuous and kinetic times, the time of actualized desire, I myself had only the one desire. And that was, for everything to stop.

I became a hero only because I survived. I survived because I could not surrender to the flux of mirages. I could not merge and blend with them; I could not abnegate my reality and lose myself for ever as others did, blasted to non-being by the ferocious artillery of unreason. I was too sardonic. I was too disaffected.

When I was young, I very much admired the Ancient Egyptians, because they searched for, arrived at and perfected an aesthetically entirely satisfactory pose. When every single one of them had perfected the stance which had been universally approved, profiles one way, torsos another, feet marching away from the observer, navel squarely staring him in the eye, they stayed in it for two thousand years. I was the confidential secretary to the Minister of Determination, who wanted to freeze the entire freak show the city had become back into attitudes of perfect propriety; and I had this in common with him – an admiration for statis. But, unlike the Minister, I did not believe statis was attainable. I believed perfection was, per se, impossible and so the most seductive phantoms could not allure me because I knew they were not true. Although, of course, nothing I saw was identical with itself any more. I saw only reflections in broken mirrors. Which was only natural, because all the mirrors had been broken.

The Minister sent the Determination Police round to break all the mirrors because of the lawless images they were disseminating. Since mirrors offer alternatives, the mirrors had all turned into fissures or crannies in the hitherto hard-edged world of here and now and through these fissures came slithering sideways all manner of amorphous spooks. And these spooks were Dr Hoffman's guerrillas, his soldiers in disguise who, though absolutely unreal, nevertheless, were.

We did our best to keep what was outside, out, and what was inside, in; we built a vast wall of barbed wire round the city, to quarantine the unreality, but soon the wall was stuck all over with the decomposing corpses of those who, when they were refused exit permits by the over-scrupulous Determination Police, proved how real they were by dying on the spikes. But, if the city was in a state of siege, the enemy was inside the barricades, and lived in the minds of each of us.

But I survived it because I knew that some things were necessarily impossible. I did not believe it when I saw the ghost of my dead mother clutching her rosary and whimpering into the folds of the winding sheet issued her by the convent where she died attempting to atone for her sins. I did not believe it when Dr Hoffman's agents playfully substituted other names than Desiderio on the nameplate outside my door – names such as Wolfgang Amadeus Mozart and Andrew Marvell, for they always chose the names of my heroes, who were all men of pristine and exquisite genius. And I knew that they must be joking for anyone could see that I myself was a man like an unmade bed. But, as for my Minister, he was Milton or Lenin, Beethoven or Michelangelo – not a man but a theorem, clear, hard, unified and harmonious. I admired him. He reminded me of a string quartet. And he, too, was quite immune to the tinselled fall-out from the Hoffman effect, though for quite other reasons than I.

And I, why was I immune? Because, out of my discontent, I made my own definitions and these definitions happened to correspond to those that happened to be true. And so I made a journey through space and time, up a river, across a mountain, over the sea, through a forest. Until I came to a certain castle. And . . .

But I must not run ahead of myself. I shall describe the war exactly as it happened. I will begin at the beginning and go on until the end. I must write down all my memories, in spite of the almost insupportable pain I suffer when I think of her, the heroine of my story, the daughter of the magician, the inexpressible woman to whose memory I dedicate these pages . . . the miraculous Albertina.

If I believed there were anything of the transcendental in this scabbed husk which might survive the death I know will come to me in a few months, I should be happy, then, for I could delude myself I would rejoin my lover. And if Albertina has become for me, now, such a woman as only memory and imagination could devise, well, such is always at least partially the case with the beloved. I see her as a series of marvellous shapes formed at random in the kaleidoscope of desire. Oh, she was her father's daughter, no doubt about that! So I must consecrate this account of the war against her father to the memory of the daughter.

She closed those eyes that were to me the inexhaustible wellsprings of passion fifty years ago this very day and so I take up my pen on the golden anniversary of her death, as I always intended to do. After all these years, the clothes of my spirit are in tatters and half of them have been blown away by the winds of fortune that made a politician of me. And, sometimes, when I think of my journey, not only does everything seem to have happened all at once, in a kind of fugue of experience, just as her father would have devised it, but everything in my life seems to have been of equal value, so that the rose which shook off its petals as if shuddering in ecstasy to hear her voice throws as long a shadow of significance as the extraordinary words she uttered.

Which is not quite like saying that my memory has all dissolved in the medium of Albertina. Rather, from beyond the grave, her father has gained a tactical victory over me and forced on me at least the apprehension of an alternate world in which all the objects are emanations of a single desire. And my desire is, to see Albertina again before I die.

But, at the game of metaphysical chess we played, I took away her father's queen and mated us both for though I am utterly consumed with this desire, it is as impotent as it is desperate. My desire can never be objectified and who should know better than I?

For it was I who killed her.

But you must not expect a love story or a murder story. Expect a tale of picaresque adventure or even of heroic adventure, for I was a great hero in my time though now I am an old man and no longer the 'I' of my own story and my time is past, even if you can read about me in the history books – a strange thing to happen to a man in his own lifetime. It turns one into posterity's prostitute. And when I have completed my autobiography, my whoredom will be complete. I will stand forever four square in yesterday's time, like a commemorative statue of myself in a public place, serene, equestrian, upon a pediment. Although I am so old and sad, now, and, without her, condemned to live in a drab, colourless world, as though I were living in a faded daguerreotype. Therefore –

I, Desiderio, dedicate all my memories

to

Albertina Hoffman

with my insatiable tears.

1. The City Under Siege

I cannot remember exactly how it began. Nobody, not even the Minister, could remember. But I know it started well after my abysmal childhood was mercifully over. The nuns who buried my mother fixed me up with a safe berth; I was a minor clerk in a government office. I rented a room with a bed and a table, a chair and a gas ring, a cupboard and a coffee pot. My landlady was still comparatively young and extremely accommodating. I was always a little bored yet perfectly content. But I think I must have been one of the first people in the city to notice how the shadows began to fall subtly awry and a curious sense of strangeness invaded everything. I had, you see, the time to see. And the Doctor started his activities in very small ways. Sugar tasted a little salty, sometimes. A door one had always seen to be blue modulated by scarcely perceptible stages until, suddenly, it was a green door.

But if remarkable fruits, such as pineapples with the colour and texture of strawberries or walnuts which tasted of caramel, appeared among the apples and oranges on the stalls in the market, everyone put it down to our increased imports, for business had boomed since the man who later became the Minister of Determination took over the post of Minister of Trade. He was always the model of efficiency. I used to put away the files in the Board of Trade. After that, I used to help the Minister with his crossword puzzles and this mutual pastime bred a spurious intimacy which made my promotion parallel his own. He admired the indifferent speed with which I led him up and down the tricksy checkerboard of black and white and I do not think he ever realized the speed was bred only of indifference.

How was the city before it changed? It seemed it would never change.

It was a solid, drab, yet not unfriendly city. It throve on business. It was prosperous. It was thickly, obtusely masculine. Some cities are women and must be loved; others are men and can only be admired or bargained with and my city settled serge-clad buttocks at vulgar ease as if in a leather armchair. His pockets were stuffed with money and his belly with rich food. Historically, he had taken a circuitous path to arrive at such smug, impenetrable, bourgeois affluence; he started life a slaver, a pimp, a gun-runner, a murderer and a pirate, a rakish villain, the exiled scum of Europe – and look at him lording it! The city was built on a tidal river and the slums and the area around the docks still pullulated with blacks, browns and Orientals who lived in a picturesque squalor the city fathers in their veranda'd suburbs contrived to ignore. Yet the city, now, was rich, even if it was ugly; but it was just a little nervous, all the same. It hardly ever dared peer over its well-upholstered shoulder in case it glimpsed the yellow mountains louring far towards the north, atavistic reminders of the interior of a continent which inspired a wordless fear in those who had come here so lately. The word 'indigenous' was unmentionable. Yet some of the buildings, dating from the colonial period, were impressive – the Cathedral; the Opera House; stone memorials of a past to which few, if any, of us had contributed though, since I was of Indian extraction, I suffered the ironic knowledge that my forefathers had anointed the foundations of the state with a good deal of their blood.

I was of Indian extraction. Yes. My mother came from feckless, middle-European immigrant stock and her business, which was prostitution of the least exalted type, took her to the slums a good deal. I do not know who my father was but I carried his genetic imprint on my face, although my colleagues always contrived politely to ignore it since the white, pious nuns had vouched for me. Yet I was a very disaffected young man for I was not unaware of my disinheritance.

When I had enough money, I would go to the Opera House for the inhuman stylization of opera naturally appealed to me very much. I was especially fond of *The Magic Flute*. During a certain performance of *The Magic Flute* one evening in the month of May, as I sat in the gallery enduring the divine illusion of perfection which Mozart imposed on me and which I poisoned for myself since I could not forget it was false, a curious, greenish glitter in the stalls below me caught my eye. I leaned forward. Papageno struck his bells and, at that very moment, as if the bells caused it, I saw the auditorium was full of peacocks in full spread who very soon began to scream in intolerably raucous voices, utterly drowning the music so that I instantly became bored and irritated. Boredom was my first reaction to incipient delirium. Glancing round me, I saw that everyone in the gallery was wearing a peacock-green skull cap and behind each spectator stirred an incandescent, feathered fan. I am still not sure why I did not instantly clap my hand to my own arse to find out whether I, too, had become so bedecked – perhaps I knew the limitations of my sensibility positively forbade such a thing might happen to me, since I admired the formal beauty of peacocks very much. All around me were the beginnings of considerable panic; the peacocks shrieked and fluttered like distracted rainbows and soon they let down the safety curtain, as the performance could not continue under the circumstances. It was Dr Hoffman's first disruptive coup. So I went home, disgruntled, balked of my Mozart, and, the next morning the barrage began in earnest.

We did not understand the means by which the Doctor modified the nature of reality until very much later. We were taken entirely by surprise and chaos supervened immediately. Hallucinations flowed with magical speed in every brain. A state of emergency was declared. A special meeting of the cabinet took place in a small boat upon so stormy a sea that most of the ministers vomited throughout the proceedings and the Chancellor of the Exchequer was washed overboard. My Minister dared walk on the water and retrieved his senior dryshod since there was, in fact, not one drop of water there; after that, the cabinet gave him full authority to cope with the situation and soon he virtually ruled the city single-handed.

Now, what Dr Hoffman had done, in the first instance, was this. Consider the nature of a city. It is a vast repository of time, the discarded times of all the men and women who have lived, worked, dreamed and died in the streets which grow like a wilfully organic thing, unfurl like the petals of a mired rose and yet lack evanescence so entirely that they preserve the past in haphazard layers, so this alley is old while the avenue that runs beside it is newly built but nevertheless has been built over the deep-down, dead-in-the-ground relics of the older, perhaps the original, huddle of alleys which germinated the entire quarter. Dr Hoffman's gigantic generators sent out a series of seismic vibrations which made great cracks in the hitherto immutable surface of the time and space equation we had informally formulated in order to realize our city and, out of these cracks, well – nobody knew what would come next.

A kind of orgiastic panic seized the city. Those bluff, complaisant avenues and piazzas were suddenly as fertile in metamorphoses as a magic forest. Whether the apparitions were shades of the dead, synthetic reconstructions of the living or in no way replicas of anything we knew, they inhabited the same dimension as the living for Dr

Hoffman had enormously extended the limits of this dimension. The very stones were mouths which spoke. I myself decided the revenants were objects – perhaps personified ideas – which could think but did not exist. This seemed the only hypothesis which might explain my own case for I acknowledged them – I *saw* them; they screamed and whickered at me – and yet I did not believe in them.

This phantasmagoric redefinition of a city was constantly fluctuating for it was now the kingdom of the instantaneous.

Cloud palaces erected themselves then silently toppled to reveal for a moment the familiar warehouse beneath them until they were replaced by some fresh audacity. A group of chanting pillars exploded in the middle of a mantra and lo! they were once again street lamps until, with night, they changed to silent flowers. Giant heads in the helmets of conquistadors sailed up like sad, painted kites over the giggling chimney pots. Hardly anything remained the same for more than one second and the city was no longer the conscious production of humanity; it had become the arbitrary realm of dream.

The boulevards susurrated with mendicants who wore long, loose, patchwork coats, strings of beads and ragged turbans; they carried staffs decorated with bunches of variegated ribbons. They claimed to be refugees from the mountains and now all they could do to make a living was to sell to the credulous charms and talismans against domestic spectres who turned the milk sour or lurked in fireplaces eating up the flames so the fires would not light. But the beggars possessed only the most dubious reality status and at any moment might be caught in the blasts of radar emanating from the Ministry of Determination, when they would vanish with a faint squeak, leaving some citizen with his proffered pennies still clutched in his hand, gazing at empty air. Sometimes the talismans they sold vanished with them even though they had already been stowed away in the household shrines of their purchasers; and sometimes not.

The question of the nature of the talismans was one of both profane and profound surmise, for in some instances the spectral salesmen must have carved their crude icons out of solid wood which did not have the faculty of vanishing but, if so, how could a knife of shadows cut real flesh from a living tree? Clearly the phantoms were capable of inflicting significant form on natural substances. The superstitious fear of the citizens rose to a pitch of feverish delirium and they often raised hue and cries against any unfortunate whose appearance smacked in some way of transparency or else who seemed suspiciously too real. The suspects were often torn to pieces. I remember a riot which began when a man snatched a baby from a perambulator and dashed it to the ground because he complained that its smile was 'too lifelike'.

By the end of the first year there was no longer any way of guessing what one would see when one opened one's eyes in the morning for other people's dreams insidiously invaded the bedroom while one slept and yet it seemed that sleep was our last privacy for, while we slept, at least we knew that we were dreaming although the stuff of our waking hours, so buffeted by phantoms, had grown thin and insubstantial enough to seem itself no more than seeming, or else the fragile marginalia of our dreams. Sheeted teasing memories of the past waited to greet us at the foot of the bed and these were often memories of someone else's past, even if they still wished us 'Good morning' with an unnerving familiarity when we opened our enchanted eyes. Dead children came calling in nightgowns, rubbing the sleep and grave dust from their eyes. Not only the dead returned but also the lost living. Abandoned lovers were often lured into the false embrace of faithless mistresses and this caused the Minister the gravest concern for he feared that one day a man would impregnate an illusion and then a generation of half-breed ghosts would befoul the city even more. But as I often felt I was a half-breed ghost myself, I did not feel much concerned over that! Anyway, the great majority of the things which appeared around us were by no means familiar, though they often teasingly recalled aspects of past experience, as if they were memories of forgotten memories.

The sense of space was powerfully affected so that sometimes the proportions of buildings and townscapes swelled to enormous, ominous sizes or repeated themselves over and over again in a fretting infinity. But this was much less disturbing than the actual objects which filled these gigantesque perspectives. Often, in the vaulted architraves of railway stations, women in states of pearly, heroic nudity, their hair elaborately coiffed in the stately chignons of the *fin de siècle*, might be seen parading beneath their parasols as serenely as if they had been in the Bois de Boulogne, pausing now and then to stroke, with the judiciously appraising touch of owners of racehorses, the side of steaming engines which did not run any more. And the very birds of the air seemed possessed by devils. Some grew to the size and acquired the temperament of winged jaguars. Fanged sparrows plucked out the eyes of little children. Snarling flocks of starlings swooped down upon some starving wretch picking over a mess of dreams and refuse in a gutter and tore what remained of his flesh from his bones. The pigeons lolloped from illusory pediment to window-ledge like volatile, feathered madmen, chattering vile rhymes and laughing in hoarse, throaty voices, or perched upon chimney stacks shouting quotations from Hegel. But often, in actual mid-air, the birds would forget the techniques and mechanics of the very act of flight and then they fell down, so that every morning dead birds lay in drifts on the pavements like autumn leaves or brown, wind-blown snow. Sometimes the river ran backwards and crazy fish jumped out to flop upon the sidewalks and wriggle around on their bellies for a while until they died, choking for lack of water. It was, too, the heyday of *trompe l'œil* for painted forms took advantage of the liveliness they mimicked. Horses from the pictures of Stubbs in the Municipal Art Gallery neighed, tossed their manes and stepped delicately off their canvases to go to crop the grass in public parks. A plump Bacchus wearing only a few grapes strayed from a Titian into a bar and there instituted Dionysiac revelry.

But only a few of the transmutations were lyrical. Frequently, imaginary massacres filled the gutters with blood and, besides, the cumulative psychological effect of all these distortions, combined with the dislocation of everyday life and the hardship and privations we began to suffer, created a deep-seated anxiety and a sense of profound melancholy. It seemed each one of us was trapped in some downward-drooping convoluted spiral of unreality from which we could never escape. Many committed suicide.

Trade was at an end. All the factories closed down and there was wholesale unemployment. There was always the smell of dissolution in the air for the public services were utterly disorganized. Typhoid took a heavy toll and there were grim murmurs of cholera or worse. The only form of transport the Minister permitted in the city was the bicycle, since it can only be ridden by that constant effort of will which precludes the imagination. The Determination Police enforced a strict system of rationing in an attempt to eke out the city's dwindling supplies of food as long as possible but the citizens lied freely about their needs and those of their dependants, broke into shops to steal and gleefully submitted to the authorities the forged bread tickets with which Dr Hoffman flooded the streets. After the Minister sealed off the city, our only news of the country outside the capital came from the terse, laconic reports of the Determination Police and the gossip of the few peasants who had the necessary credentials to pass the guards at the checkpoints with a basket or two of vegetables or some coops of chickens.

Dr Hoffman had destroyed time and played games with the objects by which we regulated time. I often glanced at my watch only to find its hands had been replaced by a healthy growth of ivy or honeysuckle which, while I looked, writhed impudently all over its face, concealing it. Tricks with watches and clocks were pet devices of his, for so he rubbed home to us how we no longer held a structure of time in common. Inside the twin divisions of light and darkness there was no more segmentation, for what clocks were left all told a different time and nobody trusted them anyway. Past time occupied the city for whole days together, sometimes, so that the streets of a hundred years before were superimposed on nowadays streets and I made my way to the Bureau only by memory, along never-before-trodden lanes that looked as indestructible as earth itself and yet would vanish, presumably, whenever someone in Dr Hoffman's entourage grew bored and pressed a switch.

Statistics for burglary, arson, robbery with violence and rape rose to astronomical heights and it was not safe, either physically or metaphysically, to leave one's room at night although one was not particularly safe if one stayed at home either. There had been two cases of suspected plague. By the beginning of the second year we received no news at all from the world outside for Dr Hoffman blocked all the radio waves. Slowly the city acquired a majestic solitude. There grew in it, or it grew into, a desolate beauty, the beauty of the hopeless, a beauty which caught the heart and made the tears come. One would never have believed it possible for this city to be beautiful.

At certain times, especially in the evenings, as the shadows lengthened, the ripe sunlight of the day's ending fell with a peculiar, suggestive heaviness, trapping the swooning buildings in a sweet, solid calm, as if preserving them in honey. Aurified by the Midas rays of the setting sun, the sky took on the appearance of a thin sheet of beaten gold like the ground of certain ancient paintings so the monolithically misshapen, depthless forms of the city took on the enhanced glamour of the totally artificial. Then, we – that is, those of us who retained some notion of what was real and what was not – felt the vertigo of those teetering on the edge of a magic precipice. We found ourselves holding our breath almost in expectancy, as though we might stand on the threshold of a great event, transfixed in the portentous moment of waiting, although inwardly we were perturbed since this new, awesome, orchestration of time and space which surrounded us might be only the overture to something else, to some most profoundly audacious of all these assaults against the things we had always known. The Minister was the only person I knew who claimed he did not, even once, experience this sense of immanence.

The Minister had never in all his life felt the slightest quiver of empirical uncertainty. He was the hardest thing that ever existed and never the flicker of a mirage distorted for so much as a fleeting second the austere and intransigent objectivity of his face even though, as I saw it, his work consisted essentially in setting a limit to thought, for Dr Hoffman appeared to me to be proliferating his weaponry of images along the obscure and controversial borderline between the thinkable and the unthinkable.

'Very well,' said the Minister. 'The Doctor has invented a virus which causes a cancer of the mind, so that the cells of the imagination run wild. And we must – we *will*! – discover the antidote.'

But he still had no idea how the Doctor had done it although it was clear that day by day he was growing better at it. So the Minister, who had not one shred of superstition in him, was forced to become an exorcist for all he could do was to try to scare the spooks off the bedevilled streets and although he had a battery of technological devices to help him, in the last resort he was reduced to the methods of the medieval witch-hunter. I rarely had the stomach to pass Reality Testing Laboratory C for the smell of roast pork nauseated me and I wondered if the Minister, out of desperation, intended to rewrite the Cartesian cogito thus: 'I am in pain, therefore I exist,' and base his tests upon it for, in cases of stubborn and extreme confusion, they operated a trial by fire. If it emerged alive from the incineration room, it was obviously unreal and, if he had been reduced to a handful of ash, he had been authentic. By the end of the second year, most other expedients – the radar and so on – were proving fallible, anyway. The Determination Police claimed the Incineration Room had carbonized a number of Hoffman's agents but, as for myself, I was suspicious of the Determination Police for their ankle-length, truculently belted coats of black leather, their low-crowned, wide-brimmed fedoras and their altogether too highly polished boots woke in me an uncomfortable progression of associations. They looked as if they had been recruited wholesale from a Jewish nightmare.

In the early days of the war the first counter-weapon we devised was the Determining Radar Apparatus, which was both offensive and defensive as it incorporated a laser effect in its beam. The Determining Radar Apparatus worked on the theory that non-solid substance which could, however, be recognized by the senses had a molecular structure which bristled with projections. The model of the unreality atom in the Minister's office consisted of a tetrahydron improvised out of a number of hairbrushes. The radar beams were supposed to bruise themselves on this bed of thorns and certainly let out an inaudible shriek instantly visible on the screens at H.Q. This shriek automatically triggered the laser and at once annihilated the offending non-substance. For a time, during the last half of the first year, the Minister wore a faint smile for daily we disintegrated whole battalions of eldritch guerrillas but the Doctor's research laboratories must have swiftly restructured their own prototype molecule for, by Christmas time, the screens at H.Q. were gradually falling silent, letting out only a few very occasional squeaks when a beam accidentally brushed the teeth of what was now patently an obsolete illusion probably only used as a decoy – such things, for example, as a man whose hat had become his head; while more and more outrageous spectacles danced and shouted in a city only intermittently recognizable. The Minister's smile died. Our physicists, all of whom had a three-star reality rating and the patience of Job, finally turned out a new hypothetical model for this modification of the unreality atom. It was a sphere of looking glass, like a reflective tear, and the leader of the team, Dr Drosselmeier, explained to the Minister and myself how the molecules must fit together like a coalescence of raindrops.

At this point, Dr Drosselmeier went mad. He did so without warning but most melodramatically. He blew up the physics laboratory, the records which contained the sum total of his researches, four of his assistants and himself. I do not think his breakdown was caused by some obscure machination of the Doctor, even though I was beginning to feel the Doctor was probably omnipotent; I suspect Drosselmeier had unwittingly exposed himself to an overdose of reality and it had destroyed his reason. However, this disaster left us utterly defenceless and the Minister was forced to rely more and more on the primitive and increasingly brutal methods of the Determination Police while he himself supervised work on a project he believed would finally save us from the Doctor. When he spoke of this project, a guarded but Messianic gleam crept into his usually cool and sceptical eyes.

He was in the process of constructing an immense computer centre which would formulate a systematic procedure for calculating the verifiable self-consistency of any given object. He believed the criterion of reality was that a thing was determinate and the identity of a thing lay only in the extent to which it resembled itself. He was the most ascetic of logicians but, if he had a fatal flaw, it was his touch of scholasticism. He believed that the city – which he took as a micro-cosm of the universe – contained a finite set of objects and a finite set of their combinations and therefore a list could be made of all possible distinct forms which were logically viable. These could be counted, organized into a conceptual framework and so form a kind of check list for the verification of all phenomena, instantly available by means of an information retrieval system. So he was engaged in the almost superhuman task of programming computers with factual data concerning every single thing which, as far as it was humanly possible to judge, had ever – even if only once and that momentarily – existed. Thus the existence of any object at all, however bizarre it might at first appear, could first be checked against the entire history of the world and then be given a possibility rating. Once a thing was registered as 'possible', however, there followed the infinitely more complex procedure designed to discover if it were probable.

Sometimes he talked to me about politics. His political philosophy had the non-dynamic magnificence of contrapuntal, pre-classical music; he described to me a grooved, interlocking set of institutions governed by the notion of a great propriety. He called it his theory of 'names and functions'. Each man was secure in possession of a certain name which also ensured him a certain position in a society seen as a series of interlinking rings which, although continually in movement, were never subjected to change for there were never any disturbances and no usurpation of names or ranks or roles whatsoever. And the city circled in this utterly harmonious fashion with the radiant serenity of a place in which everything was inevitable for, as soon as the death of a ruler completed one movement in this celestial concerto, the inauguration of another ruler signalled the start of another move-ment precisely similar in form. The Minister had a singular passion for Bach. He thought that Mozart was frivolous. He was as sombre and sedate as a mandarin.

But although he was the most rational man in the world, he was only a witch-doctor in the present state of things, even if the spooks he was pledged to eradicate were not real spooks but phenomena per-petrated by a man who was probably the greatest physicist of all time. Yet, essentially, it was a battle between an encyclopedist and a poet for Hoffman, scientist as he was, utilized his formidable knowledge only to render the invisible visible, even though it certainly seemed to us that his ultimate plan was to rule the world.

The Minister spent night after night among his computers. His

face grew grey and drawn with overwork and his fine hands shook
with fatigue and yet he remained indefatigable. But it seemed to me
that he sought to cast the arbitrarily fine mesh of his predetermined
net over nothing but a sea of mirages for he refused to acknowledge
how palpable the phantoms were, how they could be seen and touched,
kissed and eaten, penetrated and picked in bunches, to be arranged in a
vase. The variegated raree-show which now surrounded us was as
complicated as a real man himself, walking, but the Minister saw
the entire spectacle as a corrugated surface of various greys, the
colourless corpse of itself. Yet this limitation of his imagination gave
him the capacity to see the city as an existential crossword puzzle
which might one day be solved. I passed the days beside him, making
innumerable pots of the tea he drank black, with neither lemon nor
sugar, emptying his brimming ashtrays and changing the records of
Bach and the pre-classicals he played softly all the time to aid his
concentration. I was at the hub of things but still I was indifferent.
My mother came to see me; my name fluctuated on my nameplate;
my dreams were so amazing that, in spite of myself, I had become
awe-struck at the approach of sleep. And yet I could summon up no
interest in all this.

I felt as if I was watching a film in which the Minister was the
hero and the unseen Doctor certainly the villain; but it was an endless
film and I found it boring for none of the characters engaged my
sympathy, even if I admired them, and all the situations appeared the
false engineering of an inefficient phantasist. But I had one curious,
persistent hallucination which obscurely troubled me because nothing
about it was familiar and, each time I saw her, she never changed.
Every night as I lay on the borders of a sleep which had now become as
aesthetically exhausting as Wagner, I would be visited by a young
woman in a négligé made of a fabric the colour and texture of the
petals of poppies which clung about her but did not conceal her
quite transparent flesh, so that the exquisite filigree of her skeleton
was revealed quite clearly. Where her heart should have been there
flickered a knot of flames like ribbons and she shimmered a little, like
the air on a very hot summer's day. She did not speak; she did not
smile. Except for those faint quiverings of her unimaginable substance,
she did not move. But she never failed to visit me. Now I know that the
manifestations of those days were – as perhaps I then suspected but
refused to admit to myself – a language of signs which utterly bemused me because I could not read them. Each phantom was a symbol
palpitating with appalling significance yet she alone, my visitor with

flesh of glass, hinted to me a little of the nature of the mysteries which encompassed us and filled so many of us with terror.

She stayed beside me until I slept, waveringly, brilliantly, hooded in diaphanous scarlet, and occasionally she left an imperative written in lipstick on my dusty windowpane. BE AMOROUS! she exhorted one night and, another night, BE MYSTERIOUS! Some nights later, she scribbled: DON'T THINK, LOOK; and, shortly after that, she warned me: WHEN YOU BEGIN TO THINK, YOU LOSE THE POINT. These messages irritated yet haunted me. They itched away all day inside my head like a speck of dust trapped beneath my eyelids. She was qualitatively different from the comic apparition purporting to be my mother who perched on the mantelpiece in the guise of a fat, white owl begging my forgiveness and hooting her orisons. This visible skeleton, this miraculous bouquet of bone, the formal elements of physicality, was one of the third order of forms who might presently invade us, the order of angels, speaking lions and winged horses, the miraculous revenants for whom the city sometimes seemed hushed in expectation and who themselves would only be the amazing heralds of the arrival of the Emperor of the Marvellous, whose creatures we would by that time have all become.

We knew the name of our adversary. We knew the date at which he graduated in physics with honours from the national university. We knew his father had been a gentleman banker who dabbled a little in the occult and his mother a lady who liked to organize soup kitchens in the slums and sewing schools for repentant prostitutes. We even discovered, to the Minister's tactful embarrassment, that my own mother, during one of her atoning fits, had stitched for me at one of Mrs Hoffman's schools a pathetically disintegrating flannel undergarment which I wore for a day before the seams unravelled altogether, an appropriate symbol for my mother's repentance. I suppose this coincidence gave me a certain tenuous sense of involvement with the Hoffman family – as if, one rainy afternoon, I had talked with an aunt of his briefly about the weather, on a stopping, country train. We knew the very date, 18 September 1867, on which Dr Hoffman's great-grandfather arrived in this country, a minor aristocrat of slender means fleeing from unmentionable troubles in a certain wolf-haunted mountainous Slavonic principality which was subsequently rendered into legislative non-being during the Franco-Prussian war or some such war. We knew that, when his son was born, the father cast his horoscope and then gave the midwife who had delivered him a tip of several thousand dollars. We knew the boy Hoffman had been involved in a homosexual scandal at his preparatory school and we even knew how much it had cost to hush the scandal up. The Minister devoted an entire bank of computers to data on Dr Hoffman. We even tabulated his childhood illnesses and the Minister found especially significant an attack of brain fever in his seventh year and a *crise de nerfs* in his sixteenth.

However, one day some twenty years previously, Dr Hoffman, the already enormously distinguished Professor of Physics at the University of P., dismissed with a few kind words and a handsome present the valet who looked after him; made a bonfire of his notebooks; packed in a valise a toothbrush, a change of shirts and underwear and the choicest of his father's library of cabbalistic books; took a taxi to the central railway station; bought a single ticket to the mountain resort of L.; went to the correct platform, where he purchased a pack of imported cigarettes and a net of tangerines from the kiosk; was observed by a porter to peel and consume a fruit; was seen by another porter to enter the gentlemen's lavatory; and then vanished. He vanished so expeditiously there were even obituaries in the press.

In the years preceding the Reality War, an itinerant showman who gave his name as Mendoza made a small living touring country fairs and carnivals with a small theatre. This theatre did not have any actors; it was a peep-show cum cinematograph but it offered moving views in three dimensions and those who visited it were impressed by the lifelikeness of what they saw. Mendoza prospered. In time he came to the Whitsun Fair in the capital with his theatre, but by this time his art had progressed and now he offered a trip in a time machine. Customers were invited to take off their clothes and don all manner of period costumes provided for them by the impresario. When they were suitably garbed, the lights dimmed and Mendoza projected upon a screen various old newsreels and an occasional early silent comedy. These films had, as it were, slots in them in which the members of the audience could insert themselves and so become part of the shadow show they witnessed. I spoke with a man who, as a child, had been in this fashion an eye-witness of the assassination at Sarajevo. He said it had been raining heavily at the time and everybody moved with the spasmodic jerkiness of clockwork figures. This showman, Mendoza, must have been one of Dr Hoffman's first disciples or even perhaps an early missionary. Hoffman's undergraduate class list included a fellow student named Mendoza, said to be psychologically unstable, who did not complete his course of study. But one day a drunken crowd burned down his booth and Mendoza was burned with it, so badly that he died a few days later in some anonymous charity ward, attended by Sisters of Mercy. What linked him unambiguously to Hoffman had been his repeated mutterings: 'Beware the Hoffman effect!' On his board-hard death bed, under a casque of lint, he muttered away, an elderly nun remembered. But now Mendoza was irretrievably dead and the Minister wondered if he were not a red herring.

The Minister had built up a hypothetical model of the invisible Dr Hoffman much as Dr Drosselmeier had built up a model of the unreality atom. From the scientist's academic record, we could see there was scarcely a branch of human knowledge with which he had not familiarized himself. We knew of his taste for the occult. We knew his height, his size in hats, shoes and gloves; his favourite brands of cigars, eau de cologne and tea. The Minister's model was that of a crazed genius, a megalomaniac who wanted absolute power and would go to extreme lengths to grasp it. He thought Hoffman was satanic and yet I knew my master too well not to realize he was tainted with a little envy for the very power the Doctor abused with such insouciance, the power to subvert the world. This did not lessen my admiration for the Minister. On the contrary, I was so lacking in ambition myself that the spectacle of his, which ravaged him, impressed me enormously. He was like a Faust who cannot find a friendly devil. Or, if he had done so, he would not have been able to believe in him.

The Minister had all the Faustian desires but, since he had rejected the transcendental, he had clipped his own wings. In my meditative days, I used to think that the Faust legend was a warped version of the myth of Prometheus, who defied the wrath of god to gain the prize of fire and was punished for it. I could not see what there might be wrong with knowledge in itself, no matter what the price. In spite of my post, I had taken no sides in the struggle between Dr Hoffman and the Minister. At times I even speculated that Hoffman was altogether Prometheus and no Faust at all, for Faust had been content with conjuring tricks while the manifestations around us sometimes looked as though they were formed of authentic flame. But I kept these thoughts to myself. Nevertheless, you must realize the adversaries were of equal stature. The Minister possessed supernatural strength of mind to have stood out so long and it was his phenomenal intransigence alone which upheld the city.

Indeed, he had become the city. He had become the invisible walls of the city; in himself, he represented the grand totality of the city's resistance. His movements began to take on a megalithic grandeur. He said continually: 'No surrender!' and I could not deny his dignity. I even revered it. But, for myself, I had no axe to grind.

The siege went into its third year. Supplies of food were almost at an end. An epidemic of cholera decimated the eastern suburbs and thirty cases of typhus had been reported that week. Even the discipline of the Determination Police was fraying and now and then one of them would slip into the Minister's office to tell tales on a colleague. My landlady vanished. Somehow, without anybody knowing, she was dead somewhere, so now I was alone in my house. Every day, the police suppressed riots with tear gas and machine gun fire. And it was blinding, humid, foetid summer, a summer that smelled of shit, blood and roses, for there had never been such roses as those that bloomed that summer. They clambered everywhere and dripped as if perspiring the heaviest, most intoxicating perfume, which seemed to make the very masonry drunk. The senses fused; sometimes these roses emitted low but intolerably piercing pentatonic melodies which were the sound of their deep crimson colour and yet we heard them inside our nostrils. The citronade of the pale morning sun shimmered like a multitude of violins and I tasted unripe apples in the rare, green, midnight rain.

It was the day before my twenty-fourth birthday. In the afternoon, the Cathedral expired in a blaze of melodious fireworks.

It was our greatest national monument. It had been of immense size and architecturally sublimely chaste. Until then, its severe, classical revival façade had grandly ignored all the Doctor's whimsical attempts to transform it into a funfair or a mausoleum for ships' figureheads or a slaughterhouse so he finally detonated it with pyrotechnics. The Minister and I watched the illuminations from our window. The dome rose up and dissolved against the clear blue sky of the middle of the afternoon like a fiery parasol but, while I was faintly regretting that the spectacle had not taken place at night when I should have enjoyed it better, I saw that the Minister was weeping. Berlioz crashed about us; we stood in the heart of a fantastic symphony, awaiting the climacteric, death, which would come in the form of a fatal circus.

For my supper, I ate a salad of dandelions I picked from the wall of my house, which had begun to sprout flowers. I brewed myself a pot from my four-weekly ounce ration of coffee substitute and, I remember, read a little. I read a few pages of *The Rape of the Lock*. When it was time to sleep, she came to me. For the first time, I smiled at her; she made no response. I slept; and early the next morning, I awoke and yet I knew I was still sleeping for my bed was now, in fact, an island in the middle of an immense lake.

Night was approaching although I knew it was nearly dawn for outside – outside, that is, of the dream – a cock continued to crow. However, within my dream, the shadows of evening took the colours from the shifting waters round me and a small wind rustled the quills of the pine trees, for my island was covered with pines. Nothing moved except this little, lonely wind. I waited, for the dream imperiously demanded that I wait and I seemed to wait endlessly. I do not think I have ever felt so alone, as if I were the last living thing left in the world and this island and this lake were all that was left of the world.

Presently I saw the object of my vigil. A creature was approaching over the water but it did not assuage my loneliness for though I could see it was alive, it did not seem to be alive in the same sense that I was alive and I shuddered with dread. I know I must have stood in an attitude of awed listening, as if to hear the scratching of the claws of the unknown on the outside rind of the world. The oldest and strongest emotion of mankind is fear and the oldest and strongest kind of fear is fear of the unknown; I was afraid. I had been afraid when I was a child, when I would lie awake at night and hear my mother panting and grunting like a tiger in the darkness beyond the curtain and I thought she had changed into a beast. Now I was even more afraid than I had been then.

As it drew near, I saw it was a swan. It was a black swan. I cannot tell you how ugly it was; nor yet how marvellous it was. Its vapid eyes were set too close together on its head and expressed a kind of mindless evil that was quite without glamour, though evil is usually attractive, because evil is defiant. Its elongated neck had none of the grace traditionally ascribed to the necks of swans but lolled foolishly, now this way, now that, like a length of hose. And the beak, which was the clear, pinkish scarlet of scentless roses, striped with a single band of white, was flat, broad and spatulate, fit only for grubbing worms from mud. It swam remorselessly and terribly towards me but, when only a few yards of shifting water lay between us, it paused to unfurl its enormous wings as if it were opening a heraldic umbrella.

Never have I seen such blackness, such a soft, feathered, absolute black, a black as intense as the negation of light, black the colour of the extinction of consciousness. The swan flexed its neck like a snake about to strike, opened its beak and began to sing so that I knew it was about to die and I knew, too, she was a swan and also a woman for there issued from her throat a thrilling, erotic contralto. Her song was a savage, wordless lament with the dramatic cadences of flamenco in a scale the notes of which were unfamiliar to me yet seemed those of an ultimate Platonic mode, an elemental music. The shadows deepened yet one last ray of the invisible sun drew a gleam from a golden collar around her throbbing throat and on the collar was engraved the single word: ALBERTINA. The dream broke like a storm and I woke.

The room was full of muffled sunlight. The cock had ceased to crow. But I did not wake properly even though my eyes were open; the dream left my mind full of cobwebs and I scarcely saw the morning though I went, as usual, to the office and found the Minister going through his mail. He was studying a letter which had arrived in an envelope bearing the postmark of one of the solid suburbs in the north of the city. He began to laugh softly.

'Dr Hoffman's special agent would like me to take him to lunch today,' he said and handed me the letter. 'Test this immediately.'

It went through innumerable computers. It went through Reality Testing Laboratories A and B and we photocopied it before it went through Laboratory C. This was fortunate for it was authentic.

I was to go with the Minister to the rendezvous. My task was simple. I was to record every word that passed between the Minister and the agent on a very small tape recorder concealed in my pocket. He sent me home to change my suit and put on a tie. I must say, most of all, I was looking forward to a good meal for such things were hard to come by nowadays – yet I could see what the Minister could not, that Dr Hoffman would not have sent him the invitation had he not believed we were on our knees.

The restaurant was luxuriously discreet. All its staff had unimpeachable reality ratings, even the plongeurs. We waited for our contact in a dim, confidential bar too comfortably redolent of money to be affected by the tempest of fantasy we could not glimpse outside because the windows were so heavily curtained. Sipping his gin and tonic, the Minister alternately consulted his watch and tapped his foot; I was interested to see he was unable to perform these actions simultaneously, perhaps because he was so single-minded. He emanated tension. A muscle twitched in his cheek. He lit a fresh cigarette from the butt of the one he had just put out. We knew who it was the instant our contact came in because the lights immediately fused.

A dozen tiny fireflies clicked into life at the nozzle of a dozen cigarette lighters but I could make out only the vaguest outlines of Dr Hoffman's emissary until the waiters brought in a number of branched candlesticks so that he was illuminated like the icon he resembled. A breeze seemed to play about him, tossing the small flames hither and thither, keeping constantly aflutter the innumerable ruffles on his lace shirt and casting a multitude of shadows over his face. Presumably he was either of Mongolian extraction or else he numbered among his ancestors, as I did, certain of the forgotten Indians who still linger miserably in the more impenetrable mountains or skulk along the waterways, for his skin was like polished brass, at once greenish and yellowish, his eyelids were vestigial and his cheekbones unusually high. Luxuriantly glossy hair so black it was purplish in colour made of his head almost too heavy a helmet to be supported by the slender column of his neck and his blunt-lipped, sensual mouth was also purplish in colour, as if he had been eating berries. Around his eyes, which were as hieratically brown and uncommunicative as those the Ancient Egyptians painted on their sarcophagi, were thick bands of solid gold cosmetic and the nails on his long hands were enamelled dark crimson, to match the nails on his similarly elegant feet, which were fully exposed by sandals consisting of mere gold thongs. He wore flared trousers of purple suede and used several ropes of pearls for a belt around his waist. All his gestures were instinct with a self-conscious but extraordinary reptilian liquidity; when we rose to go to eat, I saw that he seemed to move in soft coils. I think he was the most beautiful human being I have ever seen – considered, that is, solely as an object, a construction of flesh, skin, bone and fabric, and yet, for all his ambiguous sophistication, indeed, perhaps in its very nature, he hinted at a savagery which had been cunningly tailored to suit the drawing room, though it had been in no way diminished. He was a manicured leopard patently in complicity with chaos. Secure in the armour of his ambivalence, he patronized us. His manner was one of wry, supercilious reserve. He was no common agent. He behaved like an ambassador of an exceedingly powerful principality visiting a small but diplomatically by no means insignificant state. He treated us with the regal condescension of a first lady and the Minister and I found ourselves behaving like boorish provincials who dropped our forks, slopped our soup, knocked over our wine glasses and spilled mayonnaise on our ties while he watched us with faint amusement and barely discernible contempt.

In a gracious attempt to put us at our ease, he chatted desultorily about baroque music in a low, dark voice which had a singular, furry quality. But the Minister refused to talk small talk. He spooned his consommé distastefully, grunting now and then, his cold eyes fixed suspiciously on the luring siren before us who ate with an unfamiliar but graceful series of gestures of the hands, like those of Javanese dancers. I drank my soup and watched them. It was like the dialogue between a tentacular flower and a stone. A waiter took away the plates and brought us sole véronique. You would not have believed we were at war. The young man speared a grape with his fork. He folded up Vivaldi and his lesser-known contemporaries and put them away. As we dismembered our fish, the following conversation took place. I found the tape in a lead coffin in the ruins of the Bureau of Determination many years later, and so am able to transcribe it verbatim.

Ambassador : Dr Hoffman is coming to storm the ideological castle of which at present, my dear Minister, you are the king.
   (*This was a minor preliminary sortie. He fluttered his darkened lashes at us and tinkled with diminutive laughter.*)
Minister : He has made his intentions in that direction abundantly clear. As far as we can tell, he opened hostilities perhaps three years ago and by now there are no directions left in the city while the clocks no longer answer to the time.
Ambassador : Yes, indeed! The Doctor has liberated the streets from the tyranny of directions and now they can go anywhere they please. He also set the timepieces free so that now they are authentically pieces of time and can tell everybody whatever time they like. I am especially happy for the clocks. They used to have such innocent faces. They had the water-melon munching, opaquely-eyed visages of slaves and the Doctor has already proved himself a horological Abraham Lincoln. Now he will liberate you all, Minister.
Minister : But ought the roads to rule the city?
Ambassador : Don't you think we should give them a crack at the whip now and then? Poor things, forever oriented by the insensitive feet of those who trample them. Time and space have their own properties, Minister, and these, perhaps, have more value than you customarily allow them. Time and space are the very guts of nature and so, naturally, they undulate in the manner of intestines.
Minister : I see you make a habit of analogies.
Ambassador : An analogy is a signpost.
Minister : You have taken away all the signposts.
Ambassador : But we have populated the city with analogies.

Minister : I should dearly like to know the reason why.

Ambassador : For the sake of liberty, Minister.

Minister : What an exceedingly pretty notion!

Ambassador : I certainly did not think *that* answer would satisfy you. What if I told you that we were engaged in uncovering the infinite potentiality of phenomena?

Minister : I would suggest you moved your operations to some other location.

(*The Ambassador smiled and dissected a translucent sliver of sole.*)

Minister : I began to perceive a short while ago that the Doctor intended utterly to disrupt any vestige of the social fabric of my country of which he himself was once one of the finest intellectual ornaments.

Ambassador : You speak of him as if he were a piece of *famille rose*!

(*The Minister ignored this gentle reprimand.*)

Minister : I can only conclude he is motivated purely by malice.

Ambassador : What, the mad scientist who brews up revengeful plagues in his test-tubes? Were his motives so simple, he would, by now, I assure you, have utterly destroyed everything.

(*The Minister pushed back his plate. I could see he was about to speak direct from the heart.*)

Minister : Yesterday the cathedral dissolved in a display of fireworks. I suppose the childish delight many showed when they saw the rockets, the catherine wheels and the vari-coloured stars and meteors affected me most of all, for the cathedral had been a masterpiece of sobriety. It was given the most vulgar funeral pyre that could possibly have been devised. Yet it had brooded over the city like the most conventual of stone angels for two hundred years. Time, the slavish time you despise, had been free enough to work in equal partnership with the architect; the masons took thirty years to build the cathedral and, with every year that passed, the invisible moulding of time deepened the moving beauty of its soaring lines. Time was implicit in its fabric. I am not a religious man myself and yet the cathedral stood for me as a kind of symbol of the spirit of the city.

It was an artifice –

Ambassador : – and so we burned it down with *feux d'artifice* –

(*The Minister ignored him.*)

Minister : – and its grandeur, increasing year by year as it grew more massively into time itself, had been programmed into it by the cunning of the architects. It was an illusion of the sublime and yet its symmetry expressed the symmetry of the society which had produced it. The city and, by extension, the state, is an artifice of a similar kind. A societal structure –

(*The Ambassador raised his beautiful eyebrows at these words and tapped his painted nail against his teeth as though in amused reproof of such jargon.*)

Minister (*intransigently*): A societal structure is the greatest of all the works of art that man can make. Like the greatest art, it is perfectly symmetric. It has the architectonic structure of music, a symmetry imposed upon it in order to resolve a play of tensions which would disrupt order but without which order is lifeless. In this serene and abstract harmony, everything moves with the solemnity of the absolutely predictable and –

(*Here the young man interrupted him impatiently.*)

Ambassador: Go in fear of abstractions!

(*Pettishly he consumed the last crumbs of fish and fell silent until the waiters had replaced the plates with, to my delight and astonishment,* tournedos Rossini. *The Ambassador brusquely dismissed an offering of* pommes allumettes. *When he spoke again, his voice had deepened in colour.*)

Ambassador: Our primary difference is a philosophical one, Minister. For us, the world exists only as a medium in which we execute our desires. Physically, the world itself, the actual world – the real world, if you like – is formed of malleable clay; its metaphysical structure is just as malleable.

Minister: Metaphysics are no concern of mine.

(*The Ambassador's hair abruptly emitted a fountain of blue lights and, suddenly Charlotte Corday, he pointed a dagger at the Minister.*)

Ambassador: Dr Hoffman will make metaphysics *your* business!

(*The Minister cut his his meat phlegmatically.*)

Minister: I do not think so.

(*The words fell from his mouth with so heavy a weight I was surprised they did not drop straight through the table. I was deeply impressed by his gravity. It quenched even the enthusiasm I had experienced at mining a black gem of truffle from my wedge of paté, for it was the first time I had experienced the power of an absolute negative. The Ambassador visibly responded to this change in tone. If he instantly ceased to look like an avenging angel, he also instantly became less epicene.*)

Ambassador: Please name your price. The Doctor would like to buy you.

Minister : No.

Ambassador : Allow me to suggest a tentative figure . . . five provinces; four public transport systems; three ports; two metropolises and an entire civil administration.

Minister : No.

Ambassador : The Doctor will go even higher, you know.

Minister : NO!

> (*The Ambassador shrugged and we all continued to eat our delicious meat until it was gone and the salad came. We were drinking red wine. The skin of the Aambassador's throat was so luminously delicate one could see the glowing shadow of the burgundy trickle down his gullet after he had taken a sip.*)

Ambassador : The Doctor's campaign is still only in its preliminary stages and yet he has already made of this city a timeless place outside the world of reason.

Minister : All he has done is to find some means of bewitching the intelligence. He has only induced a radical suspension of disbelief. As in the early days of the cinema, all the citizens are jumping through the screen to lay their hands on the naked lady in the bathtub!

Ambassador : And yet, in fact, their fingers touch flesh.

Minister : They believe they do. Yet all they touch is substantial shadow.

Ambassador : And what a beautiful definition of flesh! You know I am only substantial shadow, Minister, but if you cut me, I bleed. Touch me; I palpitate!

> (*Certainly I had never seen a phantom who looked at that moment more shimmeringly unreal than the Ambassador, nor one who seemed to throb with more erotic promise. The Minister, however, laughed.*)

Minister : Whether you are real or not, I know for sure that I am not inventing you.

Ambassador : How is that?

Minister : I don't have enough imagination.

> (*Now it was the Ambassador's turn to laugh and then he paused and harked for a moment, as if listening to an invisible voice. It was a childish trick but remarkably effective.*)

Ambassador : The Doctor's offer has just risen by four opera houses and the cities of Rome, Florence and Dresden before the fire. We will throw in John Sebastian Bach as your *Kapellmeister*, to clinch the bargain.

Minister: (*dismissively.*) Come, now! We are well at work upon our counter measures!

Ambassador: Yes, indeed. We have been watching the progress of your electronic harem with considerable interest.

(*I had never thought of the Minister's computer centre as an electronic harem. The simile struck me as admirable. But the Minister bit his lip.*)

Minister: How?

(*The Ambassador ignored this question.*)

Ambassador: You are in the process of tabulating every thing you can lay your hands on. In the sacred name of symmetry, you slide them into a series of straitjackets and label them with, oh, my God, what inexpressibly boring labels! Your mechanical prostitutes welcome their customers in an alien gibber wholly denied to the human tongue while you, you madame, work as an abortionist on the side. You murder the imagination in the womb, Minister.

Minister: Somebody must impose restraint. If I am an abortionist, your master is a forger. He has passed off upon us an entire currency of counterfeit phenomena.

Ambassador: Do you regard the iconographic objects – or, shall we say, symbolically functioning propositions – which we transmit to you as a malign armoury inimical to the human race, of which you take this city to be a microcosm?

(*The Minister put his knife and fork together symmetrically on his empty plate and spoke with great precision.*)

Minister: I do.

(*The Ambassador leaned back in his chair and smiled the most seductive of smiles.*)

Ambassador: Then you are wrong. They are emanations only of the asymmetric, Minister, the asymmetric you deny. The doctor knows how to pierce appearances and to allow real forms to emerge into substantiality from the transparency of immanence. You cannot destroy our imagery; you may annihilate the appearances but the asymmetric essence can neither be created nor destroyed – only changed. And if you disintegrate the images with your lasers and your infra red rays, they only revert to their constituent parts and soon come together again in another form which you yourself have rendered even more arbitrary by your interference. The Doctor is about to reveal the entire truth of the cosmogony. Please wait patiently. It will not take much longer.

(*They brought us fruit and cheese. The Ambassador cut himself a sliver of brie.*)

Ambassador: You do appreciate, Minister, that very soon death, in innumerable guises, will walk these teeming streets.

Minister: She does already.

(*The Ambassador shrugged, as if to say: 'You have seen nothing yet.' He pulled off a sprig of grapes.*)

Ambassador: Are you prepared to capitulate?

Minister: What are your master's terms?

Ambassador: Absolute authority to establish a regime of total liberation.

(*The Minister ground out his cigarette and cut a portion of Stilton. From the bowl of fruit, he selected a Cox's Orange Pippin.*)

Minister: I do not capitulate.

Ambassador: Very well. Prepare yourself for a long, immense and deliberate derangement of the senses. I understand you have broken all the mirrors.

Minister: That was to stop them begetting images.

(*The Ambassador produced a small mirror from his pocket and presented it to the Minister, so that he saw his own face. The Minister covered his eyes and screamed but almost at once regained his composure and went on paring the skin from his apple. The walls of the world did not cave in and the feline smile of the Ambassador did not waver. The meal concluded. The Ambassador refused coffee but, with a return of his original, de haut en bas manner, rose to bid us farewell. As he left the restaurant, all the flowers in every vase shed every single one of their petals. I switched off the tape recorder; now I must rely on my memory.*)

I myself ordered coffee and the Minister took his habitual black tea, though this afternoon he tipped into his cup the contents of a balloon of brandy. He had me play over the recording of their conversation and then stayed sunk in thought for a while, lost inside a cloud of cigarette smoke.

'If I were a religious man, Desiderio,' he said at last, 'I would say we had just survived an encounter with Mephistopheles.'

The Minister had always struck me as a deeply religious man.

'Let me tell you a parable,' he went on. 'A man made a pact with the Devil. The condition was this: the man delivered up his soul as soon as Satan had assassinated God. "Nothing simpler," said Satan and put a revolver to his own temple.'

'Do you cast Dr Hoffman as God or Satan?'

The Minister smiled.

'As my parable suggests, the roles are interchangeable,' he replied. 'Come. Let us go.'

But, for myself, I was bewildered, for certain timbres in the young man's voice had reawakened all my last night's dream and, as if his voice had struck those mysterious notes which are supposed to shatter glass, a fine tracery of cracks had all at once appeared in the surface of my indifference. The young man fascinated me. As the Minister signed the check, I saw the curious ambassador had left behind him on the chair he had occupied a handkerchief of the same exquisite lace as the fabric of his shirt. I picked it up. Along the hem, stitched in a flourish of silk so white it was virtually invisible, was the name I had only seen before in my dream, the name: ALBERTINA. The hieratic chant of the black swan rang again in my ears; I swayed as if I were about to faint.

The Minister slipped the head waiter a fat tip and lit a fresh cigarette as he led me by the arm into the equivocal afternoon, where the sunlight was already thickening.

'Desiderio,' he said. 'How would you like to go on a little trip?'

2. The Mansion of Midnight

The Minister was clutching at straws but he clutched ferociously.

That very morning, as I tested the Ambassador's letter in another part of the Bureau of Determination, the Minister's computers had startled him by registering a significant analogy. They posited certain correspondences between the activities of the proprietor of a certain peep-show who had operated his business upon the pier at the seaside resort of S. throughout the summer and now showed signs of quartering himself there for the winter. It seemed a small enough clue to me; hardly worth the importance the Minister placed on it – and hardly enough to justify my new promotion. Nevertheless, promoted I was; between lunch and teatime, I became the Minister's special agent and my mission was, if I could find him, to assassinate Dr Hoffman as inconspicuously as possible.

I was chosen for the mission because: (a) I was in my right mind; (b) I was dispensable and (c) the Minister's computers decided my skill at crossword puzzles suggested a facility in the processes of analogical thought which might lead me to the Doctor where everyone else had failed. I think the Minister himself thought of me as a kind of ambulant computer. Even so, in spite of the encouraging voice with which he wished me farewell, I guessed it was something of a forlorn hope.

The computers constructed me an identity sufficiently foolproof to take me past the checkpoints of the Determination Police, for I was the most secret of agents. I was to pose as an Inspector of Veracity, first class. At the town of S., some sixty miles further up the coast, I was to make a special report on the mysterious affair of the Mayor, who had disappeared some time before. The inscrutable business of bureaucracy went on, war or no war, and my bureaucratic credentials were impeccable. I was issued with a small car, a complement of petrol coupons and a pocket arsenal of revolvers, etc. I packed a bag with a notebook or two and a shirt. I took with me no souvenirs or objects of sentimental value because I had none. Even though I did not know when, if ever, I would see it again I did not bother to say good-bye to my arid room. I left the city the next morning; as I passed the Bureau of Determination, I saw a slogan had appeared on the wall. It read: DR HOFFMAN PISSES LIGHTNING. I drove off through a gigantic storm. It was still before breakfast time but the sky was so black that an unnatural darkness filled the streets which today, as if on purpose to speed my departure, had reverted to the forms I had always known, streets without magic or surprise, streets as boring as only those of home can be.

I did not have much hope of returning to them; nor did I believe the city would survive very long after I had gone, not only because I had always obscurely felt I was one of the invisible struts of reason which had helped to prop it up for so long but because it seemed inevitable it would soon collapse. Yet I felt no nostalgia when, after I speeded up the interminable negotiations with the Police by the gift of several cartons of the Minister's cigarettes, I took the road that led north. I suppose I hoped that, if the city fell, at least it would coffin the environment which bred my unappeasable boredom. There was nothing in the great heap of stucco, brick and stone behind me to which I felt the least attachment except the memory of a certain mysterious dream and that I took with me. And, if I felt a certain excitement as the miles wound away beneath me, it was because of that dream and the name, which seemed to shelter three magic entities, the glass woman, the black swan and the ambassador. The name was a clue which pointed to a living being beneath the conjuring tricks, for such tricks imply the presence of a conjurer. I was nourishing an ambition – to rip away that ruffled shirt and find out whether the breasts of an authentic woman swelled beneath it; and if around her neck was a gold collar with the name ALBERTINA engraved upon it.

And then? I would fall on my knees in worship.

Under all my indifferences, I was an exceedingly romantic young man yet, until that time, circumstances had never presented me with a sufficiently grand opportunity to exercise my pent-up passion. I had opted for the chill restraints of formalism only out of sharp necessity. That, you see, was why I was so bored.

The appearance of the countryside had not altered. The flat fields of vegetables around the capital stretched, as before, to the horizon and still seemed to produce nothing but commonplace roots and tubers. The villages had put up their shutters to keep out the rain but otherwise looked as vindictively peasant as they had always done. Even the scarecrows looked only like scarecrows. The road itself was the only casualty, or the first casualty, for the volume of wheeled traffic was reduced almost to nothing and already vigorous growths of weeds and flowers pushed up through the cracks in the asphalt while no holes had been repaired, so now brown troughs of water gaped everywhere. The drive took some hours more than it should have done; I reached my destination in the middle of the afternoon when a magnificent rainbow was arching over the town and, together with a shimmering brilliance in the sky over the sea, it heralded the end of the downpour. As I drove into the suburbs, the rain first fell aslant and then ceased altogether. The sun came out and the pavements began to steam gently.

S. was a bright, pleasant, pastel-tinted town redolent of dead fish and wet face flannels, clean as if the abrasive sea scrubbed it twice a day. Before the war, families came out from the city to spend a summer fortnight at guest houses where the doormats were always full of sand and the hallways littered with tin buckets and tiny spades. There was a pier made of such lacy striations of iron it looked like the skeleton of an enormous bird or a drawing of itself made with a fine pen and Indian ink on the pale blue paper of the well-mannered sea. The fishermen lived at the other end of the beach in cheerful, white-washed cottages overgrown with that summer's abundance of roses and they hung out their nets to dry on picturesque and primordial poles, weighing them at the corners with balls of dark green glass. It was late August and the shops offered pink rock, coloured postcards, candy floss, straw hats and all the appurtenances of the holiday maker but, though all the doors were open, I could see no shopkeepers within, behind the counters, and the entire place was quite empty of humanity.

Along the promenade, striped umbrellas cast pools of shade over deserted tables at which no ice-cream eaters sat, though there were plenty of saucers smeared with residual traces and also glasses half full of pink, green and orange drinks in which the ice had not yet melted and the paper straws were still indented at the top from the pressure of lips. The pale acres of sand were empty but for a few waddling sea-birds and I noticed a corpse who lay where the sand had left him, unattended but for a cloud of flies. There was nobody at the turnstile of the pier to take my coin. Some of the sideshows were shuttered but here half a dozen ping pong balls bounced on jets of water and the rifles were laid out in invitation to no cracksmen. Though the bed was made up ready to tip the lady out, the lady herself had vanished. Yet the loudspeakers blared cheerful music and nowhere looked deserted. It was as if the entire population of the town had slipped off somewhere, called to witness some event to which I alone had not received an invitation, and would all be back at their posts in five minutes. A sea breeze blew the bright pennants this way and that way. I passed a fortune teller's booth and another booth which smelled of hot dogs simmering by themselves in a tin vat of hot water and then, with most suspicious ease, I found my first quarry, the peep-show.

It was indeed the coloured replica of the canvas tent I had seen in monochrome in the files of the Bureau – coloured but faded, left out too long in the rains of years, a sagging box of pink striped canvas with the flap drawn up and held back with a fraying cord. A yellowed play-bill in old-fashioned lettering announced that the SEVEN WONDERS OF THE WORLD IN THREE LIFELIKE DIMENSIONS awaited one inside and I bent my head and stepped into the warm, dim cave. It was lit only by the beams of the afternoon sun, creeping in through the many gaps in the structure. A startled gull started up from a perch upon an iron wheel with a wild beating of wings as I came in and swooped around the interior until it found the exit. At the sound, an old man whose sleeping shape had been obscured by the thick brown shadows awoke with shouts and curses. There was a chink and rumble of a rolling, overturned bottle and the air filled with fumes of raw spirit.

'Is there no peace?' demanded the old man, rearing like a seal from a rustling heap of straw and instantly, with a groan, falling back. He was the first living thing I had seen since I arrived in the town and he was nothing but a piece of verminous flotsam overgrown with a white weed of hair. There was not a single tooth left in his head and a stained and matted beard straggled over the lower part of his face while the upper part was hidden by a pair of wire-rimmed, green-tinted glasses, the left lens of which was cracked clean across. He wore the ruins of striped trousers and a dinner jacket, relics, perhaps, of more prosperous days, and no shirt – only a torn, filthy vest. His feet were bare; his blackened toe-nails had grown into claws. He poked about for a few moments until he gained a handhold on one of the curious machines which filled the tent and, clinging to it, steadied himself sufficiently to rise again. He looked in my direction but did not look at me; he looked all about the tent as if trying to locate me and then wearily shook his shaggy head.

'Though this is by no means Gaza, yet I am eyeless,' he said and I knew for certain he was blind.

'If you are a customer,' he said, 'please place twenty-five cents in the receptacle you will find placed for that purpose on the tea-chest beside the door and take your fill of the wonders of the world. But if not,' he added and his voice began to trail away, 'then not . . . However, whatever you are, kindly restore me my bottle.'

When it rolled out to the middle of the floor, the bottle had spilled all it contained.

'There isn't a drop left,' I warned as I handed it to him. He shook it to hear if there was a rattle, sniffed the neck voluptuously and then, leaning behind him, parted the canvas walls and dropped it into the sea below, where it gurgled and sank.

'I have drunk sufficiently deeply of humiliation, anyway,' he said. 'Please pay your quarter, do your business and go away.'

He relapsed on his pallet and made no more sounds but the murmurous roaring of his breathing. The saucer contained two trouser buttons, a shell and a coin I identified as a Japanese one-sen piece, long out of circulation, but I put a quarter there, all the same. The machines were of ancient rusted cast iron decorated with impressions of cupids, eagles and knots of ribbons. Each was the size and shape of an old-fashioned oven and, at the front, a pair of glass eye-pieces jutted out on long, hollow stalks. I examined all the exhibits in turn. Inside each one, underneath the item it represented, was a sign, clumsily lettered by hand, giving a title.

Exhibit One: I HAVE BEEN HERE BEFORE
The legs of a woman, raised and open as if ready to admit a lover, formed a curvilinear triumphal arch. The feet were decorated with spike-heeled, black leather pumps. This anatomical section, composed of pinkish wax dimpled at the knee, did not admit the possibility of the existence of a torso. A bristling pubic growth rose to form a kind of coat of arms above the circular proscenium it contained at either side but, although the hairs had been inserted one by one in order to achieve the maximal degree of verisimilitude, the overall effect was one of stunning artifice. The dark red and purple crenellations surrounding the vagina acted as a frame for a perfectly round hole through which the viewer glimpsed the moist, luxuriant landscape of the interior.

Here endlessly receded before one's eyes a miniature but irresistible vista of semi-tropical forest where amazing fruits hung on the trees, while from the dappled and variegated chalices of enormous flowers the size of millstones, perfumes of such extraordinary potency that they had become visible to the eye exuded as soft, purple dew. Small, brilliant birds trilled silently on the branches; animals of exquisite shapes and colours, among them unicorns, giraffes and herbivorous lions, cropped up buttercups and daisies from the impossibly green grass; butterflies, dragonflies and innumerable jewelled insects fluttered, darted or scurried among the verdure so all was in constant movement and besides the very vegetation was continually transforming itself. As I watched, the pent-up force of the sweet juice within it burst open a persimmon and the split skin let out a flight of orange tawny singing birds. An elongated bud on the point of opening must have changed its mind for it turned into a strawberry instead of a water-lily. A fish sprang out of the river, became a white rabbit and bounded away.

It seemed that winter and rough winds would never touch these bright, oblivious regions or ripple the surface of the lucid river which wound a tranquil course down the central valley. The eye of the beholder followed the course of this river upwards towards the source, and so it saw, for the first time, after some moments of delighted looking, the misty battlements of a castle. The longer one looked at the dim outlines of this castle, the more sinister it grew, as though its granite viscera housed as many torture chambers as the Château of Silling.

The rest of the machines contained the following items.

Exhibit Two: THE ETERNAL VISTAS OF LOVE
When I looked through the windows of the machine, all I could see were two eyes looking back at me. Each eye was a full three feet from end to end, complete with a lid and a tear duct, and was suspended in the air without any visible support. Like the pubic hair in the previous model, the lashes had been scrupulously set one by one in narrow hems of rosy wax but this time the craftsmen had achieved a disturbing degree of life-likeness which uncannily added to the synthetic quality of the image. The rounded whites were delicately veined with crimson to produce an effect like that of the extremely precious marble used in Italy during the late baroque period to make altars for the chapels of potentates and the irises were simple rings of deep brown bottle glass while in the pupils I could see, reflected in two discs of mirror, my own eyes, very greatly magnified by the lenses of the machine. Since my own pupils, in turn, reflected the false eyes before me while these reflections again reflected those reflections, I soon realized I was watching a model of eternal regression.

Exhibit Three: THE MEETING PLACE OF LOVE AND HUNGER
Upon a cut-glass dish of the kind in which desserts are served lay two perfectly spherical portions of vanilla ice-cream, each topped with a single cherry so that the resemblance to a pair of female breasts was almost perfect.

Exhibit Four: EVERYONE KNOWS WHAT THE NIGHT IS FOR
Here, a wax figure of the headless body of a mutilated woman lay in a pool of painted blood. She wore only the remains of a pair of black stockings and a ripped suspender belt of shiny black rubber. Her arms stuck out stiffly on either side of her and once again I noticed the loving care with which the craftsmen who manufactured her had simulated the growth of underarm hair. The right breast had been partially segmented and hung open to reveal two surfaces of meat as bright and false as the plaster sirloins which hang in toy butcher's shops while her belly was covered with some kind of paint that always contrived to look wet and, from the paint, emerged the handle of an

enormous knife which was kept always a-quiver by the action (probably) of a spring.

Exhibit Five: TROPHY OF A HUNTER IN THE FORESTS OF THE NIGHT

A head – purporting, presumably, to have been taken from the victim of the preceding tableau – hung in the air, again with no strings or hooks in sight to reveal how this position was maintained. From the point of severance dripped slow gouts of artificial blood, plop, plop, plop, but the receptacle into which they fell was outside the viewer's field of vision. A very abundant black wig tumbled around her pallid features, which wore a hideous expression of resignation. Her eyes were closed.

Exhibit Six: THE KEY TO THE CITY

A candle in the shape of a penis of excessive size, with scrotum attached, in a state of pronounced tumescence. The wrinkled foreskin was drawn far enough back to uncover in its importunate entirety the grossly swollen, sunset-coloured tip as far as a portion of the shaft itself and, at the minute cranny in the centre, where a wick must have been lodged, burned a small, pure flame. As the viewer watched, the candle tipped forward on its balls and pointed towards one accusingly.

I was struck with the notion that this was supposed to represent the Minister's penis.

Exhibit Seven: PERPETUAL MOTION

As I expected, here a man and a woman were conducting sexual congress on a black horsehair couch. The figures, again exquisitely executed in wax, looked as though they might have been modelled in one piece and, due to a clockwork mechanism hidden in their couch, they rocked continually back and forth. This coupling had a fated, inevitable quality. One could not picture a cataclysm sufficiently violent to rend the twined forms asunder and neither could one conceive of a past beginning for they were so firmly joined together it seemed they must have been formed in this way at the beginning of time and, locked parallel, would go on thus for ever to infinity. They were not so much erotic as pathetic, poor palmers of desire who never budged as much as an inch on their endless pilgrimage. The man's face was moulded into the woman's neck and so could not be seen but the head of the woman was constructed so as to oscillate in the socket of her neck and, as it rolled from side to side, her face was intermittently visible.

I recognized this face instantly, although it was fixed in the tormented snarl of orgasm. I remained staring at it for some time. It was the beautiful face of Dr Hoffman's ambassador. The old man interrupted my reverie. His voice was as raucous as a rooster's.

'Is there enough money in my saucer to buy me a bottle?' he demanded.

'I'll buy you a drink with pleasure,' I said.

'Thank 'ee; thank 'ee kindly,' he replied and painfully heaved himself to his feet. He fumbled around in his corner until he finally produced a peaked cap of the style worn by Lenin and the Bolsheviks. When he had set this jauntily on his head, he began another search but I soon uncovered his white stick for him.

Now the pier was peopled. A ragged youth with caked snot in the grooves under his nose stood behind the rifle range idly probing the inside of his ear with a piece of twig and a blowsy woman in a rayon slip, with hair dyed the colour of apricots, yawned and scratched her buttocks at the entrance to the fortune teller's booth. Three little boys clung to the rails by their feet holding fishing rods over the sea with one hand, and, in the other hand clutched jam jars of water by the string handles tied round the rims. The beach, too, presented an everyday holiday panorama of frisking dogs, children building sandcastles and a great deal of skin exposed to the sun. But all these Johnny-come-latelies had the yawning, vacant air of those just awakened from a deep sleep and walked uncertainly, sometimes, for no reason, breaking into a stumbling run and then halting just as suddenly to stare around them with startled, empty eyes or, turning to speak to a companion, they would stop, mouth ajar, as if they no longer recognized him. And, for so great a number of people, they made very little noise, as if they knew they had no existential right to be here.

The peep-show proprietor was blind and lame but he certainly knew his way about the town and led me unerringly to a small bar so deep inside the fishermen's quarter the streets no longer bothered to keep up appearances and relapsed thankfully into slumminess. We sat down at a marble topped table and, without waiting for our order, a black brought us two glasses of the crude spirit that passes for brandy among the poor. He left the bottle on the table. The peep-show proprietor emptied his glass at a draught.

'The purpose of my display,' he remarked, 'is to demonstrate the difference between saying and showing. Signs speak. Pictures show.'

I filled up his glass again for him and he thanked me by leaning across the table and comprehensively stroking my face with his gnarled finger-tips, as if learning my dimensions before sculpting me.

'Who sent you?' he asked abruptly.

'I've come to investigate the disappearance of the Mayor,' I replied guardedly.

'Ah, yes,' he said. 'She sits like Mariana in the moated grange, poor girl! Mary Anne, the beautiful somnambulist.'

He drank again, more slowly, and then remarked: 'My life is nothing but a wind-blown rag.'

With that, he fell silent. I was to learn he spoke only in a series of disconnected, often gnomic statements usually tinged with melancholy, bitterness, self-pity or all three together. I sipped my *eau-de-vie* quietly and waited for him to speak again. After the third glass, he did.

'I was not Mendoza. I never had that honour.'

'Who were you, then?'

He became bashful and secretive.

'Once, I was a very important man indeed. Even, you might say, a great man. Once they used to take off their hats to me as I walked down the road and murmur to me ingratiatingly and barmen were glad of my custom, yes! proud and glad! Instead of merely sullenly tolerating me.'

The barman, who must have heard all this many times before, flashed his teeth and smiled at me as if to create complicity. I poured more brandy into the old man's glass.

'They used to say, "We're honoured to have you honour us with your presence, Professor" ...' And then he stopped, as though he knew he had already said too much, which was perfectly true – he had given me the principal letters of a clue and now I had only to fill in the blanks. I made an initial guess.

'The greatest success a teacher can boast is the pupil who surpasses him.'

'Then why has he humiliated me so?' wailed the old man and I knew instantly he had taught elementary physics to Dr Hoffman at the university all those years ago. When he finished the fifth glass, the last vestiges of his discretion vanished.

'He doesn't even allow me to work in the laboratories. He gave me a set of samples and let me loose, left me to wander, up and down, here and there, hither and thither, pushing my wheelbarrow in front of me ... tripping over stones and rotting my guts with filthy liquor ...'

'His set of samples?'

'Plenty more in my sack,' he said. 'Lots and lots of samples. Dozens and scores and hundreds and thousands of samples. You'd think they breed in there and I just put them in the machines, don't I, and stick a sign along with them and sometimes people pay and sometimes they don't and sometimes they scream and sometimes they giggle and sometimes the police turn me out of town and off I go down the road again, pushing my barrow. And times grow worse, since he began to put it into practice. No more money to spare for an old man's disgusting if didactic demonstrations; you can get as good at home. Soon I'll have to charge a pin to see it – or a jamjar, or a cigarette card. And who will exchange such rubbish for liquor, then? When that day dawns, poor robin must tuck his head under his wing, poor thing, and pretend to be warm, yes!'

'But,' he added, pouring out the seventh glass for himself, 'the singular privilege of becoming Mendoza was never granted me. I was allowed to make my own transformations and if you look at me you can see how well I have succeeded.'

A tear trickled out from under his glasses so that I knew he had eyes even if they were sightless and I seemed to remember a cutting in the files that said Dr Hoffman's old professor had suffered some injuries in an accident in a laboratory many many years before. I judged the old man was now sufficiently drunk and handed the bottle back to the barman.

'I should like to kill him,' said the peep-show proprietor. 'If I were ten years younger, I would go to the castle and murder him.'

'Do you know the way to the castle?'

'I should follow my nose,' he said.

But then a cock crowed and the sound affected the old man curiously. He sat up and listened attentively; it crowed a second time and then a third.

'Get thee behind me, Satan!' shrieked the old man.

With that, he struck me full in the face with his cane so that blood streamed into my eyes from a cut above my forehead and, when I could see again, he was gone. I hurried immediately back to the pier but, though he could only hobble, I caught no sign of him along the way and when I reached the place where his booth had been, it was, of course, also completely gone. So I made my way to the Town Hall, to do my official business.

The plaster scrolls and garlands on the pompous exterior of the Town Hall were crumbling like dry sponge cake and all the windows were screened with green blinds but the heavy mahogany doors swung open readily enough and, though puffs of dust rose up when I trod on the maroon plush carpeting and most of the offices were empty but for cobwebs spun from inkwell to pen-rack across blurred surfaces of desks, at last a yawning clerk came out of the ante-room of the Mayor's office to greet me. Metal bracelets hoisted up his shirt-sleeves to bare his wrists for work; he had been left in charge.

The Mayor's office itself was a mausoleum. It had been tidied since he left so there were no papers or files to be seen and they had drawn his carved, pompous chair so tightly up to the scrupulously denuded desk that it looked as though it were denying admittance there to any future body. The Mayor's pink blotter was thickly furred with mildew and his dried-out water flask, topped with an inverted tumbler, had grown hunched shoulders of settled dust. The indefatigable spiders had woven a canopy across a photograph of the late President on the wall. The clerk opened a cupboard to reveal half a decanterful of mayoral sherry, now grown viscous as treacle, groped on a lower shelf and produced the fur-collared overcoat the Mayor had left behind him on the snowy morning he vanished. The pockets contained only a single balled glove and a dirty handkerchief, nothing of significance.

But after only the briefest search through the other offices, I found evidence that a certain peep-show proprietor had filed an official request to open a booth on the pier in the preceding month of April; this form, signed with a tentative cross, still waited for the official stamp so my ramshackle friend had clearly gone ahead on his own and set up shop regardless. It was, at least, a connection. I tucked away this form to take back to the Minister, took the clerk's name and briefly checked his reality rating with my information. It appeared satisfactory. Then I asked him to ring the Mayor's home, where his daughter still lived with a housekeeper. The clerk got through after only seven or eight minutes and I noted the services were still functioning satisfactorily though the clerk told me the telephone switchboard could neither take nor receive calls outside the immediate neighbourhood while even these local calls were constantly interrupted by voices in unknown languages. After a good deal of country town chat with the Mayor's house, he ensured me some nights' lodging there, at the probable source of my bureaucratic mystery.

'It's all got very run down since the Mayor left,' he said dubiously. 'Just the old woman and the, er, girl . . .'

Something in his voice indicated a strangeness in the girl. I pricked up the ears of my mind, briskly jotted down the directions he gave me and went to my car. It was now early evening and, since I stopped on my way to eat a supper of meat pies in a fly-blown café too squalid to be illusory, I did not reach the house until it was almost dark. It lay some way out of town at the end of an old-fashioned, rutted lane, where there were no other habitations than one abandoned barn. The sky was the tender, transparent blue of a late summer's night and a slender intimation of the moon hung above a copse of fir although the tiger lilies of the setting sun still growled in the west. I parked my car in the road and, once the engine ceased to throb, there was no other sound but a faint shimmer of birdsong and the rattle of the quilled boughs of the pines.

Although I knew it was inhabited, at first I thought the house was quite forsaken for the extensive garden which surrounded it was sunk in the neglect of years. Whoever made the garden first must have loved roses but now the roses had quite overrun the garden and formed dense, forbidding hedges that sent out such an overpowering barrage of perfume that my head was soon swimming. Besides, roses sprayed out fanged, blossoming whips from cupolas which almost foundered under their weight; roses reared up in groves of sturdy standards now the size of young oaks; and roses sent vine-like tendrils along the sombre branches of yew trees, of ornamental rowans, of cherry trees and apple trees already half-suffocated with mistletoe so this summer, which had suited roses so well, seemed to have conspired with the gardener to produce an orgiastic jungle of all kinds of roses, and though I could not distinguish any of their separate shapes or colours, their individual scents all blended into a single, intolerably sweet essence which made every nerve in my body ache and tingle.

Roses had climbed up the already luxuriantly ivied walls and lodged in knots on the roofs where flowering weeds were rooted in the gaps between the mossy tiles while a great, unlopped elm with lice of rooks in its hair towered over the house as if about to drop its great limbs upon it, to smash it, while at the same time its roots clutched the foundations under the earth in a ferocious embrace. The garden had laid claim to the house and was destroying it at its arborescent leisure. Those within the house were already at the capricious mercy of nature.

Enormous clumps of mugwort had torn apart the gate and blocked the path entirely so I had to clamber over the tumbledown wall, dislodging a few more stones as I did so. Looking towards the shaggy outlines of the house, I saw a greenish glimmer of light on the ground floor filtering through the leaves which obscured the windows and took this for my clue out of the hostile, vegetable maze which, as I moved forward, lashed me, scored me, stung me and left me sick, bleeding and dizzy with its odorous excess. As I drew nearer to the house I heard, over the pounding of the blood in my ears, notes of music falling 'plop', like goldfish in a quiet pool. Breathless, I halted for a moment to find out if the sound was true. It went wistfully on. Somebody in that ruinous place was playing Debussy on the piano.

At last I reached the lighted window and parting the foliage which covered it, I peered through. I saw a drawing room with worn Persian rugs on the floor and walls hung with a once crimson brocaded paper that was now faded and figured with damp and mould, rucking and buckling over the dank walls beneath. There was an alabaster fireplace with a bouquet of shell flowers in a misted glass dome upon it and a fan of silver paper in the grate. Oil paintings so heavily varnished one could not make out their subjects hung here and there askew in pompous frames of tarnished gilt and an unlit cut-glass chandelier in the centre of the ceiling scintillated with reflections from the two candles in a branched stick which stood on the grand piano and threw a soft light over the girl who played it.

Her back was turned towards me but when I craned my neck I could see her white, thin, nervous fingers on the keyboard and caught a glimpse of the pale curve of her cheek. Her hair, the lifeless brown of a winter forest, hung down the back of her black dress. She played with extraordinary sensitivity. The room was full of a poignant, nostalgic anguish which seemed to emanate from that slender figure whose face I could not see.

I thought it best not to disturb her and made my way round to the back of the house where I found a black cat washing itself on an upturned bucket, and inside an open door, a fat old woman who sat in a darkened kitchen to save, she said, the electricity; and that was also the reason why she made the mistress of the house play the piano by candlelight. The housekeeper guessed who I must be from my lumpish shape in the shadows. She greeted me warmly and turned on the lights in my honour to reveal a blessedly commonplace kitchen with a gas stove, a refrigerator and a saucer of milk put down for pussy. She settled me down at the scrubbed table with a cup of tea and a saucerful of shortbread biscuits, asked about my journey and hoped, too solicitously, that I would find the accommodation adequate.

'Though how could we put you up luxuriously, sir, I mean – in the circumstances . . .'

She had a slippery, ingratiating quality which was meant to disarm but somehow offended me and she loquaciously set sail on a rattling stream of nothings while the girl in the drawing room continued to play the piano exquisitely and the music echoed down a corridor into the room. The old woman spoke of the vanished Mayor with neither embarrassment nor surmise. She had apparently absorbed the fact that he was gone so well into her world that if, one day, he returned, she would feel subtly affronted. She hinted that she suspected a woman might lie behind it for, she said: 'Not many women would want Mary Anne for a step-daughter. Oh, no! Oh, no!' She rolled her eyes significantly and chatted on about the difficulty of obtaining women's magazines and knitting wool. Presently the music ceased and Mary Anne herself came into the kitchen, on some errand she forgot as soon as she saw me for the housekeeper had not bothered to tell her an unexpected guest would arrive at her home. She stood in the doorway, transfixed with surprise and apprehension; in her face, only eyes the colour of a rainy day moved this way and that, as if looking for a way out.

She had the waxen delicacy of a plant bred in a cupboard. She did not look as if blood flowed through her veins but instead some other, less emphatic fluid infinitely less red. Her mouth was barely touched with palest pink though it had exactly the proportions of the three cherries the artmaster piles in an inverted triangle to illustrate the classic mouth and there was no tinge of any pink at all on her cheeks. Now she was standing up, she was almost hidden in her dress and her tiny face, shaped like a locket, looked even smaller than it was because of a disordered profusion of hair streaming down as straight as if she had just been plucked from the river. I could see her hair and dress were stuck all over with twigs and petals from the garden. She looked like drowning Ophelia; I thought so immediately, though I could not know how soon she would really drown, for she was so forlorn and desperate. And a chilling and restrained passivity made her desperation all the more pathetic. The housekeeper clucked to see the wraith-like girl's bare feet.

'Put your slippers on at once, Miss! Bare feet on those stone flags! I never did! You'll catch your death!'

Mary Anne moved awkwardly from one foot to the other as if her chances of catching death from the stone floor of the kitchen were halved if only one foot came in contact with it at a time. She was about seventeen. Her distant gaze wandered vaguely over the table and she whispered in a pleading undertone:

'Perhaps a little tea . . .'

'Not unless you step on to the rag rug,' said the housekeeper, too authoritatively for the circumstances perhaps.

The girl edged into the room until she stood on the bright strip of carpet, allowing her eyes to rest on me again while the housekeeper got her a cup and even a biscuit, although she muttered to herself as she did so.

'I am Mary Anne, the Mayor's daughter. Who are you?'

'I am a civil servant and my name is Desiderio.'

She repeated the name quietly to herself but with a curious quiver in her voice which might have been pleasure and eventually she confided:

'Desiderio, the desired one, did you know you have eyes just like an Indian?'

The housekeeper went 'tsk! tsk!' with annoyance for we whites were not supposed to acknowledge the Indians.

'My mother always found it embarrassing,' I replied and at that the girl seemed obscurely pleased and thrust out her hand in such a sudden, unexpected gesture of goodwill it was more like a thwarted blow than an offer to shake. But I took her hand and found it was icy. She would not let go of me for a long time.

'Mr Desiderio is going to stay in the spare room for a while,' said the housekeeper grudgingly, as if reluctant to share the information with her mistress. 'He's come from the government.'

Mary Anne found this very mysterious; her eyes grew wide.

'You won't find my father, you know,' she informed me.

'Why not?' I asked. My fingers were still in the snow trap of her clutch.

'If he didn't come back in time to prune the roses, he won't come back at all,' she said, and shook with such silent but vigorous laughter her tea slopped from her cup on to her dress, which was already stained with all manner of other spilled food and drink.

'What do you think happened to him, Mary Anne?' I asked gently for, though I knew from the records and my own intuition she was quite real, I had never before met a woman who looked so conversant with shadows as she.

'He disintegrated of course,' she said. 'He resolved to his constituents – a test-tube of amino-acids, a tuft or two of hair.'

She gestured with her cup for more tea. She had not given me any answer I might have expected and, when I tried to question her further, she only giggled again and shook her head so that a twist of apple leaves fell to the floor and her hair flopped over her eyes. Then she put her cup down on the table with the excessive care of the born clumsy and ran up the dark corridor again. She must have left the door of the drawing room open, for her piano sounded louder this time, and she must have changed her music, for some irrational reason; now she played the lucid nonsense of Erik Satie. With a sigh, the housekeeper gathered up the cups.

'A screw loose,' she said. 'A piece missing.'

Soon she took me to a bed with a patchwork quilt in a simple but pleasant room at the back of the house. It was a soft, warm night and the girl at her piano picked out an angular fretwork of audible lace on the surface of my first sleep. I think I woke because the music stopped. Perhaps her candles had burned out.

Now the moon had fully risen and shone straight into my room through the screen of ivy and roses so that dappled shadows fell with scrupulous distinction on the bed, the walls and the floor. Inside looked like the negative of a photograph of outside and the moon had already taken a black and white picture of the garden. I woke instantly and completely, with no residue of sleep in my mind, as though this was the proper time for me to wake although it could only have been a little past midnight. I was too wakeful to stay in my bed and got restlessly up to look out of the window. The grounds were far more extensive than I had at first thought and those behind the house were even further on the way to wilderness than those through which I had passed. The moon shone so brightly there was not a single dark corner and I could see the dried-up bed of a large pond or small lake which was now an oval of flat-petalled lilies while the roses had entirely engulfed in their embrace a marble Undine who reclined on her side in a touching attitude of provincial gracefulness. Delineated with the precision of a woodcut in the moonlight, a family of young foxes rolled and tumbled with one another on a clearing which had been a lawn. There was no wind. The night sighed beneath the languorous weight of its own romanticism.

I do not think she made a sound to startle me but all at once I grew conscious of a presence in the room and cold sweat pricked the back of my neck. Slowly I turned from the window. She lived on the crepuscular threshold of life and so I remember her as if standing, always, hesitantly in a doorway like an unbidden guest uncertain of her welcome. Her eyes were open but blind and she held a rose in her outstretched fingers. She had taken off her plain, black dress and wore a white calico nightgown such as convent schoolgirls wear. As I went towards her, so she came to me and I took the rose because she

55

seemed to offer it to me. A thorn under the leaves pierced my thumb and I felt the red rose throb like a heart and saw it emit a single drop of blood as if like a sin-eater it had taken on the pain of the wound for me. She wound her insubstantial arms around me and put her mouth on mine. Her kiss was like a draught of cold water and yet immediately excited my desire for it was full of an anguished yearning.

I led her to the bed and, in the variegated shadows, penetrated her sighing flesh, which was as chill as that of a mermaid or of the marmoreal water-maiden in her own garden. I was aware of a curiously attenuated response, as if she were feeling my caresses through a veil, and you must realize that all this time I was perfectly well aware she was asleep, for, apart from the evidence of my senses, I remembered how the peep-show proprietor had talked of a beautiful somnambulist. Yet, if she was asleep, she was dreaming of passion and afterwards I slept without dreaming for I had experienced a dream in actuality. When I woke in the commonplace morning, nothing was left of her in the bed but some dead leaves and there was no sign she had been in the room except for a withered rose in the middle of the floor.

Mary Anne did not appear at breakfast though the housekeeper supplied me so amply with eggs, bacon, sausages, pancakes, coffee and fruit that I guessed, for whatever reasons, she was well satisfied with her house guest. In the bright light of morning, the old woman's plump, lugubrious face looked indefinably sinister, even malign. She pressed me to return to the Mayor's house for supper and at last, to quiet her, I agreed to do so and gave seven o'clock as the probable hour of my return, although I did not know if I would still be in the town at that time. When I went to my room to collect my briefcase, I passed an open door and, glancing inside, saw my nocturnal visitant sitting in front of a dressing-table mirror in an untidy room full of scores. She was still in her austere night-shift as she gave her tangled hair its (probably) single combing of the day.

'Mary Anne?'

She smiled at me remotely in the mirror and I knew she was awake.

'Good morning, Desiderio,' she said. 'I hope you had a good night's sleep.'

I was bewildered.

'Yes,' I stammered. 'Oh, yes.'

'Though occasionally people are frightened by the nightingales, because they make such a noise, sometimes.'

'Mary Anne, did you dream last night?'

Her comb caught in a knot and she tugged it impatiently.

'I dreamed about a love suicide,' she said. 'But then, I always do. Don't you think it would be very beautiful to die for love?'

It is always disquieting to talk with a person in a mirror. Besides, the mirror was contraband. Her voice was high and clear and, though she always talked softly, very sweetly piercing, like the sight of the moon in winter.

'I'm not at all sure it would be beautiful to die for anything,' I said.

'One only resolves to one's constituents,' she said with a trace of precocious pedantry. I stepped into the room, leaving a crude trail of heavy footprints on her white carpet, and, lifting her hair, I bent to kiss the nape of her neck. As I did so, I saw my own reflection for the first time since the beginning of the war. I saw that I had aged a little and was now as cynical as a satyr in a Renaissance painting. My face, poor mother, had all the inscrutability of the Indian. I greeted myself like a friend. Mary Anne allowed me to kiss her but I do not think she noticed it.

'What will you do today, Mary Anne?'

'Today, I shall play the piano, of course. Unless I think of something better to do, that is.'

And I do not know if, for a moment, I saw another person glance briefly out of her eyes for I was not looking at her in the mirror, only myself.

By the time I left the house, it had become a musical box for she was already playing. Now she was practising Chopin's *Etudes*. By daylight, I could see the house was very large, one of those rambling country houses, half farmhouse and half mansion, though it must already have been three-quarters tumbledown when the Mayor himself lived there for whole sections of the roof had caved in beneath the monstrous burden of vegetation upon it while what had once been stables and outhouses now lay open to the weather and nature had already thrown too thick a green blanket over them to have been woven in only a few months. In the pure light of the morning, the fallen bricks, the exposed beams, the roses and the trees still seemed to sleep, murmuring and stirring a little as if a vague, unmemorable dream disturbed a slumber as profound as that of their mistress, the beauty in the dreaming wood, who slept too deeply to be wakened by anything as gentle as a kiss.

I slipped into the Town Hall and glanced desultorily once more through the Mayor's files but I could find nothing that threw any further light on a disappearance I was now inclined to believe was quite unconnected with Dr Hoffman but just a simple suicide which might have taken place anywhere, at any time, on the spur of a despairing moment, for somehow I guessed the Mayor had been prone to anguish. When I had satisfied the conditions of my post as an Inspector of Veracity, I once again left the Town Hall in the sole hands of the yawning clerk and went to the bar where the peep-show proprietor had taken me. But even the massive black presided there no longer. Only a golden girl far more Indian than I, in a skimpy dress of bright striped cotton, wiped glasses as she stared aimlessly at the sunlight in the street outside, where only blow-flies buzzed in the choked gutters and, though I described the peep-show proprietor to her, she did not remember ever seeing him.

So I downed a single brandy and then sauntered along the Promenade, a place now dedicated solely to the joys of summer, although these joys were undertaken with a singular, silent listlessness. As I leaned on the iron railing gazing out over the prim corrugations of the ocean, I heard a tapping behind me. As inconspicuously as I could, I looked round. He scuttled past me, accompanied by the staccato rattle of his cane, muttering to himself; at a discreet distance, I followed him.

I cannot begin to describe his crabbed, crouched, scrambling walk – how first he tapped with his cane, then set it upon the ground and half swung himself forward on it with a wheezing, triumphant gasp as if at every step he defied and vanquished the ordinary laws of motion. And he managed to perform these senile acrobatics with immense speed, as if there were springs in his stick and the worn heels of his boots, too. He was indescribably filthy. He might have spent the night in a sewer.

He had moved his pitch to a dreary quarter of creosoted warehouses in which, from the stench, dried fish was stored. At the end of the alley hung with banners of washing, was a small shrine to a fisherman's madonna with a few dead flowers stuck before it in a chipped coca-cola bottle and, behind it, a little bare plot of grass now almost filled by the familiar, pink-striped tent. And here I lost him. One moment he was there, hopping jerkily through the thick barriers of wet laundry, and the next he was gone, slipped, perhaps, into one of the hovels along the way. So I decided to wait for him in his own booth for a while.

This time, the poster read: SEE A YOUNG GIRL'S MOST SIGNIFICANT EXPERIENCE IN LIFELIKE COLOURS. To while away the time, I strolled from machine to machine, unaccountably disturbed by the things I saw there although, unlike the seven wonders of yesterday's world, none contained any element of the grotesque. All were as haunting as the cards in Tarot and the very titles of each set-piece were set like an integral medallion into each elegant design. These new tableaux were not, like yesterday's, models but actual pictures painted with luscious oils on rectangular plates in such a way that the twin eye-pieces of the machine created a stereoscopic effect. These plates were arranged in several layers which slid in and out of one another by means of a system of programmed clockwork which announced itself with a faint click and gave the impression of stilted movement in the figures. It also allowed sudden transformation scenes. Each picture was lit from behind and glowed with an unnatural brilliance so that the moonlight which suffused the first scene was far more luxuriously pure than everyday moonlight and looked like the Platonic perfection of moonlight. This transcendental radiance bathed ivied ruins and the slide shifted back and forth to allow bats to flit stiffly around them. A lugubrious owl perched on the crumbling chimney stack and slowly beat its wings upon the darkened air where hung in iridescent characters the words: THE MANSION OF MIDNIGHT.

In the second machine, the mansion split in half to reveal a crimson room and the warning: HUSH! SHE IS SLEEPING! She was as white as my last night's anaemic lover and, like her, she was dressed in black, but this one had a medieval gown of sheer black velvet with sleeves that came to points on the backs of her hands while her streaming hair contained several shades of darkness. She lay back in the voluptuous abandonment of sleep in a carved armchair where spiders propelled themselves up and down on the high-wires they had spun themselves among the hangings.

When I looked into the third machine I saw a ferocious hedge of thorns; but then, before my very eyes, a young prince with juicy bunches of golden ringlets hanging on the shoulders of his slashed and padded doublet was superimposed on the hedge in a balletic attitude of pleading and from his mouth issued a scroll which read: I COME! The hedge parted forthwith to reveal, in a set of cunning perspectives, the sleeper *inside* the haunted house of the first machine complete with owl above, etc.

A KISS CAN WAKE HER. In the crimson room, the pretty prince with skin as pink as sugar candy and lips like strawberry ice cream bent over the sleeping girl; another slide slipped into place and showed them so close together, his ringlets mixed with her locks and his face pressed so close to hers her pallor took his colour and blushed. A click of the internal mechanism. The tints of warm flesh rushed back into her face. Her eyes opened. Her newly red lips parted.

With that, the poignant charm vanished. Inside the fifth machine, all was rampant malignity. Deformed flowers thrust monstrous horned tusks and trumpets ending in blaring teeth through the crimson walls, rending them; the ravenous garden slavered over its prey and every brick was shown in the act of falling. Amid the violence of this transformation, the oblivion of the embrace went on. The awakened girl, in all her youthful loveliness, still clasped in the arms of a lover from whom all the flesh had fallen. He was a grinning skeleton. In one set of phalanges he carried a scythe and with the other pulled out and squeezed a ripe breast from the girl's bodice while his bony knees nudged apart her thighs. The emblem read: DEATH AND THE MAIDEN.

The remaining two machines were empty.

It was now in the middle of the day and the heat inside the tent grew oppressive. I went outside and sat on a doorstep, smoking and waiting, but still there was no sign of the peep-show proprietor. A child with crinkled hair tied up in the innumerable pigtails the poor and superstitious adopt for, I think, reasons of voodoo approached and stared at me. Her plaits were so tight they revealed wide areas of the glossy, brown skin covering her skull and, though I questioned her, she answered me incomprehensibly in the multi-lingual patois of the slums and began to poke indifferently in a clogged drain with a stick. Her face was covered with the whorled eruptions of a skin disease. The good nuns had taken me away from such pastimes and such afflictions but, all the same, you will have noticed I possessed a degree of ambivalence towards the Minister's architectonic vision of the perfect state. This was because I was aware of what would have been my own position in that watertight schema.

No shadows fell in the drowsing noonday. I inquired at several houses but even those who spoke the standard language knew nothing of the peep-show proprietor except that his booth had suddenly arrived in the shrine garden the previous evening. My shirt was soaked with sweat and at last I walked down to the ocean to catch the possibility of a breeze.

I wondered if all the holiday makers were nothing but phantoms. Nevertheless, most of them had dispersed for lunch and an afternoon nap and the beaches were again deserted. I strolled beside the margin of the water, among a detritus of discarded sandals and plastic sun-tan lotion jars the sea could not digest, watching the dancing white lace hems of the petticoats of the ocean and so, while I was thinking of nothing but sunshine, the breakers delivered her to my feet.

Mary Anne had indeed found something else to do that day besides play the piano. And now she had suffered a sea change, already. She was wreathed and garlanded in seaweed and shells clung to her white night shift. When I lifted her up, water spouted from her mouth. Dead, she could not have had a whiter skin than when she lived. She was dead. But still I tried to revive her.

I was overwhelmed with shock and horror. I felt I was in some way instrumental to her death. I crouched over the sea-gone wet doll in an attitude I knew to be a cruel parody of my own the previous night, my lips pressed to her mouth, and it came to me there was hardly any difference between what I did now and what I had done then, for her sleep had been a death. The notion ravaged me with guilty horror. I do not know how much time passed while I attempted to manipulate her lifeless body but, when the sound of voices at last broke into my waking nightmare, the sun was far in the west and cast long beams which fell with a peculiar lateral intensity over the sand. She and I were now both utterly bedaubed with wet sand, so that we looked like those Indian shamans who paint themselves with coloured mud when they want to summon back the spirits of the departed. And I was attempting to do no more than that. I looked up.

On the promenade I saw a dark, hump-backed figure who gesticulated in my direction with a white stick. Down the iron steps to the beach clattered a posse of the Determination Police in their long, leather overcoats and, at their head, ran the clerk from the Town Hall, an unusual animation contorting his features, and the housekeeper from the Mayor's house, still in her white apron, plumply stumbling, crimson and breathless but radiating a horrid gratification. These two formed the very picture of malevolent glee and I was seized with the conviction they had, in collusion, murdered the Mayor for reasons of their own, probably connected with money or property, and trusted to the confusion of the times to hide their guilt. They thought I might discover it. Perhaps they had even murdered poor Mary Anne, too, and dropped her into the sea, in order to frame me, for how could I accuse them if I was myself accused?

They all came nearer and nearer and nearer and I realized I must quickly run away.

I do not know why I scooped up the dripping corpse of the girl in my arms and tried to make my escape with her. I think I wanted to rescue her from the housekeeper for I knew with instantaneous clairvoyance the old woman hated her, dead or living. Burdened with Mary Anne, I lurched along the beach for perhaps a hundred yards while she, twice her weight with water, slithered about so that it was like carrying a huge fish. Then one of the Determination Police drew his pistol and fired. I felt a tearing pain in my shoulder and fell. The second bullet whistled past my ear and, while I watched, shattered the exquisite rind of the dead girl's features so that her blood and brains spattered over my face. At that, I fainted.

I was charged on four counts.

(1) obtaining carnal knowledge of a minor (for, in fact, Mary Anne had been even younger than she looked, only fifteen years old);

(2) procuring death by drowning of the said minor;

(3) practising necrophily on the corpse of the said minor, which act the police had witnessed with their own eyes; and:

(4) posing as an Inspector of Veracity Class Three when I was really the fatherless son of a known prostitute of Indian extraction, an offence against the Determination Regulations Page Four, paragraph 1 c, viz.: 'Any thing or person seen to diverge significantly from it or his own known identity is committing an offence and may be apprehended and tested.'

From the look in the eyes of the Determination Police, it seemed very likely to me that I would not survive the testing in order to stand my trial.

I was terrified to realize how much the autonomous power of the police had grown. Although I pleaded with them to let me telephone the Minister's private number, they laughed at me and beat my head with the butts of their pistols. The papers in my briefcase had, of course, all been altered so that they presented masterpieces of the dubious; this was clearly the work of the clerk, done while I examined the files. My weapons were all gone, every one. I was uncertain of the role of the peep-show proprietor in all this except that clearly he wished to be rid of me and all the time I was waiting for him, he had himself been blindly spying on everything I did.

All the cells in the Police Station were filled with reality offenders so they took me to the Town Hall and put me in the Mayor's office. They had tied up my wounded shoulder in a rough sling and treated it only with a douse of dilute carbolic acid but at least they were sensitive enough to let me wash away Mary Anne's blood. They gave the clerk an overly melodramatic machine gun and posted him outside the door, to make sure I did not escape. I heard the key turn in the lock and the harsh, retreating clang of the heels of their jackboots. After a while, I heard a cackle of female laughter and then nothing more.

It was now night and the room was in utter darkness. I was in considerable pain but a seething fury kept me from despair. I knew I should sleep a little to clear my disoriented brain enough to face the ordeal I knew next day would bring but sleep was out of the question. Besides, I was ravenously hungry and as dry as a bone. I felt my way to the bureau to grope for the decanter of Mayoral sherry and discovered there an airtight tin of Marie biscuits, too, so I munched them all down, in spite of their earthy flavour. I pulled the stopper from the decanter with my teeth. The sherry had turned to liquid demerara sugar but I managed to keep it down and it and the food gave me sufficient strength to seat myself at the Mayor's desk and look at my situation coolly. When I did so, I found it hopeless enough to be risible.

The moon soon came up and since it was full, shone through the blind over the window and let me see my makeshift prison fairly well. I listened carefully but could hear no sound in the corridor outside. I stood up, went to the window and pulled the blind aside a little. The room was on the second storey at the front of the building and the window was flanked on either side by a pair of stone goddesses. Anyone could have scaled that façade easily for the stucco breasts, rumps, pillars and pediments which covered it offered a multiplicity of foot- and handholds but, on the window-ledge itself, I would have been visible to any watcher in the square as if it had been daylight and, when I let the blind fall with a faint rattle, the sound provoked a volley of knocking on the door so I knew the guard was wakeful. I looked around the room for a better exit and my eyes fell upon the fireplace.

It, too, was flanked by a brace of caryatids who bore the massive, brown marble mantelpiece on their serene foreheads. In the grate was a screen embroidered with the town coat of arms. Although my shoulder was badly inflamed and I could hardly use my right hand, I managed to move the heavy screen without a clang or rattle and I poked my head into the fireplace. Looking up, I saw a disc of pure blue sky on which shone a few stars. A light fall of soot showered my head and I withdrew it but when I re-examined the interior of the chimney, I saw that, although caked with the soot of years, a series of clefts cut in the sides of it to facilitate the work of the chimney sweep made a staircase to the roof all ready for me. I could hardly believe my luck.

I waited until I judged from the position of the moon it was some hours past midnight. By then, my entire right arm was gripped rigid in a vice of pain and of no further use. Besides, my rising fever parched and racked me though there was nothing left to drink and I had to fight against a growing light-headedness which verged on delirium. Yet I was determined to escape. At last I crept to the door and listened. I thought I heard a faintly sawing snore and, fevered as I was, this was enough to encourage me. I had been stripped of everything but my trousers and my bandage; I was quite suitably dressed for climbing a chimney. I approached the fireplace.

Dank, powdered soot filled my mouth and nostrils and, before I had effortfully ascended three or four yards, my left hand before me was as black as the wall on which it rested and blood ran out of the rough bandaging, trickling down my right arm. The sky watched me from above with a single blue eye that looked so blithely indifferent to my predicament that tears of self-pity carved deep channels in the filth on my cheeks. The sweep had used a child to clamber up and down the chimney for him with the brushes but I was a grown man and it was a chamber of unease to me, an unease which increased with every moment of tortured confinement for my movements were too restricted to allow me to progress with any speed and the necessity for absolute silence forbade me to so much as clear my throat. Besides, my overwrought senses soon convinced me the passage was steadily growing narrower and the walls were shrinking to crush me. The building was some six storeys high. I shuddered at every dark mouth announcing the fireplace of some other room for fear a fall of soot would betray my ascent to anyone who waited there and when, now and then, one-handed, I mishandled a cleft, I nearly died with fear to hear how my own struggle betrayed me.

But up, up, I went, like an ambitious rat traversing an unaccommodating, horizontal hole and I gradually grew certain there was nobody in the upper storeys but my striving self. Yet, for some reason, this did not diminish my fear for the memory of the blasted face of the dead girl visited me very often and it seemed at times I still carried all her weight on my throbbing right arm and saw her teeth gleam from a mass of pulped flesh whenever I glanced down. At times, the sky seemed a mile away and at others I felt I could touch it if I stretched out my hand so the moment when my head broke into the fresh air surprised me as much as if I were a baby suddenly popped from the womb. At first I could only drink the fresh air in thirsty gulps, still half wedged within the chimney, but as soon as I got my breath back, I managed to clamber perilously out of the stack and rolled down the roof until I came to rest in the gutter where I lay still for a long time, for I was almost at the end of my strength.

The gutters were mercifully wide and a pediment of carved stone some three feet high concealed the domestic look of the furniture of the roof from the street, so I, too, was quite hidden. As soon as I returned to myself a little, I saw that the moon was setting and soon would come an hour or two of perfect darkness before the first signs of dawn. I waited for that darkness as for a friend. The dressings on my wound were so torn and filthy I ripped them off and flung them away. A persistent dull pulse like the pulse of pain itself reminded me they had not taken out the bullet and, unless I went to a doctor very soon, I might not last much longer. But I still had enough endurance left to escape.

The nearest building was the town bank. It lay across a narrow alley a mere six feet away and, by some miracle, it had a flat roof; but it was built on only three floors so the drop was of some eighteen feet. However, I could see the most inviting fire escape on the shady side of the building which, if I could reach it, offered me a clear route to freedom. But I do not think I would have attempted that frightful, downward plunge if my wits had not been shaking with fever. When it was quite dark, I made it; I pitched forward into the abyss and the sprawling fall winded me completely – but I landed on the other side, alive.

On this roof was a water tank and, though it contained no more than a puddle of scum, I scooped up a little in fingers where soot was now grained in the very whorls and was refreshed in proportion to the quality of the refreshment – that is, not much; but a little. I could see the silver salver of the ocean dewed at the rim with a pale shadow of dawn but otherwise the night was profound, for the street lights did not work any more. So I walked down the fire escape on my bruised, bare feet as bravely as you please and crept off down the alleys, steering clear of guard dogs, keeping my eyes skinned for the gleam of a patrolling policeman's torch – though the fever was in my eyes and I trembled unnecessarily many times before I had left the town behind me.

On my way, I stole fresh trousers and a shirt from a clothesline and took the sandals from the feet of a drunken peasant sleeping in a doorway but I did not stop to wash myself at any of the dripping waterpumps. I waited until I came to a stream well away from the last of the suburbs and there sluiced myself down with the icy water. I screamed out loud when it touched my wound. I buried my rag of an old garment under a stone and dressed myself in my new clothes. Now nothing at all was left of the brisk young civil servant who had left the city such a short while ago. I looked the perfect offspring of the ancestors my mother had so strenuously denied and to that, perhaps, I owe my life.

I came to the main road and found a telephone box where I tried to ring the Minister but all the lines were out of order or had been cut for the instrument did not even crackle. So I left the highway and took a green path between hedgerows drenched with dew where soon the sweet birds sang. The day had begun and, moment by moment, the early morning mists grew brighter. I wished I did not keep glimpsing Mary Anne's face behind the hawthorns where the hips were red already. I passed a public house, miles from anywhere, and resting against the rustic bench outside the door, wet with dew like everything else, lay a bicycle. I mounted the bicycle and rode on, though I could only steer with the one hand for a bicycle may be ridden only by a continuous effort of will and the will to live was all I had left.

I do not possess a very clear memory of this part of my journey. I was consumed by a terrible sickness and weak from hunger, too; I had eaten nothing but the dead Mayor's biscuits since the treacherous housekeeper's breakfast twenty-four hours before. I know I came to a very wide river towards the end of the morning and cycled along the embankment as the sun beat down on my uncovered head. My tyres described great, crazy arcs behind me. I was now, I think, very near to the end.

I saw a dappled horse cropping grass beside the path and, leaning against a post, a tall, brown, rangy man in rough garments smoking a meditative pipe. He watched me curiously as I wobbled faintly towards him and held out his arms to catch me before I fell. I remember his lean, dark face, almost the face I had seen so recently in Mary Anne's mirror; and I remember the sensation of being carried through the air in a pair of strong arms; and then the creaking of boards and the motion of rocking on water, so I knew I had been placed in some kind of boat on the river. I recall the touch of fresh linen against my cheek and the sound of a woman's voice speaking a liquid and melodious language which took me back to my earliest childhood, before the time of the nuns.

Then, for a long time, nothing more.

3. The River People

The Portuguese did us the honour of discovering us towards the middle of the sixteenth century but they had left it a little late in the day, for they were already past their imperialist prime and so our nation began as an afterthought, or a footnote to other, more magnificent conquests. The Portuguese found a tenuous coastline of fever-sodden swamp which, as they reluctantly penetrated inland, they found solidified to form a great expanse of sun-baked prairie. Lavishly distributing the white spirochete and the word of God as they went, they travelled far enough to glimpse the hostile ramparts of the mountains before they turned back for there was no gold or silver to be had, only malaria and yellow fever. So they left it to the industrious Dutch a century later to drain the marshes and set up that intricate system of canals, later completed and extended during a brief visit by the British, to which the country was to owe so much of its later wealth.

The vagaries of some European peace treaty or other robbed the Dutch of the fruits of their labours, although some of them stayed behind to add further confusion to our ethnic incomprehensibility and to the barbarous speech which slowly evolved out of a multiplicity of elements. But it was principally the Ukrainians and the Scots–Irish who turned the newly fertile land into market gardens while a labour force of slaves, remittance men and convicts opened up the interior and a baroque architect imported for the purpose utilized their labours to build the capital, which was founded in the early eighteenth century at a point where the principal river formed an inland tidal basin. Here they built a house for Jesus, a bank, a prison, a stock exchange, a madhouse, a suburb and a slum. It was complete. It prospered.

During the next two hundred years, a mixed breed of Middle Europeans, Germans and Scandinavians poured in to farm the plains and even though a brief but bloody slave revolt put a stop to slavery at the time of the French Revolution, enough black slaves ran away from the plantations of the northern continent to provide cheap labour in the factories, shipyards and open-cast mines which brought the country prosperously enough into the twentieth century. You could not have said we were an undeveloped nation though, if we had not existed, Dr Hoffman could not have invented a better country in which to perform his experiments and, if he brought to his work the ambivalence of the expatriate, then were we not – except myself – almost all of us expatriates?

Even those whose great, great, great grandfathers had crossed the ocean in wooden ships felt, in the atavistic presence of the foothills, that they were little better than resident aliens. The expatriates had imposed a totally European façade on the inhospitable landscape in which they lived nervously, drawing around them a snug shawl of re-membered familiarities although, with the years, this old clothing grew threadbare and draughts blew in through the holes, which made them shiver. The very air had always been full of ghosts so that the newcomers took their displeasure into their lungs with every breath. Until the introduction of D.D.T., the area between the capital and the sea was a breeding ground for fever mosquitoes; until the drinking water was filtered, it was always full of cholera. The country itself was subtly hostile.

It turned out that the extremely powerful bourgeoisie and by far the greater part of the peasantry around the capital, from the rich farmers to the white trash, was of variegated European extraction, united by the frail bond of a language which, although often imperfectly understood, was still held in common while the slum dwellers presented an extraordinary racial diversity but were all distinguishable by the colour black, for that pigmentation, to some degree, was common to them all. But, if the conquistadors had found nothing they valued, the Jesuits who sailed with them discovered a rich trove of souls and it is to the accounts of attempted conversions and the journals of those indefatigable storm-troopers of the Lord that we owe most of our knowledge of the aborigines. Certain of the tribes and many of the customs the Jesuits ascribe to those days are certainly fallacious; the famous stories of highlanders with such stiff, muscular spikes at the base of their spines that all their stools were perforated do not even need to be discredited. But not one of the tribes could write down the language they spoke, could tame horses nor could build in stones. They were no Aztecs or Incas but brown, naïve men and women who fished, hunted, trapped birds and then died in great numbers, for those who did not become running targets for the crossbows of the Portuguese survived as quarries for the bluff English, who hallooed and tally-ho'd after them in imported red coats. While most of the rest succumbed to smallpox, syphilis, tuberculosis or those sicknesses of the European nursery, measles and whooping cough, which prove deadly if exported to another hemisphere.

But those defunct Amerindians had possessed a singular charm. Near the coast, a certain tribe had lived in reed hutches on islands in the marshes and they used to paste feathers together to make themselves robes and mantles, so they darted about on stilts above the still water like brilliant birds with long legs. And they used to make tapestries which showed no figures, only gradations of colour, woven out of feathers in such a way the colours seemed to move. I have seen the tattered ruins of one of these feathered mantles in the unfrequented Museum of Folk Art; ragged, now, but still unwearied by time, the pinks, reds and purples still dance together. Another tribe which lived beside the sea, a glum, deferential people who subsisted on raw fish, had a dialect which contained no words for 'yes' or 'no', only a word for 'maybe'. Further inland, people lived in mud beehives which had neither doors nor windows so you climbed into them through a hole in the roof. When the spring rains washed their homes away, as happened every year without fail, they stoically retired to caves where they carved eloquent eyes in stone for reasons the Jesuits never fathomed. Here and there, in the dry tundra and even the foothills, the Jesuits set the Indians, who were all sweet-natured and eager to please, to build enormous, crenellated churches with florid façades of pink stucco. But when the Indians had completed the churches and had gazed at them for a while with round-eyed self-congratulation, they wandered away again to sit in the sun and play tritonic melodies on primitive musical instruments. Then the Jesuits decided the Indians had not a single soul among them all and that wrote a definitive *finis* to the story of their regeneration.

But not all the Indians died. The Europeans impregnated the women and the children in turn impregnated the most feckless of the poor whites. The blacks impregnated the resultant cross and, though filtered and diffused, the original Indian blood finally distributed itself with some thoroughness among the urban proletariat and the occupations both whites and blacks deemed too lowly to perform, such as night-soil disposal. Yet it was perfectly possible – and, indeed, by far the greater majority of the population did so – to spend all one's life in the capital or the towns of the plain and know little if anything of the Indians. They were bogeymen with which to frighten naughty children; they had become rag-pickers, scrap-dealers, refuse collectors, and emptiers of cess-pits – those who performed tasks for which you do not need a face.

And a few of them had taken to the river, as if they had grown to distrust even dry land itself. These were the purest surviving strain of Indian and they lived secret, esoteric lives, forgotten, unnoticed. It was said that many of the river people never set foot on shore in all their lives and I know it was taboo for unmarried girls or pregnant women to leave the boats on which they lived. They were secretive, proud, shy and rigidly exclusive in their dealings with the outside world. Those who married outside the river clans were forbidden to return to their families or even to speak to any member of the tribe again as long as they lived but taboos against any kind of exogamy with the fat Caucasians who rooted themselves at ease along the river banks were so rigid I do not think above half a dozen of the women and, among the men, only the masters of the boats – or, rather, barges – had ever so much as exchanged a score of sentences with any except their own. Besides, they retained a version of one of the Indian dialects and I rather think they were the remote and however altered descendants of the birdmen of the swamps, for the meaning of their words depended not so much on pronunciation as intonation. They speak in a kind of singing; when, in the mornings, a flock of womenfolk twitter about the barge emptying the slops over the side and getting the breakfast, it is like a dawn chorus. The only way to transcribe their language would be in a music notation. But I have found very few of their customs in the writings of the Jesuits.

Over the years, their isolated and entirely self-contained society had developed an absolutely consistent logic which owed little or nothing to the world outside and they sailed from ports to cities to ports as heedlessly as if the waterways were magic carpets of indifference. I soon realized they were entirely immune to the manifestations. If the hawk-nosed, ferocious elders who handled their traditional lore said such a thing was so, then it *was* so and it would take more than the conjuring tricks of a cunning landlubber to shake their previous convictions. Since, however, they bore no goodwill to the whites and very little to the blacks, if it came to that, they took a cool pleasure to witness from the security of their portholes the occasional havoc in the towns through which they passed.

I blessed that touch of Indian blood my mother had all her life cursed for it gave me hair black enough and cheekbones high enough to pass among the river people for one of their own, when they were the only ones who could help me. The bargemaster who took me in knew quite well I came from the city but he spoke enough of the standard tongue to reassure me they were well disposed to fugitives from justice, provided they were of Indian extraction. He told me that during my faint he had dug the bullet out of my shoulder with a knife while his mother held an infusion of narcotic herbs under my nose when I showed signs of regaining consciousness. Now he applied a boiling poultice of leaves to the wound, bandaged it and left me in the care of the old woman.

When she smiled at me, I thought at first she did not have a tooth in her head for my eyes were still dim with fever, but soon I learned it was the custom for all the women to stain their teeth black. Every time she came into the cabin she shut the door sharply behind her but not before I saw a curious press of children crowding outside on deck to catch a glimpse of me. But I did not meet his family until Nao-Kurai had taught me to sing something of his language.

The speech of the river people posed philosophical as well as linguistic problems. For example, since they had no regular system of plurals but only an elaborate system of altered numerals for denoting specific numbers of given objects, the problem of the particular versus the universal did not exist and the word 'man' stood for 'all man'. This had a profound effect on their societization. Neither was there a precise equivalent for the verb 'to be', so the kernel was struck straight out of the Cartesian nut and one was left only with the naked, unarguable fact of existence, for a state of being was indicated by a verbal tag which could roughly be translated as 'one finds oneself in the situation or performance of such and such a thing or action', and the whole aria was far too virtuoso a piece to be performed often so it was replaced by a tacit understanding. The tenses divided time into two great chunks, a simple past and a continuous present. Neither contained further temporal shading. A future tense was created by adding various suffixes indicating hope, intention and varying degrees of probability and possibility to the present stem. There was also a marked absence of abstract nouns, since they had very little use for them. They lived with a complex, hesitant but absolute immediacy.

Besides her blackened teeth, Nao-Kurai's mother – whom I was quickly invited to call 'Mama' – used a great deal of paint on her face, in spite of her age. The paint was applied in a peculiarly stylized manner. A coat of matt white covered her nose, cheeks and forehead but left her neck and ears as brown as nature made them. On top of this white crust she put a spherical scarlet dot in the middle of each cheek and over the mouth a precisely delineated scarlet heart which completely ignored the real contours of the lips, which one could make out beneath as vague indentations, like copings under snow. Thick black lines surrounded her eyes, from which radiated a regular series of short spokes all round the circumference. The eyebrows were painted out and painted in again some three inches above the natural position, giving her an habitual look of extreme surprise. Sometimes she would also paint, in black, a crescent, a star or a butterfly at the corner of her mouth, on her temples or in some other antic position. I could see that the young girls who came to peek at me were decorated in much the same way, though less elaborately. This traditional maquillage could not have originally been intended to repel landsmen, but, however fortuitously, it repelled them completely, if ever one chanced to see it.

Mama hid her coils of black hair in a coloured handkerchief tied loosely over her head and knotted in the nape. She always wore loose trousers nipped in at the ankle with green or red cords; split-toed socks of black cotton which allowed her to keep thonged sandals on her feet; a loose blouse of checked or floral cotton; and protecting that, a short, immaculate, white starched apron which had armholes and tied at the back of both neck and waist, so that it covered her upper part almost completely. The aprons and also the bed-linen and the curtains at the portholes were all trimmed with a coarse white lace the women made themselves in the evenings, three or four of them clustered round a single candle. I think it was a craft the nuns had taught them in the seventeenth century, before the river people signed their quittance to the world, for the designs were very old-fashioned.

Mama's costume was universal among the women. It gave them a top-heavy appearance, as if they would not fall down if you pushed but only rock to and fro. I realized that, though I had sometimes seen the dark barges moving slowly along the river, I had never seen this characteristic shape of a woman on deck and later I learned the women were all ordered below whenever they reached a place of any size.

Mama always smelled faintly of fish but so did my sheets and blankets and the smell had soaked into the very wood of the bulkhead beside me for fish was their main source of protein. When she brought me my food, Mama never brought me a fork or knife or spoon to eat it with – she only brought a deep plate of a stiff kind of porridge made from maize topped with fish in a highly flavoured sauce and I was to discover the whole family habitually ate together round a round table in the main cabin, each scooping a handful of maize from the common bowl, rolling it in the palm until it was solid and then dipping it into another common bowl and scooping up the sauce with it.

Whenever she offered me my dinner, or dressed my wound, or washed me, or smoothed my bed, or undertook the more intimate tasks she performed without distaste or embarrassment, she used a limited repertoire of stiff, exact gestures, as if these gestures were the only possible accompaniments to her actions and also the only possible physical expressions of hospitality, solicitude or motherly care. Later I found that all the women moved in this same, stereotyped way, like benign automata, so what with that and their musical box speech, it was quite possible to feel they were not fully human and, to a certain extent, understand what had produced the prejudices of the Jesuits.

The appearance and manners of the men were by no means so outlandish, perhaps because, although reluctantly, they were forced to mix more with the shore people and so had adopted a rough version of peasant manners and also of peasant dress. They wore loose white shirts over loose trousers with a loose, sleeveless waistcoat usually made from a web of small, knitted, multi-coloured squares, which they donned when the weather grew cool. In winter, both men and women would put on jackets of padded cotton. Mama was already patching and refurbishing a trunkful of these jackets ready for another season's wear.

The men sometimes wore earrings and various talismans on chains around their necks but did nothing to their faces except grow on them flamboyant moustaches whose drooping lines stressed the brooding shapes of the Indian nose and jaw. Since nobody offered to shave me and I could not shave myself, I, too, sported one of those moustaches before I was up and about again and, once I was supplied with it, I did not bother to remove it for I found I liked my new face far better than my old one. The weeks of pain and sickness passed with the remains of the summer; through my porthole, I saw the shorn cornfields of the great plain and the colours of autumn glowing, then falling, from the trees. My best companion was the ship's cat, a thick-set, obese, skulking beast, white, with irregular black patches on the rump, the left fore-quarter and the right ear, who became very attached to me for some reason – perhaps because I kept so still he could sleep undisturbed on the warm cushion of my stomach for hours, where he made me throb with the vibrations of his purr. I was fond of him because he was painted up like Mama.

When Nao-Kurai told me I was well enough to go on board, I

saw that the entire boat was strung with chains made, each one, of hundreds of little birds folded out of paper and I learned this was not only to advertise to the other river dwellers the presence of a sick man on board but was also an offering to the spirits who had caused my sickness. These birds increased my conviction that Nao-Kurai's tribe was descended from the painters in feathers. When I learned more of their medicine, however, I began to wonder why I had survived his doctoring for Mama had sterilized the knife with which Nao-Kurai had performed his surgery by dipping it in the fresh urine of a very healthy virgin while reciting a number of antique mantras.

Nao-Kurai occupied an important position in the tribe and I was very lucky to have fallen under his protection. Their business consisted of the marine transportation of goods from one part of the central plain to another via the waterways and, since Dr Hoffman had put the railways out of action, business was enjoying a boom. We drew behind us a whole string of barges which carried imported timber up to a city in the north where work still went on as usual. The entire country was poorly afforested and we were forced to import timber for building or even for the manufacture of furniture from other sources along the sea-board. Nao-Kurai owned the longest string of barges among all the river people and his skill at the standard speech and a remarkable flair for mental arithmetic had made him the spokesman and administrator for the whole community. To a considerable extent the tribe held all its goods in common and tended to think of itself as a scattered but unified family. When I lived among them, there were some five or six hundred river people who travelled mostly in convoys of five or six chains of barges each but I should think their numbers have greatly dwindled since then and perhaps by now they have all abandoned the river, the women have washed their faces for good and they have become small tradesmen on dry land.

Nao-Kurai was a gaunt, hollow-eyed man of somewhat embittered integrity and, though he had a very quick intelligence and, indeed, considerable intellectual powers, even if he were extremely cynical, he was – like the entire tribe – perfectly illiterate. When I was well enough to get up every day, had enough phrases on the tip of my tongue to chirrup morning greetings to the family and could share the porridge bowl at mealtimes without spilling my food, Nao-Kurai took me more and more into his confidence and finally told me he wanted me to to teach him to read and write for he was sure the shore people cheated him badly on all the consignments he undertook. When we stopped at a village, he sent one of his sons off to buy pencils, paper and any book he could find, which happened to be a translation of *Gulliver's Travels*. So, after that, every evening, when the barges were moored for the night, the supper cleared away and the horse attended to, we sat at the table under a swinging lantern, smoking and studying the alphabet while the boys, under strict orders to be good, sulked in the corners or sat on the deck, too intimidated even to play quietly, while Mama and two of the daughters sat in smiling silence, making lace, and the littlest girl belched and gurgled to herself like a faulty tap, for she was simple-minded.

I had been given Nao-Kurai's cabin but he would not let me move out of it now that I was well again though it placed a great strain on the sleeping quarters, for all the family had to fit themselves somehow into the main cabin by dint of hammocks slung from hooks and mattresses spread on the boards. The only other room in the barge was a cramped galley where Mama prepared our meals on two little charcoal stoves, using extremely simple, even primitive utensils.

There were six children. Nao-Kurai's wife had died at the last birth, a boy now three years old. The eldest was also a boy, who suffered from a hare lip; for two centuries of inbreeding had produced a generation of webbed hands, ingrowing eyelashes, lobeless ears, a number of other slight deformities and, Nao-Kurai told me, a high rate of idiocy. The youngest daughter was five years old and still could only crawl. But his other children were strong and healthy enough. I still remember the two elder boys, strapping, handsome lads, diving into the river every morning to wash. But I could not tell what the girls looked like because of their thick, white crust. Even the five-year-old was painted over, although she drooled so much it made the red and white grease run comically together. The next girl was seven and the eldest nine. Though this one, Aoi, was a great big girl and worked hard all day at household chores under her grandmother's supervision, she still played with dolls. I often saw her cradling in her arms and lullabying a doll dressed like the river babies, a knitted skull cap on its head to stop the demons who grabbed hold of babies' topknots and pulled them bodily through the portholes, and the rest of it stuffed into a tailored sack, to stop other demons who sucked out babies' entrails through their little fundaments. And the sack was bright red in colour because red kept away the demons who gave babies croup, colic and pneumonia. But when she offered me the doll so that I could play with it myself, I saw it was not a doll at all but a large fish dressed up in baby clothes. Whenever the fish began to rot, Mama exchanged it for a fresh one just like it so that, though the doll was always changing, it always stayed exactly the same.

That she showed me the doll at all shows on what close terms I had grown with her for even with their own menfolk the girls displayed a choreographic shyness, giggling if addressed directly and hiding their mouths with their hands in a pretty pretence of being too intimidated to reply. But as the weeks went by, I grew more and more attuned to the slow rhythms and amniotic life of the river, I learned to trill their speech as well as anyone and I became, I suppose, a kind of elder brother to them, although Nao-Kurai half hinted at certain plans for me which would make me closer than a brother. But I took no notice of him because I thought Aoi was clearly too young to be married.

As for myself, I knew that I had found the perfect place to hide from the Determination Police and, besides, some streak of atavistic, never-before-acknowledged longing in my heart now found itself satisfied. I was in hiding not only from the Police but from my Minister as well, and also from my own quest. I had abandoned my quest.

You see, I felt the strongest sense of home-coming.

Soon my new language came to my tongue before my former one. I no longer relished the thought of any food except maize porridge and well-sauced fish. Even now, I carry the memory of that barge and my foster family warmly at my heart's core. I remember one evening in particular. It must have been late November, for the nights were chilly enough for Mama to have lit the stove. The stove burned wood and its long chimney puffed smoke out above the cabin in a homely fashion; it warmed us with its great, round, metal belly that glowed red from the heat it contained. Mama set down the bowl of stiff porridge on the table and Aoi brought us the bowl of stewed fish. Nao-Kurai said a few words of pagan blessing over the food and we began sedately to ball our porridge to a firm enough consistency to sustain its freight of fish. We ate sedately; we always ate sedately. And during the meal we exchanged a few domestic trivialities about the weather and the distance we had come that day. Aoi fed the youngest girl because she could not feed herself. The lamp above us moved with the motion of the boat at the whim of the current and rhythmically now illuminated, now shadowed the faces around the table.

I saw no strangeness in the whitened faces of the girls. They no longer looked like pierrots in a masquerade for I knew each individual feature under the cosmetic, the hollow in the seven-year-old's cheek that showed where she had lost the last of her milk teeth the previous week and the little scratch the cat had given Aoi's nose. And Mama looked just as every mother in the world should look. The limited range of feeling and idea they expressed with such a meagre palette of gesture no longer oppressed me; it gave me, instead, that slight feeling of warm claustrophobia I had learned to identify with the notion, 'home'. I dipped my fist into the pungent stew and, for the first time in my life, I knew exactly how it felt to be happy.

The next day we came into the town of T. and the girls all went below when we moored beside the woodyard. Nao-Kurai asked me to go with him to the wood merchant and so I left the barge for the first time since I had boarded it. I found I was walking with a rolling gait. I was able to convince him that the wood merchant, at least, was one of the honest shoremen, but when we went to the market to get in stocks of maize for the long journey back down the river, I was able to render the river people a service which Nao-Kurai valued more highly than it was worth.

T. was a small, old-fashioned town so far to the inland north that a few sandstone outcrops of the mountains lay beyond the river. Yet here life seemed relatively unaffected by the war and people went about their daily business as if it were nothing to them that the capital had been cut off for three and a half years. This sense of suspended time comforted me. It made me feel that the capital, the war and the Minister had never existed, anyway. I had quite forgotten my black swan and the ambiguous ambassador for I had come back to my people. And Desiderio himself had disappeared because the river people had given me a new name. It was their custom to change a given name if someone had suffered bad luck or misfortune, as they guessed I had done, so now I was called Kiku. The two syllables were separated by the distance of a minor third. The name meant 'foundling bird'; it seemed to me most wistfully appropriate.

In the market-place, peasant farmers displayed baskets of gleaming eggplants, whorled peppers, slumbrously overripe persimmons and blazing tangerines – all the fruits of late autumn. There were coops of live chickens, tubs of butter and cartwheel cheeses. There were stalls for toys and clothes, cloth by the yard, candy and jewellery. A ballad singer stood up on a stone to give us a vocal demonstration of his Irish origins and a bear in an effeminate hat trimmed with artificial daisies lumbered through the parody of a waltz in the arms of a gipsy woman with red ribbons in her hair. The market-place was full of the liveliest bustle and there were enough Indian faces in the crowds of country people to make us feel a little more at ease than we usually did on dry land, for this town was a kind of headquarters for the river people, for reasons I was to learn later.

First, we went to the corn chandlers and ordered fourteen stone of hulled maize to be delivered to the boat; then we wandered about the market making Mama's commission of purchases. As they thrust three squawking chickens into paper bags for us, a man whose features and dress showed he was one of the clan came rushing up breathlessly and poured out a complaint as dramatically as Verdi.

Pared of the histrionic grace notes, it was a simple story. He had brought a consignment of grain from the plains to a seed-broker here. He had made his mark on a contract he could not read with the farmer and now the broker claimed he had contracted to carry a whole two tons more than had now been removed to the godowns and our brother, Iinoui, must pay the difference from his own pocket. Which would ruin him. Tears ran down his brown cheeks. He was fat, old, poor and quite at a loss.

'This will be easy to settle!' said Nao-Kurai. 'Kiku here can read and write, you see.'

Iinoui's eyes grew round with awe. He bowed to me stiffly and made one or two flattering remarks in the heightened language of respect they used when they wished to honour somebody's skill or beauty, for they loved to abnegate themselves before one another. So we went all three together to the seed-broker's. On the way, in the glass of a shop-window, I saw the reflections of three brown men in loose, white, shabby clothes, with tattered straw hats pulled down over our oblique eyes, a deep thatch of black hair above our upper lips and below austere noses that expressed contempt for those unlike themselves in the very whorls of our nostrils. I could have been Nao-Kurai's eldest son or youngest brother. This idea gave me great pleasure.

The seed-broker was a pale, flabby, furtive man. When I broke into a flood of invective in the standard speech, he began to quail already and when I demanded to see the contracts, his blustering protests were adequate proof that he was hopelessly in the wrong. I threatened to find a lawyer and sue him for ten thousand dollars' worth of defamation to Iinoui's character. Sweat beaded his unhealthy-looking forehead. I had already developed a marked distaste for the insipid colouring and limp bodies of the shore people; they looked like the comic figures Mama would sometimes mould out of the porridge to make the idiot daughter giggle. The broker offered Iinoui five hundred dollars' compensation for his 'clerk's mistake' and when I told Iinoui this, both he and Nao-Kurai looked at me as though I were a magician. With a good deal of instinctive graciousness, Iinoui accepted the sum in cash but while the broker counted out the notes, the two barge-masters conferred together and then with me so that when Iinoui had stowed the money away in the pouch of his inner belt, I had the pleasure of informing the merchant that none of the river people would henceforward handle goods for him any more. Since the barges were the only remaining form of internal transport, it was he and not his prey who now found ruin staring him in the face. We left him shaking with impotent rage.

Iinoui insisted I take half his profits but I would not have done so had Nao-Kurai not told me that if I did not, I would hurt Iinoui's feelings. Then we went to a bar which served Indians and drank a good deal of brandy and all the time they both flattered me unmercifully, so I felt almost ashamed. You must realize that, in spite of his quick wits and native intelligence, Nao-Kurai was not making good progress at his lessons. For one thing, he was far too old for the first grade. After so many years of hauling rope and heaving sacks, his fingers were too gnarled and stiff to handle a pencil with sensitivity. And, for another thing, his mind, which held the patterns of the currents in every river in the country and remembered the sites and quirks of all the locks on each one of half a thousand canals; his mind, a fabulous repository of water-lore, folkways and the mythology of the past; that mind which could calculate like lightning how much freight a barge could carry or how much coal made up a load – this crowded and magnificently functioning mind no longer had a stray corner left in which to store the Roman alphabet. Besides, he did not think in straight lines; he thought in subtle and intricate interlocking circles.

He conceived of certain polarities – light and darkness; birth and death – which, though they were immutable, existed in a locked tension. He could comprehend orally the most sophisticated concepts in a flash but co-ordinate his hand and eye sufficiently to form a linear sequence as elementary as 'the cat sat on the mat', he could not. 'But, Kiku!' he would say. 'The cat sits there, upon your knee, and though she is not the only cat in the world, she is for me the very essence of cat.' The very shapes of the letters led him astray. He fell to musing on their angularities and traced and retraced them, chuckling to himself with pleasure, until they became cursive abstracts, beautiful in themselves but utterly lacking in signification. Our evenings of study had become a mutual torture. I knew he would never learn to read or write. And his failure only made him respect me more. My success with the seed-broker clinched a decision that must have been growing in his mind for some time.

At last we broke away from Iinoui and went off to finish our shopping, belching fumes of brandy at one another companionably through our moustaches. I paused to spend some of my new wealth on a bunch of speckled dahlias for Mama and then I bought a cheerful silk handkerchief with violets painted on it.

'Is that a present for someone?' asked Nao-Kurai with the beautiful, tentative tact of my people.

'For Aoi,' I replied.

He had the chickens bundled in the crook of one arm and a whole still life of vegetables crammed in his other while I carried a cheese, a mound of butter wrapped up in straw and a basket containing four dozen eggs. But still he managed to reach out and grasp my hand.

'Does my Aoi please you?'

We stood in the market and it was the middle of the afternoon. The gipsy girl still danced with her bear and their money box now glinted like a box of herrings from all the silver they had been given. The Irishman had just embarked on an endless lament for dead Napoleon and a few pennies lay in his proffered cap. I remembered the city, the opera-house and the music of Mozart. The voices of Mama and Aoi were now to me the music of Mozart and as I remembered the city, so I gladly said good-bye to it. The brandy I had drunk and Iinoui's gift and pretty speeches made me warm and sentimental. And then Nao-Kurai might have been my father, from appearances; and I loved him already.

The river people had evolved or inherited an intricate family system which was theoretically matrilinear though in practice all decisions devolved upon the father. The father – or, nominally, mother – adopted as his son the man whom his eldest daughter married. When he died, this son-in-law inherited the barge and all that went with it. Therefore Nao-Kurai offered me far more than a bride; he offered me a home, a family and a future. If I murdered Desiderio and became Kiku for ever, I need fear nothing in my life ever, any more. I need not fear loneliness or boredom or lack of love. My life would flow like the river on which I lived. I would become officially an outcaste but, since I had signed my allegiance with the outcastes, I would no longer linger on the margins of life with a delicate sneer on my face, wistfully wishing that I were Marvell or that I were dead. My eyes filled with tears. I could hardly speak.

'Yes,' I stammered. 'She pleases me.'

'Then she is yours,' he said with Arab simplicity and with one accord we dropped all our parcels and embraced one another.

As we did so, the gipsy girl flung back her head at the conclusion of a fandango and I caught sight of her face over Nao-Kurai's shoulder. For a single, fleeting second, she wore the face of Dr Hoffman's beautiful ambassador and all my resolution failed, for I would have followed that face to the end of the world. But she raised her hand to wipe the sweat away and it was as if she wiped the ambassador's face away. She was once again an ordinary gipsy girl, even an ugly gipsy girl, with a wide flat nose, small eyes and gold coins dangling from her pierced ears. So I knew my eyes had deceived me but, all the same, a little of my glory evaporated and I returned to the barge more soberly, though Nao-Kurai laughed all the time from pure joy.

Because Aoi was only nine years old, I thought there would be a long period of betrothal but everyone assured me she had reached puberty and offered me visual proof if I did not believe them. So I abandoned the last vestiges of my shore-folk squeamishness and Nao-Kurai fixed the date of my wedding for a few weeks ahead, the time of the winter solstice, when we would return to the town of T. after a trip to take a load of manufactured paper goods across the country on the canal system for, beyond the town of T., the river widened to form a natural basin where the river people traditionally met to celebrate weddings, which were always occasions of great festivity among them.

Mama kissed me and told me how happy she was. Aoi jumped straight up into my arms as if propelled upwards by the force of her own giggling; the middle sister shyly tugged my shirt-tails and asked me if I would marry her as well; while even the youngest seemed to drool with unusual enthusiasm and all the brothers shook my hand and murmured more reticent congratulations. They hung all the barges in our chain with flowers made from golden paper to tell the waterways there was to be a wedding and men from every barge we passed came aboard to embrace me. It was the ritual commencement of the ritual of adoption. Mama and the girls began to stitch a very elaborate trousseau for both my bride and myself and also to make lists of the food they would need for the wedding feast. But when I asked them what kind of dishes they would serve up, they giggled convulsively and said it was to be a surprise.

Now Aoi began to treat me with a great deal of familiarity. She came and sat down on my knee whenever she had any time to spare and tweaked the ends of my moustaches, she planted wet, childish kisses on my cheeks and mouth, and taking hold of my hands firmly, inserted them under the folds of her apron and her blouse, demanding me to tell her if her breasts had grown since the last performance and if so, how much. On the third night of our betrothal, we had a special supper – oyster soup thickened with beaten eggs as well as the usual cereal and fish. We drank this soup from special cups with a pink and purple glaze. I had not seen these cups before; apparently they were kept specially for weddings. Aoi knelt down in front of me to hand me my soup and accompanied her offering with certain verbal formulae too archaic and complex for me to understand but Nao-Kurai, laughing suggestively, refused to translate them. For the first time I felt, however slightly, that they were making my ignorance of their ways the butt of a private joke.

Indeed, in a curious way, I had become less sure of myself among the river people since that curious trick of eyesight which made me put the ambassador's face on top of that of the gipsy girl, even though now I had an accredited part to play in their opera. I began to sense, or thought I sensed, a new kind of ambivalence in, especially, Nao-Kurai's behaviour. For one thing, he had dropped *Gulliver's Travels* over the side of the barge and announced, with rather a childish glee, that our lessons were at an end. Well, I could only be thankful for that but I could not by any means interpret the expression of what I can only call incipient triumph I sometimes caught in the fathomless depths of his brown eyes, which were shaped like commas and, as I already knew, in no way expressed his soul. But the principal source of my unease was just this: the betrothal and subsequent marriage already involved me in a whole intricate web of ritual which I knew I must negotiate unerringly – and yet my new almost-father seemed to take a strange pleasure in refusing to give me any clues as to how to traverse it. I already guessed it was part of my function to enthusiastically massage my fiancée's breasts whenever she offered them to me, even if it were in front of everybody. I assumed by the presence of the oysters that the soup was an aphrodisiac so I drank the three bowls she gave me, smacking my lips ostentatiously, and then I guessed I ought to ask for more. The entire cabin rocked with mirth so I knew my guess was correct and, as I expected, a little scrabbling knock came on my door some time past midnight.

'Who's there?' I said softly.

'A poor girl a-shivering with cold this night,' she answered in the voice of a child who recites a poem she has learned by heart. Her diction was as old-fashioned as her invitation to soup but this time I understood her perfectly and got up to let her in.

She had washed off the paint for the night, tied up her hair in pigtails with yellow bows and put on a plain white nightdress that reminded me of poor Mary Anne, whom I would much rather have forgotten. However, I was touched to see she still clutched her fish-doll by the tail of its red night-shirt; she must have brought it with her out of habit, for company. She scampered immediately to my bed and jumped between the sheets, arranging her doll neatly with its gills on the white-frilled pillow beside her. She was rather more solemn than usual but still she seemed to have studied every word and movement from a book of manners. Mama must have taught her everything. When I climbed into the bed beside her, she snuggled very prettily in my arms, reached down for my penis in a very businesslike way and began to stroke it with very considerable dexterity.

Now the sexual mores of the river people were a closed book to me though I felt I could learn them very quickly once I had started; but in this particular situation I simply did not know if actual coitus was expected of me. The heating soup seemed to indicate it was but somehow I thought Aoi would not have been quite so forward in her manner unless it was not. My increasing excitement under her diabolically cunning little fingers made it all the more difficult to decide but when I turned her emphatically over on to her plump backside, she let out an unpremeditated caw of shock and affront so I stopped what I was about immediately and lay quite still, contenting myself with tweaking her pubescent nipples, until, by her own un-aided work, she procured me an orgasm I was quite unable to forestall even though, as I sobbed it out, I wondered anxiously that it might be out of order and the whole exercise had been designed to test my stoicism, for they set great store by stoicism and never wept at funerals.

But Aoi seemed quite content and curled up to sleep until Mama brought us our breakfast in bed next morning, with many expressions of approval and kisses for both of us. When I met Nao-Kurai on deck, he roared with approbation and clapped my back. Since I was half expecting him to be sullen because I had passed another test successfully, I was more taken aback than ever.

The next night there was no soup but Aoi visited me promptly on the hour. This time she wore green bows on her pigtails. I guessed that Mama, Nao-Kurai and probably the entire family had their ears pressed to the bulwark in order to miss no sound we made and it was probably my duty to come as noisily as possible; so I did. This time she allowed me to caress her diminutive slit and I found, to my astonishment, her clitoris was as long as my little finger. This genuinely puzzled me. I had never encountered anything quite like it and, though I was sure it was against the rules, I decided to ask Mama about it the very next day. I thought she was more likely to explain the phenomenon to me than her son was, for she showed – so far as I could tell – nothing but honest pleasure at the impending marriage.

I trapped her by herself, for a wonder, as she prepared some savoury messes for our lunch and she embarked on a warbling recitative clotted with archaisms and references to traditions of unspeakable antiquity which boiled down to the following: it was the custom for mothers of young girls to manipulate their daughters' private parts for a regulation hour a day from babyhood upwards, coaxing the sensitive little projection until it attained lengths the river people considered both aesthetically and sexually desirable. The techniques of these maternal caresses were handed down from mother to mother but, when Aoi's mother died, Mama had undertaken the indispensable handling of her grand-daughters and felt a justifiable pride in having done so well by the girls. She asked me, had she not achieved wonders? And in all sincerity I answered, yes. The origins of this elongatory practice were lost in the mists of myth and ritual; she used the pentatonic phrase that meant 'snake' at one point and there were extraordinary snakes in their mythology. But the practice itself was, perhaps, an equivalent of the circumcision ceremonies among the males. Nao-Kurai had told me that the inevitable circumcision always took place without exception in mass surgical ceremonies when a boy reached the age of twelve and, for three weeks after the operation, the barges on which the boys who underwent it lived flew a number of bright red paper kites from flagpoles. Fortunately, the nuns had had me tidied up in that way when I was far too young to notice so I was spared the fear that a belated knife would descend on my foreskin before I could be married.

When she saw my curiosity about these customs, perhaps she wondered if I thought she might be lying to conceal a natural deformity of her granddaughter's, so Mama closed the galley door and told me to turn my back. I heard the slithering of garments and, when she told me to look again, she had taken off her trousers and, with those elegant gestures of refined invitation which always moved me so much, she invited me to inspect her own projection, which formed a splendid, quivering growth at the head of the dark red nether lips. The skin of her thighs was still supple and I realized I was quite unable to guess how old she was or even whether she was still attract- ive because of her white paint. Since all the river women married at puberty, she need not be older than her late forties and when I experimentally caressed her, I found she was already slick with secretions. She twittered a few words of admonition but, at the same time, slid fast the wooden bolt on the galley door and took me against the bulwark with a great deal of gasping, while a pan of shrimp danced and spluttered on the charcoal stove.

I experienced an almost instantaneous regret as soon as the act was over for I could hardly imagine there was any society in the world which would not think that gaining carnal knowledge of one's hostess and foster grandmother was a gross abuse of hospitality but Mama, smiling (as far as I could tell), sighing and fluttering butter- fly kisses all over my remorseful face, told me she had not enjoyed sex since the last circumcision festival in the town of T., the previous April, and that was a very long time ago; that my performance, although improvised, had been spirited enough to give her a great deal of pleasure; and that she was always available in the galley every morn- ing after breakfast and before lunch. Then she wiped us both dry with a handtowel, put on her trousers again and turned her attention back to the shrimp, which had scorched a little.

I went to lie down on my bunk for a while and examined the situ- ation. Once again, I thought I had gone down a snake when in fact I was climbing up a ladder. Now I had acquired a very powerful ally indeed. Mama's kindness to me increased enormously. The break- fast she brought Aoi and me included, now, all manner of specially juicy tidbits, such as grilled eel. Sometimes I heard her fluting my praises to her son when they were alone together. The promiscuity I had inherited from my mother, so often an embarrassment in the past, was standing me in very good stead. Indeed, I was growing almost reconciled to mothers.

I thought that night I would come to grips with my child bride because she was wearing purple ribbons but she moved on to fellatio and so it went. Mama confirmed my suspicion that actual intercourse was forbidden until the wedding night itself, so the groom would still have some first fruits to pluck, and those nights of autumn passed in elaborate love play with my erotic, giggling toy, every night adorned with different coloured bows, while in the mornings I screwed the toy's grandmother up against the wall. I began to feel like a love slave.

They fed me very rich food and nobody called on me to perform any tasks on shipboard at all except occasionally to check bills for loading or bills for purchases for, after we delivered our paper goods, were honestly paid for them and turned about for the return journey to the town of T., Nao-Kurai began to lay in sumptuous stocks for the wedding. He bought five dozen jars of the very sweet wine they make in this part of the country from plums and honey; a ten gallon cask of raw brandy; a fifteen pound drum of dried apricots; and all manner of other things, including a live sheep which would be slaughtered for the feast. The dry goods were stored down below in the hold but the sheep was tethered to the deck of the barge which followed us and given boiled barley and oats to eat. It grew fatter as one looked at it, until it was almost too fat to bleat. But when I asked if it was to be the main course, roasted whole as a pièce de résistance, they said, no; there would be something even better. But they would not tell me what it was because, they said, they wanted to astonish me. Then they would laugh softly.

So we drifted back past the melancholy landscape of early winter, through terrain so flat the light fell from an excess of sky with a peculiar, visionary intensity. These would be the last days of freedom of choice; I could still choose to leave them now, but after my wedding the barge and the river would have to be sufficient world for me and though I was kept busy enough oscillating between my two lovers, I sometimes felt an acrid nostalgia for those ugly streets where nobody cared for me and I cared for nothing, though I instantly quenched this nostalgia for I thought it must be nothing but a marsh-fire of the mind. There was no news at all of the capital in any of the villages along the canals and although at nights extraordinary lights played around the mountains we now approached again, there were no other signs of the war itself in this forgotten, pastoral country which seemed to have turned so deeply inward on itself under the great burden of sky which pressed down upon it that nothing outside itself had any significance. This was the sky which covered the world of the river people. I felt intolerably exposed to those enormous heavens. In self-defence, I became introspective but the more I brooded, the more convinced I grew that this meandering formalization of life they offered me was worth the trouble of the risky ritual of induction into it.

The canals were full of barges and by the time we reached the great river, we headed a long convoy all flying paper streamers. In the evenings other barge-masters joined us in the cabin while the women were relegated to the galley or to my little bedroom and we drank brandy, smoked our corn-cob pipes and I listened to many discussions of their politics, which seemed mainly to turn on the maintenance of the barges and the arrangements of the adoption-marriages which linked them all together. More than ever I realized their life was a complex sub-universe with its own inherent order as inaccessible to the outsider as it went unnoticed by him. And yet they were somehow frozen in themselves. Even the method of pouring a drink was hallowed by tradition and never altered. One held out one's glass to the offered jug, then took the jug after one's own glass was filled and filled the other's glass, so nobody ever poured out a drink for himself. The community spirit reigned among them to that extent! And in this lack of self, I began to sense a singular incapacity for being, that sad, self-imposed limitation of experience I recognized in myself and must also, like my cheekbones, be my inheritance from the Indians. And yet I knew it was in me and though I felt constraint, I was learning to love that constraint. Nao-Kurai treated me with overt pride, yet more than ever I sensed an undertow of veiled hostility until I wondered if it were simply this – he was scared that, at the last moment, I would get away from him.

So we entered the town of T. again and did the last of our festival shopping in a market full of tinsel, Christmas trees and other souvenirs of a festival we ourselves were too pagan to comprehend. There were posters everywhere advertising a fair that would come to town on Christmas Eve and the church announced it would celebrate Midnight Mass but we would burn our candles only to the primordial spirits of the solstice whose roots lay in the turn of the seasons and the principle of fertility. It was, said Nao-Kurai, the most suitable time for a wedding. This time we took no orders in the town but sailed further up the river a little way to the basin, where it seemed all the barges in the world were waiting for us, garlanded with paper emblems and each one flying a blaze of paper candle-lanterns decorated with phallic symbols in my honour, for tomorrow was my wedding day.

For inscrutable, hieratic reasons, Aoi did not come to my bed that night and the winter moon shone so brightly through the white curtains at my porthole that it hurt my eyes and I could not sleep. At last I went up on deck and found Nao-Kurai, wakeful too, was sitting on a coil of rope beneath a great cloud of pipe-smoke, sipping at a jug of brandy decanted from his big barrel. He seemed pleased to see me, though he did not greet me by name. He fetched me a glass and poured me a drink. I could tell by the way he walked to the galley that he had already been drinking on his own for some time.

For a long time, we watched the moonlight on the water together in silence. Then he began to speak and I soon realized he was very drunk for the words seemed to drift up at random out of a mind which had become a pool of memory in which an idea or two rose up to the surface now and then, like hazy strands of water-weed. As he went on, I became less and less sure that he remembered who I was and by the end of the story I was certain of it. Perhaps he had mistaken me for the eldest boy or for one of the bargees who had come aboard to pay their respects. He spoke the thickest version of the river argot and used many expressions that had long fallen out of common use but I could make out the drift of his story well enough.

'It was a long time ago – oh! such a very long time ago, it was, before we got to living on the water. And then we used to live in huts made out of down and bits of feather and to make tough enough fabric to keep the weather out we stuck them all together with spit, or so Mama's mama used to say and she never told a lie. Besides, she was quite old enough to remember everything and she'd been hatched from a parrot's egg when she was a little girl, oh, yes she had. She said so. She was old enough to remember everything and she was such an old lady when she died of the coughing she was bent right over like a snake eating its tail and she'd eaten snakes herself, you know. I'm coming to that in a moment.

'She was so bent over when she died a great to-do we had of it to straighten her out enough to fit her into a natural coffin, oh, yes! what a time we had! But all this was such a long time ago, all this when it happened what I'm remembering tonight, it was such a long time ago there was hardly any dark at night and, on the whole, it was a good time, because there weren't any shore folk, but, then, it was a bad time, because we didn't know how to make fire, did we. So it was always a wee bit cold and we couldn't cook nothing, of course, because of not having fire.

'But it's a lie to say we didn't know how to make fire until the black ships came! What a lie! But even so, in those days, the days I'm talking about, we ate nothing but slugs and snakes and crawly things that lived in the water because if we didn't actually live *on* the water, then, we lived, so to speak, in it. Or rather, there wasn't much difference in those days, none of your harsh divisions. No day, no night, but light sufficient; no solid, no fluid, but footholds a-plenty; no hard, no soft but everything chewable . . . everything all at once, just as it should be. Or so my granny used to say. Except it was just a wee bit cold.'

Most of the last sequence issued from his mouth in the weird chant of one who recounts details of a legendary past and I was pleased to find more evidence that my family might derive from the beautiful bird-people of antiquity. The night air chilled me so I took another mouthful or two of brandy. Around us the sleeping boats rocked gently at anchor, each one decorated with paper garlands to celebrate my wedding, and my wife slept beyond the bulkhead behind me, probably nursing her curious doll in her innocent arms. Nao-Kurai rambled on in a drowsy voice, inadvertently flattening notes here and there, which subtly altered various meanings, but I continued to listen because these picturesque ancient survivals were, were they not, the orally transmitted history of my people.

'Now in those days, the women weren't supposed to touch the snakes, not with their hands, that is. But one young girl picked off of the floor this head of a snake her father had caught and it spat its venom right up between her legs and she conceived straight off, didn't she. So she had this snake in her belly and it rattled around and writhed and she got very uncomfortable and said: "Mr Snake, won't you come out, please?" And Snake said: "All in my own good time." So she went on doing her chores but the wonder of it was, she never got cold, no matter how hard the wind blew. So Snake said: "That's because I've built my little fire. Don't you know what a fire is?" And the girl said: "Well, no. Not precisely." So out pops Snake from her hole with a bit of fire in his jaws and she rubs her hands to feel the glow and jumps for joy and says: "It's good!" So he taught her the word for "warm", which she needed to know, see, because she'd never felt like that before.

'Well, she was just going to eat her dinner, a little bit of lizard, that's what she'd got for dinner, and Snake says: "Why don't you toast your bit of lizard over my fire? I'm sure you'll find it ever so much more tasty." So she did and it was the most savoury thing she'd ever eaten, much more savoury than all those raw slugs and snails and things. Then they heard somebody coming and Snake slithered back up inside her quick as a flash and all was as it had been before. Except, after that, whenever she was by herself, Snake came out and she toasted and roasted her dinners and kept lovely and warm all winter, too.

'Now her father and brothers began to prick up their nostrils and lick their lips when they smelled the lovely savoury smells in the hut and they found some bones she hadn't picked quite clean and chewed the crumbs of meat off them and oh! it *was* nice but they hadn't the least idea why. But they saw the girl round as a ball and still she showed no signs of going into labour, though when they leaned against her belly, they would have thought it was as hot as an oven if they'd known what an oven was, of course.

'So, one day, the youngest brother hid in the cabin trunk and saw Snake come out of his sister and a big flame flickered all round the hut and cooked her dinner. "What's this?" he thought and he jumped out and caught hold of Snake and said: "Show me your trick or I'll kill you!" But Snake slithered out of his hands and vanished up the sister before you could say "Jack Robinson" and Sister cried and pleaded but it wasn't any good because *she* didn't know how to make fire, did she.'

Nao-Kurai spoke more and more slowly and began to leave great gaps between the sentences to be filled by the mournful lapping of the waters against the sides of the barge, while his head slid further down his chest. Somewhere, a tethered dog howled.

'When Father and the other Brothers came back, Youngest Brother told them what he'd seen so they picked up their big knives and cut Sister open just like you'd fillet a fish. But Snake was sulking and wouldn't show them how to make fire. They teased him and bullied him and dangled Sister's head in front of him by the hair so at last he consented to give them lessons. Every day, in the evenings, after supper, he'd rub two sticks together and make the flame and say "See! It's easy!" But they couldn't learn, no matter how they tried. They racked their poor old brains and inked their fingers but they could never learn as much as A, B, C, or what spells "cat", could they. So then they knew it was magic and they killed Snake and cut him into little pieces. Then they each ate their piece and . . . after that . . . they could all make fire . . .

' . . . every one of them could *scribble* away in fire in a twinkling, easy as anything . . .'

With that, his eyes closed and he spoke no more except to mumble, with intense satisfaction, 'Do anything easy as anything,' before he passed entirely into a thick sleep. I seized the jug and gulped down a great slug of brandy for I was shaking though not, this time, with cold; I shook with terror and despair. I remembered a story I had read once in an old book about some tribe of Central Asia who 'made a point of killing and eating in their own country any stranger indiscreet enough to commit a miracle or show any particular sign of sanctity, for thus they imbibe his magic virtue.' The name of the tribe, Hazara, had once helped me in a difficult crossword puzzle; now the remembered information helped me solve another clue. If the bird-people had wanted the Jesuits' magic, they would have eaten the priests to get it. As they would eat me.

All at once I filled in the suspicious gaps my lonely sentimentality had refused to acknowledge. Nao-Kurai's air of furtive triumph after I had accepted his daughter; Mama's excessive cordiality; their suspicious eagerness to adopt me when they knew, against all appearances, I was really nothing but a feared, mysterious dweller upon the shore all the time, one who had not all his life felt beneath him only the shifting motion of the insubstantial river yet who owned the most precious, most arcane knowledge they could only gain for themselves by desperate measures. And I knew as well as if Nao-Kurai had sung it out that they proposed to kill me and eat me, like Snake, the Fire-Bringer, in the fable, so that they would all learn how to read and write after a common feast where I would feature as the main dish on the menu at my own wedding breakfast. I was torn between mirth and horror. At last I got up, covered my father-in-law with my jacket to stop him catching cold and went silently below, prowling for further evidence.

In the main cabin my brothers and sisters lay sweetly sleeping and the moonlight mixed with festive lantern light slanted through the portholes and shone on their beloved faces. Because, yes, I am not ashamed to say I loved them all, even the dribbling baby who could not speak her name and peed on my lap when I took her on my knee. Mama and my child bride shared the same mattress and when I saw in one another's arms the old flesh and the young flesh which were, in some sense, interchangeable and whose twinned textures was already part of my flesh, then I fell down on my knees beside them, ready at that moment to pledge myself entirely to them and even to give my own flesh to them, in whatever form they pleased, if they thought it would do them any good. I was almost overcome with trust and good faith. I do believe that I was crying, young fool that I was. And Aoi had her doll beside her; her hand clasped its red dress. It was an inexpressibly touching detail.

Then the child shifted position in her sleep and muttered something. As she stirred, so she uncovered what should have been the scaled head of her baby in its white cap. I saw there was no fish's head under the lace but the tip of the blade of one of the very large knives Mama used in the kitchen. The boat swayed with the current and Aoi, half-waking, drowsily clutched the knife to her bosom. With great distinctness, she said, 'Tomorrow. Do it tomorrow.'

Then she turned on her back and began to snore.

Perhaps the knife was involved in some bizarre ritual of defloration. And, again, perhaps not. I sat back on my heels and wiped the sudden sweat from my forehead; then I realized I was not willing to take the slender chance they did not mean me harm. But, all the same, I kissed their cool cheeks before I left, first poor Aoi, who would have murdered me because they told her to, a programmed puppet with a floury face who was not the mistress of her own hands, and then Mama, whose skin I had never tasted before without savouring the odour of the mutton fat base of her cosmetics. I do believe my heart came as near as it ever did to breaking, that night – as near as it came to breaking, that is, before I said good-bye to Albertina, when my heart broke finally and forever.

I had nothing to take with me from the ship except memories. I went outside and said a silent good-bye to the stupefied figure of my father-in-law, who had tumbled from his seat and sprawled beside the brandy bottle that had betrayed him. As I let myself noiselessly over the side down into the freezing water, the candles in the paper lanterns began to gutter and by the time I reached the river bank, they were beginning to go out, one by one.

The wind blew through my soaking clothes and the cold woke up the old Desiderio. As I turned my back on the barges and set my face towards the distant lights of the town, I welcomed myself to the old home of my former self with a bored distaste. Desiderio had saved Kiku from the dear parents who would have dined off him but Kiku still could not find it in his heart just yet to thank Desiderio for it, as all his hopes of ease and tranquillity ran off and away from him like the river water that dripped from his clothing at every step.

The clock in the market square told me it was a quarter to four in the morning and the market square was full of the booths and side-shows of the Christmas fair, all locked, shuttered and deserted at this hour. I thought I might find a little shelter against what remained of the night in one of the tents and so I went down the canvas alleys until I found an entrance held open by a rope, as if someone inside were waiting for me. I recognized the booth instantly. This time, the sign outside said: EVERYBODY'S SPECIAL XMAS PRESENT. I went inside. He rustled in his straw.

'Candle and matches on the box,' he said. 'And close up the flap now you're inside, boy. Brass monkey weather, dammit.'

As I expected, I saw in the machine, rotating as on a pole, a woman's head flung back as if in ecstasy, so that the black hair unfurled like grandiloquent flags around her. The head of Dr Hoffman's ambassador turned like the world on its axis and one severed hand pressed its forefinger against her lips as if to tell me she was keeping a delicious secret while the other was extended as if to joyfully greet my return to her.

It was titled: PRECARIOUS GLIMMERING, A HEAD SUSPENDED FROM INFINITY.

4. The Acrobats of Desire

'If you've seen all you want, you can save me the candle,' he said and I blew it out so that the only light was the serrated luminous disc cast upwards on to the ceiling by a small oil stove. I knelt gratefully beside the stove for I was shivering while he, muttering, began to potter about making a meal for me. I was surprised and touched by these unhandy preparations. He opened a cardboard box, his larder, and took out half a loaf and a heel of rat-trap cheese on a tin plate; then he poured cold coffee from a bottle into a chipped enamel saucepan and set it on top of the stove to warm.

'I had a change of orders,' he explained. 'Got to look after you. Got to see you get there safe and sound. *She* came herself and told me.'

'She?'

'The she of she's. His daughter.'

'Albertina?'

I had never spoken the name aloud before.

'You're smart,' he applauded. 'Oh, you know the nature of plus all right"

'I can,' I said, 'put two and two together.'

'Where've you been since you did for poor Mary Anne?' But he leered and grimaced as he spoke so I knew he knew I knew he knew I

93

had not, in fact, murdered the unfortunate girl but that, for some reason, I was now forced to pretend that I had. However, I was too tired to continue with such Byzantine perplexities.

'Hiding,' I said briefly.

'They thought you'd most likely try to find me sooner or later, if you were still alive, that is.'

He tested the temperature of the coffee with his thumb.

'Seeing,' he added with a certain smugness, 'that I'm your only clue.'

So he gave me back my quest but I could not think about it yet. I ate his food and let him wrap a blanket round me for I had taken a violent chill and, no matter how closely I hugged the stove, my teeth would not stop chattering.

'You mustn't get sick, you know,' he said. 'We've got a goodish long trip before we get there.'

'I'm to go with you, am I?'

'Oh, yes. I'm to give you a job as my assistant and also identification: to wit, my nephew. You'll drive my little new old truck for me and put up the tent for me and oil the machines for me and so on, for I am getting on in years and not so active as I was.'

'How long will it take to reach there?'

'Oh, there'll be ample *time*,' he said. 'He's coped wonderfully with time, hasn't he. Worried about your city, are you?'

'Not particularly,' I confessed.

'He could probably use a smart young man like you in his organization.'

He gave me a mug of hot coffee and I warmed my hands on it.

'But I do have my own orders, you know.'

My tongue tripped on the standard speech and, as I had become aware of positive happiness among the river people for the first time in my life, now I knew at last the flavour of true misery for I would never speak their musical tongue again. The old man cocked his head inquisitively and I waited for him to ask me where I had been hiding but he was attending only to what I said, not the manner in which I said it.

'Licensed to kill?' he queried.

'What is your precise relationship to Dr Hoffman?' I parried.

He motioned me to pass him the mug and took some bitter sips before he replied. When he did so, his voice had lost something of its querulous senescence, so that I wondered to what extent he covered an authentic role in the Doctor's play with that of an embittered old sot.

'I am not necessarily connected with him,' he said. 'There are no such things as necessary connections. Necessary connections are fabulous beasts. Like the unicorn. Nevertheless, since things occasionally *do* come together in various mutable combinations, you might say that the Doctor and I have made a random intersection. He remembered me in my blindness. I was blind and old and had half drunk myself to death. He remembered me and he saved me. He even made me the curator of his museum.'

There was a note of quiet pride in his voice that did not suit the rotting old hut in which we sat and bed of straw on which he slept so I knew he was of more importance than he seemed and the Minister's computers had known what they were about when they put me on his trail.

'His museum?' I asked tentatively.

'The sack ... behind you. Look.'

The sack was immensely heavy and contained innumerable small boxes each marked on the lid with an indented device so that the old man in his blindness could inform himself of their contents by a single touch. Each one of these boxes contained, as I expected, the models, slides and pictures which went inside the machines and were there magnified by lenses almost to life-size. A universality of figures of men, women, beasts, drawing rooms, auto-da-fés and scenes of every conceivable type was contained in these boxes, none of which was bigger than my thumb. I spilled out a mass of variegated objects on my lap, each a wonder of miniaturization and some of scarcely credible complexity.

'The set of samples,' he explained. He was beginning to address me as if I were a lecture theatre. As I watched them, they seemed to wriggle and writhe over my knees with the force of the life they simulated but I knew it was only a trick of the vague light from the oil stove.

'I am proud to say he was my pupil,' said the peep-show proprietor. 'If I feel a little resentment against him from time to time, when my bones ache with the travelling – well, it is only to be expected. I wasn't even his John the Baptist, you know. I queried his doctoral thesis. I mocked his friend, Mendoza. Yet he trusts me with his set of samples.'

He leaned over and plucked out a handful of figures.

'Look at them. Do they look like toys?'

'Yes. Like toys.'

'They are symbolic constituents of representations of the basic constituents of the universe. If they are properly arranged, all the possible situations in the world and every possible mutation of those situations can be represented.'

'Like the Minister's computer bank?'

'Not in the least,' he snapped. 'By the correct use of these samples, it would be possible to negate the reality of the Minister of Determination. Ironically enough, your Minister seeks the same final analysis my former pupil made long ago. But then the Doctor transcended it.'

He held out a bouquet of ferocious images of desire in my direction. They seemed almost to leap from his hand, such was their synthetic energy.

'The symbols serve as patterns or templates from which physical objects and real events may be evolved by the process he calls "effective evolving". I go about the world like Santa with a sack and nobody knows it is filled up with changes.'

I poured myself more coffee for I needed to keep my wits about me. After all, he had once been a rationalist even if now he were a charlatan.

'I am very confused,' I said. 'Give me at least a hint of his methodology.'

'First theory of Phenomenal Dynamics,' he said. 'The universe has no fixed substratum of fixed substances and its only reality lies in its phenomena.'

'Yes,' I said. 'I comprehend that.'

'Second theory of Phenomenal Dynamics: only change is invariable.'

This sounded more like an aphorism than a hypothesis to me but I held my peace.

'Third theory of Phenomenal Dynamics: the difference between a symbol and an object is quantitative, not qualitative.'

Then he sighed and fell silent. I saw through a rent in the canvas wall that though it was still night inside the booth, the dawn began in violet outside; and then I fell asleep.

Now I was in hiding from both the police – for my picture with a WANTED sign was posted outside the town police station – and also from the river people. I passed myself off as the peep-show proprietor's renegade nephew. My new identity was perfect in every detail. I tailored my hair and moustache to new shapes and threw away my Indian clothes, putting on instead some dark, sober garments which came with my new identity. I guessed that in the Minister's reckoning I was listed dead, among the casualties of the war, and that was why Dr Hoffman was taking such pains over me but all I had to do was to hide in the shadows of the booth, polish the lenses of the machines, watch my master arrange each day's fresh, disquieting spectacles and listen to the various accounts of his former pupil's activities that he gave me in the evenings as we sat beside the stove after our business was done for the day.

I was not competent, then, to comment on any of the information I received and I am not competent to do so now, even though I have seen the laboratories themselves, the generators and even the inscrutable doctor himself, at work among them with the awful conviction of a demiurge. But from the notes I made at the time, I extracted the following unlikely hints as to the intellectual principles underpinning the Doctor's manifestations.

His main principles were indeed as follows: everything it is possible to imagine can also exist. A vast encyclopedia of mythological references supported this initial hypothesis – shamans of Oceania who sang rude blocks of wood ship-shape without the intervention of an axe; poets of medieval Ireland whose withering odes scalded their kings' enemies with plagues of boils; and so on and so forth. At a very early point in his studies Hoffman had moved well out of the realm of pure science and resurrected all manner of antique pseudo-sciences, alchemy, geomancy and the empirical investigation of those essences the ancient Chinese claimed created phenomena through an interplay of elemental aspects of maleness and femaleness. And then there was the notion of passion.

In the pocket of my dark suit I found a scrap of paper with the following quotation from de Sade written on it in the most exquisite, feminine handwriting; though the message was undirected and unsigned, I knew it was meant for me and that it came from Albertina.

'My passions, concentrated on a single point, resemble the rays of a sun assembled by a magnifying glass; they immediately set fire to whatever object they find in their way.'

Yet I could see no personal significance in these words and finally decided they must refer to the machinery of the peep-show itself for I had even begun to believe that the manipulation of those numinous samples might indeed restructure events since, in a poetic and circuitous fashion, they had certainly helped to organize my disastrous night at the Mayor's house.

But I was wistfully impressed by the grandiloquence of both de Sade and the girl who quoted him to me for I knew myself to be a man without much passion, even if I was a romantic. If I once again existed only in the vague hope I would one day see Albertina herself again, I could not imagine this desire might make me incandescent enough to glimpse her whereabouts by my own glow – let alone to utilize what my instructor in hyperphysics described to me as the 'radiant energy' which emanated from desire to blaze a path to her. A blind old man, playing with toys in a fairground, lost in a mazy web of memories of things he had not seen ... it was a case of the blind leading the blind, for he could never have been a man who burned with passion himself, either! So when he spoke of Albertina as if she were lambent flame made flesh, his words rang curiously false, although I could remember my dream of the inextinguishable skeleton and wonder if she had visited him in a dream, too, for he could only see when he was asleep.

He had formed a loose attachment with the fairground people and so the old man, the carnival and I travelled on together. I found that the peep-show proprietor, anticipating my arrival, had rented a broken-down truck from the Armenian who operated the wheel of fortune. This was his new little old truck and I drove it for him as we moved with our new companions from place to place, part of a tumultuous cavalcade moving towards other towns along the winter roads. On the road I was as safe from the Indians as I had been from the police while I lived on the river. I was as safe from everything as I would have been in the Opera House, listening to *The Marriage of Figaro*, because the road was another kind of self-consistent river.

The travelling fair was its own world, which acknowledged no geographical location or temporal situation for everywhere we halted was exactly the same as where we had stopped last, once we had put up our booths and sideshows. Mexican comedians; intrepid equestriennes from Nebraska, Kansas or Ohio whose endless legs and scrubbed features were labelled 'Made in U.S.A.'; Japanese dwarfs who wrestled together in arenas of mud; Norwegian motor-cyclists roaring vertically around portable walls of death; a team of dancing Albinos whose pallid gavottes were like those of the luminous undead; the bearded lady and the alligator man – these were my new neighbours, who shared nothing but the sullen glamour of their difference from the common world and clung defensively together to protect and perpetuate this difference. Natives of the fairground, they acknowledged no other nationality and could imagine no other home. A polyglot babel manned the sideshows, the rifle ranges and coconut shies, dive-bombers, helter-skelters and roundabouts on which, hieratic as knights in chess, the painted horses described perpetual circles as immune as those of the planets to the drab world of the here and now inhabited by those who came to gape at us. And if we transcended the commonplace, so we transcended language. Since we had few tongues in common, we mostly used a language of grunt, bark and gesture which is, perhaps, the common matrix of language. And as we rarely had anything more complicated to say to one another than how miry the roads were, we all got on well enough.

They were not in the least aware how extraordinary they were because they made their living out of the grotesque. Their bread was deformity. Their biographies, however tragic or bizarre, were all alike in singularity and many of them, like myself, were permanently in hiding from a real world which they understood so badly nobody knew how much it had changed since the war began. Sometimes I thought the whole savage and dissolute crew were nothing but the Doctor's storm troops but they did not know anything at all about the Doctor. Nobody had heard his name. They only knew a little about themselves and this knowledge, in itself, was quite sufficient to create a microcosm with as gaudy, circumscribed, rotary and absurd a structure as a roundabout.

I often watched the roundabouts circulate upon their static journeys. 'Nothing,' said the peep-show proprietor, 'is ever completed; it only changes.' As he pleased, he altered the displays he had never seen, murmuring: 'No hidden unity.' The children of the fairground pressed their snot and filth-caked faces to the eyepieces and giggled at what they saw. Nothing was strange to those whose fathers rode the wall of death three times a day while their mothers elegantly defined gravity on a taut, single leg atop the white back of a pirouetting horse. And they seemed to see so little of their parents they might have been spontaneously generated by the evanescent paraphernalia of the passing show around them which, no sooner had it been set up, was dismantled, piled up in segments on erratic trucks and shifted in its entirety to some other new venue. The fairground was a moving toyshop, an ambulant raree-show coming to life in convulsive fits and starts whenever the procession stopped, regulated only by the implicit awareness of a lack of rules.

'First will come Nebulous Time, a period of absolute mutability when only reflected rays and broken trajectories of an entirely hypothetical source of light fitfully reveal a continually shifting surface, like the surface of water, yet a water which is only a reflective skin and has neither depth nor volume. But you must never forget that the Doctor's philosophy is not so much transcendental as incidental.

It utilizes all the incidents that ripple the depthless surfaces of, you understand, the sensual world. When the sensual world unconditionally surrenders to the intermittency of mutability, man will be freed in perpetuity from the tyranny of a single present. And we will live on as many layers of consciousness as we can, all at the same time. After the Doctor liberates us, that is. Only after that.'

The toasting cheese sweated a few drops of grease on to the flame in the stove so that it flared and stank. I filled the glass he held out to me, watching as I did so the reflected flame splutter on the cracked lenses of his dark glasses. Sometimes he looked like an old, blind evangelist. As he grew more used to having once again an audience, he ordered his periods more and more succinctly and phrased his lecturettes with more resonance. He started to impress me not so much with the quality of his discourse as with the awed wonder with which he delivered it. He often combined prophetic fervour with sibylline obscurity. Since I always got up before him in the mornings, sometimes I caught sight of him waking up. It was always poignant to watch him open his sightless eyes and blink a little as if this time there might be a chance he would blink away the darkness forever.

Thrust as I was into such intimacy with the peep-show proprietor, I could not help beginning to feel affection for him and I found myself ministering to the needs of an occasionally incontinent, always foul-mannered old man with a generosity I would never have expected of myself, though he made few demands upon me and those were mostly upon my attention.

My tasks were simple and housewifely, for he did not allow me to meddle with the set of samples. I assembled our meals, swept out the booth, shook out our sleeping straw, dusted the machines and, behind a spare pair of discreet sunglasses, sat at the counter during his frequent absences in bars, for his drunkenness was real enough. Then I would make notes of the things he told me and try to tease out from them some notion of the practical means by which his former pupil performed his conjuring tricks, though this was a very difficult task for the essence of the Hoffman theory was the fluidity of its structure and, besides, I was constantly interrupted by visits from the roving packs of children and their elders also.

A clatter of scales announced the arrival of *homo reptilis* for a bleak chat and several of my cigarettes, a whiff of gunpowder and imported perfume, that of Mamie Buckskin the sharp-shooter, while a more fragile and tentative clearing of the throat told me Madame la Barbe was here. Madame la Barbe kept her chestnut moustache to neat, discreet, Vermeer proportions and it disguised an uncommonly maternal nature. She would bring me a brioche freshly baked in the oven she had installed in her French provincial caravan full of plants in pots, pet cats, over-upholstered sofas and framed photographs of kin. On the frames of those of her relatives who were deceased she hung rosettes of black ribbons.

I must admit that all my guests enchanted me and I, in turn, enchanted them for, here, I had the unique allure of the norm. I was exotic precisely to the extent of my mundanity. The peep-show proprietor's nephew was a small businessman bankrupted by the catastrophe in the capital and all those freaks could not get enough of my accounts of the world of typewriters and telephones, flush toilets, tiled bathrooms, electric lights and mechanical appliances. They wondered at the masterpiece of sterility I remembered for them as if it were an earthly paradise from which they were barred forever. So I gave them an imitation of another reality while the peep-show proprietor offered me far stronger meat.

Proposition: Time is a serial composition of apparently indivisible instants.
Since the inception of the mode of consciousness we refer to as 'the world', man has always thought of time as in itself a movement forward, an onward flow leaving only a little debris behind it. Evanescence is the essence of time. And since temporality is the medium in which this mode of consciousness has itself been expressed, since time is, as it were, the canvas on which we ourselves are painted, the empirical investigation of the structure of time poses certain acute methodological problems. Could the Mona Lisa turn round, scratch her own background and then submit to a laboratory analysis the substance she found under her nail?

No, indeed!

Now this analogy, a striking one, implies that all phenomena are necessarily temporal in nature and roll forward en masse on wheels at the corners of the four-square block of space-time they occupy, shoulder to shoulder and bearing always at their backs the wall against which they all must meet that shooting-squad, mortality. Yet this model of the world does not make even so much as the formal acknowledgement of the synthesizable aspect of time as was made to space by the introduction of perspective into painting. In other words, we knew so little about the geometry of time – let alone its physical properties –

that we could not even adequately simulate the physical form of so much as a single instant.

The introduction of cinematography enabled us to corral time past and thus retain it not merely in the memory – at best, a falsifying receptacle – but in the objective preservative of a roll of film. But, if past, present and future are the dimensions of time, they are notoriously fluid. There is no tension in the tenses and yet they are always tremulously about to coagulate. The present is a liquid jelly which settles into a quivering, passive mass, the past, as soon as – if not sooner than – we are aware of it *as* the present. Yet this mass was intangible and existed only conceptually until the arrival of the preservative, cinema.

The motion picture is usually regarded as only a kind of shadow play and few bother to probe the ontological paradoxes it presents. For it offers us nothing less than the present tense experience of time irrefutably past. So that the coil of film has, as it were, lassooed inert phenomena from which the present had departed, and when projected upon a screen, they are granted a temporary revivification.

My student, Mendoza, offered me some investigations along these lines to justify the many hours he spent each day in the neighbourhood fleapits gazing at the panorama of revived phenomena with glazed, visionary eyes. Once he remarked to me in conversation: 'Lumière was not the father of the cinema; it was Sergeant Bertrand, the violator of graves.'

The images of cinematography, however, altogether lack autonomy. Locking in programmed patterns, they merely transpose time past into time present and cannot, by their nature, respond to the magnetic impulses of time future for the unachievable future which does not exist in any dimension, but nevertheless organizes phenomena towards its potential conclusions. The cinematographic model is one of cyclic recurrences *alone*, even if these recurrences are instigated voluntarily, by the hand of man viz. the projectionist, rather than the hand of fate. Though, in another sense, the action of time is actually visible in the tears, scratches and thumbprints on the substance of the film itself, these are caused only by the sly, corrosive touch of mortality and, since the print may be renewed at will, the flaws of ageing, if retained, increase the presence of the past only by a kind of forgery, as when a man punches artificial worm-holes into raw wood or smokes shadows of fresh paint with a candle to produce an apparently aged artefact.

Mendoza, however, claimed that if a thing were sufficiently artificial, it became absolutely equivalent to the genuine. His mind puffed out ideas like the dandelion seed-head his chevelure so much resembled but we did not take any of his ideas seriously, not one of us, not any of them. Yet Hoffman refined Mendoza's initially crude hypotheses of fissile time and synthetic authenticity and wove them together to form another mode of consciousness altogether. But we did not know that. We were content to laugh at Mendoza. We laughed uproariously.

He dreamed of fissile time – of exploding the diatonic scale with its two notes, past and present, into a chromatic fanfare of every conceivable tense and many tenses at present inconceivable because there is no language to describe them. He produced sheet after sheet of mathematics in an exceedingly neurotic script to prove to me that time was amenable to the rigours of scientific analysis as any other notion; and, indeed, he convinced me, at least, that time was elastic for it always seemed to stretch out to eternity as I read them through!*

His attitude to abstractions was this: abstractions only were true because, since they did not exist, they could be proved or disproved entirely at the whim of the investigator. How his wild eyes flashed as he spoke!

By the end of his sophomore year, Mendoza was the clown of the senior common room. We looked forward to his essays much as London clubmen look forward to their weekly *Punch*. How we chuckled richly over our port as I read aloud the choicest tidbits! His classmates mocked him, too. Only Hoffman, with his Teutonic lack of humour, listened to the outrageous Mendoza with a straight face. In time, he and Mendoza became almost inseparable, though they made a strangely ill-assorted couple and together gave an impression of vaudeville rather than the laboratory for Mendoza sported flowing hair, abundant neckties, herbaceous shirts and suits of black velvet while his gleaming, impassioned gaze seemed to warn one to weave a circle round him thrice before approaching him. As for Hoffman, *he* was a model of propriety, well starched and stiffly suited, one of his cold, blue eyes wedged open with a monocle. His handshake was moist and chill; his smile was alpine in its austerity and he always smelled of medicated soap. He was already unnaturally brilliant and even his teachers feared him. Mendoza was his only friend.

They worked together and they played together. Soon we began to hear the most disreputable stories of their exploits in the red light quarter. Now Mendoza had a streak of Moorish blood and read Arabic fluently. He followed up certain hints from obscure books

* A pastel-coloured joke, designed to produce a discreet titter among freshmen. Desiderio.

and became more and more obsessed with the nature of time in relation to the sexual act. At length he devised a hilarious thesis concerning the fissile/tensile nature of the orgasm. He claimed that the actual discharge took place in neither past, present nor future but precipitated an exponential polychromatic fusion of all three, especially if impregnation were effected. He submitted to me an end of term paper titled, I recall: 'The Fissile Potential of the Willed Annihilation of the Orgiastic Instant'. It described an experiment utilizing the talents of seven of the town's most notorious whores and, if it proved nothing else, it showed that Mendoza was something of an athlete while his technical assistant, none other than our decorous Hoffman, possessed, against all appearances, quite remarkable sexual versatility.

Mendoza described his results as 'the perpetration of a durationless state possibly synthesizing infinity'. He claimed their enthusiasm had set up such intense vibrations every clock in the establishment burst its case. He submitted to the university bills not only for the services of the prostitutes but also for those of the clock-repairer. So we dismissed Mendoza. When he learned he had been sent down, he broke into the laboratory and smeared faeces all over the blackboards. After that, we heard no more of him. But Hoffman, of course, kept in touch with him. Indeed, it was the beginning of the first great period of their research . . .

And so on and so on and so on.

As he grew used to my continual presence, he gave me such heady blends of theory and biography three or four times a week and various forgotten tricks of the lecturer came back to him. He often hunted for forgotten chalk to draw diagrams on a blackboard which existed only in a memory of the university and bunched his fingers in an invisible academic gown. I found these gestures unspeakably moving. I filled his glass and listened.

But none of these gobbets and scraps issuing from a mind blunted by age and misfortune made much sense to me. Sometimes a whole hour of discourse plashed down on me like rain and I would jot down from it only a single phrase that struck me. Perhaps: 'Things cannot be exhausted'; or 'In the imagination, nothing is past, nothing can be forgotten.' Or: 'Change is the only valid response to phenomena.' I grew aware that Hoffman's Phenomenal Dynamics involved a hypothetical dialectic between mutuality and transformation; the discovery of a certain formula which speeded up the processes of mutability; and that he had often spoken to his teacher of a 'continuous improvisation of correlatives'. But, for the most part, I was utterly mystified. And I would toast a little cheese on top of the stove, to eat with bread and beer for our suppers, rumble vague, indeterminate sounds I hoped the old man would interpret as those of a quickened interest and brood upon the changes I myself had undergone.

'Mutable combinations,' he would say, swig beer and belch. Then, scooping up a handful of magic samples, he tossed them in the air as in the game of five-stones, letting them fall with such solemnity I was almost tempted to believe, with him, that the haphazard patterns they made as they fell at the blind dictation of chance were echoed in flesh in the beleaguered city which, he informed me with irritation, was still managing to hold out.

Now and then I asked a few questions, though these were mainly concerned with the facts of Hoffman rather than his conceptual framework.

'Why did he and Mendoza quarrel?'

'Over a woman,' he said. 'Or so Hoffman once told me, in a voice choked either with tears or with anger – I could not tell which for by then, of course, I was blind and reduced to nothing more than a cipher in his formulae.'

It was a long time before he told me that woman had been the mother of Albertina.

'And what happened to Mendoza?'

'In the end, he spattered himself over infinity in a chromatic arc, like a rainbow.'

Well, nobody would ever know, now, the cause of the fire that destroyed his itinerant time machine!

And then there were my other distractions.

Madame la Barbe was as reticent as a young girl. She raised the flap of the tent, deposited her gifts of cake, smoking pots of delicious coffee and now and then a savoury cassoulet on our counter and vanished with the most fleeting of smiles. Without her beard, she would have been a fat, aproned, hard-mouthed, grim-visaged French countrywoman who never stirred one half kilometre from her native ville. Bearded, she was immensely handsome, widely travelled and the loneliest woman in the world. She sat in her caravan and picked out sentimental songs on a parlour organ, crooning the wistful words of love and longing in a high-pitched, over-elocuted voice. Slowly, when she saw I found her neither risible nor disgusting, she started to confide in me.

She had only the one dream: to wake up one day in the town where she was born, in her bed of childhood, the geranium on the windowsill, the jug and basin on the wash-stand. And then die. I found her sympathetic. She exposed her difference to make her living and had done so for thirty years, yet each time the gawping peasants came into her booth as she posed for them in white satin and artificial orange blossom, the Bearded Bride felt all the pangs of defloration although, of course, she was a virgin. 'Each time,' she said in her prettily broken accent, 'a fresh violation. One is penetrated by their eyes.'

The beard appeared with her breasts; she was thirteen. Never a pretty girl, always bulky and dowdy, she had hoped only to pass unnoticed. Perhaps a neighbouring tradesman in that grey, sedate town in the Loire valley where all the chairs wore antimacassars and even the shadows fell with propriety might marry her for her *dot*. Her father was a notary. The daughter took her first communion with a blue stubble of five o'clock shadow showing under the veil. The mother died of cancer and the father took to peculation. He was found out; he slit his throat with the common razor. It was an utterly commonplace tragedy. She started to live alone in the echoing, narrow house, hiding behind the shutters. She was fifteen. Soon there was nothing left to sell and the charity of the neighbours was exhausted. A circus came to town. Trembling, in mourning, muffled in veils, she visited the ringmaster and next day she was a working woman. She celebrated her sixteenth birthday at the carnival in Rio and had visited in the course of her career all the fabled cities of the world from Shanghai to Valparaiso, Tangiers to Tashkent.

It was not her beard that made her unique; it was the fact that, never, in all her life, had she known a single moment's happiness.

'This,' she would say, touching the frilled leaves of one of her potted plants, 'is my *monstra deliciosa*, my delicious monster.'

And her eyes would involuntarily stray to the little mirror on the wall. She had fixed one of her black mourning rosettes to its gilt frame. I visited her caravan with great circumspection and never without a small gift – a bunch of violets, candy, a French novel picked up in a second-hand bookstore. In return, she brewed me hot chocolate and played and sang for me.

'*Plaisirs d'amour ne durent plus qu'un moment . . .*'

But she herself had known no pleasure at all. She was a perfect lady. She had the wistful charm of a flower pressed inside a perfectly enormous book. She always used to call me 'Désiré'. It was always refreshingly boring to call on her, like calling on an aunt one had loved very much in childhood.

In the oracular limbo between sleeping and waking, my master once cried out: 'Everything depends on persistence of vision.' Did he refer to the peep-show alone or to the phantoms in the city? I took advantage of his blindness and his sleeps to go through the set of samples and, as far as I could, make a comprehensive catalogue of them, though this self-imposed inventory was complicated by the difficulty of ascertaining how many samples there were, since the numbers in the sack varied constantly and the work of classifying was almost impossible because they were never the same if you looked at them twice.

I lost the notebooks containing the rough, inadequate list in the earthquake which, according to Mendoza's theory, was already organizing the events which preceded it with the formal rhetoric of tragedy. And, with reference to the landslide, I do not know if I would remember Madame la Barbe as so pitiful, Mamie Buckskin as so ferocious or my master with such affection if I did not know, with hindsight, how soon they were all going to die. However, I remember that, however much the symbolic content of the samples altered, they all came in one of three forms e.g.:

(a) wax models, often with clockwork mechanisms, as described;
(b) glass slides, as already described;
and:
(c) sets of still photographs which achieved the effect of movement by means of the technique of the flicker books of our childhood.

These sets usually consisted of six or seven different aspects of the same scene which might be, typically, a nursemaid mutilating a baby, toasting him over a nursery fire and then gobbling him up with every appearance of relish. As one moved from machine to machine watching the various panels of this narrative unfold each one another facet of the same action, one had the impression of viewing an event in, as it were, temporal depth. The photographs themselves had every appearance of authenticity. I was particularly struck by a series showing a young woman trampled to death by wild horses because the actress bore some resemblance to Dr Hoffman's own daughter. There were also pictures of natural catastrophes such as the San Francisco earthquake, but I did not feel a shudder of anticipatory dread as I handled these; indeed, I even played through one set of theme and variations upon the subject of an earthquake through the machine, when my master was away drinking. And perhaps I should not have meddled with the machines, just as he warned me, at that . . . though Albertina told me her father always retreated in front of the boundaries of nature, so I do not think I had anything to do with the landslide, in reality.

From my investigations in the sack, I came to the conclusion that the models did indeed represent everything it was possible to believe by the means of either direct simulation or a symbolism derived from Freud. They were also, or so the peep-show proprietor believed, exceedingly numinous objects. He would never let me put them in the machines for him; he had even forbidden me to peek in the bag.

'Just let me catch you poking in my sack,' he remarked, 'and I'll cut your hands off.'

But I was too cunning to be caught.

Mamie Buckskin lived alone in a rifle range. Every morning she set up a row of whisky bottles along a nearby fence and shot the neck off each one. So she practised her art. She claimed she could shoot the tail-feathers off a pheasant in flight; she claimed she could shoot out the central heart of the five of hearts at twenty paces; she claimed she could shoot a specified apple from the bough of a specified tree at forty paces; and she often lit my cigarettes for me with a single, transverse bullet. Her rifles were fire-spitting extensions of her arms and her tongue also spat fire. She always dressed herself in fringed leather garments of the pioneers of the old West yet her abundant yellow hair was always curled and swept up in the monumental style of the saloon belle while a very feminine locket containing a picture of her dead, alcoholic mother always bounced between her lavish breasts. She was a paradox – a fully phallic female with the bosom of a nursing mother and a gun, death-dealing erectile tissue, perpetually at her thigh. She boasted a collection of more than fifty antique or historic rifles, pistols and revolvers, including specimens once owned by Billy the Kid, Doc Holliday and John Wesley Hardin. She spent three hours a day polishing them, oiling them and lovingly fingering each one. She was in love with guns. She was twenty-eight years old and as impervious as if shellacked.

Imprisoned in the far West for shooting the man who held the mortgage when he tried to take possession of her dying father's farm, she easily seduced the gaoler, escaped and disposed of the sheriff's posse by shooting them too. But she soon grew weary of a life of crime for she was an artist with her weapons; killing was only an effect of her virtuosity. A Winchester repeater was a Stradivarius to her and her world was composed only of targets. Sexually, she preferred women.

At one time she had worked a double act in an American burlesque house, where, in the trappings of a cowboy hero, she shot every stitch of clothing off her beloved mistress, a fluffy exuberant blonde of Viennese extraction whom she had abducted from a convent. But this soubrette ran off with a conjurer and took up a fresh career in which she was sawn in half nightly. After that, Mamie, made only the more cynical by this brush with love, blazed away by herself.

She loved to travel and joined the fair only to see the world. Besides, if she ran her own sideshow, she could keep her hands on all the profits and, next to guns and the open road, she loved money. She took a great liking to me for she admired passivity in a man more than anything and she offered me a job as her straight man, to set up her targets and let her blast hats and oranges off my head on stage. But I told her my uncle could not manage without me. Her strident vigour was both exhilarating and exhausting. Now and then, when she could not entice an equestrienne into her fur-lined sleeping bag, she morosely made do with me and these nights were as if spent manning a very small dinghy on a very stormy sea. Her caravan contained nothing but racks of guns, targets and a tiny, inconspicuous afterthought of a cooking stove on which she occasionally cooked burning chili and the leaden biscuits she consumed with syrup and a slug of rye for breakfast. Yet, sometimes, in sleep, I surprised her brass features relaxed and then she looked once more the wistful, belligerent tomboy who stole her father's Colt 45 to roar away at rattlers but wept when she shot the family German shepherd dog in the paw, in error. And I occasionally caught her glancing at Madame la Barbe's beard with a certain envy. Mamie, too, was a tragic woman.

I see them all haloed in the dark afterlight of accomplished tragedy, moving with the inexorability of the doomed towards a violent death.

In the fairground, it was a fact of nature that things were not what they seemed. Mamie once took me to watch the pretty riders servicing their horses in the privacy of the loosebox. We lay concealed in the hay as they conjugated the ultimate verb below us. The whinneys we heard could have come from the throats of either the stallions or their riders and the violence of their movements rocked the box so tempestuously back and forth that at every moment we threatened to fall from our perch. The swaying paraffin lamps which hung from the roof lent the lurid scene a dramatically expressionist chiaroscuro so intermittent I began to doubt some of the things I saw and I remembered how the peep-show proprietor had muttered in his sleep: 'It all depends on persistence of vision.' Meanwhile, my virile mistress, reeking already with sympathetic lust, pawed and clawed me so our position was all the more insecure and, in that resounding box of passion, I must admit I did indeed experience Mendoza's durationless infinity. I should say I substantiated his theory for I have no idea how long the orgy lasted after we did indeed tumble into the morass of satin limbs and flailing hooves and, had there been a clock in the van, I am sure it would have exploded. I was also disturbed because the scene had certainly some resemblances to the sequence of photographs in the sack of samples showing a girl trampled by horses; yet it was teasingly different. Even so, I wondered how far I might have prefigured it. Though often, the whole fair seemed only another kind of set of samples, anyway.

Mamie broke a rib where a horse kicked her and went about in an unbecoming corselet of bandages for a while. Her eyes, grey as a rifle barrel, took on a curious expression of surmise when she saw me, as though I had revealed unsuspected talents during the evening, and finally she astonished me by offering to teach me how to improve my draw.

I discovered the peep-show proprietor was in the habit of performing some kind of divination by means of the samples though I never found out what it was, precisely, he divined or forecast; nor how he did it; nor – for that matter – why. Certainly he got no previous information about the landslide from his investigations, or he would have run away. But he would sometimes thrust blindly into the neck of the sack and pull out the first boxes he touched. He would read the braille inscriptions sometimes with a worried frown, sometimes with shrill squeaks of glee.

'To express a desire authentically,' he told me, 'is to satisfy it categorically.'

I puzzled over this gnomic utterance for a long time. Did he merely mean what he said – which was patently nonsense? Or was he referring to Mendoza's other theory, that if a thing were artificial *enough*, it became genuine?

I touched his shoulder lightly to wake him for his morning tea and in his sleep he exhorted: 'Objectify your desires!'

This seemed somehow very important but I was not at all sure why.

The third of my friends, the Alligator Man, gave me the simplest pleasure. He was a Creole and sometimes played the mouth organ and sang to me rough, dark melodies in a uniquely savorous French. Born in a Louisiana swamp, his affliction was genetic; he owed it to an unhappy interlocking of the genes of his picturesquely fey mother, who rocked all day on the porch in a white nightdress while her home went to rack and ruin, and his picturesquely crazy father, who spent his time building an ark on the bayou, for he believed the second Flood was imminent. The Alligator Man spent his childhood up to his neck in another part of the same bayou because he found his own company more stimulating than that of his family and so lolled all day among the weeds under the drifting ghosts of Spanish moss, playing his harmonica and doing nobody any harm. When he was twelve, his father sold him to a travelling showman for the price of fourteen pounds of nails and that was the last he saw of his parents, who did not even bother to wave him good-bye. He spent the rest of his life similarly immersed up to the neck in a glass water tank where he lay somnolently as a log, staring at those who came to stare at him with an unblinking malice.

For a man who had spent most of his life under water, he had a remarkable knowledge of the world and, of all the fairground people, he was the only one with some inkling of the war or the way in which it was conducted. He and his tank had spent three months in a Gallery of Monsters in the slums of the capital when the hostilities were beginning and he had grasped to a surprising extent what was going on, though he was as bored by mutability as any immutable stone must be. In his tank he had learned patience, cunning and duplicity. He had trained himself in the spiritual discipline of absolute apathy.

'The freak,' he said, 'is the norm.'

He was fond of the peep-show and sometimes came out of his tank, leaving a watery trail behind him, to visit us, moving from machine to machine, his flat feet sonorously slapping the ground with the sound of flaccid applause. The scales covered his entire face and body except for a small patch of infantine softness, pale peach in colour, above his genitals, which were perfectly normal. He could not bear the sunlight and had shivering fits if he were out of the water for more than two or three hours. As far as I could tell, he suffered from no human feelings whatsoever but I grew very fond of him for he had refined his subjectivity until he believed in absolutely nothing. He taught me to play the harmonica and finally gave me his very own spare one. I think it was the first gift he had made in his entire life. Though I was very pleased to receive it, I was sorry to see the Alligator Man's inflexible misanthropy soften a little.

So, with one thing and another, life passed pleasantly enough and I was never bored. The travelling fair tacked back and forth across the uplands, now teasingly taking me high into the foothills and then

withdrawing far back, almost into the plain. But, in his sleep, the
peep-show proprietor murmured: 'The way South lies along the
Northern road' and I knew I must leave myself in his hands and
dare not hurry things, even when I realized the tentative beginnings of
spring were already here.

As I drove our ramshackle truck along the rutted roads, I saw
the fresh young grass disturbing the drifts of last year's leaves and
Madame la Barbe shyly gave us little bunches of fragile snowdrops
which she crept out to gather in the concealing dusk. It was now six
months since I left the capital and I still had no means of communi-
cating with the Minister. I tried to telephone his private number
from time to time but all the lines were defunct. Yet I felt a vague
stirring in my blood which was almost the prickings of incipient action,
as if I, too, were awakening with the spring and now the cavalcade
turned incontrovertibly towards the spires of the mountains and the
road began to climb all the time. We were to provide the Easter fair
at the highest city in the country, a place where eagles were said to
nest in the steeples. Our wheels consumed the pocked asphalt.

'Nebulous Time,' said the peep-show proprietor with a certain
anticipatory excitement, 'will be succeeded by synthetic time.'

However, he did not elaborate on the statement.

At our last stop before a destination that would be a terminus for
all my companions, had they but known it, we were joined by a team
of Moroccan acrobats. There were nine of them and a musician, yet
somehow they all packed themselves neatly into a slickly vulgar motor-
ized trailer in the latest American style, sprayed the luscious pink of
plastic orchids yet ornamented with various Islamic talismans such
as black-inked prints of hands to keep away the Evil Eye. They spoke
with others infrequently and then in a French more dislocated even
than the Alligator Man's but my French had grown very supple
during my conversations with Madame la Barbe and I managed to
gain their confidence sufficiently for them to let me watch them as they
rehearsed their extraordinary performance, though talking to them
was like gossiping with hyenas, for they had a slippery viciousness of
manner. I was a little afraid of them, even though I thought they
were wonderful.

All nine were the same height and shared a similar, almost female
sinuosity of spine and marked development of the pectorals. In the
daytime, they wore sharp, flared trousers and bright shirts painted
with flowers and palm trees, styles more suited to Las Vegas or the
Florida beach resorts than to the arid, yellow peaks through which our

road now took us; for their stunning gyrations they donned costumes which might have been designed by Cocteau ... or Caligula – brief tunics made of a network of gold crescents with a central projection between the horns, so their amber skin looked netted with hooked freckles and they did not look clothed at all, only extravagantly naked. A larger half moon hung from the left ear of each of them and they painted their eyes thickly with kohl and curled their hair so tightly their heads looked like bunches of black grapes. They gilded their finger and toenails and rouged their lips a blackish red. When they were dressed, they negated physicality; they looked entirely artificial.

To enter their circular arena was to step directly into the realm of the marvellous. To the weird music of a flute played by a veiled child, they created all the images that the human body could possibly make – an abstract, geometrical dissection of flesh that left me breathless.

When I told the peep-show proprietor about them, he cursed his blindness.

'The acrobats of desire have come!' he said. 'Nebulous Time is almost upon us!'

But they had never even heard the name, Hoffman, although four times a day they transcended their own bodies and made of themselves plastic anagrams. I suspected an arrangement of mirrors. I inspected their arena and found nothing but sawdust in which ashed half moon glittered here and there. Their act went something like this.

A clumsy spotlight focussed on their minuscule sawdust ring. The flute wailed a phrase. A faint tintinnabulation of their metallic shifts heralded their coming. They entered one by one. First they formed a simple pyramid – three, three, two and one; then they reversed themselves and formed the pyramid upside down – one on his hands, whose feet supported two, and so on. Their figures flowered into one another so choreographically it was impossible to see how they extricated or complicated themselves. They did not give out an odour of sweat; no effortful grunt escaped any of them. For perhaps thirty minutes they went through the staple repertory of all acrobats anywhere, though with incomparable grace and skill. And then Mohammed, the leader, took his head from his neck and they began to juggle with that until, one by one, all their heads came off and went into play, so that a fountain of heads rose and fell in the arena. Yet this was only the beginning.

After that, limb by limb, they dismembered themselves. Hands, feet, forearms, thighs and ultimately torsos went into a diagrammatic multi-man whose constituents were those of them all. At times, the juggled elements composed an image like those of the many-handed Kuan-Yin of the Four Cardinal Points and the Thousand Arms whose multiplication of limbs and attributes signified flashing action and infiinite vigour to the ancient Chinese; but this Arab image was continually in motion, a visual synthesis of the curves and surfaces along which any single body always moved suddenly happening all at once.

And then, the *pièce de résistance*, they began to juggle with their own eyes. The severed heads and arms and feet and navels began to juggle with eighteen fringed, unblinking eyes.

I would repeat to myself as I watched them the peep-show proprietor's maxim: 'It all depends on persistence of vision', because, of course, I could not entirely suspend my disbelief, although I might lay it aside for a while. I knew there was more to it than met the eye although, in the finale, so many eyes met and greeted one's own! Such a harmonious concatenation of segments of man, studded with incomplete moons and brown pupils!

And then this demonstration of juxtaposition and transposition was over. Each torso took from the common heap its due apparatus back again and, composed again as nine complete Moroccans, they took their bows.

I went to watch them whenever I could and I haunted their tent. But I never managed to discover their secret.

The chill brilliance of early spring struck a dazzle of mica from the sandstone enfilades of the mountains. They were appallingly barren, for the scanty soil could support only those plants that love dry, arid places, spiny cacti and low-growing, warped, daisy-like things with stems wiry enough to cut your fingers. The gloomy road took us to a gloomy destination for the city, which functioned only as a trading post, was as sullen as the perpendicular perspectives around us. We crossed an enormous bridge above a mighty river in the bleakest of valleys and saw the town perched, itself like an eagle, on a precipitous outcrop of rock above the rushing torrent. This town was full of malevolent saints. Shut in on themselves in their isolation, they were an inbred mixture of Carpathian Poles and mountain French whose forefathers had fled to Europe in the late seventeenth and early eighteenth centuries due to persecutions of the scrupulous sects of the reformed religion to which they belonged. There had been both Calvinists and Jansenites among them and the town itself had finally evolved such a rigorous blend of the more mortifying aspects of both that I was astonished they allowed a carnival there at all, for they usually entertained themselves only with hymns of the simplest melodic structure. But the high, rarefied air had caused some singular mutations of their practices. After the fast of Lent, when they drank only water and ate only beans, they spent the whole of Good Friday without stirring from shuttered houses in which they brooded on the inherent evil of all mankind, and then devoted Easter Week itself to exposing themselves to the temptations of the flesh. Which the fair was judged to represent well enough. My cynical friend, the Alligator Man, was delighted to find himself defined as a siren and took to preening himself lasciviously in his tank. To some degree we all became more voluptuous, in self-justification.

But the townsfolk were kindness itself to us and brought us all small presents of wine and cake. I soon realized their charity sprang from pity. They thought we were all hopelessly damned.

The peep-show proprietor industriously changed his samples daily. They were all the most outrageous tableaux of blasphemy and eroticism, Christ performing innumerable obscenities upon Mary Magdalene, St John and His Mother; and, in this holy city, I was fucked in the anus, against my will (as far, that is, as I was conscious of my desires), by all nine of the Moroccan acrobats, one after the other.

Those who had caravans parked them in a paddock near the market square usually used for grazing goats and drying linen; the booths were set up in the square itself. After we closed up for the night, the old man, who had drunk a gift of dandelion wine with his supper, nodded off to sleep by the stove and I slipped out to watch the Arabs' last performance. The day had lowered with incipient storm and now violent winds whipped about the square, blowing the posters and bunting in all directions. It was so cold that only the intense puritanism of the inhabitants kept them out enjoying themselves. In the acrobats' tent, the sober clothes of the customers ringed the spangled contortionists in solid shadow and their massed conviction that they watched the devil's work weighed the air with disapproval. The white faces, arranged on the darkness in concentric circles around the ring, were inexpressive as teeth in a maw although the Arabs pelted them with a confetti of fingers and gilded fingernails and when the last atom of flesh was retrieved from the sawdust and slotted back into place, the audience heaved a great, convulsive sigh that billowed the canvas, a sigh of gratification that not one of them had succumbed to delight.

They filed out in silence.

Mohammed and his tinkling brethren rubbed themselves briskly with huckaback towels and invited me to take coffee with them in their mobile home, an unexpected gesture of hospitality I attributed to an appreciation of the enthusiasm I had often expressed for their work. The storm had already risen to a tempest and we sprinted to their van through sheets of rain. Lightning flashed and all nine, in their Heliogabalian finery, flared briefly like magnesium, reflecting a glare so harsh and violent it wounded the retina. And then the rain obscured them again.

A coke stove filled the van with choking warmth. Inside, the van was as soft and excessive as a whore's bed for they slept three apiece on three divans piled with satin cushions in lingerie tones and these filled up most of the interior. The smell of sweat, liniment and spent semen was almost overpowering. There were no windows and one could not see the walls for they were covered with mirrors and photographs which captured them all in every segmented attitude so that, now stripped of their tunics down to briefs of iridescent elastic, arranged upon their beds, they and their reflected or pictured parts – here, a bubbled head, there a shoulder, elsewhere a knee – seemed to continue, in a subtly enervated fashion, the climax of their act.

Had I not known all along it was all done with mirrors? I had never seen so many mirrors since the war began.

Mohammed brewed Turkish coffee in a brass pot on the stove and they made room for me on a pink cushion decorated with a mauve, appliquéd nude. The musician took off his yashmak and crouched down on a strip of white bearskin laid on what of the floor there was. He was a boy of six or seven, quite black, perhaps an Ethiopian; he was a eunuch. He seemed to go in almighty fear of his protectors. He lay in an attitude of utter submission. They suggested I would be more comfortable without my shirt and most comfortable of all without my suit but I insisted on retaining my trousers. After that, they jabbered to themselves in Arabic for a while and I leafed through some of the many body-building magazines that littered the beds until Mohammed served us each a syrupy thimbleful of his concoction.

We sipped. There was silence and soon I became a little uncomfortable. I realized I was there for a reason and I could hardly believe my intuition as to what that reason was. Out of sheer nervousness, I found myself complimenting them again on their virtuosity.

'We are,' said Mohammed, with a faint undertone of menace, 'capable of virtually anything.'

So I could not say I was not warned. The coke rattled in the stove and the wind buffeted the sides of the van. With a slithering movement, the castrated black boy took his flute from the pile of his discarded veils. He sat down crosslegged on a couch and began to trace on the air an angular, tritonic tune which repeated itself over and over again like a wordless incantation.

The mirrors reflected not only sections of the Arabs; they reflected those reflections, too, so the men were infinitely repeated everywhere I looked and now eighteen and sometimes twenty-seven and, at one time, thirty-six brilliant eyes were fixed on me with an intensity which varied according to the distance between the images of the eyes and their originals. I was surrounded by eyes. I was Saint Sebastian stuck through with the visible barbed beams from brown, translucent eyes which spun a web of fine, shining threads on the air like strands of candified sugar. Once again, they juggled with their hypnotic eyes and used their palpable eye strings to bind me in invisible bonds. I was trapped. I could not move. I was filled with impotent rage as the wave of eyes broke over me.

The pain was terrible. I was most intimately ravaged I do not know how many times. I wept, bled, slobbered and pleaded but nothing would appease a rapacity as remorseless and indifferent as the storm which raged outside and now reached a nightmarish hurricane. They stretched me on my face on a counterpane of pale orange artificial silk and took it in turns to pin down my arms and legs. I ceased to count my penetrations but I think each one buggered me at least twice. They were inexhaustible fountains of desire and I soon ceased to be conscious of my body, only of the sensation of an arsenal of swords piercing sequentially that most private and unmentionable of apertures. But I was so far outside myself they might just as well have cut me up and juggled with me and, for all I know, they did. They gave me the most comprehensive anatomy lesson a man ever suffered, in which I learned every possible modulation of the male apparatus and some I would have thought impossible.

And then, as if obeying an inaudible whistle, they stopped. The wind and the rain still beat down but the acrobats were done with their display though they showed no signs of satiation or weariness, only of conclusion. It was as if they had only been going through a gymnastic exercise and now they once again towelled themselves, searched for their discarded briefs and drew them again over the pistons of their loins with the most offensive insouciance. A blubbered wreck, I lay on the coverlet and I think that I was calling for my mother, though it was probably Albertina. After a time, Mohammed came, fed me more coffee and, I think, a little arak and held me in a fairly warm and comforting embrace, murmuring to me in his vile French that I had been initiated – though into what I had no idea. The liquor stung my throat and slowly brought me back to my senses.

Mohammed dressed me and then, after a murmured consultation with his colleagues, dug about in a drawer concealed in the lower part of one of the divans. The many coruscating surfaces and the reflections of men were still at last. The men themselves lay on their sides propped on one elbow, with a childlike brightness in their faces as if their innocence had been, somehow, refreshed. I felt a nervous agitation. I longed to be gone but did not dare move until they ordered me for fear of unleashing a fresh assault. Mohammed turned to me holding something coyly concealed behind his back. His g-string throbbed like a sling full of live fish.

'*C'est pour toi*,' he said. '*Un petit cadeau.*'

He pressed into my hands a little purse of coloured, cut and ornamented leather such as they sell to tourists in Port Said. It was decorated with the picture of an Egyptian king listening to his musicians and the sight almost made me weep, to think of Ancient Egypt preserved in the gelid amber of the time it had sustained for all of two thousand years. Then Mohammed drew me gently from the bed and wrapped me in one of those great, dark, hooded, enveloping, desert Arab cloaks to protect me, he told me, from the weather. And after that he put me outside the door, sent me into the teeth of the whirlwind. It hurt me dreadfully to walk.

The air was full of blown tiles, chimneypots, washing poles and dustbins. The wind had seized the town by the throat and particularly tormented the flimsy tents of the carnival, tossing them about this way and that. The rain came in black, wind-swept palls and the river below the city was fearfully swollen, a concourse of angry waters. I walked up the road, away from the inhabited places, as rapidly as the storm and my pain would let me. I had a great need to leave humanity behind for a while.

I stumbled over a scrubby field or two and discovered a narrow lane which took me out on to a cliff overhanging the river. Now I had to crawl, for fear the wind would blow me into the gorge. The path took me down on to the face of the cliff itself and when I saw the mouth of a small cave, I instantly clambered into it, drew my Bedouin coverall snugly about me and tried, as best I could, to compose myself a little, though I was in the grip of a terrible reactive shock. Presently I remembered I still clutched the purse Mohammed had given me and I opened it. It contained twenty-seven eyes, brown as ale and shaped like oblate spheroids. I thought he must have plucked these spare eyes off the mirrors. I was a little light-headed and, I remember, must have spent most of that tempestuous day playing a solitary but elaborate game of marbles with those objects, rolling them across the sandy floor of the cave and laughing with childlike pleasure when they bounced off one another. About noon, I remember, I heard a tremendous, roaring crash and part of my roof came down, swallowing up half a dozen of my toys, which irritated me. But I paid no further attention to the world outside until, one way and another, all the marbles were gone, lost in ratholes or crevices or rolled into the dry undergrowth at the mouth of the cave where I did not have the patience to retrieve them.

When the last one disappeared, I found I was recovered. I felt light-headed and still severely wounded but I discovered I was very hungry and thought my master, if he was sober, probably needed me. Besides, the storm had spent its fury and the rain ceased almost altogether. So I came out of my cave to find that most of the track that had taken me to it was obliterated. I scrambled hand over hand up the cliff while the river gnashed teeth of foam in the ravine below and all manner of refuse drifted past.

I saw there had been a total realignment of the landscape during my oblivion. Everything had a blasted look and the wind still bit and whipped me as I anxiously made my way back to the town, as if tormenting me for being still alive. And I found the town was there no longer.

The town had vanished from the face of the earth, leaving behind it only its sandstone corpse as its own gravestone. The crag on which it had perched was now as bald of habitations as an egg and, smoking in the midst of the turbid river, lay a mound of yellow rubble through which, here and there, poked a steeple or a weather-cock. The bridge began at its other end and then stopped in mid-air. A jutting, truncated thrust of masonry hung over the valley, endlessly about to fall, and all signs of the bridge on this side were gone forever because the town had been plucked from its foundations in the earth and tossed carelessly into the ravenous water. Bathed in the grey, dying light of the afternoon, the ruins were already indistinguishable from the rest of the tumbled rocks in that hellish valley, through which the hungry waters roared. When I looked at the river more closely, I saw it was full of corpses, plentiful and insignificant as driftwood. Saints and damned had died together and only a few ravens of the peaks drifted above the desolation on the wild currents of the air, uttering inconsolable cries. Nothing human moved.

The catastrophe was too immense for me to take in at once. I sank down on a stone and buried my head in my hands.

5. The Erotic Traveller

At first I thought the landslide must have been the Doctor's work, but no logic of any kind, no matter how circuitous, could have justified that disaster. He could have gained no tactical advantages by destroying that forgotten place. Besides, his set of samples had perished completely and the peep-show was the greatest single weapon in his armoury; he would never have destroyed it. So the landslide could only be a simple assertion of the dominance of nature herself who, in the service only of the meaningless, reintegrated the city with chaos and then, her business done, casually abandoned it. It was an event of too massive arbitrariness for me to comprehend but, as the rain-washed light fell more and more wistfully on the gigantic tip of sandstone that killed my bearded lady, my reptilian friend, my shooting star and my blind philosopher, I became most deeply aware of mortality. Even the acrobats of desire could not put themselves together again after this dissolution. No phantom dared float above the desolation, though the water roared with as violent a display of energy as I have ever seen. A stranger would never have guessed that, at this same hour, the previous evening, the peak had been crowned with prim streets full of freaks and puritans. Light died on the rocks. I turned my back on a whole sub-universe that had been wiped out as if with a huge eraser and on the corpse of yet another of my selves, that of the peep-show proprietor's nephew. I stumbled away over the rough fields, vanquished again, now beyond tears.

I was in altogether unknown country. After a while, I found a rough farmstead built of great blocks of windowless sandstone but they set a pack of lean, snarling dogs on me so I could not even beg a crust of bread there. Then a fat, white moon rose and I wandered down a rugged pathway with only my bleached shadow for company, two pale ghosts against a backdrop of mountains as sharply pointed and unnatural looking as those outlined by the brusque crayon of a child. I thought that if I wandered far enough, I would certainly reach Hoffman's castle. I was sure I only had to put one foot before the other, indefatigably in the wrong direction, as the old man had told me, and my instinct would guide me there, although I did not know what I would do when I arrived except to look for Albertina. So I lurched on drearily, until I came to a defile through which ran a narrow road.

At the roadside grew a withered tree and a night-bird perched on one bare branch emitting a hoarse, rasping rattle, the antithesis of song. I looked along the road in both directions and all at once hope deserted me entirely for I did not know which was north and which was south. Suddenly I grew very, very weary. I heard, from far away, the shriek of a mountain lion and wondered indifferently if I might not be eaten during the night. The notion did not affect me one way or the other. I sat down under the tree and drew my hood up over my head for the high, thin air sang bitterly in my ears and made my temples throb. I watched the moon move across the white, cloudless sky and saw many unfamiliar stars. I sank into a mindless reverie. I was altogether drained of thought.

Presently I heard the clatter of wheels and hoofbeats echoing among the rocks. After some time, a light carriage, a trap of somewhat eighteenth-century design, appeared upon the road and I saw two persons shared the narrow seat, a tall, black-clad figure with a startling air of authority and a slender boy who held the reins. The hooves of the black horses struck sparks from the flinty track. The wheels revolved more slowly. The travellers halted.

'If you are an Arabian, why do you not sleep?' demanded the older man in the standard speech, which he spoke fluently, though with a slight foreign accent and a very formal intonation.

'I fear my dreams,' I replied and, looking up, met eyes as ghastly as burned-out coals set in a face so thinly fleshed the bones pushed sharply against the skin.

'Then ride with us,' he invited. I was willing to go anywhere so I climbed over the wheel into the space they made for me and we drove on through the moonlight in silence. My host's profile was as craggy and arrogant as those of the mountains. He was in his late forties or early fifties. His face was ravaged with pride and bitterness.

He wore a black cloak with many layers of capes on the shoulders and a top-hat from which trailers of black crepe depended at the back. He was ready for any funeral and he carried a cane tipped with a silver ball that looked as if it could kill. His diabolical elegance could not have existed without his terrible emaciation; he wore his dandyism in his very bones, as if it was a colour that had seeped out of his essential skeleton to dye his clothes, and he never made a single movement that was not a gaunt but riveting work of art.

I discovered this road must be the low road to the devastated city for soon it found the river, which had so entirely encroached on it I thought we could go no further. The frightened horses bucked and whickered but the driver whipped and cursed them so we went on, though the water swirled around their hocks. When I realized I would see the graveyard of the city again, I moaned involuntarily.

'Music!' muttered the older man. 'Music!'

But I could not tell whether he meant the sound of my pain or that of the gushing swirl of the waters, which rang out like a carillon. When this road also vanished under the surface of the water, the driver urged the horses into the river itself. The carriages floated buoyantly and the horses began to swim. So we went down the river and drove on the moonlit flood over the very heart of the ruins, which were rapidly sinking under the tempestuous waves.

The driver exclaimed: 'Oh! What an appalling tragedy!'

But my host cuffed him sharply and snapped:

'Lafleur, do I have to warn you again against softness of heart? Do as I do; salute nature when she offers us another *coup de théâtre*!'

Then he took a flask from his pocket and fed me brandy.

'Did you witness it? Did many die?'

'The whole population of the town and also the members of a travelling fair.'

He sighed with gratification.

'How I should have liked to have seen it! And gloried in the Wagnerian clamour of it all ... the shrieks, the crash of rending stone. And little children dashed to smithereens by bounding boulders! What a spectacle!

'You must know that I am a connoisseur of catastrophe, young man. I witnessed the eruption of Vesuvius when thousands were coffined alive in molten lava. I saw eyes burst and fat run out of roast crackling in Nagasaki, Hiroshima and Dresden. I dabbled my fingers in the blood beneath the guillotine during the Terror. I am a demon for a cataclysm.'

He flung down this speech as if it were a gauntlet but I was far too awestruck by his misanthropy to pick it up. At last we saw signs of a road again on the bank and soon the horses were once more galloping on dry land, by the light of too much indifferent moon.

'Where are you going?' I asked. He did not so much reply to my question as speak out of the depths of some unknowable reverie of his own.

'The journey alone is real, not the landfall. I have no compass to guide me. I set my course by the fitfulness of fortune and perceive my random signposts only by the inextinguishable flame of my lusts.'

That silenced me. The wheels of the carriage wound the road on to an invisible spool and I began to feel the effect of a strange heaviness exerted on me, a perverse, negative fascination exercised by the gaunt aristocrat who sat beside me, though a shudder went through me when I saw his curiously pointed teeth for they were exactly the fangs with which tradition credits vampires. All the same, he drew me. His quality of being was more dense than that of any man I have ever met – always excepting the Minister, of course. Yet, apart from his mind, which was a bruising heavy-weight, I think what made him so attractive to me was his irony, which withered every word before he spoke it. Everything about him was excessive, yet he tempered his vulgarity – for he was excessively vulgar in every respect – with a black, tragic humour of which he was only occasionally conscious himself.

He was particularly extraordinary in this: he had a passionate conviction he was the only significant personage in the world. He was the emperor of inverted megalomaniacs but he had subjected his personality to a most rigorous discipline of stylization so that, when he struck postures as lurid as those of a bad actor, no matter how ludicrous they were, still they impelled admiration because of the abstract intensity of their unnaturalism. He had scarcely an element of realism and yet he was quite real. He could say nothing that was not grandiose. He claimed he lived only to negate the world.

'It is not in the least unusual to assert that he who negates a proposition at the same time secretly affirms it – or, at least, affirms something. But, for myself, I deny to the last shred of my altogether memorable being that my magnificent denial means more than a simple "no". Sometimes my meagre and derisive lips seem to me to have been formed by nature only to spit out the word "no", as if it were the ultimate blasphemy. I should like to speak an ultimate blasphemy and then bask in the security of eternal damnation but, since there is no God, well, there is no damnation, either, unfortunately. And hence, alas, no final negation. I am the hideous antithesis in person and I swear to anyone who wants the word of a hereditary count of Lithuania for it that I am not in the least secretly benignly pregnant with any affirmation of any kind whatsoever.'

He paused to caress his valet, who, with the submissiveness of the born victim, turned to him a face as livid as putrefaction. After my first shock of horror, I saw this was not a real face but one quite covered up with white bandages. This pliant valet was almost extinguished by subservience. His very walk was a kind of ambulant cringe. He abased himself obsequiously at all times. He was only a tool of the Count's will.

'Is there nothing in the world you do not to some degree condemn?' I asked the Count.

He was silent for a long time. I thought he had not heard me and repeated my question; I had not yet grown used to the utterly self-centred nature of his discourse. He only answered questions when he thought that he had posed them to himself. But when he eventually spoke, he did so without his customary disdain.

'The death-defying double somersault of love.'

The valet made some kind of repressed exclamation at that, probably applause, and the Count sombrely rested his chin on the top of his cane, fixing his eyes only on the road before us. When I spoke a little of the war, I met such a blank wall of unresponsiveness I realized the Count knew nothing at all about it and the journey continued in the silence of the morgue, until, as we were descending to the plain, the Count spoke again.

'I ride the whirlwind of my desires and I would give this whirlwind, which has driven me to all the four rounded corners of the globe, the emblematic form of a tiger, the most ferocious of beasts, whose pelt yet bears the marks of a flagellation which must have taken place before the dawn of time.'

It was impossible to converse with him for he had no interest in anyone but himself and he offered his companion only a series of monologues of varying lengths, which often apparently contradicted themselves but always, in a spiral-line fashion, remained true to his infernal egoism. I never heard another man use the word 'I', so often. But I sensed an exemplary quality in his desperate self-absorption. I had not met anyone who lived with such iron determination since I left the Minister. He reminded me of the Minister.

'Yet I am always haunted by a pain I cannot feel. Isolated in my invulnerability, yet I am nostalgic for the homely sensation of pain . . .'

A bloody froth blew back in our faces from the mouths of the straining horses and yet we galloped on without sparing them until we reached a strange place, one of those flamboyant chapels built by the Jesuits in the fallacious expectation of mass conversions among the Indians and long since abandoned. The moon was dying but still fitfully illuminated the crumbling façade and the bushes which grew in the roofless interior, where a startled frog splashed out of the pool of rainwater in the font when we entered with the picnic basket, for the Count wanted to eat breakfast. As if from habit, he pissed on the altar while the valet set out the meal; the Count was always iconoclast, even when the icons were already cast down.

Out of the basket came a feast such as I had not eaten since that memorable luncheon with the Minister and Albertina. There was a can of truffled goose liver paté; glasses of game in aspic; a flock of cold roast pheasant; imported cheese whose savourous reek stung the nostrils; a side of smoked salmon from which the valet shaved curling strips; an exotic gravel of various caviars; an insulated box of salad and another filled with grapes and peaches, while an ice-chest contained a dozen bottles of Veuve Clicquot. There was china and sparkling glassware of the finest quality. The cutlery was of solid silver. The boy laid out an incomparable *fête champêtre* and we all fell to with a will. The Count ate very heartily; indeed, he ate with a blind voracity that demolished the spread so speedily the valet and I were hard put to it to seize enough to satisfy ourselves, although there was so much. When nothing was left but gnawed bones, dirty plates, peach stones, and empty bottles, the Count sighed, belched and grasped the valet. His mute's hat tumbled to the ground.

'Watch me! Watch me!' he cried as though, in order to appreciate the effect of his own actions, he had to know that he was seen. But it was far too dark in the ruined church to see anything. I heard the grunts and whimpers of the valet and the amazing roars which accompanied the Count's lengthy progress towards orgasm. The vault of heaven above us darkened and all the time frightful cries and atrocious blasphemies issued from the Count's throat. He whinnied like a stallion; he cursed the womb that bore him; and finally the orgasm struck him like an epilepsy. Ecstasy seemed to annihilate the libertine and there was a silence broken only by the pathetic whimpering of the valet until, in the velvet and luminous darkness, the Count spoke, in a voice drained of all vigour.

'I have devoted my life to the humiliation and exaltation of the flesh. I am an artist; my material is the flesh; my medium is destruction; and my inspiration is nature.'

Now the valet moved painfully about, gathering together the dishes, and it grew light enough to make out the Count's shape as he lolled against the desecrated altar, his head bare. His hair, a coarse and uniform grey, hung down to his shoulders.

'I am impregnable because I always exist in a state of dreadful tension. My crises render me utterly bestial and in that state I am infinitely superior to man, as the tiger, who preys on man if he has any sense, is superior. My anguish is the price of my exaltation.'

I began to wonder if the Count was one of the Doctor's agents and then I thought, no! This man might be the Doctor himself, under an assumed identity! The suspicion made me quiver.

I can hardly describe to you the man's appalling, cerebral lucidity. He was like a corpse animated only by a demonic intellectual will. When he had rested a little, we climbed back into the carriage and rolled off across the green, spacious countryside, under a vertiginous arc of sky which began to clear and sparkle. The mountains dwindled behind us. The dew glittered in the budding hedgerows. A lark rose, singing. It was a beautiful morning in early spring.

'The universe itself is not a sufficiently capacious stage on which to mount the grand opera of my passions. From the cradle, I have been a blasphemous libertine, a blood-thirsty debauchee. I travel the world only to discover hitherto unknown methods of treating flesh. When I first left my native Lithuania, I went at once to China where I apprenticed myself to the Imperial executioner and learned by heart a twelve-tone scale of tortures as picturesque as they are vile. When my studies were complete, I tied my tutor to the trunk of a blossoming apricot tree so the rosy petals showered down upon his increasing mutilations as, with incredible delicacy and a very sharp knife, I carved out little oysters of his living flesh – the torture known as the "slicing", the dreaded *ling ch'ih*. What a terrible sight he was to behold! The apricot tree wept tears of perfumed flowers over him; that was Nature's pity, decorative but unhelpful.

'Subsequently I visited the rest of Asia, where, among other infamies too numerous to mention, I amputated the scarcely perceptible breasts of all the occupants of a geisha house in the exquisitely bell-haunted city of Kyoto. Then I left my crest stamped in wax plugs in all the capacious anuses of the royal eunuchs of the court of Siam. Subsequently I visited Europe where, as a reward for my villainies, I was condemned to burn at the stake in Spain, to hang by the neck in England and to break upon the wheel in a singularly inhospitable France, where, sentenced to death *in absentia* by the judiciary of Provence, my body was executed in effigy in the town square of Aix.

'I fled to North America, where I knew my barbarities would pass unnoticed, and in Quebec I hired my valet, Lafleur, whose interesting nose has quite caved in under the weight of a hereditary syphilis. Young as he is, his face has already been totally obliterated by the ghastly residue of past pleasures he never tasted personally. Together we travelled the various states. I gave certain evidence in the trials at Salem, Mass., which condemned eighteen perfectly innocent persons to death by pressing. I instigated a rebellion among the slaves on a plantation in Alabama which led to bloody and wholesale retribution; they were all tied to bales of cotton and ignited by ululating Klansmen. Then, in a perfumed bordello in New Orleans, I strangled with my legs a mulatto whore just as she coaxed the incense from my member with a mouth the shape, colour and texture of an overripe plum.

'But after that, I became the object of the vengeance of her enraged pimp, a black of more than superhuman inhumanity, in whom I sense a twin. And that is why I must not let him catch up with me for I know too well what he would do to me if he did so. So Lafleur and I drove over the neck of the continent, through deserts that delighted me since they were far too atrociously barren to sustain life, through jungles altogether envenomed with hatred for the brown maggots of men who dare to try to live in that green, festering meat; and then across those rearing mountains that now lie behind us than which, even in the steppes of Central Asia, I have seen nothing more arid or inimical. Refreshed, we now travel towards the coast for I feel stirring within me a strange desire to return to the peaks where I was born and perhaps I shall try to die there. Unless, that is, the vengeful pimp ensnares me first. Which is a horror beyond thought.'

When noon came, he bought me beer and bread and cheese at an inn. He had not asked a single question of me or even seemed to ask himself what this stranger was doing in his company but I realized he regarded me as part of his entourage, now. I made a few tentative guesses as to what my role might be. Was I his observer, whose eyes, as they watched him, verified his actions? Did his narcissism demand a constant witness? Or had he other plans for me – would I, perhaps, figure among his amusements? The masked, unspeaking valet and I formed his little world. If one was his hireling victim, for what purpose was the other hired? But I wondered if his servant had more autonomy than he thought. Something in the texture of the valet's presence hinted he was self-consciously the slave. Occasionally, when he whimpered, he seemed altogether too emphatically degraded. But perhaps he was not yet altogether inured to his position. What would I myself become when I, too, knew what my position was?

But though the Count had given me a very detailed autobiography, I still suspected he might really be the Doctor and so I knew I must travel with him, no matter what happened. And then again, he was so remarkable! He seemed to cast a shadow as solid as lead. We drove on through the afternoon until we came to a lonely crossroads where suddenly the Count announced:

'I know it, I know it! We must turn right!'

The signpost which pointed north bore only, in faded blue paint, the legend: THIS WAY TO THE HOUSE OF ANONYMITY and a lonely path overgrown with grass and primroses stretched far away across the faintly burgeoning prairies. There was no sign of any building along its course. The sun had gone in and the sky was now a leaden grey. Because everywhere was so flat, this sky was swollen and inflated; it occupied so much more space in the world than the earth beneath it that the sky seemed to smother us under a transparent pillow. The day had not fulfilled the bright promise of the morning; the weather was full of foreboding. But Lafleur turned the horses to the north, though now they were so overdone they ran with sweat and rolled their eyes until the whites showed. The Count was very excited. He cried out and muttered to himself as we took the deserted track and now clouds began to pile heavily in the sky and a few drops of heavy rain spattered on our faces.

'Faster! Faster!'

The horses strained their coal-black loins and neighed beneath Lafleur's whip. Then, at the side of the road, we saw a scarecrow and although there was nothing in the bare field where it stood for it to protect, it carried a bow and arrow. There was no head inside the hat it wore, only a human skull, and the wind, laden with rain, flapped its ragged jacket miserably around its broomstick bones. Round its neck hung a tattered paper sign which read: I AM PERFECTLY EMPTY. I HAVE FORGOTTEN MY NAME. I AM PERFECT BUT YOU ARE ON THE RIGHT ROAD. CONTINUE.

The Count laughed aloud and we drove on until we came to a door set in a white wall. Here, the road stopped short. Lafleur climbed down and rapped upon the door. A grille opened and we saw a pair of eyes.

'Who is it?' asked a woman's voice.

'A hereditary count of Lithuania,' Lafleur introduced his master.

'Show us the colour of your money,' said the voice and the Count gave Lafleur a thick roll of banknotes to show. The mere sight of it satisfied her; she nodded approvingly and said: 'Your bill will be presented upon departure, sir.'

After some more minutes' waiting, while the dismal rain sluiced down, the door opened inward with a heavy thunder of bars and chains and we drove into the courtyard. The door banged to behind us and the porteress, a fat woman with a puffed, pale face and haggard lips, came to help us down from the carriage. She wore a black dress and a white apron. She did not know how to smile. But she did not wear a mask. None of the servants were masked; their roles made them sufficiently anonymous.

The Count sharply dismissed his valet, who drove the carriage round to the stable. As I glanced after Lafleur, I saw, once he left his master, he sprang up again like a branch which has been tied back and is now released. His slight figure took on a sudden, sprightly decisiveness; then he was gone. So the Count and I stood in front of the House of Anonymity, whose door was always open to anyone with a fat enough wallet.

It was a massive, sprawling edifice in the Gothic style of the late nineteenth century, that poked innumerable turrets like so many upward groping tentacles towards the dull, cloudy sky and was all built in louring, red brick. Every window I could see was tightly shuttered. The porteress rang peremptorily for a maid and a woman who might have been her sister appeared and led us into the house, through a series of dark, gloomy corridors where our footsteps echoed on flags until we came to more formal, carpeted quarters and ascended a winding stair to a little dressing-room done up in moist red velvet, like the interior of a womb. She invited us to undress and while we did so, she took from a cupboard two pairs of black tights made in such a way that, once we put them on, our genitals remained exposed in their entirety, testicles and all. Then she offered us short waistcoats of a soft, suède-like substance which she assured us was the tanned skin of a young negro virgin. The Count began to murmur softly with anticipation and already his prick, which was of monstrous size, stood as resolutely aloft as an illustration of satyriasis in a medical dictionary. Then the maid handed us hood-like masks which went right over our heads, concealing them, and were attached by buttons to buttonholes in the collars of our waistcoats, so that our heads were changed into featureless, elongated, pinkish, rounded towers. The only indentations on these convex surfaces of pink cardboard were two slits, to look through. These masks or hoods completed our costumes, which were unaesthetic, priapic and totally obliterated our faces and our self-respect; the garb grossly emphasized our manhoods while utterly denying our humanity. And the costumes were of no time or place. Now we were ready. With our expressions hidden and the most undifferentiated parts of our anatomies exposed, she led us down another stair to a reception room where she bowed, smiled formally and opened the door for us.

'Welcome to the Bestial Room,' she said.

With that, she left us.

The insides of the windows had all been painted black, so even if you opened the black velvet curtains, nothing disturbed the artificial night inside them. The walls were covered with a figured brocade of such a slumbrous purple the Count murmured: 'It is the very colour of the blood in a love suicide.' Everywhere, clinging to the curtains, perched on the heavy gold frames of innumerable immense mirrors or crouched on the swags of a marble fireplace, were dozens of chattering monkeys smartly dressed like bellboys in bum-freezer jackets of braid-trimmed crimson plush. These monkeys were living candelabra; they clutched black candles in their paws, wedged in the coiled kinks of their tails or stuck in sockets in the metal circlets they all wore round their heads. When the hot wax dripped on to their fur or into their eyes, they squealed pitifully.

The furniture was also alive.

They had employed a taxidermist instead of an upholsterer and sent him a pride of lions with instructions to make a sofa out of each pair. At both ends of the sofas, flamboyantly gothic arm-rests, were the gigantically maned heads of these lions. Their rheumy, golden eyes seeped gum and their cavernous, red mouths hung sleepily ajar, gaping wider, now and then, in a sleepy yawn or to let out a low, rumbling growl. The serviceable armchairs were brown bears who squatted on their haunches with the melancholy of all the Russias in their liquid eyes. When a girl sat on his shaggy lap, the bear grunted, leaned back and spread her legs out wide apart with his blunt forepaws. The occasional tables ran about, yelping obsequiously; they were toadying hyenas and on their brindled backs were strapped silver trays containing glasses, decanters, bowls of salted nuts and dishes of stuffed olives. Other hyenas crouched in corners, their endless tongues lolling like sopping lengths of red flannel, balancing between their pricked ears a pot of carnivorous flowers or else jars of Japanese porcelain containing tasteful arrangements of bodiless hands. The dark, polished floorboards were scattered with vivid pelts of jaguars that stirred and grumbled underfoot; their hot breaths blasted the ankle as you stepped over them. In all the room, only the prostitutes, the wax mannequins of love, hardly seemed to be alive for they stood as still as statues. But they were the only beings kept in cages.

Though the bars of these cages were exceedingly stout and enamelled a glistening black, the shapes of the cages and the whimsical elaboration of the intricate wrought ironwork itself resembled those of the cages in which singing birds were housed in Victorian drawing rooms, though each container was some seven feet high in order to accommodate its inmate, who looked more than humanly tall because each cage was mounted on an ivied marble pedestal, three feet high. The doors of the cages were secured by very large padlocks and all the keys hung from a length of ribbon around the Madame's neck, though she, too, sat so still you could not hear them jingle. And the candlelight danced on locked-up breasts, breasts as white as immortelles, the only flowers that blossomed in this zoological garden that stank vilely of the reek and echoed hideously with the cries of the wild beasts who furnished it.

Though the mirrors reflected the hangings, sofas, chairs, tables, candlesticks and every cageful of venereal statuary, they did not give the Count and me our blank, pink faces back to us because here we had no names.

The Madame sat beside the door behind an elaborate wrought iron cash register in the *fin de siècle* style one finds in suburban Parisian brasseries, on which she rang up each item her customers purchased. She was still a young woman and she was quite naked but for her necklace of keys and a *cache-sexe* made of sequined eyes; stockings of coarse black mesh; and a mask of supple, funereal black leather like the masks worn by old-fashioned executioners. This mask covered her entire face except for the drooping peony of her mouth and the area around it. She was naked because she was human and she did not have a reflection either. Her skin had the blurred sheen of a yellow metal which has been attacked by verdigris and sweated out a scarcely bearable stench of musk.

She spoke. I am ashamed to say I did not recognize her voice, although it stirred me.

'My house is a refuge for those who can find no equilibrium between inside and outside, between mind and body or body and soul, vice versa, etcetera, etcetera, etcetera.'

A hyena sprang up, eager to curry favour, and the Madame poured us each a glass of curaçao from the battery of beverages it carried. She rang up the price on her till and, glass in hand, we went to inspect the merchandise.

'A meridional vigour arises within me,' confided the Count. (Was I, then, to be his confidant?)

The costume the House forced upon us may have hidden his appearance but it also transfigured him. He stalked, erect, among this garden of artificial delights with a crazy, apocalyptic grandeur. He was so magnificently, preposterously obscene that the sofas bowed their heads to see him pass and the tables all ran up to lick his hands and fawn over him. As we approached each girl, the monkeys darted up to her cage and hung in furry clusters from the bars, holding out their candles so that all her subtly spurious charms were clearly visible and she extended her arms while opening and closing her eyes with every mannerism of the siren.

There were, perhaps, a dozen girls in the cages in the reception room and, posed inside, the girls towered above us like the goddesses of some forgotten theogeny locked up because they were too holy to be touched. Each was as circumscribed as a figure in rhetoric and you could not imagine they had names, for they had been reduced by the rigorous discipline of their vocation to the undifferentiated essence of the idea of the female. This ideational femaleness took amazingly different shapes though its nature was not that of Woman; when I examined them more closely, I saw that none of them were any longer, or might never have been, woman. All, without exception, passed beyond or did not enter the realm of simple humanity. They were sinister, abominable, inverted mutations, part clockwork, part vegetable and part brute.

Their hides were streaked, blotched and marbled and some trembled on the point of reverting completely to the beast. If beasts of prey had become furnishings, some of the sexual appliances of the establishment were about to become their victims. Perhaps that was why they kept them in cages. The dazed, soft-eyed head of a giraffe swayed on two feet of dappled neck above the furred, golden shoulders of one girl and another had the striped face of a zebra and a cropped, stiff, black mane bristling down her spine. But, if some were antlered like stags, others had the branches of trees sprouting out of their bland foreheads and showed us the clusters of roses growing in their armpits when they held out their hands to us. One leafy girl was grown all over with mistletoe but, where the bark was stripped away from her ribcage, you could see how the internal wheels articulating her went round. Another girl had many faces hinged one on top of the other so that her head opened out like a book, page by page, and on each page was printed a fresh expression of allure. All the figures presented a dream-like fusion of diverse states of being, blind, speechless beings from a nocturnal forest where trees had eyes and dragons rolled about on wheels. And one girl must have come straight from the whipping parlour for her back was a ravelled palimpsest of wound upon wound – she was neither animal nor vegetable nor technological; this torn and bleeding she was the most dramatic revelation of the nature of meat that I have ever seen.

A sweating, odoriferous heat filled the salon and all their thighs were opulent but I shivered as though they breathed out gusts of iced air, though I do not think that any of them breathed. The libidinous images all bared their sexual parts with a defiant absence of provocation that was not bred of innocence, for in their primitive simplicity the dozen orifices were shockingly made manifest, the ugly, undeniable, insatiable nether mouths of archaic and shameless, anonymous Aphrodite herself, the undifferentiated partner in the blind act who has many mouths, even if not one of them ever asks for a name. And I had come with orders to worship here, I, Desiderio, the desired one, to kneel down before the twelve hairy shrines of this universal church of lust in a uniform that made of me only a totem of carnality myself.

The Count now ostentatiously and continually increased his stature by such an effort of will I thought the swollen veins of his forehead would burst. His breast heaved like thunder. He seemed to graze the ceiling with the round tip of that bland, peachy, concupiscent hood, which turned his head itself into a monumental symbol of sexuality. He took on a ponderous and ecclesiastical gait, as if it were a kind of mitre that he wore – he, the Pope of the profane, officiating at an ultimate sacrament, the self-ordained, omnipotent, consecrated man–phallus itself; and when he snatched a candle from a monkey's paw and used it to ignite the rosy plumage of a winged girl, I knew he was about to preach us a sermon and she was to be his text.

His eyes rolled in delirious agitation, as if they might start out of the holes in his mask. Striking the pose of a man possessed, he flung back his head and there issued from his thunderous mouth the following, agonized psalm in the intervals and cadences of plainsong, while the girls silently opened and closed their arms with the helpless, automatic reaction of so many sea anemones behind their black bars, and the furniture snuffled, howled and grunted, and the angel burned so quickly, with such a smoky flame, I realized she had only been a life-like construction of papier mâché on a wicker frame.

'I am the zodiacal salamander man
because flesh is a constellation of flame
and I am universal flesh
I am an oxyacetylene pen
who scrawled all over the face of the sky
in my incendiary rage
segmented constellations fleshly novas.

'I am the willed annihilation of the orgiastic moment in person, ladies.'

I pricked up my ears at that. Could he be, not the Doctor, but that other mystery man, Mendoza, who had written on just such a theme before he annihilated himself in a manner unknown? Could Mendoza have reconstituted himself out of infinity – perhaps by running a film of his own explosion backwards, so that he hatched out of the inward-turning egg of an implosion without a stain upon him? But the Count did not allow me to ponder this sufficiently; he surged on down a remorseless torrent of metaphor.

'I ride the pyrotechnic tiger
that eats nothing but fire

'I burn away inexorably
until nothing is left but bare, rhetorical bone
that burns and burns and is not consumed

'I burn in my white-hot, everlasting, asbestos flesh!'

At that, I thought immediately of Albertina, but he turned all the imagery of desire on its head and diabolically inverted its meanings, like a warlock saying the Pater Noster backwards. He bewildered me utterly. And he swept on like the landslide that devoured the set of samples.

'I, the bane of bone!
I, the denuded skeleton comet!
I, volcanic enigma, phallic aspiration, unfallen Icarus!'

So I came to the conclusion he was only lamenting his own frigidity. Then his voice dropped an octave as if he were about to intone a blessing.

'I am my own antithesis.
My loins rave. I unleash negation.
The burning arrows of negation.
Come!
Incinerate yourself with me!'

The paper angel flickered and went out. Her ashes crumbled into a surprisingly small heap. The Madame rang up the price of a replacement on her till.

'Yes,' she said in the voice of a governess congratulating a child who has recited well. 'There is no matter more grave than pleasure.'

The Count rattled the bars of the cage of the whipped girl.

'Give me my striped tiger woman! Flagellated past the bone, she is bleeding fire, a cannibal feast.'

The madame obligingly unlocked the door and the Count seized the meat voraciously. As he humped it towards the door on his back, like a porter, he snapped at me:

'Select your harlot immediately! I must have a stimulus.'

I was in a quandary. None of the metamorphosed objects before me aroused the slightest desire in me. Even though they came in all the shapes of every imaginable warped desire, they seemed to me nothing but malicious satires upon eroticism and I felt the same mixture of laughter and revulsion that the Count's ode had inspired in me. But I was his creature and so I must do whatever he wanted. The Madame rescued me. After she rang up the Count's purchase, she stepped from her post and clasped her yellowish hand firmly round my wrist.

'I shall come with you myself,' she said and her fingers tightened so authoritatively I did not have much option but to go with her. Because I had never touched her before, nobody could have expected me to know her from her touch, although her touch was thrilling. Besides, we were in the House of Anonymity and had put away ourselves when we put on our masks.

The whole house had the close humidity of a groin and the blue smoke of the incense burning everywhere in faience bowls made it smell like an embalming shop. She led us up a formal staircase with carpets of black panther under foot but now we were out of the Bestial Room, the furs were safely dead. Light came from the glowing eyes of bronze birds with outspread wings hanging from the basalt vaulting over our heads and both these and also the eyes in her loincloth winked lasciviously now and then. She walked with a free, proud, sensual grace. She smelled like a rutting leopard. Her skin was almost green.

The heavy, mahogany door of our common bedroom was guarded on either side by jasper colossi, Babylonian monsters with curved, brooding beaks and feathered arms that brushed the faces of those who went inside with a menacing voluptuous caress.

'We call this room the Sphere of Spheres,' she said.

She ushered us into a circular chamber filled with a shifting medley of colours from a lamp with a stained glass shade that turned in a slow circle in the middle of the ceiling. The Count carried his victim to the bed as ceremoniously as if it were a sacrificial altar but I did not bother to watch him or even to look more closely at this place of consummated desires for the Madame had turned towards me and placed her finger on her incomparable lips. I remembered that mouth and that gesture perfectly. I gasped. I think I sobbed. She plucked away my mask and kissed me lightly on the lips. I saw her eyes through the clefts of her sheath of black leather; their incalculable depths were blurred with tears.

'I am Albertina,' she said.

She pulled off her head covering and her black hair fell down around her well-remembered face.

I do not know why she loved me at first sight, as I loved her, even though I first saw her in a dream. Yet we pursued one another across the barriers of time and space; we dared every vicissitude of fortune for a single kiss before we were torn apart again and we saw the events of the war in which we were enlisted on opposite sides only by the light of one another's faces.

I took her in my arms. We were exactly the same height and the arches of our bosoms met with a sonorous clang. A terrible cry from the Count's whore did not interrupt our first embrace. The earth turned on the pivot of her mouth. The sense of seraphic immanence which had afflicted me in the city was now fulfilled. Her arms clasped my neck and her belly pressed against my nakedness as if striving to transcend the mortal flaw that divided us and so effect a total, visceral mingling, binding us forever, so that the same blood would flow within us both and our nerves would knit and our skins melt and fuse in the force of the electricity we generated between us.

We moved towards the round bed that spun round like the world on an axis in the middle of the room. Here the Count crouched slavering over the ruins of his unfortunate prostitute who was now only a bleeding moan. We glanced at them with the indifference natural to lovers and I turned back the coverlet of dark fur to lay my Albertina down on sheets that bore stains as tragic and mysterious as those on a pavement after a nude had been thrown down from a balcony. I knelt above her and kissed her cool breasts. I sucked great mouthfuls of the cold water of her breasts, as though my thirst would never be slaked. The eyes on her single garment closed one by one.

At that very moment a hail of machine-gun fire crashed through the windows, tore through the velvet curtains and ploughed into the mattress beneath us.

The Count darted to the shattered window, yelling an invitation to further violence. An inrushing gale pattered a tattoo of fragmented glass against the cardboard hood he still wore. Fresh bullets spattered into the whipped woman, who danced and opened out beneath them. Albertina lay quite still and did not move at all. She let me drag her off the bed and bundle her safe out of range of the bullets, while she lay limp as a doll and all the time she wept very bitterly.

'They've come for you,' she said. 'I can't do anything about it. All hell has been let loose since we lost the set of samples.'

She clung to me and cried like a child.

Then came running footsteps outside the room and a pounding at the door.

'The police!' cried the porteress. 'The police are looking for two murderers! There's two murderers in bed with you!'

Albertina pushed me away and opened the door.

'She'll take you out the back door,' she said through her tears. 'Go, now.'

'Tears?' said the Count, sliding towards her. 'Whorish tears?'

He unmasked himself in order to savourously lick her face but she was crying too much to notice.

'I won't leave you,' I said and took her into my arms again.

'No!' she said. 'That's quite impossible.'

I felt I was stronger than anyone in the world.

'How can your father's daughter possibly say anything is impossible?'

I picked her up and carried her bodily into the passage but there she began to melt like a woman of snow. As I was holding her, she grew less and less. She dissolved. Still weeping, she dissipated into the air. I saw her. I felt her. I felt her weight diminish. I saw her, first, flicker a little; then waver continuously; then grow more and more indistinct, as if she herself were gradually erasing the pattern she made upon the air. Her eyes vanished last of all and the last tears that fell from them hung for a little while on the air after she had gone, like forgotten diamanté ear-drops. Then all that was left of this fragile bequest of tears was an evanescent trace of moisture on my shoulder. In the midst of my grief and bewilderment, bullets crashed round me from within the house and I heard the cruel voices of the Determination Police and heard their voices clang and rattle like sabres.

It had suddenly grown very cold.

The lights of their own electric torches glimmered on the leather coats of the police, for all the lights had gone out though terrified monkeys, their fur ablaze, flashed past like meteors. The candles they had dropped rolled underfoot, and here and there the hangings were already on fire. The Count picked up a fallen candle and lighted whatever curtains we passed with such rapidity it seemed the fir : sprang from his fingers rather than from the flame. The porteress led us this way and that, threading us like a cunning needle through narrow, unused corridors, up unexpected spiral staircases, through echoing galleries full of instruments of torture and the apparatus of fetishism. We could hear the oceanic roaring of the lions for the furniture was running loose. Once we pushed past a lumbering chair; a howling pack of tables fled away from us down a hall of dark mirrors as we ourselves ran through – just in time, for, as we pushed past the bead curtain hanging over the outer doorway, bullets shivered the mirrors back to chips of unreflecting silvered glass. Albertina must somehow have let all the prostitutes out of their cages for, freed from the petrification of their profession once they were free of bars, the prostitutes, too, were trying to escape the police, who were the sworn enemies of objects so candidly unreal. We often glimpsed a leafed or feathered shape transfixed in the beam of a torch upon a staircase; it would let out a shuddering cry before disintegrating at the impact of an authentic bullet or it would collapse in a whispering rustle of waste paper or the bullets cracked open the carapace and all the springs and wheels sprang whizzing out.

Then, as we waited on an obscure gallery while the porteress wrestled with a rusty lock, the Count, who had been peering at the holocaust through the banisters with an eager but detached interest, slumped against me, quivering.

'He is there,' he said with a certain wry pleasure, as if savouring an unfamiliar sensation which might have been fear.

A shape had materialized in the shadows below us, a black some six and a half feet tall, with shoulders of a bison and a Plutonian head, armed with a knife, waiting in the well of the stairs. He wore the leather overcoat of a policeman but I knew he was no other than the man who searched for the Count because of the baleful mass of his presence and the appalling pressure it exerted, so that my eardrums throbbed as though I stood in a great depth of water. He seemed to wait only for the Count to show himself. He bore his vigil like a cloak and a certain quality in his waiting indicated the Count would come to him, in time; that the Count would roll to him as one drop of mercury rolls to another across a plate. He was like a man made of magnetic stone.

'That man – if man he be – is my retribution,' said the Count. 'He is my twin. He is my shadow. Such a terrible reversal; I, the hunter, have become my own prey. Hold me or I will run into his arms.'

Fortunately the porteress impatiently tugged his shoulder for she had unlocked the door to another staircase which took us to the roof, out into the wind and rain, and so the Count was saved from himself for the time being. We went down a root of ivy hand over hand, the porteress last, and she led us dexterously through a formal garden where we could see nothing except the spurt of flame from the mouths of the machine guns stationed there. When I looked back, I saw that most of the house was burning, now, but there was no time to look back more than once. The porteress took us through a little gate and here was Lafleur, with travelling cloaks and horses. I was extraordinarily pleased to see him. It was about nine o'clock. Behind us the burning brothel already tinted the sky with crimson. The porteress reached into her pocket and now presented us with a lengthy roll of bill. The Count, stupendously ironic, swung on to his mount and, leaning down, pressed his wad of banknotes into her hand.

'One must pay for one's pleasures,' he said.

Despising roads, we galloped over the open country in headlong flight, the Count and I still in our phallic carnival costume, riding as widely as crazed psychopomps. When we came to a spinney of poplars, we halted briefly to see what lay behind us. All within the House of Anonymity had turned to air and fire in an awesome, elemental transmutation and rising above the high walls, the fireball seemed to tug impatiently at its moorings within the earth while the turrets spouted jets of flame directly into the hearts of the rainclouds. Even from the distance of a mile, we could hear a symphony of agony and crashing brick, orchestrated like Berlioz. But the Count's satanic laughter rang more loudly than all that tumult of destruction.

'I, the lord of fire!' he said in a low but piercing voice and I knew he thought his hunter must be destroyed. But I was too stunned by my own misery to rejoice with him for he meant nothing to me.

To have her so unexpectedly thrust into my arms and, the next minute, to have her vanish! As if, all the time she kissed me, she had been only a ghost born of nothing but my longing – the first ghost who had deceived me in all those years of ghostly visitants! I felt I was nothing but a husk blown this way and that way by the winds of misfortune and the only light that guided me was the deceitful iridescence on the face of my beloved. The Japanese believe that foxes light bonfires on marshland and lure travellers towards them. The Japanese fox is a beautiful lady, a marvellous prestidigitator with a whole boxful of tricksy delights and, once she has you in her luring arms, then, with a whiff of rancid excretions, she derisively shows you the real colour of her brush and vanishes, laughing. Albertina's face was the treacherous mask of the rarest of precious black foxes; and yet her tears were the last thing of all to disappear. Could tears be a token of deceit? Ought I to trust the authentic grief of her tears?

Then we saw the headlights of the police cars coming towards us and by their straightforward beams, the massive figure of the black pimp leading them on a motorcycle. The Count blasphemed horribly and moaned. We spurred on our horses.

Much later, we stopped by a stream to let the beasts drink and Lafleur came up to me as I sat gazing abstractedly at the dark water. He knelt beside me. The submissive curve of his back was exquisitely graceful. He spoke to me gently. His voice was muffled by his bandages.

'You haven't lost her,' he said. 'She is safe.'

Though I did not know why he spoke with such assurance, he comforted me a little. Then we rode once more. The countryside sped by us in the changing light of night and day. We went in silence, stopping only to buy a loaf of bread or a length of sausage and cram it hastily into our mouths as we stood in the shop. I was very much afraid of the Determination Police but I was not half so scared of them as the Count was of the black pimp. His pursuit was the impulse of our desperate career. The Count's terror showed itself in fits of hysterical laughter and outbursts of crazed blasphemies. His fear had a theatrical intensity not at all out of the character of a self-created demiurge – which is how I saw the Count. I did him the courtesy of seeing him as he wished to be seen, as the living image of

ferocity, even if sometimes I found him risible. And yet his fear
infected us all with such a quaking fever I wondered again if he
might not be the Doctor in disguise, for he could communicate to
us so well his own imaginings. Each time a twig snapped as we passed
by, we all shuddered together.

But, if he were the Doctor, why had his daughter not acknowledged
him in the brothel? Out of tact and discretion?

The first chance I had, I took off the uniform of the customers in
the House of Anonymity and got the Count to buy me new clothes.
He chose me as elegant and sober an outfit as he could find in a little
country haberdashers, for he had offered me the post of his secretary
and wanted to see me well dressed. I did not know what the job would
entail, except for admiring him all the time, but I accepted it because I did not have much choice although I knew the Count was
going to take a ship as soon as we reached a seaport and I must go
with him to Europe, to another continent, to another hemisphere,
where everything would be new because it was so old and there was
no war, no Dr Hoffman, no Minister, no quest, no Albertina – nothing familiar except myself. I cannot say I made a conscious decision
to abandon everything and go with the Count. Under the influence
of his shadow, it was possible to do only as he desired, though I did
not even like him much. Already I was just as much his creature as was
the miserable Lafleur.

The Count refused to take off his tights and waistcoat, though the
costume was even more paradoxical without the mask.

'The livery of hyper-sexuality becomes me,' he said, though he
was hypocrite enough to keep his cloak wrapped tightly round him
when it came to encounters with shop-keepers.

Days melted into nights until, in my weariness, I could hardly
sort out the one from the other. At last, one morning, we saw a grey
ribbon of ocean on the horizon and, before sunset, we entered the
port, our spent and weltered horses foundering beneath us. We went
at once to the docks to find a ship and, after speaking to innumerable
captains, we found a cargo vessel sailing under the Liberian flag for
The Hague on that very evening's tide, whose captain was willing
to take us with him for a very substantial sum. We went aboard at
once, abandoning our horses in the stable of a public house.

They gave the three of us a single, narrow cabin with two hard
bunks one above the other and a hammock for Lafleur. Stretching
out immediately, we all fell into the profound sleep of absolute ex-
haustion and, when we woke the next day, we had been delivered

over entirely to the grey, wet, shifting hands of the waters and there was no sign of land anywhere.

It seemed to me I sailed unwillingly against the strongest current in the world, a current of tears, because I thought the boat was taking me away from Albertina. I did not then understand that the reciprocal motion of our hearts, like the oscillation of the waves, was a natural and eternal power and those who tried to part us were like men who take a great comb and try to make a parting through the ocean. I did not know then that she travelled with me for she was inextricably mingled with my idea of her and her substance was so flexible she could have worn a left glove on her right hand – if she had wanted to, that is.

6. The Coast of Africa

Now the world was confined to the ship and its crew of sullen Lascars, dour Swedes and granite Scots, who raucously shouted lewd shantys as they swung about the rigging hauling on great hawsers and performed all the other tasks that, added together, kept this fragile shell of wood and canvas on its course across a sea which blurred into the sky in the morning haze and at night contained as many stars in its bosom as blazed above us, for we were very exposed to the heavens and to the weather. At first, I was plagued with sea-sickness and could not stir from my bunk but soon I got my sea legs and then I fell prey to the dreadful boredom of the traveller by sea.

There was nothing to do all day but keep out of the way of the crew, to watch the cyclorama of the sky, to applaud the dances of seabirds and flying fish, to listen to the wind in the canvas and to wait for the thick stews of salt fish and potatoes, all the menus at mealtimes offered. The Count bore this ennui with a stoicism I would not have expected of him. Perhaps he was restoring his energies with a period of silence for he rarely, if ever, spoke, lying all day in our cabin as still as a corpse to emerge only in the evenings, when he would come out just as the sailors, the deck swabbed down for the night, sat sipping from their cans of watered rum upon the coops that housed the hens who gave the captain eggs for breakfast, puffing on their pipes, or else danced together to the wheezing music of an accordion. I sometimes joined in these diversions exercising the skills the Alligator Man had taught me on a borrowed harmonica to give them a barn dance or two from the bayous and Lafleur, also, crept out to join us, slight and shy and bandaged, adding a husky, hesitant, still unbroken voice to the choruses, a voice which sometimes seemed to me disguised for occasionally it woke in me strange, vibrating echoes as mysterious as if it were the sea who was singing to me.

But the Count scorned these simple pleasures. He stalked straight to the prow, whirling in the folds of his cloak, and sat there in aquiline solitude, gazing into the night towards which we sailed, for we left the sun folding up its crimson banners in the west behind us. He sat there sometimes all night, like the very figurehead of the ship if it had been called *The Wandering Jew* or *The Flying Dutchman;* he had retreated into an impenetrable impassivity and yet sometimes he seemed to have become the principle that moved the ship, as if it were not the wind that drove us towards Europe but the power of that gaunt, barbarous will. His conviction that he was a force of nature always suspended my disbelief for a time, if never for long.

Woman-starved, dreaming of mermaids, satisfying themselves desultorily with one another, the sailors cast scowling but hungry eyes on little Lafleur and on myself, too, but I had learned enough to keep them at their distance. Strange, blue days at sea! One day so like another I often went to gaze at our creaming wake for visible proof we had budged an inch. But, in this constriction and this apparent immobility, the sea-miles strung one upon the other like beads on a thread of passage until no weed bobbed on the water and soon we were too far from land to sight any but the most intrepid of sea-birds. I slept but did not dream. All my life now seemed a dream from which I had woken to the boredom of the voyage. We endured a storm; we endured a torrid calm. I reconciled myself to the gnawing longing for the sight of a girl I would never see again unless her father cramped the world into a planisphere and I had not the least idea what time or place the Count might take me to though, since his modes of travel were horseback, gig and tall-masted schooner, I guessed, wherever it was, it would be somewhere in the early nineteenth century.

A kind of silent camaraderie had sprung up between Lafleur and myself. He often came to sit beside me, a little black shadow with a concealed face in which only the eyes were visible, eyes that seemed gentle enough and were of such an immense size and so liquidly brown they reminded me of those of a sad, woodland animal. We deceive ourselves when we say the eye is an expressive organ; it is the lines around the eye that tell their story and, with Lafleur, these lines were hidden. But I sensed a certain wistful kindliness in that abused little valet, though he hardly ever spoke to me and seemed only to communicate in sighs. Yet he pointed out to me one or two teasing anachronisms on shipboard.

The cook, a sour, dyspeptic Marseillais, had a wind-up gramophone with a large horn on which, all through the starry nights, he played hiccoughing records of Parisian chanteuses whose voices, brought to us fitfully on the breeze, mingled with the plash of the waters, were the essence of a nostalgia which affected me strangely for it was an entirely vicarious emotion for places I had never seen. The obnoxious Finn, a first mate of memorable ill-temper and vile oaths, had a sea-chest full of magazines containing photographs of plump girls in corsets and boots laced up to the thigh; he showed them to me, once, in a rare fit of good nature. The cabin-boy once told Lafleur of a motorbike he kept in his father's house in Liverpool but when, curious, I asked him about his toy, he shook his head blankly and, denying all knowledge of it, hurried off pretending he had to feed immediately the stinking pig they kept on deck to supplement our fare when the salt fish ran low.

The sailors would sometimes halt, open-mouthed, in the middle of a shanty, as if they were actors who had suddenly forgotten their lines, and mouth away vacantly for a few seconds, their hands suddenly dangling as if they had forgotten how to hold the ropes. But these lapses of continuity lasted no more than a moment. Then all would be saltily nautical again, in the manner of an old print. But sometimes there was a jarring effect of overlapping, as if the ship that bore us was somehow superimposed on another ship of a quite different kind, and I began to feel a certain unease, an unease which afflicted me most when I heard the sounds the Captain coaxed out of the air as he twisted the dial of his radio when he relaxed in his private cabin at the end of the day. Lafleur seemed to catalogue these puns in the consistency of the vessel with a certain relish but the Count did not even notice them. He noticed nothing. He even ignored his servants.

I decided that, after all, he was not the Doctor, unless he was some bizarre emanation of the Doctor. I concluded he was some kind of ontological freelance who could certainly determine the period in which the ship sailed and this was quite enough to speculate upon. I would not have believed such a thing possible before I started on my journey. His monumental silence continued and then, before my eyes, he crumbled away to nothing so that I never admired him again. For we were betrayed.

The Captain's little radio betrayed us.

One bright, azure morning, the Captain listened in on the short waves as he ate his eggs in bed and, though his native language was Dutch, he made out enough of the standard speech of my country to hear how the Count and I were both wanted for murder. And there was a price on my head, for I was a war criminal.

They came for us with guns as we lay sleeping. The Captain and the first mate came. They handcuffed us and took us down to the malodorous hold where they chained us to rings in the floor and left us there in misery and deprivation while the Captain turned the ship round in mid-ocean and steered back on our course, for the Determination Police and the State of Louisiana both offered rewards to those who delivered me to the one, and the Count to the agents of the other.

I expected the Count to bear this reversal with ironic self-containment, but no. For the first twenty-four hours of our incarceration, he screamed all the time on a single, high-pitched note and when the first mate came in with our meagre rations, he cowered away as if he expected the Finn to kick him, a perfectly justified fear. This display of quivering pusillanimity fascinated me. I waited eagerly for the Count to speak. I had to wait for only two days.

What were our rations? Traditional fare. The first mate put a tin platter down on the floor twice a day. It contained three segments of ship's biscuit alive with weevils and we had to scrabble for it as best we could, all encumbered with our irons. He brought us a small can of stale water, too, and was at least sufficiently humane to free us for a few moments so that we could attend to the needs of nature in a bucket provided for the purpose. I never dreamed I could regret those rank fish stews but otherwise I found I bore up to captivity well enough, perhaps because we were returning to my lover's country, even if I could hope for nothing but the torture chamber once I got there. Lafleur, however, seemed curiously content. Perhaps he felt the gloomy period of his bondage to the Count was over. Sometimes, in the rolling darkness of the hold, the seeping bilge washing around my feet, I even heard him chuckling to himself.

On the third day, the Count spoke. I could tell it was about sunset because the accordion was playing and the feet of the dancing sailors beat a tattoo overhead. We had no other means of marking the time in the close darkness below. The Count's screams had modulated to a low, dull moaning and this moaning, in turn, seemed to alter quantitatively until it was a moan in words.

'These men are not my equals! They have no right to deprive me of my liberty! These adversaries are unfit for me! It is unjust!'

'No such thing as justice,' observed the valet with unaccustomed briskness but the Count ignored him. All this time he had been preparing another oration and would not be interrupted.

'By all the laws of natural justice, I was pre-eminent because I, the star-traveller, the erotic conflagration, transcended all the laws! Once, before I saw my other, I could have turned this mountain into a volcano. I would have fired these rotten timbers round us with a single sneeze and risen from the pyre, a phoenix.

'Terror of a fire at sea! How the tars brutally trample each other down; they stab and murder their comrades in the mad tussle for the lifeboat but the lifeboat was the first to blaze. My tumultuous bowels vomit forth flaming wrack! And I did not forget to invite the sharks to dinner, oh, no. They have formed up around the ship, their dinner table; they wait for their meal to cook. They wait for the involuntary tributes of sea-boys' sinewy limbs.

'But when I opened my mouth to order the *plat du jour*, I found my grammar changed in my mouth. No longer active; passive.

'He has tampered with my tongue. He has bridled it.

'I always eschewed the Procrustean bed of circumstance until he pegged me out on it.'

(Lafleur was seized with a fit of coughing but it only lasted a few moments.)

'If I am indeed the Black Prometheus, now I must ask for other guests to dine. Come, every eagle in the world, to this most sumptuous repast, my liver.'

(His chains clanged as he tried to throw himself backwards in an attitude of absolute abandonment but he did not have enough room for such exercises. His moaning again intensified to a scream and then diminished to a moan again.)

'They have eaten me down to an immobile core. I, who was all movement. My I is weaker than its shadow used to be. I is my shadow. I am gripped by the convulsive panic of a mapless traveller in a virgin void. Now I must explore the other side of my moon, my dark region of enslavement.

'I was the master of fire and now I am the slave of earth. Where is my old, invincible I! He stole it. He snatched it from the peg where I hung it beside the mulatto's mattress. Now I am sure only of my slavery.

'I do not know how to be a slave. Now I am an enigma to myself. I have become discontinuous.

'I fear my lost shadow who lurks in every shadow. I, who perpetrated atrocities to render to the world incontrovertible proof that my glorious misanthropy overruled it, I – now I exist only as an atrocity about to be perpetrated on myself.

'He let his slaves enslave me.'

During the lengthy, wordless recitative of shuddering groans that followed, Lafleur said unexpectedly, in the voice of a scholarly connoisseur:

'Not a bad imitation of Lautréamont.'

But the Count, unheeding, sang out with delighted rapture:

'I am enduring the keenest, most piercing pangs of anguish!'

With that, he concluded his aria. The renewed silence was broken only by the sound of waves and the tread of the dancers above us, until Lafleur, with more insolence than solicitude, demanded:

'Do you feel any pain?'

The valet was undergoing some kind of sea change.

The Count sighed.

'I feel no pain. Only anguish. Unless anguish is the name of my pain. I wish I could learn to name my pain.'

This was the first time I ever heard him, however obliquely, answer a question, though it was hard to tell whether, in his reply, he acknowledged the presence of the person who posed it or if he thought the question was a fortuitous externalization of the self-absorption which had already doubled or tripled the chains with which he was bound, until he could no longer breathe without our hearing them rattle. But, to my astonishment, Lafleur coughed again to clear his throat and, with a touch of pedantry, in a curiously gruff, affected voice, gave the following exposition.

'Master and slave exist in the necessary tension of a twinned actuality, which is transmuted only by the process of becoming. A sage of Ancient China, the learned Chuang Tzu, dreamed he was a butterfly. When he woke up, he was hard put to it to tell whether a man had dreamed he was a butterfly or a butterfly was still dreaming he was a man. If you looked at your situation objectively for a moment, my dear Count, you might find that the principal cause of your present discomfort is a version of Chuang Tzu's dilemma. You could effectively evolve a persona from your predicament, if you tried.'

But the Count was incapable of the humility of objectivity and took only a few hints to further his soliloquy from Lafleur.

'Am I the slave of my aspirations or am I their master? All I know for certain is, I aspired to a continuous sublimity and my aspirations accentuate the abyss into which I have fallen. In the depths of this abyss, I find the black pimp.'

But Lafleur continued to expand his theme.

'You were a man in a cage with a monster. And you did not know if the monster was in your dream or you were the dream of the monster.'

The Count clanged his chains with dreadful fury.

'No! No! No!'

But this triadic reiteration was addressed to the shadows, not to Lafleur, who commented with some asperity:

'Now you believe yourself to be the dream of the black pimp, I suppose. That is the reverse of the truth.'

But the Count did not hear him.

'I toppled off my pyrotechnic tiger and, as I plunge downwards, endlessly as Lucifer, I ask myself: "What is the most miraculous event in the world?" And I answer myself: "I am going to fall into my own arms. They stretch out to me from the bottom of the pit."

'I am entirely alone. I and my shadow fill the universe.'

Lafleur gasped at that and so did I for I felt myself instantly negated. To my horror, I discovered I immediately grew thinner and less solid. I felt – how can I describe it? – that the darkness which surrounded us was creeping in at every pore to obliterate me. I saw the white glimmer of Lafleur's face and held out my hands to him imploringly, beseeching him to go with me together into the oblivion to which the Count had consigned us, so that I should have some company there, in that cold night of non-being. But, before my senses failed me, there was a sudden, dreadful clamour on deck.

The accordion sputtered a final, distracted, terrified chord. There were screams, thuds and an awful wailing, suddenly cut short, that the pig must have made when the pirates cut its throat, while a hundred tongues announced that chaos was come. Abruptly I fell out of the magic circle of the Count's self-absorption; my dissolution was cut short. The end of our imprisonment had come. The ship had been attacked by pirates.

They were swart, thick-set, yellowish men of low stature, equipped with immense swords and massive moustaches. They spoke a clicking, barking, impersonal language and never smiled though, when they decapitated the crew in a lengthy ritual by the light of flares on the deck, they laughed to see the heads roll and bounce. Once they knew we were murderers, they treated us with respect, cut off our chains with swift blows of their heavy swords, which were of incredible sharpness, and let us up on deck to watch the débâcle.

No one was spared except ourselves. After all their heads were off, the torsos went into the sea, while the pirates set about improvising small fires to cure the heads, which they proposed to keep as souvenirs. The Count visibly grew fatter at the smell of blood. He watched the ghastly ballet of the execution with the relish of a customer at a cabaret. When he flung off his cloak and the pirates saw he still wore the uniform of the House of Anonymity in all its arrogant exoticism, they gasped with admiration and bowed deeply to him in a display of servility. Another reversal had re-established his continuity. He was in the ascendance again.

But Lafleur lost all the crispness he had displayed in the cabin. He became wary and uneasy and stayed close beside me. Later, I learned he was very much afraid and almost about to reveal himself so that we might not die without knowing one another again, for the pirates were the mercenaries of Death itself.

They sailed these angry waters, far from the land that spawned them, in a black ship with eyes painted on the bows and the stern fashioned into the shape of the tail of a black fish. The triangular sails were black and they flew a black flag. They were some mixed tribe of Kurds, Mongols or Malays but their saturnine visages hinted at an infernal origin and they worshipped a sword.

As soon as the crew was dead, they set about stripping the cargo vessel and transferring its contents to their own boat. When they found the casks of rum in the forecastle, they greeted them with obscure grunts of glee but they did not broach them immediately. Instead they piled them as a votive offering around the altar of the sword they kept on the poop of the black ship. Now Lafleur and I clung to the Count like scared children for the pirates offered him instinctive reverence. When they saw our wrists were chafed from the manacles, they wrapped rags soaked in oil and spices round them and gave us for nothing a far more spacious cabin than the one the Count had hired – a wide room – with straw mats on the floor, mattresses for sleeping and a tasteful water-colour of a black cockerel, a little sea-stained, hanging on the wall. They brought us satisfying and delicious meals of rice, curried fish and pickles. The ship was frail and lightly built. I felt far closer to the sea than I had done before and hence far nearer to death, for the slightest breeze could tip it over and fling us and our hosts into the sea. But they were the most expert sailors.

During his adventures in the East, the Count had picked up a smattering of many tongues and found some words and phrases he could share with the pirate leader, so he spent most of his time with this brooding, diminutive killer whose face was as unyieldingly severe as the object he worshipped, intent on learning some of their art of swordsmanship. He also learned our destination. We would cross the Atlantic in their mournful cockleshell, boarding whatever craft we passed, round the Cape of Good Hope, cross the Indian Ocean and any other ocean that lay in our path and eventually drop anchor in an island off the coast of China where they kept their booty, their temples, their forges and their womenfolk. A long, weary journey full of dangers lay before us and a landfall I was sure we should find replete with horrors. Now we were free, I was far more frightened than I had been in chains.

The shrine on the deck consisted of a sword laid between two ebony rests. From a pole above it hung a number of garlands of heads, all smoked a dusky, tan colour and shrunk to the size of heads of monkeys by the process of curing. Every morning, after prayers, the pirate leader removed the black loincloth which was his only garb and bent over on the poop in front of the altar while each of his men filed past him in devout silence, kissed his exposed arse and emitted a sharp bark of adulation while slapping his buttocks briefly with the flat of their blades. Their fidelity to their lord was so great one could have thought each pirate was only an aspect of the leader, so that the many was the one. They were indistinguishable from one another. They were like those strings of paper figures, hand in identical hand, that children cut out of sheets of paper. After this display or refreshment of fidelity, they practised with their swords.

These were heavy, double-bladed shafts of steel half the height of the pirates themselves, with handles constructed in such a way they had to be grasped with both hands. Though their use required great skill, it needed no finesse for the most telling stroke was a murderous, chopping blow that easily split a man in half. It was impossible to fence with such a sword. It was equally impossible to defend oneself except by attacking first. They were weapons which denied forethought, impulses of destruction made of steel. And the pirates themselves, so slight, so silent, so cruel, so two-dimensional, seemed to have subsumed their beings to their swords, as if the weapons were their souls or as if they had made a pact with their swords to express their spirit for them, for the flash of the sword seemed by far a more expressive language than the staccato monosyllables that came so grudgingly to their lips. Their exercises lasted for six hours a day. They transformed the decks into an arcade of flashing light, for the blades left gleaming tracks behind them that lingered in the air for a long time. After they had finished, they polished their swords for another hour and, as the sun went down, joined together to sing a tuneless hymn which might have been a requiem for the day they had killed with their swords. After that came a night of perfect silence.

The pirates fed us and left us alone, for which I was heartily thankful. The ship was a black sea-bird, a marine raven. It skimmed over rather than cut through the waves and though there was only this thinnest of matchwood skins between us all and death, the sheer virtuosity of their seamanship maintained us in a position something like that of a ship navigated along a tightrope. Their seamanship was as amazing as their swordsmanship and, from the risks they took, seemed also to imply an intimate complicity with death. Lafleur and I, alone in our cabin, spent the days in quiet and foreboding. I discovered his hooded, luminous eyes watched me all the time with affection, even devotion, and I began to feel I had known him all my life and he was my only friend; but you could not have said this new warmth blossomed for now he took on an almost Trappist speechlessness and scarcely said more than 'Good morning' or 'Good evening' to me. I began to feel I would soon lose the use of my tongue. I counted the days by scratching a line with my fingernail on our cabin wall. On the twelfth monotonous day, it was the full moon and when they staved in the covers of the rum barrels, I realized they meant to release their pent-up inhibited passions in a debauch.

They set about the initial processes of becoming drunk with the same glum diligence that characterized all their actions. It was a night of sweltering, ominous calm. A gibbous moon fired the phosphorescence in the waters so that the black ship rocked on a bed of cold, scintillating flame and they wreathed the sails so that the ship could look after itself for the rest of the night and most of the next day, if need be, for every single one proposed to drink himself to complete insensibility. Then they arranged themselves in ranks on the deck, cross-legged on round straw mats, as was their custom, facing the poop where their leader sat facing them under the shrine with his guest, the Count, beside him and the cask of rum before him. Each man held his cannikin ready and the leader, after barking a grace before drink, scooped out a ladleful of rum from the cask into the Count's cannikin and then helped himself. The pirates went up one by one for their shares. The outlines were as distinct as those of Indonesian shadow puppets. They each wore a black loincloth and each carried at his side a sword in its scabbard. They twisted black sweatbands round their heads and none of them was taller than four and three-quarter feet, death's weird hobgoblins. As he took hold of his spilling portion, each pirate took off his sword and put it down on a growing pile beside the leader, either in a gesture of trust or as a hygienic precaution intended to forestall the ravages they might wreak with their weapons when they had drunk enough.

As the crew passed up its cans for its rations, Lafleur, gazing beside me through the window, softly tugged my sleeve.

'Look!' he said. 'There is land against the sky.'

Across the undulating plateau of bright water, far, far away, the shapes of a tropical forest flung up their fringed arms against the white sky. We had already travelled many hundreds of miles to the south; the distant landscape was as unfamiliar to me as that of another planet and yet it was land and the sight of it cheered my heart, although I would be denied the comfort of it.

'The currents around here are deceitful and the tornadoes come swiftly, unheralded and treacherous,' said Lafleur. 'They have chosen a foolish time for a drinking bout.'

'The demands of ritual are always stronger than those of reason,' I replied. 'When the full moon comes, they must get drunk even in the teeth of a hurricane.'

'I wish they did not worship steel,' he said. 'Steel is so inflexible.'

It was delightful to talk to somebody again and to feel his good-will beside me, although again his disguise was far too cunning and complete for me to penetrate.

'Well, we can't persuade the hurricane to smash the ship and let us live through it,' I said.

'No, indeed,' said Lafleur. 'But the hurricane is governed only by chance and chance at least is neutral. One can rely on the neutrality of chance. And when I look at the sky, I think I see a storm.'

I, too, looked at the sky but saw only moonlight and the drifting banks of cloud. But as the pirates lined up for their second round, they were already grunting with savage mirth and poking one another, for they had only the most primitive idea of fun. Their behaviour moved between only the two poles of melodrama and farce. As soon as they took off their frivolous armour, laid by their swords and had a drop or two of rum inside them, they frolicked with the mindlessness but not the innocence of infants. Even from our cabin, I could see the Count was growing disillusioned with them. He had admired their deathward turning darkness yet, after a third round, they stripped off their loincloths and, one and all, embarked on a farting contest. They made the radiant welkin ring with a battery of broken wind. Exposing to the moon the twin hemispheres of their lemon-coloured hinder cheeks, each banged away as loudly as he was able, amid a great deal of unharmonious laughter, and soon they began to set light to the gases they expelled with matches, so a blue flame hovered briefly above every backside.

'The clouds are piling up,' said Lafleur breathlessly and, indeed, the sky was growing sullen so that now the moonlight fell with a baleful glare the convives were too drunk to see.

They fell to wrestling and horseplay, tripping one another over as they passed on an endless chain to receive the apparently inexhaustible rum and their leader, who took two or three drinks for each one the men received, often missed their cannikins altogether and upset the ladle on his creature's head. This convulsed them with laughter. Someone untied the trophies from the shrine and they began to play a stumbling game of football with them. The Count sat quite still above them, brooding above these Breughel-like antics, his face set in lines of aristocratic distaste.

'The moon has put on a halo,' said Lafleur excitedly.

When I looked up, I saw the angry moon was surrounded with a sulphurous aura and from its white mouth now belched vile, hot gusts. The pirates, however, were beyond knowing or caring. Some, as if felled, tumbled down where they stood and snored immediately. Others first puked weakly and staggered before they slumped to the deck. But most simply sank down and slept the deep sleep of the newly purified. The cries, laughter and bursts of drunken song slowly faded away. Though he had absorbed most, the leader was the last to go. He slithered slowly from an upright position, clasped the rum-tub to break his fall and then he and the tub together rolled along the poop for a while and lay still in a pool of spilled liquor. The Count rose up and seized the holy sword from its shrine with a gesture that implied their god was too good for them. He was as tall as a stork and as wild as the spirit of the storm, which now broke upon us in a sudden squall. Lightning danced along the blade and the rain struck the oblivious revellers with tropic fury while the Count hissed: 'Scum!' and spat upon the pirate leader. Stepping through the bodies and the puddles of vomit and excrement with fastidious distaste, he went to the stern of the ship and inexorably directed us into the eye of the whirlwind.

We ran from the cabin to crouch at his side, like his dogs, for his protection, for now again we saw him in his tempestuous element. The tempest seemed his tool; he used this tool to destroy the black ship and its sailors.

The very air turned to fire. The topmast, an incandescent spoke, snapped and crashed; storm-born luminescence danced upon every surface and the rain and driving waves lashed us and soaked us until we were half-drowned before we sank. Lafleur and I clung to one another while the ship tilted this way and that, tossing its freight of sleeping swine hither and thither, flinging them senseless into the boiling sea or crushing them beneath its disintegrating timbers. The black sails unfurled and flew away on the wings of the storm; he flourished the sword like a wand or a baton, for he conducted the tempest as though it was a symphony orchestra and again we heard his dishevelled laughter, louder than the winds and waters put together. The currents and the wind were driving us nearer and nearer land in the random flares of the lightning. We saw the giant palms threshing and bowing double as if in homage to the Count. Yet we could see nothing clearly for our motion was too uncertain and soon the ship broke up in a succession of shivering concussions and all who sailed in it were flung into the water.

Yet not a single one of the sodden pirates flickered so much as an eyelid while the sea engorged them and we, the living, were washed up on a white beach which the wind moulded into fresh dunes at every moment, together with a great quantity of black driftwood and yellow corpses.

Yes, we were saved – Lafleur, the Count and I; though we were little more than skins swollen with salt water and our ears were still as full of the hurricane as if shells were clapped to them, blotting out all other sounds. But the great-grandfather of all breakers tossed me negligently on the spar to which I clung almost to the margin of the forest and Lafleur followed me on a lesser wave, holding on to the rudder. I stumbled down the beach and dragged him up the sand, out of harm's way, and then a lightning flash showed me the Count walking out of the water as simply as if he had been bathing, in his eyes a strange glow of satisfaction and, in his hand, still the mighty blade.

We followed him a little way into the forest and there Lafleur and I made ourselves a kind of nest in the undergrowth and slept as soon as our battered heads touched the grassy pillow, but the Count sat up awake all night, keeping some kind of vigil with his sword. He was still kneeling among the brushwood when we woke. The playful monkeys were pelting us with leaves, twigs and coconuts. The sun was high in the sky. The mysterious susurration of the tropic forest trembled sweetly in my ears after the clamour of the oceans. The air was soft and perfumed.

The storm was over and a miraculous peace filled the vaulted, imperial groves of palms. A web of lianas let a translucent green light down upon us three, ill-assorted babes in the wood and it was already so hot that steam was rising in puffs from our drenched clothing and the now filthy bandaging Lafleur obstinately refused to take off his face. It was marvellous to feel the solid ground beneath my feet again, even if I was not at all sure to which continent the ground belonged. I thought it must be my own far American South but the Count opted hopefully for savage Africa while Lafleur observed remotely that we had not the least notion where we really were but had probably been blown willy-nilly on to the coast of some distant island. When we went down to the beach to wash ourselves, we soon saw the inhabitants were black and so felt certain we were in Africa.

The tide, in receding, had left corpses strewn with shells all along the endless, white beach and the glistening purity of the sand emphasized the surpassing ebony of the inhabitants who, clad in long robes of coloured cottons and necklaces of dried beans, diligently searched among the debris for its trove of swords. They were men and women of great size and dignity, accompanied by laughing children of extraordinary charm, and when they saw us, they lowed gently among themselves like a congregation of wise cattle. Our garments smoked. We stood still and allowed them to approach us. They did so slowly, some trailing the pirates' swords unhandily behind them. Their faces and chests were whorled and cicatrized with tribal marks, knife cuts discoloured because white clay had been rubbed into them. As we waited, more and more of them came out of the margin of the jungle, walking with such grace they might all have been carrying huge pots on their heads, while their naked children danced round them like marionettes carved out of coal. When he saw their colour, the Count began to shiver as if he had caught a fever in the sea but I knew he shivered out of fear. But these solid, moving shadows showed no fear of us though soon they formed a great ring about us, hemming us in on all sides, and we knew we had been captured.

Then we heard the sound of crude but martial music and a jaunty detachment of Amazons marched out of the forest. These women were elderly and steatopygous. They were the shapes of ripe pears bursting with juice and their wrinkled dugs swung loosely back and forth, inside and outside the silver breastplates they wore but, all the same, they were a splendid sight, some with scarlet cloaks and loose white breeches made of swathes of cloth tucked up between the legs, others with cloaks of chocolate brown and dark blue breeches, all with metal helmets crowned with decorations of black horsehair. Their officers, chosen, it would seem, as much for the size of their bottoms as anything, marched beside them playing long-stemmed, brass trumpets and little hand drums and these female soldiers were aggressively armed with duck-guns, blunderbusses, muskets and razor-like knives, a museum of ancient weapons. They easily made us understand by signs we were under arrest again and took us, heavily if quaintly guarded, down the green path to a clearing where their village lay, while the black host fell in behind us with the same decorum that marked all they did.

The village was a seemly place of roomy huts made of dried mud and we were taken into a neat, clean house and offered a breakfast of some kind of pounded grain mixed with minced pork, served on fronds of palm. Lafleur and I ate heartily but the Count, unmanned again, a quaking skeleton, ate nothing. He cowered deep under the quilts they had given us to rest on, repeating over and over again: NEMESIS COMES. But they were far too polite to even raise their eyebrows when they saw him. Indeed, the only discordant notes in all this sober, harmonious decency were the low stools on which we were invited to sit and the low tables off which we ate, for they were ingeniously fashioned out of bones which, from their shapes, could only have been human. But these bones were dressed up so prettily that at first one hardly realized they were bones at all for they had been painted dark red and then adorned with tessellations of gummed shells and feathers.

They took away our ragged, filthy clothes with polite exclamations of distaste and Lafleur hid himself in a corner with a touching, virginal modesty until they brought us some of their lengths of cotton printed in blacks, indigos and crimsons so that we could cover ourselves. We made ourselves togas after the Roman fashion and then Lafleur and I sat at the door of our hut in the sunshine, trying to chat wordlessly with the little children who stared at us with huge, solemn eyes. The children fingered Lafleur's bandages curiously because they thought the covering was a kind of upper face and he laughed with them with such affecting motherliness I ought to have suspected ... but I suspected nothing! Shape-shifting was so much hocus-pocus to me. So the morning whiled away peacefully enough with never a hint of dread though we saw the women were busily tending huge cauldrons which hung over fires in the open air and, when the sun stood directly overhead, the captain of the female soldiers came to us and informed us that now we must go and pay our respects to the village chief whose grand ceremonial hut lay a little way out of the village. So we straightened our togas and combed our fingers through our hairs. But the Count would not come of his own free will so the captain had to poke him with the butt of her musket until he crept reluctantly out to join us.

Oh, what a bedraggled demiurge he was! His black tights were all tattered and torn, so a fringe of toe peeped out at the foot of each, and his prick hung out of the aperture as limp and woebegone as a deflated balloon. He limped like an eagle with a broken wing. Poor, yellow tiger! And yet he had ridden out his tempest in triumph the previous night and even as we walked through the village, he took on, as if he summoned up all his flagging courage to do so, a few shreds of enigmatic charisma, enough to fling back his head proudly, as if, perhaps, invigorated by the high, brazen clamour of the trumpets which accompanied us.

The path climbed steeply through the vaulted architraves of the palms which sprang straight up to the sky in soaring, prodigious, bluish-greyish columns towards the tasselled parasols of emerald feathers which formed the capitals of this vegetable cathedral. A muted solemnity governed the tread of our guards. They changed their music to a more mournful key and played what was almost a lament and when we came to a waterfall, everyone fell on their faces to worship it. Beyond this waterfall was a cave in a rock face, with its entrance curtained in the printed cotton that covered us. The soldiers prostrated themselves again so we knew this was where the chief lived and also that his people held him in religious awe. The Count had turned pale as if all the blood had been drained from his body but still he held his ground with something of his old, defiant spirit. The brass and the kettledrums fell silent but we could hear the liquid music of the waterfall and the crackling of the wood that burned under a great pot outside the cave.

When I looked behind me, I saw the entire village had followed us, and in the arborescent silence we were the only men left standing up for everyone else crouched with their faces deep in grass or flat on earth. The presence of a hundred silent people filled the green twilight with a sacral quietude that made me uneasy. And then a sensuous parade of the chief's wives and concubines came from the cave without drawing the curtains apart so we could not see what lay beyond them. Intensely black and perfectly naked, these women wore plumes of ostrich in their hair and arranged themselves around the entrance to the cave in a frame of submissive adoration. Many bore the bleeding marks of gigantic bites in their breasts and buttocks. Some had a nipple missing, most were minus one or several toes and fingers. One girl had a ruby set in the socket in place of a lost eyeball and some wore false teeth carved in strange shapes out of the tusks of elephants. Yet all had been beautiful and their various disfigurements lent them an exquisite pathos. After them came a number of eunuchs and then the royal castrater, the royal barber and several other barbarous officials, until the whole court was displayed before us, lined up before the cave as if they were posing for a group photograph.

The drums now began to play again, a dismal throbbing like the palpitation of a dying heart. The tribe lay still on their faces but two of the royal wives crawled forward and at last drew back the curtains as the drums rolled and the trumpets suddenly whined. And we saw him. The chief.

He sat on a throne of bones on a dais of bones which, as we watched, rolled ponderously forward on four wheels made of skulls, wheels that crushed the hands of half a dozen concubines before it came to a halt. Seated, he was six and a half feet high. He was far, far blacker than the blackest night. He was a very sacred and very monstrous idol.

On his head he wore a ceremonial wig consisting of three thick fringes arranged in concentric rings. That next to the skin of his head was brown; the middle one was crimson; and the outside fringe was of bright gold, like a diadem. Through this arresting chevelure was wound a chain of mixed carbuncles and round his neck, virtually clothing the upper part of his body, were a great many golden chains with pendants, charms and skulls of babies dangling from them. His face was brilliantly painted with four discs on either cheek, each one rimmed with white and coloured inside yellow, green, blue and red. A brown, white-rimmed eye was painted on his forehead between and above his own eyes. He carried the thigh-bone of a giant for a sceptre, painted scarlet and once again decorated with inlay and feathers. He wore the pelt of a tiger wrapped round his middle and the root-like toes which protruded from his sandals were stuck with rings containing gems of amazing size and peerless water, as were his hands, which were so heavily be-ringed they looked as if they were mailed with jewels. His appalling face suggested more than Aztec horrors and, now the curtain was open, I could see that the cave behind him was an arcade of human skeletons.

'Welcome to the regions of the noble children of the sun!' he said in a cavernous voice that sank to thrilling depths, while the drums pounded on and on. But he did not speak to Lafleur and me; he addressed himself only to the Count.

'You are my only destination,' replied the Count. 'You altered my compass so that it would point only to you, my hypocritical shadow, my double, my brother.'

Then I saw this dreadful chieftain was indeed the black pimp who was now about to avenge his lover's murder, for such was the Count's desire he should be and do so. The chieftain rose from his throne, stepped from his dais on to a footstool of grovelling concubines and took the Count into the warmest, most passionate embrace. But he concluded it by striking the Count such a heavy blow that he reeled out of the great black arms and fell to the ground. The chief set one foot on the Count's chest in the attitude of a successful hunter and spoke, it seemed, to the sky above us, which showed in patches of azure electricity through the vivid fronds of the palms.

'The customs of my country are as barbarous as the propriety with which they are executed. For example, not one of those delightful children who seem, each one, to have stepped straight off the pen of Jean-Jacques Rousseau but has not, since he put forth his first milk teeth, dined daily off a grilled rump, or roasted shoulder, a stew, a fricassée, or else a hash of human meat. To this usually most abhorred of comestibles they owe the brightness of their eyes, the strength of their limbs, the marvellous gloss of health on their skins, their longevity and a virility as great as it is discreetly practised, since this diet is certain to triple the libidinal capacities, as my wives and concubines can willingly testify. But we have learned to let circumspection sharpen our pleasures and we conduct the most loathsome profligacy with no public show of indecency at all.

'How do I rule my little kingdom? With absolute severity. Only if a king is utterly ruthless, only if he hardens his heart to the temper of the most intransigent metal, will he maintain his rule. I am a ruler both secular and divine. I hedge about my whims, which I term my "laws", with an awesome incomprehensibility of superstitious fears. The least rebellious thought rising weed-like in my subjects' hearts is instantly transmitted to me by my espionage system of telepaths whose minds are magic mirrors and reflect not only faces but thoughts. Those incipient rebels and their entire families are condemned for the most fleeting wish alone for we do not give them time to act. They are forthwith shipped directly to the army catering staff and boiled down to nourishing soups which contribute towards the excellent, indeed, prolific physique of my army while my punishments extend even towards that insubstantial part of themselves, their souls, for I encourage a belief in the soul in order to terrify them better. The least rebellious inclination rising weed-like condemns the subject and his seed to damnation for three generations. So it behoves them to tend their gardens well and only let the lilies of obedience grow there!'

The Count now rose painfully to his feet but the chieftain instantly kicked him back into a kneeling position and the Count knelt at his feet for the rest of the interview.

'Why, you may ask, have I built my army out of women since they are often held to be the gentler sex? Gentlemen, if you rid your hearts of prejudice and examine the bases of the traditional notions of the figure of the female, you will find you have founded them all on the remote figure you thought you glimpsed, once, in your earliest childhood, bending over you with an offering of warm, sugared milk, crooning a soft lullaby while, by her haloed presence, she kept away the snakes that writhed beneath the bed. Tear this notion of the mother from your hearts. Vengeful as nature herself, she loves her children only in order to devour them better and if she herself rips her own veils of self-deceit, Mother perceives in herself untold abysses of cruelty as subtle as it is refined. Not one of my callipygian soldiery but has not earned her rank by devouring alive, first gnawing limb from limb and sucking the marrow from its bones, her first-born child. So she earns her colours. To a woman, they are absolutely ruthless. They have passed far beyond all human feeling.'

The army, as one woman, lifted its head and smiled to hear this tribute so I guessed they were still capable of responding to flattery.

'And, since my early researches soon showed me that the extent of a woman's feelings was directly related to her capacity for feeling during the sexual act, I and my surgeons take the precaution of

brutally excising the clitoris of every girl child born to the tribe as soon
as she reaches puberty. And also those of my wives and concubines
who have been brought from other tribes where this practice is
not observed. Therefore I am proud to say that not a single one of my
harem or, indeed, any of the tribe of more than Roman mothers you
see before you, has ever experienced the most fleeting ecstasy, or
even the slightest pleasure, while in my arms or in the arms of any
of my subjects. So our womenfolk are entirely cold and respond only
to cruelty and abuse.'

At that there was a rumbling murmur of approbation from all the
men and many broke into spontaneous applause. The soldiers jumped
at once and ran among the ranks of the tribe, beating them with the
flats of their swords until they were quiet.

'In these regions, you may observe Man in his constitutionally
vicious, instinctively evil and studiously ferocious form – in a word, in
the closest possible harmony with the natural world. I am, in my
hard-hearted way, most passionately in love with harmony. As an
emblem of harmony, I would take the storm that rent your ship last
night, resolving that poignant little fabrication of the human hand to
constituents in harmony with this world as it would be without man –
that is, natural. I would take the lion rending the lamb as an emblem.
In a word, I would take all images of apparent destruction – and mark
how I use the word, "apparent", for, in essence, nothing can be created
or destroyed. My notion of harmony, then, is a perpetual, convulsive
statis.

'I am happy only in that I am a monster.'

Now, when I thought about it, I knew that this man-eating hiero-
phant who recounted his proclivities to us with such pompous arro-
gance could not possibly be the black pimp of New Orleans; he was
only his living image. But the Count identified him rightly in that
this princeling of the anthropophagi was yet another demiurge and the
Lithuanian aristocrat and the savage were twinned in that both
were storm-troopers of the world itself. The world, that is, of earthquake and cataclysm, cyclone and devastation; the violent matrix,
the real world of unmastered, unmasterable physical stress that is
entirely inimical to man because of its indifference. Ocean, forest,
mountain, weather – these are the inflexible institutions of that world
of unquestionable reality which is so far removed from the social
institutions which make up our own world that we men must always,
whatever our difference, conspire to ignore them. For otherwise we
would be forced to acknowledge our incomparable insignificance

and the insignificance of those desires that might be the pyrotechnic tigers of our world and yet, under the cold moon and the frigid round dance of the unspeakably alien planets, are nothing but toy animals cut from coloured paper.

All this ran through my mind as the monster harangued the Count and Lafleur's little hand reached out and grasped hold of mine for comfort.

'Nothing in our traditions suggests history. I have been very careful to suppress history for my subjects might learn lessons from the deaths of kings. I burned all their former idols as soon as I came to power and instituted a comprehensive monotheism with myself as its object. I allowed the past to exist as a series of rituals concerning the nature of my omnipotent godhead. I am a lesson, a model, the perfect type of king and of government. I am far more than the sum of my parts.'

And now he smiled gently at the Count; and, to my amazement, I saw that he reflected the Count's face perfectly, as if his own face were only a pool of dark water, and the paintings upon it a few blossoms floating on the surface.

'In a certain brothel in the city of New Orleans, once, I saw you strangle a prostitute solely to augment your own erotic ecstasy, my dear Count. Since that time, I have pursued you diligently across space and time. You excited my curiosity. It seemed I might be able to crown my own atrocities by making my brother in atrocity my victim. That I might, as it were, immolate myself, to see how I should bear it.

'I wish, you understand, to see how I would suffer.

'I have a great deal of empirical curiosity. A Jesuit in his black cassock once came to my tribe and lived among us for a year. When he learned my manners, he rebuked me so sternly, in the name of pity, that first I had him crucified – for he professed to admire so much this form of torture – and, while he was still quivering on the tree, I cut out his heart with my own hands, to see if such a professedly compassionate an organ had a different structure from the common kind of heart. But no! it did not.

'Now I should like to see if we have a heart at all, dear Count. Are we ourselves so much the physical slaves of nature?

'And I wish to see if I can suffer, like any other man. And then I want to learn the savour of my flesh. I wish to taste myself. For you must know I am a great gourmet.

'Bind him.'

Two female officers pounced on the Count and tied his wrists together with cords. From the ranks of the chief's retinue a plump, giggling being wearing only a white chef's cap and a girdle hung with ladles stepped forward with a jar of salt in one hand and a nosegay of potherbs in the other. He lavishly seasoned the water that now bubbled in the cauldron while the Count began to laugh softly.

'Don't you think I'm too old and tough and starveling to make a savoury dish?'

'I thought of that,' said the cannibal. 'That is why I'm going to boil you up for soup.'

The soldiers slit the Count's tights with the points of their swords so they fell like opening petals from his white, scrawny legs. They slit his waistcoat and it fell. Naked, his tall, skeletal form and great mane of iron grey hair were still clothed in that strange, intangible cloak of exalted loneliness. He was a king whose pride was all the greater because he lacked a country. The chef flung a string of onions into the pot, thoughtfully stirred in more salt, stirred and sipped the stock from his ladle. He nodded. The lady soldiers marched the Count between them to the fire, took firm hold each one of an elbow, lifted him bodily and plunged him feet first into the water, so that his head stuck over the rim. But his face did not change expression as it began to grow rosy. And he endured in perfect silence for far longer than I would have thought possible.

And then, when he was red as a lobster, he began to laugh with joy – pure joy.

'Lafleur!' he called from the pot. 'Lafleur! I am in pain! I've learned to name my pain! Lafleur –'

And, using the very last of his strength, he rose up out of the cauldron in an upward surging leap, as of a fully liberated man.

But when he reached his apex his heart must have burst for his mouth sagged, his eyes started, blood leaked out of his nostrils and he fell back with a splash that scalded half the court with broth. This time, his head disappeared entirely beneath the rim of the stew pot and presently a delicious steam began to drift from the simmering concoction, so that the entire audience licked its lips in unison. At that, the chef clapped a lid on him.

I was touched to see Lafleur's bandages were soaking up a trickle of tears but then I realized he and I were also to feature as *entremets* for the ensuing feast. The chef ordered a team of apprentices to prepare long beds of glowing charcoal and himself busily began to grease a gridiron.

'Skin the smallest rabbit first,' commanded the chieftain negligently and he did not bother to season us first with verbiage since we were only so much meat to him.

Two privates seized Lafleur's shoulders and dragged him away from me. They cut off his robe, although he struggled, and I saw, not the lean torso of a boy but the gleaming, curvilinear magnificence of a golden woman whose flesh seemed composed of the sunlight that touched it far more kindly than the black hands of the fiendish infantry did. I recognized her even before they sheared away the bandages and showed no noseless, ulcerated, disfigured face but the face of Albertina herself.

Never before, in all my life, had I performed a heroic action.

I acted instantly, without thought. I grasped the knife of one of my own guards and the musket of the other. I stabbed them both in their bellies and then I stabbed the women who were preparing her for the pot. I flung away my knife and embraced her with one arm while, with the other, I pointed the musket at the chieftain's head and pulled the trigger.

The antique bullet, larger than a grape, pierced the painted eye in the centre of his forehead.

A great spurt of blood sprang out as from an unstoppered tap in such a great arc that it drenched us. He must have died instantaneously but some spasm of muscle jerked him to his feet. The juggernaut rose up on his car and stood there, swaying, a fountain of blood, while the crowd moaned and shivered as if at an eclipse. Somehow his uncoordinated shuddering freed the wheels of his trolley and, at first slowly, it began to move, for there was a downward inclination to the earth. And still the corpse stayed upright, as if rigor mortis had set in straight away. And still it jetted blood, as if his arteries were inexhaustible. So it started on a headlong career, crushing wives and eunuchs and those of his tribe who, maddened at the sight, out of despair or hysteria at the sudden extinction of their autocratic comet, now flung themselves under the wheels of its chariot with maenad shrieks.

Bouncing over a path of flesh, bearing a tottering tower, the car's mad career took it to the bank of the river and there it plunged into a foaming torrent that carried it to the edge of the waterfall within seconds. There car parted company with rider for the water flung them both high up into the air and they swept separately over the lip of the cascade, to dash to pieces on the rocks below.

Albertina and I kissed.

The soldiers should have killed us, then, for then we should have been perfectly happy. But now the utmost confusion reigned among them for the pole of their world was gone. Their wives, concubines and eunuchs tore their hair and wailed for they could think of nothing else to do but set out at once on the elaborate ritual of mourning. The necromancers had drawn a circle and were standing inside it, attempting to summon back the chieftain's spirit; while the lady general called a common drill so, as the populace ran this way and that, lamenting, the soldiers ceremoniously formed fours and shifted their blunderbusses from one shoulder to the other with a discipline which, in other circumstances, might have been almost inspiring to watch, since it demonstrated a devotion to duty carried far beyond the point of absurdity. But I was kissing Albertina and so I did not watch them, although I could tell by the heavy odour on the air that the Count had almost finished cooking. Albertina stirred in my arms.

'I must pay him my last respects,' she said. 'We travelled a long way together. And, after all, I admired him.'

Naked as a dream, she lifted the lid of the pot and stirred the scum that had risen with the bay leaves to the surface.

'And I can't deny he was a worthy adversary. His slightest gesture created the void he presupposed.'

She clapped back the lid and with businesslike precision started to undress the corpse of one of the female soldiers. When she had dressed herself up in dark blue apron and chocolate brown cloak, she made an armful of as many weapons as she could and said to me purposefully:

'Come!'

Nobody tried to stop us. Soon even the noises of the convulsive wake were silenced by the massive, viridian door of the forest that we closed behind us.

7. Lost in Nebulous Time

There was once a young man named Desiderio who set out upon a journey and very soon lost himself completely. When he thought he had reached his destination, it turned out to be only the beginning of another journey infinitely more hazardous than the first for now she smiled a little and told me that we were quite outside the formal rules of time and place and, in fact, had been so since I met her in her disguise. We moved through the landscape of Nebulous Time her father had brought into being but could no longer control because the sets of samples were buried under a mountain. She appeared abstracted and remote.

At first the landscape looked only like that of any tropical forest, though this in itself was marvellous enough to me. Nothing I had seen in the low-lying, poorly forested temperate zones that bore me had prepared me for the supernal and tremendous energy of the rearing colonnades of palm which concluded in an interwoven roof of limbs and lianas high above our heads. I would have experienced a green panic there, among those giant forms far older than even my antique race if Albertina had not walked beside me, picking us a safe path as delicately as a cat through undergrowth where strange, flesh-eating flowers writhed as if in perturbed slumber for this forest was also cannibal and full of perils.

All the plants distilled poisons. This essential hostility was not directed at us or at any comer; the forest was helplessly, motivelessly malign. The blossoms on the creepers snapped their teeth at nothing or something, dragonfly or snake or hushed breeze, with an objective spontaneity. They could not help but be inimical. The leaves let through only a greenish dazzle and a lonely silence pressed against our ears like fur for the trees grew too close together for birds to fly or sing. Heavily armed, Albertina walked with the proud defiance of an Empress of the Exotic.

'My Albertina, how could you possibly have been both Lafleur and the Madame at the same time?'

'Nothing simpler,' she replied. She had the slightest trace of an unfamiliar accent and she chose her words and organized her sentences with the excessive pedantry of one who uses a second language perfectly, though I never found out exactly what her first tongue had been. But her mother tongue, or the tongue of her mother, was Chinese.

'I projected myself upon the available flesh of the Madame. After all, was it not put out for hire? Lafleur in the stable, among the whickering horses, projected himself, myself, into the Bestial Room, myself in the bodily clothing of the Madame. She was a real but ephemeral show. Under the influence of intense longing, the spirit – or, let us even say, the soul – of the sufferer can create a double which joins the absent beloved while the original template goes about its everyday business. Oh, Desiderio! never underestimate the power of that desire for which you are named! One night, Yang Yu-chi shot what he thought was a wild ox and his arrow pierced a rock up to the feathering because of his passionate conviction the rock lived.'

I did not mind her lecturing me because she was so beautiful. I told her that, at that moment, I desired her with the greatest imaginable intensity but she only said she had been given her orders and was afraid that we must wait.

'Let us be amorous but also mysterious,' she said, quoting one of her selves with so much ironic grace that I was charmed enough to shrug away my disappointment and resign myself to walking through the wood beside her. Presently she shot a small, rabbit-like animal as it sat on a boulder washing its face with its paw and when we came to a clearing as the shadows deepened into those of evening, I skinned it while she lit a fire with the tinder box she found in the soldier's girdle and then cooked supper. After we ate, we sat together watching the red embers dissolve and we talked.

'Yes; the Count was dangerous. I was keeping him under the closest surveillance. It was my most important mission of the whole war. I would have taken him to my father's castle if I could, to enlist him in our campaign for he was a man of great power though he was sometimes a little ludicrous because the real world fell so far short of his desires. But he did what he could to bring it up to his own level, even if his will exceeded his self-knowledge. And so he invented those macabre clowns, the Pirates of Death.

'What was chilling, even appalling, in the Count's rapacity was its purely cerebral quality. He was the most metaphysical of libertines. If he had passions, they were as lucid and intellectual as those of a geometrician. He approached the flesh in the manner of one about to give the proof of a theorem and, however exiguous those passions seemed to him, they were never unpremeditated. He acted the tyrant to his passions. However convulsive the grand guignol in his bed, he had always planned it well beforehand and rehearsed it so often in his brain that his performance perfectly simulated an improvisation. His desire became authentic because it was so absolutely synthetic.

'Yet it remained only a simulation. He may have jetted his sperm in positive torrents but he never released any energy. Instead, he released a force that was the opposite of energy, a devitalizing force quite unlike – though just as powerful as – the kind of electricity which naturally flows between a man and a woman during the sexual act.

(She gently took my hand away from her breast and murmured in parenthesis: 'Not yet.')

'Yet his performance was remarkable. In bed, one could almost have believed the Count was galvanized by an external dynamo. This galvanic mover was his will. And, indeed, his fatal error was to mistake his will for his desire –'

I interrupted her with a certain irritation.

'But how is one to distinguish between the will and a desire?'

'Desire can never be coerced,' said Albertina with the crispness of a pedagogue even though, at that moment, she was coercing mine. She immediately resumed her discourse.

'– and so he willed his own desires.'

I interrupted her again.

'How was it he never found out you were a woman?'

'Because he only ever took me backwardly, i.e. *in anum*,' she explained patiently. 'And, besides, his lusts always blinded him completely to anything but his own sensations.'

Then she took up her thread again.

'His self-regarding "I" willed himself to become a monster. This detached, external yet internal "I" was both his dramatist and his audience. First, he chose to believe he was possessed by demons. Next, he chose to believe he had become a demon. He even designed himself a costume for the role – those gap-fronted tights! That vest of skin! When he reached a final reconciliation with the projective other who was his self, that icon of his own destructive potential, the abominable black, he had merely perfected that self-regarding diabolism which crushed and flattened the world as he passed through it, like an existential version of the cannibal chief's chariot. But his insistence on the authority of his own autonomy made him at once the tyrant and the victim of matter, for he was dependent on the notion that matter was submissive to him.

'So, when he first felt pain, he died of shock. And yet he died a happy man, for those who inflict suffering are always most curious about the nature of suffering.

'As soon as I took service with him, I realized I must abandon my plan of enlisting him for I soon realized he would never serve any master but himself. However, if he had wanted to, or willed it, he could have flattened my father's castle by merely breathing on it and burst all the test tubes only with laughing at them. After that, I travelled with him to keep him in a kind of quarantine.'

'At first, I thought he was your father, the Doctor.'

'My father?' she cried in astonishment and laughed very musically for a long time. 'But at first we thought he was the Minister! Even after I met the Minister, I thought it might be possible. Both of them had such earth-shaking treads.'

'When did you cease to regard me as an enemy agent?'

'As soon as my father verified you were in love with me,' she said, as though it were obvious.

Night had completed itself and lesser lights, eyes of snakes and effluvia of fireflies, spangled the black velvet surfaces around us but the eyes of Albertina shone continually, like unquenchable suns. Her eyes were an unutterably lambent brown and the shape of tears laid on their sides. But shape and colour were not the primary quality of these unprecedented eyes; that was the scandalous cry of passion ringing out clamorously from their depths. Her eyes were the voice of the black swan; her eyes confounded all the senses and sleep nor death cannot silence nor extinguish them. Only, they are lightly veiled with incandescent dust.

During the first part of the night, she slept while I kept watch for wild beasts. She watched over me all the second part of the night and so we continued to arrange our rests during the remainder of the journey though days and nights soon resolved together and we had no notion of how much time had passed, or even if any at all of the cloudy stuff had drifted away before the great rain forests thinned out a little. Then we came to a gentler, more feminine country full of jewelled birds with faces of young girls and oviparous trees, where there was nothing that was not marvellous.

'Because all this country exists only in Nebulous Time, I haven't the least idea what might happen,' she said. 'Now the Professor and his sets of samples are gone, my father cannot structure anything until he makes new models. And desires must take whatever form they please, for the time being. Who knows what we shall find here?

'If his experiment is a failure, we shall, of course, find nothing.'

'Why is that?'

'Because the undifferentiated mass desire was not strong enough to perpetuate its own forms.' When she saw I did not understand her, she grudgingly amplified: 'It would mean that the castle is not yet generating enough eroto-energy.'

I did not understand her but I nodded, to save face.

'Anyway, we must watch the sky by day and keep a fire burning at night and then one day we may make contact with one of my father's aerial patrols.'

'Has he extended the boundaries of the war so far?'

'Oh, no,' she said. 'But he keeps most deserted places under continuous air reconnaissance to discover what, if anything, is peopling the emptiness.'

All this sounded like *folie de grandeur* to me but I was content to leave my fate in her hands, now that I had found her, and we went on through a dangerous wonderland.

We soon learned to identify the grey-green shrubs we called 'pain trees' because of the invisible patches scattered over their leaves and bark that stung us when we touched them and left great areas of scarlet inflammation on our skins that irritated us for a long time. But the trees whose trunks were scaled like fish did not harm us, though they stank horribly when the sun was high, unlike the lucidly fragrant white gardenias that wept such hard tears of perfumed gum that I threaded some of them into a necklace of scented amber and gave it to Albertina. Often we walked through intoxicating odoriferous copses composed only of incense trees and we found ourselves in groves of a strange, tall plant which must have been some variety of cactus for its flesh, though soft and white as snow, was formed all over into round bosses tipped with red knobs. When we put our mouths to these nipples we found ourselves drinking sweet milk and were refreshed. These luscious cacti grew all together in tracts of many hundreds at a time and if the country had shown any signs of being inhabited we would have thought that they were farmed in enormous, free-form fields. But we saw no sign of man at all, though we sometimes found the marks of hoofprints of wild horses.

Creeping along the ground and wreathed around branches was an auriculate morning glory with purple ears where the blossoms should have been and often we heard the singing of flowers we never saw. A certain bush with speckled plumage laid clutches of six or seven small brown eggs at a time, eggs the size of pullet's eggs, in the sandy hollows at its roots. When the bush was laying, it shuddered and clucked; then sighed. In this forest, it seemed that nature had absolved her creations from an adherence to the formal divisions so biology and botany were quite overthrown and the only animals we saw, green-fleshed, marsupial, one-eyed, crawling things, seemed more an ambulant vegetable than anything else. Roasted on a spit, they tasted like barbecued celery.

As far as I can remember, we had been about three days in this *terra nebulosa* before we came to the strangest of all the trees. It grew by itself on the crown of a low hill, and though it was firmly rooted into the earth by four, quivering legs and a massive trunk topped with branches resembling those of a European oak sprang from its neck, beneath the trunk and above the legs was the skeleton of a horse with its entrails visible. A green sap pulsed and throbbed through the entrails, emitting as it did so a hum like that of a hive of happy bees. The first evidence of the hand of man we had seen since we entered the forest was pinned to the branches of this equine tree. It was decorated with ornaments of wrought iron which jangled together in the wind; with what seemed to be amulets in the shape of horseshoes; and on a prominent branch, a very large longbow abruptly broken in half. Every available spot on the trunk was crowded with votive tablets and inscriptions carved in a brusque, cuneiform script, and here and there votive nails were hammered in while little switches of horsehair were tied to all the twigs in neat bows. And the springy turf around the tree was deeply crusted with droppings of horses and indented with the marks of hooves.

We stood on the hill beside the buzzing, bi-partite thing, half horse, half tree, and looked down on the lyrical contours of a Theocritan valley that opened out before us in rich, unfenced fields of ripe corn that rippled under the soft wind. Albertina pointed to them at the very same moment I saw the series of magnificent forms break the cover of the wheatfield and come towards us, moving as soundlessly on the green carpet underfoot as horses in a dream, though only their bodies were those of horses for they were centaurs.

There were four of them, one bay, one black, a dappled grey and one all unspotted white, but their imposing torsos were mostly gleaming bronze though it seemed, from a distance, almost as if spiders had woven webs all round their shoulders for they were covered with mazy decorations like hug-me-tights of lace. The hair they all wore falling straight down their backs accorded to their horse-like colouring, russet, black or white, but their features were cast in the sternest, most autocratic mould of pure classicism. Their long noses were so straight you could have rolled a ball of mercury down them and their lips were set in austere, magisterial folds. All were clean shaven. They wore their genitalia set at the base of the belly, as on a man; because they were animals, they were without embarrassment but, because they were also men, even if they did not know it, they were proud. And, as they trotted towards us, their arms folded on their breasts, the light of a setting sun glittered upon them so they looked like Greek masterpieces, born in a time when gods walked among us. However, they did not believe they were gods; they believed they walked a constant tightrope above damnation.

As they came closer, I saw they were entirely naked for what I had taken for clothing was the most intricate tattoo work I have ever seen. These tattoos were designed as a whole and covered the back and both arms down as far as the forearms; and the middle of the chest, the upper abdomen and the throat and face were all left bare on the males though the womenfolk were tattooed all over, even their faces, in order to cause them more suffering, for they believed women were born only to suffer. The colours were most subtly woven together and the palette had the aesthetic advantages of limitation for it consisted of only a bluish black, a light blue and a burning red. The designs were curvilinear, swirling pictures of horse gods and horse demons wreathed in flowers, heads of corn, and stylized representations of the mammiform cacti, worked into the skin in a decorative fashion that recalled pictures in embroidery.

When they reached the hill, they turned their faces towards the tree and three times uttered, in unison, a singularly piercing neigh, while each dropped a turd. Then the bay, in the most thrilling baritone I have ever heard, began a sacerdotal song or hieratic chant something in the style of the chants of orthodox Jewry, though with the addition of a great deal of dramatic mime. It was the hour when the Sacred Stallion in his fiery form, the Sun Horse, entered the Celestial Stable and closed the bars on himself for the night and the bay was giving thanks for the day's ending, because, in their theology, every event in the physical world depended solely on the ongoing mercy of the Sacred Stallion and on his congregation's ongoing atonement for the unmentionable sin at the dawn of time that recurred inexorably every year. But I did not know that then. The bay used his voice like a musical instrument and, since I did not understand their language, I thought it was a wordless song. The other centaurs lent their voices at intervals in a magnificently polyphonic counterpoint and also beat their hooves on the turf to provide rhythm. It was stupendously impressive.

When the bay finished, he bowed his head to show his orisons were over. His black mane and tail were grizzled and his face showed the marks of age in a weathering that added to its heroic beauty. Then he spoke to Albertina and myself in a sonorous sequence of deep, rumbling sounds.

But we could not understand a single word and that, I realized when I learned a little of their speech, was because it possessed neither grammar nor vocabulary. It was only a play of sounds. One needed a sharp ear and a keen intuition to make head or tail of it and it seemed to have grown naturally out of the singing of the scriptures, which they held to be vital to their continued existence.

When he saw our perplexity, the bay shrugged and indicated by gesture we should throw down our weapons. When we had done so, he gestured us to mount the dappled grey and the black. I demurred in pantomime, mimicking our unworthiness to ride them and at that he smiled, and told us wordlessly that, even though we were unworthy, we must ride just the same. Only much later, when I learned we had ridden two of the princes of their Church, did I realize how privileged we had been for the black was the Smith and the dappled grey the Scrivener and these were posts the equivalent of cardinals. Each centaur picked one of us up in his brawny arms and swung us up behind him on to his broad back as easily as if we had been children. Although I should not think they had ever carried passengers before, they moved at a stately walk, though less out of consideration for our precarious seats than that they never strolled or ambled but always only processed. We rode through the sea of corn to the cluster of homesteads that lay, half-smothered in vines and flowers, beyond the fields. And there they gently put us down in a kind of agora or meeting place, in the centre of which was a very large wooden rostrum with a brass trumpet hanging from its rail. The bay put his trumpet to his lips and blew.

The centaurs lived in enormous stables fashioned from the trunks of trees, with deep eaves of thatch, a style of architecture with a Virgilian rusticity for it had the severe, meditative quality of classicism and yet was executed in wood and straw. The lofty proportions of these stables were dictated by the size of our hosts; a half-grown centaur, part yearling, part adolescent, was already a whole head taller than I so the doors all had wooden archways more than fifteen feet high and ten feet broad, at least. It was the hour of the evening meal when we arrived and woodsmoke drifted into the fading sky from various holes in the roofs but, as soon as the bay sounded the horn, every inhabitant of the place came trotting from his house until we were surrounded by a throng of the fabulous creatures, inquisitively snuffing the air that blew about us, arching their necks and blowing thoughtfully through their nostrils for, though they were men, they had all the mannerisms of horses.

They thought that, since they had found us on the Holy Hill, we too must be holy in spite of our unprepossessing appearance.

If they had not decided we were holy, they would have trampled us to death.

Though they were men, they did not know what a man was and believed themselves to be a degenerate variety of the horse they worshipped.

Herds of wild horses often came to trample down their plantations of grain and their cacti dairies, to plunge through the townships like a hooved river in full spate and to mount the centaurs' womenfolk, if they found them. They believed the Sacred Stallion housed the souls of the dead in the wild horses and called their depredations the Visitation of the Spirits. They followed them with weeks of fasting, of the self-mortification to which they were addicted and to the recital of the part of their equine scripture which celebrated the creation of the first principle, the mystic essence of horse, the Sacred Stallion, from a fusion of fire and air in the upper atmosphere. Even before I understood their language, I found myself profoundly moved to hear the impassioned recital of their mythic past, which only the males of a certain caste were allowed to perform. Though they all sang constantly and all their songs were hymns or psalms, sacred narrative poetry was the exclusive property of a single cantor, who to earn the right to sing it had to run with the wild horses for an entire season, an ordeal few candidates for the post survived. Then, when he reached the age of thirty, he began to study the arcane classics under the elder who alone knew them all. By his forty-fifth birthday, he had learned the complete canon and its accompanying gestures and footwork, for this poetry was both sung and danced; then he would present for the first time in public, in the earth-floored agora, the song of the horse who penetrated to the shades to retrieve his dead friend.

They prized fidelity above all other virtues. An unfaithful wife was flayed alive and her hide given to her husband to cover his next marriage bed, a mute deterrent to his new bride to keep from straying, while her lover was castrated and forced to eat his own penis, uncooked.

Since they all had the most profound horror of meat, they termed this method of execution 'Death by Nausea'. However, this rigorous puritanism did not prevent every male in the village from raping Albertina on the night we arrived and their organs were so prodigious, their virility so unmentionable, that she very nearly died. While, as for me, they forced on me the caresses of all their females for they had no notion of humanity in spite of their extraordinary nobility of spirit. Because they were far more magnificent than man, they did not know what a man was. They did not have a word for shame and nothing human was alien to them because they were alien to everything human.

These hippolators believed their god revealed himself to them in the droppings excreted by the horse part of themselves since this manifested the purest essence of their equine natures, and it was quite as logical an idol as a loaf of bread or a glass of wine, though the centaurs had too much good sense to descend to coprophily. The community was governed by a spiritual junta comprising the Cantor, the repository and interpreter of the Gospel; the Scrivener; the Smith; and the Tattoo-master. It went on four legs, as was only natural.

The centaurs did not give one another personal names for they felt themselves all undifferentiated aspects of a universal will to become a horse. So these cardinals were referred to in common speech by the symbols of their arts. The Cantor was called Song, though never to his face; the Tattoo-master Awl, Gouge or Aspiring Line; the Smith Red Hot Nail and the Scrivener, Horse Hair Writing Brush. But this terminology was necessary not because the individuals needed names but because the tasks they performed distinguished them from the others, so that it was not precisely the bay who was known as Song but the idea of the Cantor which he represented. They did not have much everyday social intercourse. The women did not gossip at their work, although they always sang. Daily life was meaningless to them for all they did was done in the shadow of the continuous passion of the Sacred Stallion and only this cosmic drama was real to them. They had no vocabulary to express doubts. Nor were they able to express the notion 'death'. When the time came to identify this condition, they used for it the sounds that signified also 'birth' for death was their greatest mercy. In giving them death, the Sacred Stallion gave them an ultimate reconciliation with Him; they were reborn in the wild horses.

Music was the voice of the Sacred Stallion. Shit signified his presence among them. Their Holy Hill was a dungheap. The twice daily movement of their bowels was at once a form of prayer and a divine communion. Every aspect of their lives was impregnated by the pro-foundest religious feeling for even the little foal child whose milk teeth were not yet through was a kind of priest, or medium for the spirit, in this faith. But only the males held the secrets of these mysteries. The women were the rank and file of the devotees and had so much to do, working the fields, bearing the children, milking the cacti, making the cheese, grinding the corn, building the houses, they could spare time only to pray, beating staccato patterns of hoofbeats and uttering the shrieking neigh that meant: 'Hallelujah!' The females were ritually degraded and reviled. They bore the bloody brunt of the tattooing. They dragged whole trunks of trees to build the stables while their menfolk prayed. Yet the women were even more beautiful than the men, each one both Godiva and her mount at the same time. They walked like rivers in floods of variously coloured hair and carried their crimson holes proudly beneath tails that arched like rainbows. It was a heraldic sight to see a pair of centaurs mating.

And now, on our first evening, the setting sun cast a magic aurefac-tion on their hocks and shoulders and all those profiles off Greek vases and I felt the strange awe I had experienced in the choirs and naves of the forest, for once more we were surrounded by giant and indifferent forms. I felt myself dwindle and diminish. Soon I was nothing but a misshapen doll clumsily balanced on two stunted pins, so ill-designed and badly functioning a puff of wind would knock me over, so grace-less I walked as though with an audible grinding of rusty inner gears, so slow of foot our hosts could run me down in a flash for I might even be stupid enough to try to escape. And when I looked at Albertina, I saw that though she was still beautiful, she also had become a doll; a doll of wax, half melted at the lower part.

When the bay spoke to me, I answered him in my own tongue; then French; then the already half-forgotten language of the river people; then my faulty English; then my even scantier German. He rumbled deeply in the back of his throat, possibly in admiration of my facility for making noises, and then Albertina spoke a few phrases in, among other languages I could not even identify, Chinese and Arabic. But the bay shrugged, making a kaleidoscopic confluence of the colours on his shoulders and, gripping me tightly in his mighty fist, began a mute inspection of me, while the dappled grey investigated Albertina.

They soon discovered that our clothes came off and the sight of these flapping, detachable integuments provoked a sweet thunder of laughter among a breed used to garments embroidered in pain that fitted so intimately they came off only if a back was pared like an apple.

Kneeling down in the fashion of horses, the bay and the grey prised, poked and handled every part of our bodies, especially our forked, insubstantial, lower halves, for they had nothing to compare Old Two Legs with. Our feet, especially, were objects of the greatest wonder and, by the sonorous exclamations, clearly also of considerable surmise. When a yearling ran up with an axe, I guessed the bay planned to cut off a foot in order to take it in his hands and examine it more closely. I was interested to see he interpreted my involuntary cry as one of outraged protest and waved the hatchet away. A look of intense curiosity crossed his face while he subjected me to a fresh barrage of incomprehensible questions. But I did not know how to reply except with a few, wordless murmurs because I had not yet grasped the essentially nonverbal nature of the language and he soon abandoned all attempts to talk to me and bent over me afresh to count my toes and exclaim over my toenails, which clearly fascinated him.

As it grew darker, they brought flaming brands set in iron torches to light up the piazza and left us lying on our backs on the stage while the bay conducted vespers. The service consisted of a recital from the scriptures and prayers. The recital of their scriptures *in toto* occupied the entire year, which concluded with the death and resurrection of the Sacred Stallion at midwinter. Then forty days' mourning was succeeded by a three-day feast and the entire cycle began again. Now, by one of the temporal metastases which occurred constantly in Nebulous Time, we happened to have fallen into their hands at the very time in which they were living again the season, recurring every year in the timeless medium which regulated all their actions, when the Sacred Stallion from the depths of his compassion teaches them the art of tattooing, so that, though the sins of their father had denied them the true shape of horses, they could at least carry the shapes of horses upon their altered skins. So the lesson for today had the text: TRANSMISSION OF THE DIVINE ART NUMBER ONE. Though this was neither more nor less significant to them than any other phase in their theological dramaturgy, for all were of the utmost significance, it had certain repercussions upon the nature of the hospitality they eventually offered us. For their ritual was by no means inflexible; it could be altered and broadened to incorporate any new element they happened upon. As it incorporated the incursions of the wild horses, so eventually they modulated it in order to incorporate us. But that came later.

By its nature, the TRANSMISSION OF THE DIVINE ART NUMBER ONE was one of the less choreographic of their recitals, though the staging was sufficiently impressive. Nevertheless, it was awesome.

First of all, the assembled women began to beat a subdued rhythm with their hooves and an acolyte, a sorrel-coloured foal, ceremoniously brought on to the stage a wooden tray containing a whip, a paintbrush, a saucer full of black liquid and some kind of metal instrument I could not identify. He knelt before the bay who at first seemed sullen and impassive, adopting a statuesque pose with his arms folded. But, as the drumbeats quickened, he began to sing in that most glorious baritone and in response came the nasalized hallelujah chorus that is my strongest memory of our life among the centaurs for it greeted the dawn and foreclosed the day, every day, inevitably, and is inseparably mingled in my mind with the rich smell of fresh horse-dung.

As the music he and his congregation made grew quicker and louder, the bay's excitement began to rise. He sought after atonement and he chastised himself. He moaned and grovelled and quarrelled with himself until, seizing the whip, he beat his own flanks until the blood came. When they saw the blood, some of the women went off into strange, lonely ecstasies. Puffs of blue flame came out of their holes and they reared, threshed about with their hooves and whinnied convulsively. But when the Cantor dropped his whip and sank to the ground, covering his face, in an attitude of complete abnegation, everyone grew tremulously silent and I saw that even the grown males were weeping.

Now a second actor entered the spectacle and engaged him in a duet. The white centaur stepped forward. The persistent beat changed to almost a waltz rhythm. The white was a seductive tenor and, though I only understood the meaning through the tones of the sound itself, I knew he was singing of forgiveness and the baritone was beseeching him to be allowed to suffer more. But the mercy of the tenor was inexorable. At last he took from the tray the paintbrush and the metal object, which I saw was some kind of gouge, parted the bay's tributaries of hair to reveal his back, dipped the brush in the saucer of ink and made a number of obviously highly stylized passes over the exposed flesh of the kneeling bay, who responded by throwing such a contagious ecstasy that he took most of his audience with him and, in a clamour of tears, abandoned laughter and signs everywhere of the most delirious joy, the service ended with an explosive shedding of all the dung in every bowel present, Albertina's and mine excepted.

After the god had visited them, the women went to fetch brooms and wooden buckets from their stables and swept up all the manure into heaping piles, which they used to fertilize their fields, for they wasted nothing. While the women tidied up by the light of the torches, the Cantor and the Tattoo-master turned their attention back to us. Now they concentrated their fingerings upon our private parts and seemed reassured by the familiar shapes although they were lodged between such unfamiliar legs. The white centaur thoughtfully pushed three fingers bunched together up Albertina's vagina and listened to her scream judiciously, with his head on one side. He lowered his muzzle and began to sniff her comprehensively. His working nostrils travelled over every inch of her skin and occasionally he licked her, to let his palate verify the evidence collected by his nose. His warm breath and rough tongue tickled her; she began to laugh and, when the bay followed suit and started to snuffle over me, soon I was laughing too, though it was a laughter close to hysteria.

These two elders raised their heads and engaged in a baying colloquy which ended in the following manner. We were both carried bodily to the bay's stable and laid down on the table from which his wife hastily cleared the supper dishes when they brought us in. The rest of the villagers followed us, so there was a great crowd, every male, female and infant in the village gathered in the enormous room. When I tried to scramble over the great board of oak to reach her and protect her, the bay easily held me down with one hand. His strength was immense. Then the white spread her legs wide and investigated the aperture involuntarily offered him, clearly comparing it with the size of his tumescent organ, which was that of a horse rather than a man. Nevertheless he pulled her down to the edge of the table and in it went, after a hideous struggle.

The audience, rapt with wonderment, neighed softly and pawed the ground and then, one after the other, all the males took their turn at her. She was soon mired with blood but, after the first exclamation, she did not cry again. I struggled and bit the bay but still he would not let me go though he murmured to himself as if surprised to see evidence of a bond between two members of a species that must have seemed to him the lowest form of horse he had ever seen. They were all bathed in ruddy light and the tattoos performed *danses macabres* across their backs. None of them seemed to extract the least pleasure out of the act. They undertook it grimly, as though it were their duty.

And I could do nothing but watch and suffer with her for I knew from my own experience the pain and indignity of a rape. But the centaurs let me alone in that way, either because my offering was too narrow or else that mode of congress was unknown to them. At the back of my mind flickered a teasing image, that of a young girl trampled by horses. I could not remember when or where I had seen it, such a horrible thing; but it was the most graphic and haunting of memories and a voice in my mind, the cracked, hoarse, drunken voice of the dead peep-show proprietor, told me that I was somehow, all unknowing, the instigator of this horror. My pain and agitation increased beyond all measure.

While the males made this prolonged and terrible assault upon Albertina, the bay was organizing the females into a line and I knew I would not be left out of the savage game. But me they treated with far less severity because they respected the virile principle and reviled the female one. So my torment was intended only to humiliate their own womenfolk who one by one caressed me, as they were ordered, but only with the gentlest of fingers. I was subjected to the ministrations of twenty or thirty of the tenderest, if the most perverse, of mothers and some even bent to kiss me with mouths like wet velvet in faces covered with permanent masks of lace, so I could not help but quicken with pleasure while the bay held me down so firmly I could only moan. And this was the subtlest of tortures – that I was bathed in a series of the most exquisite sensations on the very table where they cruelly abused the flesh of the one I loved best. My nostrils were full of the mingled stench of horses, of the smoke from their pine wood torches, of the perfumed oil with which the women dressed their hair, of blood, of semen and of pain; the very air thickened and grew red. And though Albertina was the object of a rape, the males clearly did not know it was a rape. They showed neither enthusiasm nor gratification. It was only some form of ritual, another invocation of the Sacred Horse.

They had a deeply masochistic streak. They did not reserve the whip only for religion but used it continually on themselves and one another, making the slightest real or imagined fault the pretext for a beating. It was a matter of pride as to how thin one could bear one's bed of straw. They loved to feel the hot steel on their fetlocks when the priest shod them, for the Sacred Horse had taught them the art of the smith and if he had ordained them bits and bridles stuck with inward-turning spikes, they would have donned them luxuriously. The centaurs had all the virtues and defects of a heroic style.

The bay serviced Albertina last of all, while the white Tattoo-master took a turn at holding me down. Of all the rapists, the bay was most impassive. Then, in silence, they dispersed to their homes and the stable was empty but for the family of the bay.

The bay's mate, a Junoesque roan mare, put a great cauldron of water to heat on a hook over the fire and I wondered if they were going to end the evening by boiling us alive. But the bay snorted, wiped himself down with a wisp of hay, took a leather-bound book from a high shelf and sat down before the fire. The three children – a male of perhaps twelve by human reckoning, as yet unshod; a female of about fifteen, part wood nymph and part Palomino; and a foal baby who hardly knew, yet, how to tumble about on her four legs, lined up in front of him and all went down on their front legs. And then he began to hear their catechism.

The girl–female was already completely sheathed with a pattern of horses and grapes that made her look as if she were peering through a vineyard but the artist had only just begun to work on the boy and nothing more than the centrepiece of a full design, a rampant stallion, was traced in outline on his skin. He went to the Tattoo-master every morning after prayers and a little more was filled in every day so that, under our eyes, the living picture was to grow more and more emphatic the longer we lived there and we could mark the passage of time by the creeping tendrils of the work on his back. Their father asked the questions and the children made the ritual responses; they seemed to have forgotten us and I crawled across the table top to Albertina. She had lost consciousness. I took her in my arms and buried my face in her forlorn hair.

The proportions of the stable and of the beings who lived there were only just a little larger than those suited to a man but the slightness of the excessive size of everything together with the superhuman strength and flawless gravity of our hosts or captors made me feel like a child at the mercy of uncomprehending adults rather than of ogres. Even the rape had had elements of the kind of punishment said to hurt the giver more than the receiver though I do not know what they were punishing her for, unless it was for being female to a degree unprecedented among them. Now, when the roan mare looked up from tending the fire and saw me grieving over my fainting lover, she did not change mood so much as allow her essential motherliness to intensify. She came and looked at Albertina and then she spoke some low, submissive but reproachful words to her master and stroked Albertina's face with a piteous hand. I think she had meant to wash the table top with the water she was heating, for the table was now very dirty and her house was very clean, but instead she took the pan off the hook and invited me to clamber in and wash myself while she herself made a soft pad of hay, moistened it and gently wiped the blood and muck from Albertina. The centaur's saucepan made me a snugly fitting hip bath and, when I had finished, she indicated I should sit in front of the fire and dry myself while she put Albertina to bed on the straw but I saw Albertina's eyelids flutter and went to her at once.

Again the mare spoke to her husband and then to me, with the intonation of a question. I thought she must be asking me if Albertina was my mate so I repeated the sound she had made back to her in a strongly affirmative tone. She looked exceedingly surprised; and then she smiled most tenderly and let us both lie down together while she covered us up with straw and the catechism droned softly on.

The mare must have talked to her husband during the night because he came to our bed in the morning, abased himself and kissed my feet because she was my mate, therefore my property, and so he must apologize to me. Tears ran out of his eyes. He whipped himself for me. Then he went out to conduct morning service and after that I ate my breakfast with the family, sitting on a stump of wood his wife found for me while the males all sat on their haunches and ate with their hands from wooden dishes like sylvan men and the women waited until the men had finished before they took their own meal. But Albertina could not stir from her bed and only feebly sipped a mouthful or two of the milk I tried to feed her.

Their diet was one of rustic simplicity. The women ground their corn in stone querns and made flat, tortilla-like pancakes which they ate with the wild honey in which they also deliciously preserved fruit. They sometimes roasted the ears of corn on hot coals. Morning and evening, they milked the cactuses into wooden buckets, fermented the milk to make a sour but invigorating drink and also made flat, white cheeses with a sweet, bland flavour and a crumbling texture. They cultivated orchards of fruit and vegetable gardens of roots and tubers; they gathered salads in the forests and also mushrooms, which they particularly liked to eat raw, dressed with oil and vinegar. They made sweet syrup from berries but the Sacred Horse had not revealed to them the mysteries of alcohol so their religion was only a spartan, teetotal variation upon Dionysianism and their grapes went only into jellies and salad dressings. Their abstemious, vegetarian diet filled them out with iron muscle. Their teeth were white and perfect. They died only of accident and old age and old age took a long time to come to them.

But their lives were only apparently tranquil. Every day of the week and every week of the year was irradiated by the continuous divine drama unfolding in the voices of the singers and the turning of the year so they lived primarily on dramaturgical terms. This gave the women a certain dignity that would otherwise have been denied them for every one of the most insignificant household tasks, mucking out, bringing water from the spring, picking the lice from one another's manes and tails, was performed as if in a divine theatre, as if, for example, each mare was the embodiment of the archetypal Bridal Mare as she cleaned the Celestial Stable; even if the Bridal Mare was only a penitent sinner, still she was essential to the Sacred Horse's passion.

Therefore, every minute of the day, they were all, male and female alike, engrossed in weaving and embroidering the rich fabric of the very world in which they lived and, like so many Penelopes, their work was never finished. The whole point of their activity was th; t it was endless, for they unravelled their work at the end of the year and then, with the return of the sun after the shortest day, began on it again. The horse-tree on the Holy Hill was the central node of their world, for it was the living skeleton of the Sacred Stallion left them as an authoritarian reminder by the deity himself; their conduct was regulated by the tree's responses to the seasons and the Sacred Stallion died when the leaves fell. Yet, for all its sanctity, the tree was really no more than a kind of anthropoid vegetable clock, for it only told them when it was proper to perform certain choric cantatas. For, as I say, their drama was comprehensive enough to be extremely flexible and if the tree had been blasted one night by lightning the Church of the Horse would have absorbed this event into a new mutation of the central myth, after a period of spiritual reorientation.

They were not fabulous beasts; they were entirely mythic. Sometimes I thought they were not really centaurs at all but only men who possessed such a deep conviction the universe was a horse that it was impossible for them to see any evidence that hinted things might be otherwise.

Their language was far simpler than it seemed at first. It consisted primarily of sound clusters and intuition and, though it was quite different from any human language, it was easy enough for a man to grasp and before three weeks passed both Albertina and I had enough of the rudiments to make simple conversation with our hosts and so learn something of the consternation into which our arrival had plunged them. We had disrupted their cycle and they were still going through a painful period of readjustment. They had searched all through their holy books and found there no formulas of hospitality. We were the first visitors they had ever had in their entire legendary history and when we learned to say their equivalent of 'good morning', their consternation reached a giddy height for there was no sound in their language with which to define a sentient, communicable being who was not mostly horse.

But, since they had found us on the Holy Hill, they knew we were a sign from heaven though they had not yet decided just what it was we signified. While they racked their brains over the problem, they took certain hygienic precautions. They would not let us go and watch their matins and their evensong and they never left us entirely alone together, for fear we might propagate other as yet indigestible marvels before they could find a means of digesting us. Apart from that, they treated us kindly and, after I received permission from the bay to browse among his books, I soon filled my days by turning my old talents at the crossword puzzle to solving the riddle of their runes.

Poor Albertina took a long time to recover from her ordeal. The roan mare and I looked after her and fed her warm milk mixed with honey and a rich porridge made from corn, kept her warm and attended to everything but her fever did not leave her for three days and she could hardly walk but only hobble for more than a fortnight. She was brave and soon stopped flinching when she saw the bay while the children shyly brought her wild strawberries arranged on platters of fresh leaves or bunches of the poppies and moon daisies that grew in the corn, because she was so holy. I sat beside Albertina with my books as the roan mare did the housework and Albertina told me, in the way of those who are sick far from home, of her childhood in Hoffman's *Schloss*, of her rarely seen father, who had seemed so formidable to the little Albertina, of the frail mother with bridled eyes who died so soon and of certain pet rabbits, birds and other playthings. She did not speak of the war or of her father's researches; she seemed content to rest for a while and gather her strength. She begged me to watch for the aerial patrols and so I went up to the Holy Hill every morning and scanned the sky; though I always saw only clouds and birds, she never gave up hope but said: 'Perhaps, tomorrow ...' My trips to the hill only helped confirm our host's theory that we must be numinous.

The more I was beside her, the more I loved her.

At last I began to gain some glimmerings of the centaurs' cosmogony.

The Books of the Sacred Stallion were painted with the brushes they used in the tattooing operation on a kind of parchment made from the barks of certain trees characterized by a leaf formation like a horse's tail, for they believed in an elaborate system of correspondence. Their cuneiform script was based on the marks of their own hooves and, though all men could read, only the Scrivener was allowed to practise the art of writing. It was hermetic knowledge and handed down only from eldest son to eldest son. When the Scrivener's wife bore him no sons, they considered the sequential inheritance so important he was permitted to put his old wife away and take a new one, the only circumstances in which they allowed divorce. But the script was simplicity itself; it was a system of marks corresponding in size exactly to sounds and, after a few lessons from the astonished bay, I was soon able to figure it out well enough.

They called themselves the Distorted Seed of the Dark Archer, although this name was so terrible it could not be spoken aloud, only whispered from one cantor to his successor during the course of his three-week-long initiation. It was an awareness of imminent damnation that kept them at their devotions with such fervour and the mark of Cain they printed upon their backs. It was clearly a matter of pride with them to grow as glorious in their mutilations as they possibly could. And all this was the brooding counterpoint, unspoken yet known, that lent such passion to their worship.

I sheared the thick flesh of rhetoric from the contents, ignored the stories of lesser heroes and was left with this skeleton: the Bridal Mare marries the Sacred Stallion, who instantly impregnates her but, while in foal, she deceives him with a former suitor, the Dark Archer. Spurred by jealousy, the Dark Archer shoots the Sacred Stallion in the eye with an arrow. As he dies, the Sacred Stallion tells the Dark Archer his children will be born in degenerate forms. The Dark Archer and the Bridal Mare cook and eat the Sacred Stallion to hide their crime, but a desolation immediately comes upon the country and, repentant, they whip themselves ferociously for thirty-nine days. (This corresponded to the fast at midwinter and must have been truly astonishing to watch; but we did not stay among them long enough to have the chance of seeing it.) On the fortieth day, the Mare, in a uroboric parturition, gives birth, with extraordinary suffering, to none other than the Sacred Stallion himself, who ascends into the Celestial Stable in the shape of his own foal. The remainder of the liturgical year was taken up with lengthy and overbearing forgiveness and his many teachings – of the art of singing; of the techniques of the smithy; of corn growing; of cactus culture; of cheese-making; and of writing – and all the almost countless ways in which they must conduct their lives in order to atone for their sins. And then, matured, the Sacred Stallion descends from the sky and once again marries the Bridal Mare.

So that was why they held women in such low esteem! And why they would not touch meat! And why they hung a broken bow on the horse-tree! And now I understood they were not so much weaving a fabric of ritual with which to cover themselves but using the tools of ritual to shore up the very walls of the world.

Albertina was as concerned as I with the texture of the life of our hosts but not from any simple, childish curiosity such as mine. She had become engrossed in the problem of the reality status of the centaurs and the more she talked of it, the more I admired her ruthless empiricism for she was convinced that even though every male in the village had obtained carnal knowledge of her, the beasts were still only emanations of her own desires, dredged up and objectively reified from the dark abysses of the unconscious. And she told me that, according to her father's theory, all the subjects and objects we had encountered in the loose grammar of Nebulous Time were derived from a similar source – my desires; or hers; or the Count's. At first, especially, the Count's, for he had lived on closer terms with his own unconscious than we. But now our desires, perhaps, had achieved their day of independence.

I remembered the words of another German savant and quoted to her: ' "In the unconscious, nothing can be treated or destroyed." * Yet we saw the Count destroyed; and I myself destroyed the Cannibal Chief.'

'Destruction is only another aspect of being,' she said categorically and with that I had to be content.

Yet we ate the bread of the centaurs and were nourished by it. So I saw that, if what she believed were so, these phantoms were not in the least insignificant for the existence of the methodical actuality on whose beds of straw we slept, whose language we were forced to learn, this complex reality with its fires, it cheeses, its complicated theology and its magnificent handwriting, this concrete, authentic, self-consistent world was begotten from phenomenal dynamics alone, the product of a random becoming, the first of the wonderful flowers that would bloom in the earth her father had prepared for them by means she, as yet, refused to so much as hint at, except to say they had to do with desire, and radiant energy, and persistence of vision. We were living, then, according to the self-determined laws of a group of synthetically authentic phenomena.

Because they did not have a word for 'guest', or even for 'visitor', they began to treat us, at last, with a nervous compassion but until they expanded their liturgy to absorb us we were at best irritating irrelevancies, distracting them from the majestic pageant of their ritual lives. We did not even have anything to teach them. They knew

* Sigmund Freud, *The Interpretation of Dreams.* Desiderio.

all they needed to know and when I tried to tell the bay that by far the greater number of social institutions in the world were made by weak, two-legged, thin-skinned creatures much the same as Albertina and I, he told me in so many words that I was lying. For, because they were men, they had many words to describe conditions of deceit; they were not Houyhnhnms.

When we could speak the language fluently and Albertina had quite recovered, they put her to work in the fields with the women, because it was harvest time. The women reaped the corn and brought it into the village in sheaves on their backs. When all was gathered in, they would thresh it during the performance of semi-secular harvest songs on a communal threshing floor. Soon Albertina became as brown as an Indian, for the yellowish pigment of her Mongolian skin took to sunshine in as friendly a fashion as my own did. She would come home in the golden evenings, wreathed with corn like a pagan deity in a pastoral and naked as a stone, for they did not give us back our clothes and we never needed to cover ourselves, for the weather was always warm. But even when all her wounds were healed, she would not let me touch her, though she would not tell me why except to say that the time was not yet ripe. So we lived like loving brother and sister, even if I was always a little in awe of her for sometimes her eyes held a dark, blasting lightning and her face fell into the carven lines of the statue of a philosopher. At these times a sense of her difference almost withered me for she was the sole heir to her father's kingdom and that kingdom was the world. And I had nothing. Familiarity did not diminish her strangeness nor her magnetism. Every day I found her all the more miraculous and I would gaze at her for hours together, as though I were feeding on her eyes. And, as I remember, she, too, would gaze at me.

But we were prisoners of the centaurs and did not know if we would ever be free, unless her father's aerial patrols sighted us.

Because I was male, they did not let me do any work and seemed happy enough to let me wander around the village, learning what I could learn. Perhaps they even thought, when they saw me poring over their books, they might even be able to enlist me in their ceremonies, one day, as an inkbearer or an assistant fustigator. I do not know. But I do know they were making their plans for us. When the Cantor, the Tattoo-master, the Smith and the Scrivener talked together, they always talked in whispers. But now they met together more and more frequently; they vere always at their whisperings. And the Scrivener, with a choir around him, chanting, would sit at the table in his stable and write in a new big book in the evenings.

When I went to watch the tattooing, I found the art was as remarkable as the method was atrocious. First, they chose a design from the pictures in the ancient volumes of blueprints and drew it on the skin with the brush. But then the pain began for the artist did not use a relatively humane needle; he kept in a consecrated chest his artillery of triangular-shaped awls and gouges. He ground and mixed his pigments himself. He and his sons, his apprentices, went into the forest to search for the ingredients for their mixes and the colours, taken from minerals in the earth and dried, powdered plants, were often toxic enough to produce an effect as of scalding, and always a terrible itching, although the skin of the man-parts was far tougher than human skin. So one often saw young boys feverishly scratching their half-embroidered backs against rough trunks of trees in the mornings after their visits to the master. During a tattooing, the Tattoo-master's stable was half-way between an operating theatre and a chapel.

His wife scrubbed down the table and set out a pillow of straw on which the boy victim rested his head as he lay face down while the master's three sons lined up, chanting, one carrying the awls, another the paint and the third a bowl of water and a sponge. The Cantor, at the head of the table, began to sing; he sang the sympathetic magic of the emblem, how he who wore the horse indented on his skin took on the virtue of horses while the master plunged the brush in the ink with his left hand and, taking in the other an awl or gouge, depending on the thickness of the desired line, he rubbed the instrument in the wet brush and pushed the colouring matter under the skin. And then the third son wiped the blood away with a sponge. Each of the children's visits lasted an hour. The Tattoo-master always had a full day's work. The more complicated designs, those for the children of the church dignitaries, could take up to a year to complete and the women, especially, suffered terribly in the regions around their nipples. And all the time they suffered, the song went on; religion was their only analgesic.

Work on the tattoo of the bay's son was almost complete. Only another few hours' work and he would become a work of religious art as preposterous as it was magnificent. But we never saw him in his final, ridiculous splendour for one day at breakfast the bay said to me:

'She is not to go to the fields today. I shall come for both of you after prayers and you will go to the Holy Hill with me.'

He smiled grimly and with even a certain affection, or, rather, with a tolerant acquiescence in my presence at his breakfast table when I could not even sit down decently on all fours, and at Albertina's presence as she waited quietly with his mate and daughter for her own share of the meal.

We did not have the least idea what would happen to us on the Holy Hill for we were in Nebulous Time. All we could do was help the roan mare clean the wooden platters and wait for his return. I knew from my studies of their books no special ritual was scheduled for today. We were in the time of TRANSMISSION OF DIVINE KNOWLEDGE NO. TWO and that was concerned with the art of the Smith. Yet, foolishly, I felt no suspicion. When they saw how badly the rape had injured Albertina, they had realized we were both more delicately put together than they and treated us, physically, with the greatest respect. Yet I do not think they even understood quite how feeble we were. It was impossible for them to do so. And, like all grown ups, they were quite sure they always knew what was best.

Yet I felt the first misgivings when I saw a solemn procession line up before the bay's stable and the Cantor lead them all in a song I had never heard before.

It was plainly an unusual day for none of the women had gone to the field. Even the Tattoo-master had left his table to take a prominent place in the procession with his sons ranked behind him and the soot-stained Smith, the black, had abandoned his forge while the dapple grey Scrivener stood at the head of them all and his son ceremoniously carried the suspiciously new book on which he had been working. Perhaps it was a holiday, for all the women were carrying picnic baskets; but they did not have a word for 'holidays'. And then the bay took Albertina and me one by each hand and so we went out of the village and all the time he sang a new song called: CONSECRATION OF A NEWLY DISCOVERED BOOK OF THE SCRIPTURES.

A light mist lay over the fields that morning, so we could see no further than the golden tassels of ripe corn that brushed us as we passed, and hear nothing besides the bay's mahogany coloured baritone but the soft, regimented clop of their hoofbeats on the rutted path. Because it was Nebulous Time, one could have imagined it the dawn of time, the anteriority of all times, since Nebulous Time was the womb of time. For the first time, led like a child by the great bay whose form was so much nobler than mine and whose sense of the coherence of his universe was so inflexible, my own conviction that I was a man named Desiderio, born in a certain city, the child of a certain mother, lover of a certain woman, began to waver. If I was a man, what was a man? The bay offered me a logical definition: a horse in a state of ultimate, biped, maneless, tailless decadence. I was a naked, stunted, deformed dwarf who one day might begin to forget what purpose such a thing as a name of my own served. And the brown thing with breasts who held the bay's other hand was my mate. From the waist upwards, she was passable, if ugly because not equine; but, from the waist down, vile. And, besides, she was incomplete because there were none of the necessary scars on her skin. How naked we were! I had begun to think of the centaurs as our masters, you see, although Albertina had warned me: 'The pressures of Nebulous Time alone force them to live with such certitude!' And perhaps I was indeed looking for a master – perhaps the whole history of my adventure could be titled 'Desiderio in Search of a Master'. But I only wanted to find a master, the Minister, the Count, the bay, so that I could lean on him at first and then, after a while, jeer.

If Albertina had known how despicable I was, she would not have given me a second thought.

When we came to the Holy Hill, they all neighed 'Hallelujah!' and evacuated. Then they spread down straw they had brought with them under the tree so that we should not have to lie down in horse dung when they laid us down. The Scrivener nailed the new book to the tree. The prayers were interminable. The Tattoo-master and the Cantor performed an endless cantata for tenor and baritone while the three boys who bore the instruments of torture waited with the blind indifference of trees.

As I listened to the singing, I learned from the text how the master I longed for proposed to treat us.

We would be tattooed upon the Holy Hill where the Sacred Stallion had first set us down. He had sent us into the world to show his flock what fearful shapes they might all still come to if they did not adhere even more strictly than before to his dogmas. But, in his infinite compassion, the Stallion had decided to integrate us with the celestial herd. They would paint us with his picture and then, to make us resemble him even more, they would nail the iron shoes on our feet with red hot nails. After that, they would take us into the forest and give us to the Spirits. That is, the wild horses, who would certainly trample us to death.

Red Hot Nail in person threw back his mane and neighed. We heard every word. I turned my head a little and saw she was crying. I stretched out my hand towards her and grasped it. Whatever the reality status of the centaurs, they certainly had the power to deprive us forever of any reality at all for it was certain we would die together, if not from the first sacrament, then from the second, and, if we managed to survive that, the third would certainly end us. I felt a certain clarity and composure, for matters were quite out of our control; if we were the victims of unleashed, unknown desires, then die we must, for as long as those desires existed, we would finish by killing one another.

Yes. I thought so, even then.

The Tattoo-master knelt and took the brush. She shivered when she felt the chill, wet tongue of horsehair lick along her spine and I held her hand more tightly. The congregation drummed their hooves. The Cantor chanted and mimed, I think, the DANCE OF THE HORSEHAIR WRITING BRUSH. I do not know how long it took before her back was painted over completely; I do not know how long it took to paint me but when we were both finished, they stopped the ceremony to eat their lunches and brought us some milk and cold pancakes, too, though they would not let us get up because the paint was not yet dry. When the brief meal was over, our ordeal would begin in earnest. She trembled and I remembered how she had looked when she was Lafleur. And yet I knew she was far braver than I.

It was late morning and the sun was shining very brightly. The morning mist had dried and the sky was amazingly clear and blue. She raised herself up on her elbows as high as she could, and, shading her eyes with her hands, she gazed into the far distance. Again, I remembered Lafleur looking for a storm, although I knew she was searching for her father's aerial patrols. However, I did not believe in the patrols. Yet, as she trembled, I saw it was not with fear but with hope – or, perhaps, a kind of effortful strain; she gripped my hand more tightly, until her nails dug into my palm. I remembered the scrap of paper in the pocket of the peep-show proprietor's nephew. 'My desires, concentrated to a single point . . .'

I am sure what happened next was coincidence. I am positive of that. I would stake my life on it.

'Look!' she hissed on a triumphantly expelled breath.

In the far distance, the sunlight glinted on the wings of a metal bird.

But that was not the most remarkable thing; that was not the extraordinary coincidence. The litany began again and the Cantor threw almost on top of us an ecstasy so wonderful I could not see anything but his flailing hooves and sweat-drenched loins whirling above me. His consummation laid him low; he sprawled on the ground, kicking his hooves spasmodically, and in the tremendous silence I heard the whirring of an engine, but either they were too transfigured to hear it or they thought it was the sound of a clattering insect in the corn. And, yes, the sap in the horse-tree went on busily buzzing. Then came the sacerdotal moment. The Awl raised the brush and the piercing instrument. And this was the coincidence. At the very moment he bent down to make the first incision, the buzzing horse-tree went up in flames.

'. . . ignite all in their way.'

The Scrivener might have written a new book but it did not allow for so much improvisation. Besides, now the book was burning. The dried dung at the roots of the tree caught almost instantaneously and a lasso of flame captured the bay's tail. He thrashed his sparking torch this way and that way, howling, and he dropped dung not in prayer, but this time in fear. The Tattoo-master turned into a horse of ivory and flame and suddenly they were all on fire, all the priests around us and our bed of straw was blazing, too. But Albertina and I sprang out and through the wall of fire to run as fast as we could through the whinnying havoc to the helicopter that had landed in the corn field.

8. The Castle

While the co-pilot filmed the scene below with a television camera, the helicopter rose up in a rattle of whirling metal. When I looked down, I saw the wide valley of the centaurs open out like a French, eighteenth-century neo-classical fan painted by a follower of Poussin and then close up again as we flew so low above the forest itself the topmost branches scraped against the cabin walls. So all those months of our selves vanished without trace and I heard the pilot call Albertina, 'Madam', and then 'Generalissimo Hoffman'. When I turned from the window, I saw she had already put on one of their spare combat suits of drab, olive twill and was now combing out her black hair, which had grown halfway down her back during our captivity. The co-pilot put away his camera and dug into a locker to produce clothes for me, too. Now she was dressed, I was embarrassed at my nakedness and hurried to cover myself, though my fingers fumbled over the unfamiliar buttons.

'Am I the general's batman?' I asked her but she only smiled at me remotely and began to pore over a map the co-pilot handed her. He and the pilot were both swarthy, silent young men in black berets who chewed on long, black cigars. They spoke mainly a laconic French and I felt I had seen men like them very often before but only in newsreel films. I was given coffee from a thermos flask and they cleared me a place in the cramped quarters so that I could sit down. I had not been in the twentieth century for so long that I felt quite stunned. A radio began to squawk messages in the standard speech of my country. I had not heard my own language for a long time; when we were among the centaurs, Albertina and I had used it as a private language, such as secretive children invent for themselves, and I was shocked to recall the speech was common property. The coffee was hot and strong; they opened a wax-paper parcel of ham sandwiches. Albertina absently plaited her hair and, as she did so, so she put away all her romanticism. Her face was hard and brown and impersonal. I sipped my coffee. She spoke into the radio transmitter but I could make out nothing whatsoever of what she said because of the noise the engines made.

And then Albertina had finished. She gave the pilot back the microphone, sighed, smiled and came to crouch beside me.

'Not my batman,' she said. 'The Doctor will commission you. He just told me that.'

'Even though I'm enlisted on the other side?'

'You will go wherever I go,' she said with such conviction I was silent for I had just seen her passions set fire to a tree and now I was in the real world again I was not quite sure I wanted to burn with her – or, at least, not yet. I felt an inexplicable indifference towards her. Perhaps because she was now yet another she and this she was the absolute antithesis of my black swan and my bouquet of burning bone; she was a crisp, antiseptic soldier to whom other ranks deferred. I began to feel perfidious, for I had no respect for rank.

'And what of my city?' I asked her, drawing on a cigar the pilot gave me.

She frowned into her plastic tumbler of coffee.

'The course of the war was dramatically altered by the destruction of the set of samples. While my father was modifying the transmitters, the Minister completed his computer bank and then instituted a programme he called the Rectification of Names. In spite of himself, he was forced to use philosophic weapons – or, as he would probably prefer to call them, ideological weapons. He decided he could only keep a strict control of his actualities by adjusting their names to agree with them perfectly. So, you understand, that no shadow would fall between the word and the thing described. For the Minister hypothesized my father worked in that shadowy land between the thinkable and the thing thought of, and, if he destroyed this difference, he would destroy my father. Do you follow me?'

'More or less.'

'He set up a new slogan, "If the name is right, you see the light." He is a man of great intellect but limited imagination. Which is why he can hold out against my father, of course. Once the names were right, he thought perfect order and hence perfect government on his own Confucian terms would follow automatically. So he dismissed all his physicists and brought in a team of logical positivists from the School of Philosophy in the National University and set them to the task of fixing all the phenomena compiled by his computers in the solid concrete of a set of names that absolutely agreed with them. Ironically enough, their task was made all the easier because of the flexibility of identity produced in the state of nebulous time.'

She paused. A yellowish glare flooded the cabin.

'Look. Now we are crossing the desert, the mother of mirages,' she said.

There was no more forest, only sand drifting in dry spirals the very colour of sterility and, above us, a sky as lifeless as the earth.

'This is your Minister's place,' she said. 'He has not got enough imagination to realize that the most monstrous aberrations are bound to flourish in soil once it has been disinfected of the imagination.'

And, though I loved her more than anything in the world, I remembered the music of Mozart and murmured to the Queen of the Night:

'I do not think so.'

But she did not hear me because of the noise of the engines and the turning propellers.

'So, when the transmitters were operating again, the images we sent out bounced off the intellectual walls the Minister had built. My poor father – he was almost disconcerted, because I was lost in Nebulous Time just when he needed me most!'

The helicopter followed its own shadow over the realm of spiritual death.

'But now I have been in contact with him at last and he is only waiting for our return to start the Second Front.'

'For our return? For you – and for me as well?'

'Yes,' she said and turned her ensorcellating eyes on me so that all at once I was breathless with desire and the cabin dissolved in our kiss. Yet there was still that duplicity in my heart's core. I had been marked out at the beginning as the Minister's man, for all my apathy, for all my disaffection, for I, too, would have worshipped reason if I could ever have found her shrine. Reason was stamped into me as if it were a chromosome, even if I loved the high priestess of passion. Nevertheless, we kissed; and the crew of the helicopter shielded their eyes as though we were too bright for them to bear.

Then the pilot sighted a walled fort with a landing strip beside it on which stood two spare, lean, military transports. We landed in a helicopter port inside the fort itself, which I believe I had once seen in a film of the Foreign Legion. A complement of troopers manned it. They were as brown and down to earth as the crew of the helicopter and they, too, all called Albertina 'Generalissimo'. We were given a bath and I got myself a military haircut, for my hair had grown almost as long as Albertina's. Then we had an austere dinner of army rations – for, although she was a general, she was not given preferential treatment – and lay down on two hard, iron beds with flat pillows and coarse grey blankets in a barracks that smelled of disinfectant where I could not have made love to her even if she had let me because twenty other men were sleeping there. I had forgotten how convenient the real world was; how, for example, hot water came boiling out of taps marked 'hot', how good it felt to sleep between sheets, and, though there were no clocks in the fort, all the soldiers had come to an informal agreement on a common standard of time so our breakfast, full of nostalgic flavours of bacon, toast, tea and marmalade, was served at the hour we had all agreed to wake up. Then, when everything was ready, the commandant of the fort kissed Albertina on both cheeks; we climbed into a military transport and flew, far more simply though much more lengthily than in any dream, directly to Hoffman's castle. And nothing whatever happened to ripple the serene, accommodating surface of events except the constant presence of Albertina's eyes.

Ocean and jungle and, finally, remembered peaks jutting against the sky of evening. I waited expectantly for a sense of homecoming but I experienced nothing. With a faint sinking of the heart, as the plane dipped and circled, I thought that perhaps now I was a stranger everywhere.

It was a hazardous descent into the mountains for Hoffman's own landing strip was well concealed from the air and I saw nothing of the castle itself as we came down, only the reeling peaks. A jeep was waiting for us; it took us along a rough track through long, black shadows of approaching night but I saw among the rocks before me four moons were already shining high in the secret crests. They were four huge, concave saucers of very highly polished metal that circled like windmills and were all turned towards the city I knew lay below me to the south. Plainly they were part of the transmission system, even though they were so blatantly technological. I was so busy watching them I did not see the castle, though it lay before us, until the jeep stopped and Albertina, with a rush of joy in her voice, said: 'We're nearly home.'

Almost – but not entirely for we still had to cross a chasm in the earth by a wooden bridge so fragile we must walk and so narrow we could only go one at a time. The driver of the jeep spoke a strange mixture of French and Spanish and wore a battered anti-uniform of green twill; he kissed Albertina on both cheeks and roared away, leaving us alone. We went out on to the bridge. The chasm was some sixty feet wide and, from both its lips, sheer precipices fell to a depth of a thousand feet or more, so deep you could not see what lay at the bottom. Beyond the bridge was a little green grove about four acres in area, surrounded on all sides by the crags in which the transmitters were lodged. It was a sweet, female kernel nestling in the core of the virile, thrusting rock. The trees in the grove were full of fruit and the dappled and variegated chalices of enormous flowers seemed to be breathing out all the perfume they had stored up during the day in these last moments before they closed for the night. Brilliant birds sang cn the branches in which chattering squirrels swung and the luxuriant grass rustled with rabbits while beautiful roe deer sauntered among the trees, holding up their heads proudly, like princes, under the weights of their antlered crowns. It did not look as though winter had ever touched it and as we drew nearer, our footsteps ringing with a hollow sound on the wooden bridge, I remembered I had seen a picture of Hoffman's park, a magically transformed picture in which all the detail had been heightened but still recognizably a dream vision of this very park. I had seen it in the peep-show. It was the park framed by the female orifice in the first machine of all and when I looked beyond the trees, I saw the very same castle I had seen then.

The castle stood with its back up against a cliff. The battlements hinted at Hoffman's Teutonic heritage; he had built himself a Wagnerian castle like a romantic memory in stone and as the light faded, the castle began to open eyes of many beautiful colours for all the windows were of stained glass. And yet I knew I was not dreaming; my feet left prints on the grass and Albertina picked me an apple from a tree and I brushed away the bloom and bit into it and my teeth went 'crunch!' While the transmitters flashed and a roaring in the sky told us the transport had taken off again, or another transport had taken off, for there was a hangar full of the things at the military base at the airstrip.

'What a year it's been for apples!' said Albertina. 'Look how heavy the crop is. The trees are bending almost to the ground. When I went away to quarantine the Count, it was apple blossom time. You can't imagine how beautiful the apple blossom is, Desiderio!'

I finished my apple and threw away the core. So the princess was taking it for granted I was interested in her patrimonial apple blossom, was she? What presumption! Perhaps she should not have told me so plainly, in her ownership tone of voice, that all this was hers, the castle, the orchards, the mountains, the earth, the sky, all that lay between them. I don't know. All I know is, I could not transcend myself sufficiently to inherit the universe. Although it was real, I knew the perfection round me was impossible; and perhaps I was right. But now I am too old to know or care. I can no longer tell the difference between memory and dream. They share the same quality of wishful thinking. I thought at the time perhaps I was a terrorist in the cause of reason; though I probably tried to justify myself with such a notion later. Yet when I close my eyes I see her still, walking through the orchard towards her father's house, in her soldier's uniform, her heavy black plaits hanging down her back like a little girl's.

Nobody came to meet us but the front door was open, a door at the top of a not in the least grandiloquent but cracked and mossy staircase, for it was not really a castle, only a country house built after the style of a castle. We entered, first, a sombre, low-ceilinged hall scented with pot pourri and furnished with carved chairs, Chinese pots and Oriental rugs. I do not know what I had been expecting – but certainly never this tranquillity, this domestic peace, for were we not in the house of the magician himself? However, the transmitters sent out their beams high over its battlements and did not affect the fortress of the enemy itself. Here, everything was safe. Everything was ordered. Everything was secure.

All that puzzled me were certain pictures on the wall. These pictures were heavily varnished oils executed in the size and style of the nineteenth-century academician and they all depicted faces and scenes I recognized from old photographs and from the sepia and olive reproductions of forgotten masterpieces in the old-fashioned books the nuns gave us to look at when I was a child, in the evenings after supper, when we had been good. When I read the titles engraved on metal plaques at the bottom of each frame, I saw they depicted such scenes as 'Leon Trotsky Composing the Eroica Symphony'; the wire-rimmed spectacles, the Hebraic bush of hair, the burning eyes were all familiar. The light of inspiration was in his eyes and the crotchets and quavers rippled from his nib on to the sheets of manuscript paper which flew about the red plush cover of the mahogany table on which he worked as if blown by the fine frenzy of genius. Van Gogh was shown writing 'Wuthering Heights' in the parlour of Haworth Parsonage, with bandaged ear, all complete. I was especially struck by a gigantic canvas of Milton blindly executing divine frescos upon the walls of the Sistine Chapel. Seeing my bewilderment, Albertina said, smiling: 'When my father rewrites the history books, these are some of the things that everyone will suddenly perceive to have always been true.'

Though the signs of the scrupulous attentions of servants were apparent everywhere, the house seemed quite deserted. We were welcomed only by an ancient, lumbering dog who heaved himself painfully up from a rug in front of a little log fire, burning more for the sake of the scent of applewood and the sight of flame than the need for warmth, who came and thrust his wet nose in Albertina's palm, whining for joy.

'When I was little, he used to give me rides on his back,' she said. 'How white his muzzle is growing!'

Wheezing and panting, the Great Dane followed us up a staircase and along a gallery but we left him outside a room in which a stained glass window dyed the valley outside purple and crimson and Ravel was playing on a very elaborate hi-fi set. A diminutive, dark-haired woman in a long, black dress lay on a couch with her face turned away from us. There, holding her hand, sat the Doctor himself, on a low, padded stool. I knew him at once though he was far older than the pictures I had seen, of course, even if he still wedged open one eye with a monocle just as his old professor had told me he did. There was a strong smell of incense in the room which did not quite conceal the smell of incipient putrefaction. When he let go the woman's hand, it fell with a lifeless thud. The one discordant note in all this rich man's sumptuous country estate was the embalmed corpse of his dead wife he kept on a bergère settee in this white-walled room. He was grey-faced and grey-haired and grey-eyed. He wore a handsomely tailored dark suit and his hands were exquisitely manicured. His quality, whatever it had been once, was now only quiet. There was no resemblance whatsoever between the old man and his daughter.

They used the standard language with one another. His first words were:

'I go to the city tomorrow and arrive there yesterday.'

'Yes, of course,' replied Albertina. 'Because the shadow of the flying bird never moves.'

They smiled. They appeared to understand one another perfectly. Then he gave her the kisses due to a generalissimo.

They both laughed gently and I felt the hair rising on my scalp. In that room which hung in the castle like a bubble filled with quietude, faced with that strange family group, I felt the most appalling fear. Perhaps because I was in the presence of the disciplined power of the utterly irrational. He was so quiet, so grey, so calm and he had just said something entirely meaningless in a voice of perfect, restrained reason. All at once I realized how lonely we were here, far away in the mountains with only the wind for company, in the house of the man who made dreams come true.

He stroked the nocturnal hair of the corpse and whispered softly: 'You see, my dear, she has come home, just as I told you she would. And now you must have a refreshing sleep while we must have our dinner.'

But a bell rang and first, it seemed, we must all dress up. Albertina showed me to a chaste, masculine room at the front of the house with a narrow bed and a black leather armchair, many ash trays and a magazine rack containing current numbers of *Playboy*, *The New Yorker*, *Time* and *Newsweek*. On the dressing-table were silver-backed brushes. I opened the door of a closet and found a bathroom where I took a steaming shower, assisted by great quantities of lemon soap. When I came out, wrapped in the white, towelling robe they had provided for me, I found a dinner jacket and everything to go with it laid out ready for me on the bed, down to silk socks and white linen handkerchief. When I was dressed, I felt in the pocket and found a gold cigarette lighter and matching case filled with Balkan Sobranie Black Russian cigarettes. I looked at myself in the oval, mahogany mirror. I had been transformed again. Time and travel had changed me almost beyond my own recognition. Now I was entirely Albertina in the male aspect. That is why I know I was beautiful when I was a young man. Because I know I looked like Albertina.

From my window, I could see the apple orchards, the crevasse and the road that led over the bare mountain to the military installation.

The Castle

Everything was perfectly calm and filled with the mushroomy, winey scents of autumn. Another bell rang and I went down the thickly carpeted staircase to the picture gallery where Albertina and her father were drinking very dry sherry. Dinner was served off an English eighteenth-century table in another of those chaste, restrained, white-walled rooms with a flower arrangement in the disappearing Japanese transcendental style on the sideboard and china, glass and cutlery so extraordinarily tasteful one was hardly aware of its presence. The meal was very simple and perfectly in tune with the season of the year – some kind of clear soup; a little trout; a saddle of hare, grilled; mushrooms; salad; fruit and cheese. The wines all matched. With the very strong black coffee there was a selection of recherché liqueurs and we all smoked probably priceless cigars. Still no servants appeared. All the courses had been sent up from subterranean kitchens in a small service elevator from which Albertina herself served us. There was no conversation during the meal but another stereo set hidden behind a white-enamelled grille was playing a Schubert song cycle, *The Winter Journey*.

'Do you not feel,' said the Doctor in his very soft but still crisp-edged voice, 'that invisible presences have more reality than visible ones? They exert more influence upon us. They make us cry more easily.'

This was the only sentiment or expression of feeling he revealed during the time I knew him. As the silent meal went on, I began to sense in his quietness, his almost quiescence, his silence and slow movements, a willed concentration of thought that, if exploited, might indeed rule the world. He bemused me. He was stillness. He seemed to have refined himself almost to nothing. He was a grey ghost sitting in a striped coat at a very elegant table and yet he was also Prospero – though, ironically enough, one could not judge the Prospero effect in his own castle for he could not alter the constituents of the aromatic coffee we sipped by so much as an iota. Here, nothing could possibly be fantastic. That was the source of my bitter disappointment. I had wanted his house to be a palace dedicated only to wonder.

Even at the worldly level I was disappointed, for I could plainly see that, on everyday terms alone, he was very rich and I was very, very poor. As the very poor often do, I felt the rich could only justify their wealth by making a lavish and conspicuous display of it. My grill disgruntled me; I scorned his good taste. If I were as rich as he, why, I would barbecue peacocks nightly. Besides, good taste has always bored me a little and, in the enemy H.Q., I felt a little bored. It was then, to revive my flagging interest in my surroundings, that I consciously reminded myself I was a secret agent for the other side. They were not the enemy. I was.

The white evening dress of a Victorian romantic heroine rustled about Albertina's feet and clung like frost to her amber breasts yet I wished she had worn the transvestite apparel of her father's ambassador or had come to the table naked, with poppies in her hair, in the style she had adopted for dinner in the land of the centaurs. My disillusionment was profound. I was not in the domain of the marvellous at all. I had gone far beyond that and at last I had reached the powerhouse of the marvellous, where all its clanking, dull, stage machinery was kept. Even if it is the dream made flesh, the real, once it becomes real, can be no more than real. While I did not know her, I thought she was sublime; when I knew her, I loved her. But, even as I pared my dessert persimmon with the silver knife provided, I was already wondering whether the fleshly possession of Albertina would not be the greatest disillusionment of all.

The habit of sardonic contemplation is the hardest habit of all to break.

When we finished our coffee, the Doctor excused himself for he said he had some business in his study, which was housed in a tower, but he gave me another of his fine cigars and Albertina said, Would I not like to walk outside for a while and enjoy my cigar in the mild evening? So we went out into the park. I have forgotten what month it was but, by the scents, I guessed it must be October.

'Here,' she said. 'This way.'

The face of the precipice opened before her but I knew it opened only because she had pressed an unmagical switch. Her abundant skirts swirling before us, she led me up a steep cleft in the rock, a secret passage to the rooftree of the mountain, which issued among the tumbled rocks where one of the transmitters turned like a transfigured mill wheel. But she turned her back on it and led me some little distance through the dishevelled boulders, under a faint half lemon slice of moon, both of us so elegant in evening dress we were ourselves like a poignant anachronism projected backwards upon primeval wilderness. And then we came to a kind of circular amphitheatre hollowed out of the yellow rock and peopled with a silent multitude of immobile shapes in rows and columns and ranks, like the guardians of the place.

'It was a cemetery,' said Albertina. 'The Indians made it, before the Europeans came. But they did not come here. Then the Indians died, most of them. So these are all that remains of the Indians.'

In the centre of this amphitheatre was an oblong tumulus containing, presumably, the bones of my dead ancestors and all the mute spectators who surrounded it were meant to scare away grave robbers, mountain lions, or mountain dogs, or any other thing that might disturb the sleepers in the earth. The Indians had shaped unglazed pottery into men on horseback armed with swords and women with bows, into dogs that snarled, and also urns, small houses and cooking implements as if to make a city for the earthen regiments, these crude, brown figures sadly chipped by time and the weather whose eyes were holes through which you could see that all were hollow within. We went down the stepped side of the hollow through these thickets of imitation men and her skirts drifted out behind her and her hair flowed down her bare, richly coloured shoulders as freely as the hair of a Druid priestess. She, formed of the colours of the rocks and the figurines, the darkness and the moonlight.

Love is the synthesis of dream and actuality; love is the only matrix of the unprecedented; love is the tree which buds lovers like roses. In white, vestal majesty, she spoke to me of love among the funerary ornaments on the naked mountain and then I, like an intrepid swimmer, flung myself into the angry breakers of her petticoats and put my mouth against the unshorn seal of love itself. And that was as close as I ever got to consummation. It took place in the graveyard of my forefathers.

Albertina seated herself on a rock that might have been an altar, once, and motioned me to sit beside her. We were the cynosure of the sightless eyes of a countless pottery audience.

'The state of love is like the South in Hui Shih's paradox: "The South has at once a limit and no limit." Lu Teming made the following commentary on this paradox: "He spoke about the South but he was only taking it as an example. There is the mirror and the image but there is also the image of the image; two mirrors reflect each other and images may be multiplied without end." Ours is a supreme encounter, Desiderio. We are two such disseminating mirrors.'

In the looking glasses of her eyes, I saw reflected my entire being whirl apart and reassemble itself innumerable times.

'Love is a perpetual journey that does not go through space, an endless oscillating motion that remains unmoved. Love creates for itself a tension that disrupts every tense in time. Love has certain elements in common with eternal regression, since this exchange of reflections can neither be exhausted nor destroyed, but it is not a regression. It is a direct durationless, locationless progression towards an ultimate state of ecstatic annihilation.'

She lectured me and the grave ornaments with the most beautiful gravity and, if I felt my attention wandering, it was only because of the chill in the night air and the teasing presence in my pocket of the cigar the Doctor had given me that I felt would be rude to light up, now. And, besides, my nostrils were full of the musky odour of her skin. Then she put her hand on my wrist; her touch electrified me.

'My father has discovered that the magnetic field formed by our reciprocal desire – yes, Desiderio, our desire – may be quite unique in its intensity. Such desire must be the strongest force in the world and, if it could be crystallized, would show itself as a deposit which is the definitive residuum of the most powerful inherited associations. And desire is also the source of the greatest source of radiant energy in the entire universe!'

Her intellectual grasp impressed me but I could have wished she was a little less earnest. She had inherited in full her father's lack of humour. The peep-show proprietor had warned me of his lack of humour. Yet I found her most endearing when she was so serious. When I thought she was endearing, suddenly she looked exactly like the angel the nuns put on top of the convent Christmas tree. And yet she was very eloquent. Her eloquence moved me, as the music of Mozart and the wall-paintings of the Ancient Egyptians used to move me.

'In theory, one can reduce everything to a series of ultimate simples. When my father perfects this theory, which he will do in perhaps three or four years time, he will name it Hoffman's Principle of Unwrought Simplicity and once he fully understands its laws, he will reduce everything in the world to the non-created bases from which the world is built. And then he will take the world apart and make a new world.'

What? The grey man in the monocle who so hated humanity he could not bear to see a servant and reserved his affection for a wife who was safely dead? Yes. That grey man. Her black mane brushed my cheek and I touched her shoulders. The texture of her skin was like suède.

'Because, you see, the world is built from these simples. Everything else in the world is only an irrelevant accessory of certain simples. These simples have a kind of reality that does not belong to anything else. The ultimate simplicity, Desiderio, is Love. That is to say, Desire, Desiderio. Which is generated by four legs in bed.'

Roused beyond endurance, I was naïve enough to take this as an invitation and I flung her backwards on the burial mound and dived straight into her beating, foaming skirts. But, though I managed to get high enough to kiss her simplicity, she fought me so skilfully I could do nothing else. Then she began to laugh.

'Don't you see it's quite out of the question, at the moment?' she said. 'You have never yet made love to me because, all the time you have known me, I've been maintained in my various appearances only by the power of your desire.'

I was disconcerted to find my physicality thwarted by metaphysics. I struck her in the face with the heavy flat of my hand. Her cut lip bled a little but she did not flinch from the blow nor reprimand me afterwards.

'Oh, Desiderio, soon! soon! When we go to the laboratory together, you will see me as I really am.'

I did not understand her at all. The segment of moon leaked out a thin, ugly, sepia-coloured light that crumbled everything around us to degenerate forms. I was troubled in mind and very uneasy for the magician's castle was not the home of unreason at all but a school for some kind of to me incomprehensible logic and now she told me we must go back there, for her father was waiting to take me on a tour of the laboratories.

She took me up to his study high in a tower in a smoothly gliding elevator and she left me outside the door. She kissed me on the cheek and said with infinite promise: 'Tonight. Later.' She vanished inside the doors of the elevator, like a white bird, engulfed; I watched her go with I do not know what presentiment of ill-fortune. How could I know that, when I saw her next, I would have no option but to kill her?

I knocked. The Doctor greeted me. He had changed into a white coat for he was a scientist, but whatever clothes he wore he could not have been more impersonal than he had been at first. He was cold, grey, still and fathomless – not a man; the sea. I found I was afraid of him.

His study, his private work-room, his inner sanctum, his lair, his observatory, had windows from which he could check the movements of the transmitters, though he must have watched the stars, too, for there was an antique map of the heavens hanging on the wall. And now I think I must have imagined some, at least, of the décor I found in the room for it satisfied my imagination so fully I was half suspicious, even when I remembered how the peep-show proprietor had told me his former pupil had delved deeply into the Arabic and Oriental and medieval pseudo-sciences. It was half Rottwang's laboratory in Lang's *Metropolis* but it was also the cabinet of Dr Caligari and, more than either, as I remember it, very probably fallaciously, it was the laboratory of a dilettante aristocrat of the late seventeenth century who dabbled in natural philosophy and tried his hand at necromancy, for there were even martyrized shapes of pickled mandrake in bottles on the shelves and a mingled odour of amber and sulphur filled the air.

The room was cluttered with curiosities – whales' teeth, narwhals' horns and skeletons of extinct creatures left higgledy-piggledy wherever they had happened to be put down, all thick with dust and most satisfactory cobwebs, and on the right of the great, black, locked cupboard that dominated the room were alembics, furnaces, Bunsen burners and various other instruments of chemistry as well as jars of preserved monsters and heaps of fossils in forms I would not have thought possible before I had seen less of the world. The shelves to the left of the cupboard bowed in the middle under the weight of the books they bore. Most of the books were very ancient; some were in Arabic and a great number in Chinese. The bulk of his library seemed to be devoted to rare treatises on various forms of divination, though there was no branch of human knowledge that was not represented. On a workbench lay a curious collection of optical toys, a thaumatrope, a Chinese pacing horse lamp and several others, all of types which worked on the principle of persistence of vision. These were all free from dust and seemed to be the objects of his most recent researches. I remembered he had lately been trying to replace the set of samples.

The Doctor laid his hand on the work-bench.

'At this very bench, I, personally, assisted only by my daughter and my former professor whose fingers were not blind, collected, selected and graded all the complex phenomena in the universe before I could even begin to submit it to changes.'

I murmured my admiration in the back of my throat. He took a ring of keys from his pocket and unlocked the cupboard. The black door swung open to reveal three long shelves crammed with very thick files.

'Here are the tabulated records of my researches.'

But I was far more interested to see the six shelves given over to the raw materials for the fabrication of all the images in the peep-show – two shelves of trays of glass slides; two of envelopes labelled 'negs.' which must contain the negatives of the photographic sequences; and two of moulds for casting small objects in wax, neatly arranged under inscrutable headings consisting of various combinations of sets of three broken and unbroken lines, like so: ☰; and so ☷; and so ☲; and so on.

Hoffman said: 'Once the samples are selected, interpreted, painted, cast and articulated, I can exhibit pain as positively as I can exhibit red. I show love in the same way that I show straight. I demonstrate fear just as precisely as I exemplify crooked. And ecstasy and tree and despair and stone, all exhibited in the same fashion. I can make you perceive ideas with your senses because I do not acknowledge any essential difference in the phenomenological bases of the two modes of thought. All things co-exist in pairs but mine is not an either/or world.

'Mine is an and + and world.

'I alone have discovered the key to the inexhaustible plus.'

His voice never rose above a drab monotone, never expressed enthusiasm, never invited astonishment. In him, the pedantry he had handed down to his daughter went unmodified by charm or leavened by intellectual passion.

'What is the nature of that key, Doctor?'

'Eroto-energy,' he said tonelessly. 'Here. I have something that will interest you.'

He took a tape recorder from the bowels of the cupboard and switched it on. After a preliminary crackle, I heard the voice of the Minister. After all that time, all those changes, I heard him speak again. The tape must have been monitored from a propaganda broadcast to the besieged city.

'– and though real plagues have ravaged us and most of our buildings have tumbled stone from stone, so those of us who are left skulk like rats in the ruins; even if, for a time, our very spirits were tormented without cease by deceitful images springing from that dark part of ourselves humanity must always consent to ignore if we are to live in peace together; although unreason has run rampant through our streets, nevertheless, reason can – will – must! restore order in the end. For light to guide us, we have nothing but our reason. Night and day, day and night, we are tirelessly at work on the immediate problem before us. Our only weapon in the fight is inflexible rationalism and, since we brought reason into the battle, already the clocks have agreed to tell us the same time once more and, already –'

The tape registered a roaring, splintering crash and after that it was perfectly empty. It ran hissing on until the Doctor switched the machine off.

'Reason cannot produce the poetry disorder does,' he remarked without enthusiasm. 'And he thinks I only operate in the gaps between things and definitions! What scant respect he shows for me!'

But I was silent for the resolute yet unhysterical timbre of the

Minister's voice had brought back all kinds of dimly remembered certitudes, certain forgotten harmonies that had once moved me as deeply as I was capable of being moved.

I found the paraphernalia of the Doctor's science disgusted me when I saw it face to face. And his cold eyes perturbed me. I knew he could never be my master. I might not want the Minister's world but I did not want the Doctor's world either. All at once I was pitched on the horns of a dilemma, for I was presented with two alternatives and it seemed to me that the Doctor must be wrong for neither alternative could possibly co-exist with the other. He might know the nature of the inexhaustible plus but, all the same, he was a totalitarian. And I was in this unhappy position – I, of all men, had been given the casting vote between a barren yet harmonious calm and a fertile yet cacophonous tempest.

Well, you know the choice I made. Nothing in this city quarrels with its name. The clocks all run on time, every one. Time moves forward on the four wheels of the dimensions just as it always did before the Doctor's time. When I finish this chapter, they will bring me a cup of hot milk and a plate of lightly buttered digestive biscuits; when I finish my life, they will bring me a winding sheet and take me to a vault in the Cathedral. They have reconstructed the Cathedral so well you would not believe it had ever been demolished. I will never see her again. The shadows fall immutably. In the square, the chestnut tree casts leaves of autumn on my statue's shoulders. The golden bowl is not broken in this city. It is round as a cake and everyone may have a slice of it, according to his need. A need is nothing like a desire.

Old Desiderio asks young Desiderio: 'And when he offered you a night of perfect ecstasy in exchange for a lifetime's contentment, how could you possibly choose the latter?'

And young Desiderio answers: 'I am too young to know regret.'

But it was not as simple as that, of course. It is not even as though I have been contented. Yet others have certainly been contented. Nothing excessive, mind – always only a gentle contentment. Yet, because of what I did, everybody is relatively contented because they do not know how to name their desires so the desires do not exist, in accordance with the Minister's theory. So I suppose that, all in all, I acted for the common good. That is why they made a hero of me, although I did not know at the time I acted for the common good. Perhaps I acted only on impulse. Perhaps he did not offer me a high enough price; after all, he only offered me my heart's desire.

Besides, he was a hypocrite.

He penned desire in a cage and said: 'Look! I have liberated desire!' He was a hypocrite. So I, a hypocrite on a less dramatic scale, I hypocritically killed him, did I?

But there I go again – running ahead of myself! See, I have ruined all the suspense. I have quite spoiled my climax. But why do you deserve a climax, anyway? I am only trying to tell you exactly, as far as I can remember, what actually happened. And you know very well already that it was I who killed Dr Hoffman; you have read all about it in the history books and know the very date far better than I because I have forgotten it. But it must have been October because the air smelled of mushrooms.

I would have hated him less if he had been less bored with his inventions.

'The source of eroto-energy is, of course, inexhaustible, as my early colleague and co-researcher, Mendoza, surmised.'

He pointed through the window to the transmitter that turned ceaselessly at the top of the cliff beside the house.

'For the last five years those transmitters, powered by simple, radiant energy, e.g. eroto-energy, have been beaming upon the city the crude infrastructure of

(a) synthetically authentic phenomena;

(b) mutable combinations of synthetically authentic phenomena;

and have also been transmitting

(c) sufficient radiation to intensify a symbol until it becomes an object according to the law of effective evolving, or, if you prefer a rather more explicit term, complex becoming.

'By the liberation of the unconscious we shall, of course, liberate man. And the naked man will walk in and out of everybody's senses.'

But he was one of those people it is impossible to imagine without their clothes. He was taken by a fit of coughing which he smothered in a spotless white handkerchief.

'The positive is an involved correlative of the negative and, once desire *is* endowed with synthetic form, it follows inevitably that thought and object operate on the same level. This is basic to –'

And this was the man whose daughter had told the Minister to go in fear of abstractions! I interrupted him; I had a question.

'And whatever really happened to Mendoza?'

'Mendoza?'

The Doctor took down a jar from a shelf. It contained a human brain floating in formaldehyde.

'This is all we managed to salvage. He was horribly scarred. Whatever happened in his time-machine, it burned him to the bone and also utterly disordered his mind. He lingered on, raving, for five days before he died in the public ward of a charitable hospital. Mendoza and I had not been on speaking terms for years, of course. But I managed to obtain his brain as I was most curious to see it. However, whatever it had contained died five days before the rest of him and the structure was no different from that of any other brain.'

Somehow I found this recital exceedingly unnerving. He replaced the jar and smiled as well as he was able.

'Now let me take you down to visit the distilling plant and the reality modifying machines. I'm sure you'll find the reality modifying machines perfectly fascinating; they actually perform the preliminary stages in the synthesis of phenomena.'

He might have been inviting me on a guided tour round a chocolate factory. I wondered why his daughter loved him. The Count had suited my notion of Prometheus far better than the real Prometheus did; yet, now and then, the half-derisive contempt I felt for this prim thief of fire was touched with a horrid shudder when I remembered he was triple-refined Mind in person and Matter was an optical toy to him. But I could not understand why a man like him should want to liberate man so much. I could not see how he could have got that notion of liberation inside his skull. I was sure he only wanted power.

Perhaps I killed him out of incomprehension.

We descended to the underground levels of the castle in another businesslike electric elevator which took us a great distance below the earth before it stopped. Here, where the dungeons should have been, there were white-tiled corridors soundlessly floored with black rubber and lit by strip lighting far more brightly than day. All was technological whiteness and silence. Presently he pressed a button which released the catch on an impassive-looking metal door. We entered a busy, deserted laboratory filled with the apparatus of a distillery. The glass vats and tubes were bubbling with a faintly luminous, milky, whitish substance.

'We need not linger here but I thought you would like a glimpse of it. This is merely the distilling plant. Here, the secretions of fulfilled desire are processed to procure an essence which has not yet pullulated into germinal form. Even with an electron microscope it is impossible to detect the slightest speck of root, seed or fundament in this, as it were, biochemical metasoup and it is safe to say we have cooked up for ourselves in our glass casseroles a pure, uncreated essence of being.

'Now, what do we do with our metasoup? Why, we precipitate it. Come this way.'

The wall of the distilling plant opened to let us through and closed again behind us.

'Allow me to introduce,' said Hoffman with a pale smile, 'my reality modifying machines.'

The machines operated with only an occasional, internal, twanging murmur; they could have been making electronic music. They were six cylindrical drums of stainless steel rotating on invisible axes with the same ceaseless, terrifying serenity of the transmitters turning, now, perhaps a mile above our heads, for we had penetrated very deeply into the earth. The drums were as tall as a man and perhaps three feet in circumference, with a shuttered viewing window in each base. A ridged, plastic pipe emerged from the white-tiled wall to disappear into a sealed aperture in the top of each drum and the wires which led from them appeared to feed into six glowing screens a confusion of endlessly swelling and diminishing ectoplasmic shapes formed around central nuclei of flashing lights. These screens were something like TV screens and formed a bank in the wall above complicated panels of switches on the other side of the laboratory.

Though the room was brightly lit and obviously in use, the only signs of the existence of a staff of technicians were a water cooler, a number of tubular steel chairs and a table containing a number of clipboards. It was a very sterile place.

'These machines were formulated on the model of objective chance, taking "objective chance" as the definition of the sum total of all the coincidences which control an individual destiny. Just like the transmitters, they are powered by eroto-energy so their action is further modified by the Mendoza effect, that is, the temporal side-effect of eroto-energy.

'Inside the reality modifying machines, we precipitate essence of being.'

He snapped open one of the viewing windows and I glimpsed a whirling darkness shot through with brilliant sparks, like the sky on a windy night. But he closed the window again immediately.

'During the precipitation process, the essence of being spontaneously generates the germinal molecule of an uncreated alternative. That is, the germinal molecule of objectified desire.'

He paused to allow me to absorb this information. I would have expected any other man to show a certain modest pride as he exhibited devices that could utterly disrupt human consciousness but Dr Hoffman displayed only a faded weariness and a depressing ennui. He paused to take a drink of water from the water-cooler, crumpled up his used cardboard cup dispiritedly and sighed.

'Inside the reality modifying machines, in the medium of essential undifferentiation, these germinal molecules are agitated until, according to certain innate determinative tendencies, they form themselves into divergent sequences which act as what I call "transformation groups". Eventually a multi-dimensional body is brought into being which operates only upon an uncertainty principle. These bodies appear on the screen ... over there ... expressed in a complex notation of blips and bleeps. It requires extreme persistence of vision to make sense of the code at this stage. Nevertheless, those formless blobs are, as it were, the embryos of palpable appearances. Once these undifferentiated yet apprehendable ideas of objectified desire reach a reciprocating object, the appearance is organically restructured by the desires subsisting in latency in the object itself. These desires must, of course, subsist, since to desire is to be.'

So *that* was the Doctor's version of the cogito! I DESIRE THEREFORE I EXIST. Yet he seemed to me a man without desires.

'In this way, a synthetically authentic phenomenon finally takes shape. I used the capital city of this country as the testing ground for my first experiments because the unstable existential structure of its institutions could not suppress the latent consciousness as effectively as a structure with a firmer societal organization. I should have had very little success in, for example, Peking – in spite of the Chinese influence on my researches.

'My wife,' he added tangentially, 'is a very brilliant woman.'

I thought of the corpse upstairs and shuddered.

'I chose the capital only because it was so well suited to my experiments. I was rather put out when the times produced the Minister and the Minister produced his defences. I had thought there were no defences against the unleashed unconscious. I had certainly not bargained for a military campaign when I began transmission. I had not seen myself as a warlord but I effectively evolved into one.'

From his significant pause, I realized he had made a joke and laughed dutifully.

'At once I hired mercenaries and, of necessity, an element of attrition entered the deployment of my imagery since, initially, I could to some extent control the evolution of the phantoms by the use of the sets of samples and my blind old professor, who once received a little training in divination from my wife, could also suggest certain possible mutations of events which usually, in fact, transpired. However, I had always intended to phase myself out of operations when I had clear evidence of the autonomous, free-form, self-promulgation of concretized desires. But, once the set of samples was accidentally destroyed, my calculations went awry. Nebulous time arrived instantaneously rather than in the course of a programmed dissolution of time itself and I did not know if the manifestations could, as it were, stand on their own two feet. Or on whatever number of feet they decided to possess.

'But every day the aerial patrols spot more and more growths of hitherto unimaginable flora and herds of biologically dubious fauna inhabiting hitherto unformulated territory. And, of course, Albertina's detailed reports of the tribe of a quite illusory African coast and the verifiable, photographable activities of beasts with no reality status whatsoever indicate the manifestations are functioning perfectly adequately. Indeed, all have reified themselves to such an extent that they seem to believe themselves quite firmly rooted in the imaginary sub-stratum of time itself.'

Lecturing seemed to tire him. He took another drink of water and dissolved two tablets into it before he swallowed it. Yet he was the man who wanted to establish a dictatorship of desire.

'But the Cannibal Chief was real enough!' I objected.

'The Cannibal Chief was the triumphant creation of nebulous time. He was brought into being only because of the Count's desire for self-destruction.' He hid a yawn with a desiccated hand.

'But I know he was real enough because I killed him!'

'What kind of proof is that?' asked Hoffman with a chill smile and all at once I felt a twinge of doubt for killing the Chief was the only heroic action I performed in all my life and I knew at the time it was out of character.

'The existence of things is like a galloping horse,' he went on with that patronizing, Decembral smile of his. 'There is no movement through which they become modified, no time when they are not changed. What I have achieved has been accomplished only through certain loopholes in metaphysics and I was able, as it were, to base a meta-technology upon metaphysics only by the most scrupulous observance of and adherence to the laws of empirical research. And I have hardly begun, yet. Compared with what is to come, my work so far has only been a period of inactivity, such as the Ancient Chinese called: "the beginning of an anteriority to the beginning".'

I knew only that he had examined the world by the light of the intellect alone and had seen a totally different construction from that which the senses see by the light of reason. And yet he moved with the feeble effort of a man near death.

'I think you have seen enough here,' he said. 'We will move on to the desire generators.'

We left the ballet of incipient forms and the throbbing drums and once again walked those white, endless corridors that were the unprepossessing viscera of dream. I was almost in possession of the secret now, and it did not seem to me to be worth much. Was I condemned to perpetual disillusionment? Were all the potential masters the world held for me to be revealed as nothing but monsters or charlatans or wraiths? Indeed, I knew from my own experience that, once liberated, those desires it seemed to me he cheapened as he talked of them were far greater than their liberator and could shine more brightly than a thousand suns and yet I did not think he knew what desire was. At the end of the corridor was a pair of sliding doors with Chinese characters painted on them.

'My wife's work,' said Hoffman. 'She is the poet of the family. In rough translation, our motto reads: "There is intercommunication of seed between male and female and all things are produced." It is exceedingly apt.'

I was totally unprepared for what I found inside those doors.

The electricity of desire lit everything with chill, bewitching fire and the entire structure was roofed and walled with seamless looking-glass. The first technician I had seen in the laboratories sat at a steel desk, nodding over a pile of comic books. He was a beautiful hermaphrodite in an evening dress of purple gauze with silver sequins round his eyes.

'I am a harmonious concatenation of male and female and so the Doctor gave me sole charge of the generators,' he said in a voice like a sexual 'cello. 'I was the most beautiful transvestite in all Greenwich Village before the Doctor gave me the post of intermediary. I represent the inherent symmetry of divergent asymmetry.'

The Doctor caressed him affectionately on the shoulder. But the intermediary was a cripple and had to roll himself forward on a wheelchair to show us round the love pens.

They were housed in a curving, narrow room some hundreds of yards long, an undulating tentacle extending into the very core of the mountain. All along the mirrored walls were three-tiered wire bunks. In the ceiling, above each tier of bunks, were copper extractors of a funnel type leading into an upper room where a good deal of invisible machinery roared with a sound like rushing water but the noise of the

machinery was almost drowned by the moans, grunts, screams, bellow-
ings and choked mutterings that rose from the occupants of those open
coffins, for here were a hundred of the best-matched lovers in the
world, twined in a hundred of the most fervent embraces passion
could devise.

They were all stark naked and very young. They came from every
race in the world, brown, black, white and yellow, and were paired, as
far as I could see, according to colour differences. They formed a pic-
torial lexicon of all the things a man and a woman might do together
within the confines of a bed of wire six feet long by three feet wide.
There was such a multitude of configurations of belly and buttock,
thigh and breast, nipple and navel, all in continual motion, that I
remembered the anatomy lessons of the acrobats of desire and how the
Count had spoken, with uncharacteristic reverence, of the 'death-
defying double somersault of love'.

I was awed and I was revolted.

'They are paired in these mesh cubicles so that they can all see one
another – if they bother to look, of course, and hear one another, if
they can hear, that is; and so, if necessary, receive a constant refreshment from visual and audial stimuli,' commented the irrepressibly
efficient Doctor. The rubber wheels of the hermaphrodite's chair
squeaked a little on the mirrored floor as we walked slowly past the
hutches. The polished walls and floor reflected and multiplied the
visible propagation of eroto-energy as they had done that stormy night
in the orchid-coloured caravan, when the Arab tumblers and I together
must unwittingly have invoked a landslide. Our footsteps clinked. The
Doctor tugged at the brown ringlets of a plump, dimpled, pink and
white English rosebud straining beneath a diminutive but immensely
tooled Mongolian; she did not even turn her head for she was poised
on the verge of a ripping shriek as her apricot-skinned lover plunged
down.

'Look! They are so engrossed in their vital work they do not even
notice us!'

The hermaphrodite tittered sycophantically but she need not have
worked so hard at her disguise. I suspected her already. I had seen her
disguised far too often not to recognize her disguises.

'We feed them hormones intravenously,' the Doctor informed me.

'Their plentiful secretions fall through the wire meshes into the
trays underneath each tier, or dynamic set, of lovers and are gathered
up three times a day by means of large sponges, so that nothing whatsoever is lost. And the energy they release – eroto-energy, the simplest

yet most powerful form of radiant energy in the entire universe – rises up through these funnels into the generating chambers overhead.'

And these were all the true acrobats of desire, whom the Moroccans had only exemplified.

He sighed again and swallowed two aspirin, though there was no water-cooler in this laboratory so he had to chew them dry. The eyes of the hermaphrodite were the shape of tears laid on their sides and had the very colour of the tremendous clamour that rose from all those lovers caught perpetually in the trap of one another's arms, for there were no locks or bars anywhere; they could have come and gone as they pleased. Yet, petrified pilgrims, locked parallels, icons of perpetual motion, they knew nothing but the progress of their static journey towards willed, mutual annihilation.

'These lovers do not die,' said Albertina. 'They have transcended mortality.'

'After an indefinite period of dimensionless time,' amplified the Doctor wearily, 'they resolve into two basic constituents – pure sex and pure energy. That is, fire and air. It is a grand explosion. And,' he added with, I think, a faint wonder, 'every single one of them volunteered.'

Beneath the purple bosom of her ball gown, I saw an interior corsage of flame, her heart. We moved down the lines of pens, we and our reflections, he, and she, and I, until we came to the end of the line. It had taken us a quarter of an hour, walking at a good pace. And here, at the top of a tier, was an empty cubicle.

As soon as I saw it, I knew it was my marriage bed.

The time was ripe. My bride was waiting. We had her father's blessing.

'I shall go to the city tomorrow,' said the Doctor, 'and, since time will be altogether negated –'

'– you will arrive yesterday,' concluded Albertina. They both laughed gently. And now I understood this gnomic exchange perfectly. Our long-delayed but so greatly longed-for conjunction would spurt such a charge of energy our infinity would fill the world and, in this experiential void, the Doctor would descend on the city and his liberation would begin.

She wiped the silver from her eyes and the purple dress dropped away from the goddess of the cornfields, more savagely and triumphantly beautiful than any imagining, my Platonic other, my necessary extinction, my dream made flesh.

'No!' I cried. 'No, Generalissimo! No!'

And I cried out so loudly I pierced even the willed oblivion of the love slaves for, as I ran past towards the door, they bucked and thrust less violently and one or two of them even moved their eyes as far as they could without moving their heads to watch me, such vacant eyes that slowly, painfully cleared as the sweat on their limbs dried. The light began to flicker a little, as though heralding a power failure.

An alarum bell shrilled. The Doctor had a gun and sent a volley of bullets after me but my many reflections misled him and the bullets bounced back off the walls and caused great bloodshed among the woefully exposed practitioners of desire. I rattled the steel doors but they must have locked automatically when the alarum went off. So, weaponless, desperate, half-blinded by tears, I turned to face my adversaries.

The Doctor had leapt into the wheelchair to propel himself more quickly down the long room, for he was slow on his feet. He was showing some emotion at last. His face was working and he gibbered with rage as he shook his useless, empty revolver. But she – she was like an avenging angel, because she truly loved me, and in her hand she held a knife that flashed in the white, trembling, artificial light. And all the naked lovers had abandoned their communion to lament their dead and the dying on whose beautiful flesh the bright blood blossomed.

I had seen nothing in the peep-show to warn me of the grotesque dénouement of my great passion.

He came straight at me in his wheelchair, intending to run me down, but I grasped the arms of the chair and overturned it. He was as weightless as a doll. He went limply sprawling and the revolver flew from his hand to spin over the glass and crash against the wall while his head cracked down at such an awkward angle I think his neck broke instantly. A little blood trickled down his nose to meet the flow that trickled upwards from the nose in the mirror and then I was wrestling on top of his body with Albertina for the knife.

We wrestled on her father's flaccid corpse for possession of the knife as passionately as if for the possession of each other.

And then we slithered like wet fish over the mirrors but still she would not let go of the knife though I clutched her wrist too tightly for her to be able to kill me with it. She bit me and tore my clothes and I bit her and pummelled her with my fists. I pummelled her breasts until they were as blue as her eyelids but she never let go and I savaged her throat with my teeth as if I were a tiger and she were the trophy I seized in the forests of the night. But she did not let go for a long, long time, not until all her strength was gone. At that, I killed her.

It is very hard for me to write this down. And I have already told you how I killed the Doctor – that is, unintentionally. Do you not already know I do not deserve to be a hero? Why should I tell you how I killed Albertina? I think I killed her to stop her killing me. I think that was the case. I am almost sure it was the case. Almost certain.

When her fingers slackened on the handle, I seized the knife immediately and stabbed her below the left nipple. Or perhaps it was in the belly. No, it was below the left nipple for the fire vanished as the steel entered the flames but she spoke to me before she died. She said: 'I always knew one only died of love.' Then she fell back from the blade of the knife. She must have hidden the knife in her purple dress though I will never know why, of course. It was a common kitchen knife, such as is used to chop meat fine enough for hamburger and so on. Her flesh parted to let the knife out and her eyes, though still the shape of horizontal tears, were silent forever.

If the Doctor had been a real magician, the underground laboratory, the castle, the whole edifice of stone and stained glass and cloud and mist should have vanished. There should have been a crash of thunder and a strong wind would have blown away the levers and the machinery and the books and the alembics and the pickled mandrakes and the alligator skeletons; and I should have found myself alone on the mountain side, under a waning moon, with only the rags of dream in my hands. But no. The alarum bells continued to ring and some of the surviving lovers, rudely shaken from their embrace by the sound of gunfire, began to clamber from their sleepless dormitory on shaky legs, though they moved without sense or purpose, as if obeying some obscure compulsion to come closer to the spectacle of death, though none of them seemed to observe this spectacle for they still seemed half-blinded. And the one door remained remorselessly closed, while I was a mile beneath the crust of the earth, locked in a white-tiled hall of mirrors. Nevertheless, as I wiped the reeking blade on the handkerchief they had provided for my breast pocket, I felt, how can I put it? Yes; I felt the uneasy sense of perfect freedom. Freedom, yes. I thought I was free of her, you see.

But there was no way out of the laboratory except the sealed door and how could I be free of her as long as I myself remained alive?

I knew the alarum bell must rouse something and my first thought was, escape; my second, that escape was impossible. Those of the milling lovers who were not lamenting their dead or grieving over one another's wounds were as witless and uncertain on their feet as new born colts. They knew only that they had been interrupted in the middle of the most important work in the world but neither how nor why and even those whose shattered faces streamed with blood clasped their partners' arms or legs and begged them to lie down again while others, risen, tottering, befogged by mirrors, kissed the glass cases that seemed to hold such inviting lips. Yet few, if any, took any notice of me with my knife or had even seen how cruelly I had betrayed love itself. I hid myself among the wire hutches until the metal doors slid open. The alarum ceased.

But no detachment of militia appeared, only a single, white-clad representative of the hitherto invisible technical staff, armed only with a syringe. And he did not even bother to close the door behind him. Clearly the alarum had always before only indicated some slight indisposition among the lovers that could easily be righted with a shot or two of extra hormones; perhaps they interpreted the flickering of the lights as the sign of a hormonal deficiency. How could anyone know the real nature of the disturbance? What riot might the lovers make? Why should they call out the guard to deal with a lowered vitality among the love slaves? Yet I had been prepared for fifty hired rifles to level against me. I wanted a heroic struggle. I wanted a heroic struggle to justify my murder to myself. And all I did in the end was to stab the harmless technician in the back of the neck as easily as you please while he gaped open-mouthed at the splintered wheelchair, the contorted savant and the dead girl. Leaving my bag of three stiffening behind me, I walked out into the corridor and pressed the button that closed the door behind me.

If you feel a certain sense of anti-climax, how do you think I felt?

I still carried my knife. I noticed I had unconsciously tucked that handkerchief stained with Albertina's blood into my breast pocket, where it looked just like a red rose.

But the lights were all going out and I knew the rest of the castle, whoever that comprised, would soon all be roused. First, I knew I must destroy the reality modifying machines; this was clearly fixed in my mind as though to wreck them would completely vindicate me – as, indeed, in the eyes of history, it has. I ran down that ice warren of white, glittering corridors, found the laboratory, went in, smashed the dancing screens with the desk, dragged pipes and wires from the walls and set fire to the papers with my gold cigarette lighter. It was the work of moments. To complete the job, I went into the distilling plant and smashed everything I found there, though first I surprised another technician and so I had to stab him, too. These depredations set off no alarums for, by the structure of the Doctor's system, disturbances were impossible; but the lights were flickering so badly now, I knew I had not much longer at liberty in the castle and so would have to leave the workroom in the tower unharmed. But I guessed the Doctor only allowed his daughter to handle the most arcane secrets and so it proved, for everything stopped immediately as soon as he was dead, of course, and the love slaves disbanded, for concretized desires could not survive without their eroto-energy and . . . But I knew nothing of that. Those are the dreary ends of the plot. Shall I tie them up or shall I leave them unravelled? The history books tie them up far better than I can for I was deep in the bowels of the earth, was I not, with four notches on my knife. Oh, but I got out easily enough even though the elevator was no longer running. I found the emergency exit; it was beside the elevator. It spiralled me dizzily up to the hall of the castle, where the old dog still drowsed before the grey ashes of the applewood fire.

When he smelled Albertina's blood, he leapt at me with the last reserves of his senile strength and I left the kitchen knife in his throat. And so he was my last victim in the Doctor's castle.

In the beatific park, the birds now slept with peaceful heads tucked beneath their wings and the deer slept like statues of deer. One by one, the castle closed its coloured eyes behind me, like a peacock slowly furling in its spread, and its four attendant moons revolved more and more slowly and were already perceptibly fading round the edges, like the real moon towards the end of the night. And I, I was still in my dinner jacket with a black tie round my neck and a bloody buttonhole still stuck in my lapel as I fled across the dew-moistened grass as if I were an uninvited guest turned away from the door of a magnificent dinner party.

I started to run. The wooden bridge sounded off like machine-gun fire under my running feet. I pulled up a dry bush from the edge of the cliff and lit a bonfire on the bridge with my gold cigarette lighter and I burned the bridge behind me, so I could not have gone back to the castle even if I wanted to. I only burned the bridge so that I would not be able to return to her. It broke and fell blazing into the abyss; the earth swallowed it.

But now the sky filled with a locust swarm of helicopters all descending on to the roof of the dying castle and I thought the military were roused at last but then I realized they must have arrived according to a pre-scheduled plan and had come to take the Doctor into the city.

I was the only man alive under the stars who knew the Doctor was dead.

I was the only man alive who knew time had begun again.

The only road led to the air-strip and base so I did not follow any path. Once again I took to the mountains. I wandered among them for perhaps three days, hiding among the rocks when I sighted a roving helicopter overhead for they were buzzing all over the terrain like angry flies and I wondered if the militia might inherit the kingdom the Doctor had prepared for himself. On the third day, quite by accident, I found an Indian farmstead. When I spoke to them in the language of the river people, they took me in, gave me thin barley porridge and let me sleep on the common pallet. In return for my gold cigarette lighter they allowed me to ride away on a scrawny, white, starveling mare and the smallest son, in his baggy white drawers, with the open sores on his legs, came with me until I was safely on the track that took me winding down to the foothills through those cruel, yellow clefts that seared my weary brain with their infinite monotony. The helicopters monitored the white, abandoned skies less and less often; after all, the Doctor's swarthy soldiers had only been mercenaries and when their pay was not forthcoming, after they tried but failed to make sense of the books, the instrument panels and the generators, they would gut the castle and go off in search of another war, for was there not always another war to be had? And the technicians were only technicians . . . but I knew nothing of this last phase of the war, its dying fall; I only knew the helicopters came less frequently and then did not come at all.

And there were no more transformations because Albertina's eyes were extinguished.

On I went, through the lifeless vegetation of winter, and I thought myself free from all the clouds of attachment because I was a traveller who had denied his proper destination. I saw no colours anywhere around me. The food I begged from cottagers had no savour of either sweetness or rankness. I knew I was condemned to disillusionment in perpetuity. My punishment had been my crime.

I returned slowly to the capital. I had neither reason nor desire to do so. Only my inertia, dormant for so long, now reasserted itself and carried me there by its own passive, miserable, apathetic force. In this city I am, or have been, as you know, a hero. I became one of the founders of the new constitution – largely from the negative propulsion of my own inertia for, once I was placed and honoured on my plinth, I was not the man to climb down again, saying: 'But I am the wrong man!' for I felt that, if what I had done had turned out for the common good, I might as well reap what benefits I could from it. The shrug is my gesture. The sneer is my expression. If she was air and fire, I was earth and water, that residue of motionless, inert matter that cannot, by its very nature, become irradiated and may not aspire, even if it tries. I am the check, the impulse of restraint. So I effectively evolved into a politician, did I not? I, an old hero, a crumbling statue in an abandoned square.

I returned slowly through the mists of winter. Time lay more thickly about me than the mists. I was so unused to moving through time that I felt like a man walking under water. Time exerted great pressure on my blood vessels and my eardrums, so that I suffered from terrible headaches, weakness and nausea. Time clogged the hooves of my mare until she lay down beneath me and died. Nebulous Time was now time past; I crawled like a worm on its belly through the clinging mud of common time and the bare trees showed only the dreary shapes of an eternal November of the heart, for now all changes would henceforth be, as they had been before, absolutely predictable. And so I identified at last the flavour of my daily bread; it was and would be that of regret. Not, you understand, of remorse; only of regret, that insatiable regret with which we acknowledge that the impossible is, *per se*, impossible.

Well, I walked the heels out of my silk socks and the soles off my patent leather pumps and I fell down to sleep and rose to walk again until this filthy scarecrow in ragged evening dress, his matted hair falling over his shoulders and his gaunt jaw sprouting unkempt beard, his lapel still stuck through with a blackened rose of stiffened blood – until I saw before me, one moonlit dawn, the smoking ruins of a familiar city.

But as I drew nearer, I saw the ruins were inhabited.

Old Desiderio lays down his pen. In a little while, they will bring me my hot drink before they put me to bed and I am glad of these small attentions for they are the comforts of the old, although they are quite meaningless.

My head aches with writing. What a thick book my memoirs make! What a fat book to coffin young Desiderio, who was so thin and supple. My head aches. I close my eyes.

Unbidden, she comes.

READ MORE IN PENGUIN

BY THE SAME AUTHOR

Heroes and Villains

After the apocalypse the world is neatly divided. Rational civilization rests with the Professors in their steel and concrete villages; marauding tribes of Barbarians roam the surrounding jungles; mutilated Out People inhabit the burnt scars of cities.

But Marianne, a Professor's daughter, is carried away into the jungle – a grotesque vegetable paradise – where she will become the captive bride of Jewel, the proud and beautiful Barbarian. There she will witness the savage rituals of the snake worshippers, indulge her voluptuous, virginal fantasies, taste the forbidden fruit of chaos . . .

Erotic, exotic and bizarre, *Heroes and Villains* is a post-apocalyptic romance, a gripping adventure story, a colourful embroidery of religion and magic and, not least, a dispassionate vision of life beyond our brave nuclear world.

The Bloody Chamber

From the lairs of the fantastical and fabular and from the domains of the unconscious's mysteries . . .

Lie the brides in the Bloody Chamber – Hunts unwillingly the Queen of the Vampires – Slips Red Riding Hood into the arms of the Wolf – Pimps our Puss-in-Boots for his lustful master . . .

In tales that glitter and haunt – strange nuggets from a writer whose wayward pen spills forth stylish, erotic, nightmarish jewels of prose – the old fairy stories live and breathe again, subtly altered, subtly changed.

'She writes a prose that lends itself to magnificent set pieces of fastidious sensuality . . . dreams, myths, fairy tales, metamorphoses, the unruly unconscious, epic journeys and a highly sensual celebration of sexuality in both its most joyous and darkest manifestations' – Ian McEwan, author of *First Love, Last Rites*